The Shintae

BRIAN R. HILL

PublishAmerica
Baltimore

© 2005 by Brian R. Hill.
All rights reserved. No part of this book may be reproduced, stored in a retrieval system, or transmitted in any form or by any means without the prior written permission of the publishers, except by a reviewer who may quote brief passages in a review to be printed in a newspaper, magazine, or journal.

First printing

ISBN: 1-4137-8324-4
PUBLISHED BY PUBLISHAMERICA, LLLP
www.publishamerica.com
Baltimore
Printed in the United States of America

For Michael, Angela, Gary, Grace, George & Henry

I would like to thank the following for all their generous help and comments:
  Geoff Sheasby, Dorothy Sharman and John Braine

The Shintae

Chapter One

The sun's rays flickered and died as dusk stepped confidently into the glade where he rested. Only his eyes moved as he persisted there, cooled by the scented air drawn down from the surrounding wooded slopes, his mind far away on matters of great importance. He had recovered The Shintae. The long years of search and hardship had not been in vain and now, finally, the end of his mission was within his grasp. Allowing his mind to wander, he fingered the short sword at his side, remembering deeds and enemies slain in the valleys and amongst the mountains of Cantaé far to the west. Lying on the ground beside him was his trusty longbow, an old and valued friend that had saved him on so many occasions out beyond the edges of civilisation. Suddenly he stooped, gathered it from the still warm ground and turned towards a solitary timber framed cabin standing close by.

Although the last faint glimmer of light had been extinguished long since, he had no difficulty in picturing the building with its heavy planked wooden walls and angular straw thatched roof supported by wooden cross-members. Narrow openings cut into the outer walls were covered by shutters, which, when pulled back, allowed light to enter. An arched doorway led into the first of three large rooms, with several smaller chambers at the rear. Highly intricate carvings and multi-coloured tapestries covered the internal walls, whilst a variety of woven and deep furred rugs were scattered over the wooden floor. Most of all, however, he recalled the stone fireplace in the main living area and how, on winter days, a roaring fire threw out its arms of all embracing warmth. Even on a warm summer's evening it felt good to be reminded again of such protection.

With this thought in mind, he moved around the house towards the doorway, which, to his surprise, stood open. Running his fingers around the opening, he found the shattered remains of the doorframe where the entrance had been forced. For a moment he stood silently, listening intently to the sounds of the night. Detecting nothing untoward and finally satisfied he was alone, he removed a tallow lamp from his pack. Using his tinderbox to spark a flame, he succeeded in lighting the lamp whereupon, shielding his eyes from the resultant glare, he stepped carefully over the remains of the door. Halting abruptly he gazed numbly around at the scene of destruction that greeted him. Wearily he moved from room to room, but the whole building appeared to have been ransacked during his lengthy absence.

A native of the forest lands of Maraé, he was just short of six feet in height, tall for his race, with long brown hair flowing over delicately pointed ears down to broad shoulders. Brown, weather-beaten cheeks faded in to a wide and hairless chin, while piercing blue eyes gazed out from beneath broad eyebrows that angled down towards a finely chiselled nose. His clothes were old, faded and stained with constant travel. A creased brown tunic covered the upper part of his torso, hanging limply from a slightly hunched back. The garment was made to blend into the surrounding woodland, as were his deerskin trousers. A pair of stretched hide moccasins covered his feet, and a cloak the colour of grass was tightly rolled within a small pack on the floor beside him. Exhausted, he leant against a wall before sinking slowly to the floor, too tired to think clearly any more. Had his instincts not been dulled by fatigue, he would have moved on immediately; and then, perhaps, things might well have turned out so very differently. Instead, his head nodded once, twice, three times, his eyes closed, and he dropped into a deep but troubled sleep.

Silently, in the small hours, the intruders returned, a group of savage mountain men, Cantaén warriors from the far west. Taller than the average forest dweller, their heads were covered in dirty dark hair while unkempt beards, dyed ginger as was their custom, sprouted untidily. Over their muscular frames they wore tunics of dark grey, woven from rough and crudely spun yarn, designed to blend more readily into the rocky mountain sides than the forests below. The thick hide trousers worn by the Cantaéns were far more suited to the upper peaks than to the lower ground in summer.

The antithesis of the forest dwellers who, overall, were an honest and peaceable folk, the inhabitants of the mountains were evil, both in heart and mind. Just one glance into their dark eyes revealed the hatred that smouldered deep within their souls. An all-consuming loathing for most living things filled their daily lives, whether creatures of the wild or strangers from another land. Arguments and feuds were a part of daily life to them, the ones who perished during combat generally being the lucky ones. Prisoners, whether from elsewhere or their own kind, usually came to a hideous end, something that particularly applied to those from the forests.

The origins of this intense detestation of the woodland folk were to be found in the distant past when, centuries ago, the people of Maraé had come together and taken up arms against the invading mountain hordes. Driving them back to the foot of the Cantaé Mountains, they engaged in battle below the Cliffs of Sorealai, where a crushing defeat was inflicted on the forces of evil. Few Cantaéns escaped the ensuing carnage but those who did took with them the embryo of The Hatred, which had now become instinctive, the young being born with it and the elders adding to it with their teachings.

Kaér, for that was his name, came violently awake, a sharp excruciating pain in his side. Rolling around in agony, he crashed into something and, upon opening pain-filled eyes, stared straight at a pair of dirty boots, the style and origin of which was instantly recognisable. It had never been in doubt that Cantaéns had wreaked havoc within his home, but for them to have remained nearby was beyond all understanding. If there was one thing that came a close second to their hatred of the forest dwellers, it was their fear of them. Few dared venture down to the forest and those who did never stayed long in any locality. The damage to the cabin was not recent; dust had settled quite heavily over his scattered possessions and he believed the despoilers had long departed. Extraordinary circumstances currently prevailed. Kaér had reclaimed The Shintae and the Cantaéns were desperate for its return.

His mission was ended; there could be no triumphal return to Myssous, the nation's capital where the leaders of the High Council had originally charged him with the task of recovering The Shintae. He had failed them, for The Shintae was power, the power for good in the hands of the just, or a terrible potential for evil in those of the degenerate. This ancient relic had been the deciding factor at the Battle of Sorealai when wise men had transmitted its power to the warriors in the field. During the final moments of battle, the wise men had been surprised by a lone Cantaén warrior. Seizing The Stone, the warrior had fled towards the mountains, closely followed by Maraén troops determined to relieve him of his prize. Somehow, he managed to evade pursuit and disappear amongst the peaks, never to be seen again by mortals of either nation.

Although many searched for it, The Shintae had vanished without trace and, in time, both sides came to accept its loss. In fact, almost five hundred years had passed since any expedition had been organised to seek its whereabouts. The story passed into legend where it seemed destined to remain until, three years previously, runners had been hastily dispatched from the border to the High Council, warning of strange happenings taking place in Cantaé. From their homes in the foothills, lying deep in the shadow of the mountains, villagers had witnessed lightning bolts playing around distant peaks at all hours of the day and night, accompanied by faint sounds of thunder. Rarely were there other signs of a storm to account for these phenomena.

Immediately suspicions amongst the council members were raised, although none dared voice them aloud outside their chambers. Border Scouts were ordered to scour the mountains close by to gather what information they could. Returning from reconnaissance of the nearest territories, they brought news of heavily armed groups of Cantaéns flocking towards the central mountains. On hearing this, the council leaders commanded more missions be undertaken, this time to locate the exact source of the lightning, but these proved costly as not one scout returned to safety. Then, six months after the first signs of trouble had been observed, messengers were racing again towards the coast bearing ill tidings. Columns of smoke were now billowing from the tips of the highest peaks, whilst huge flashes of fire had taken the place of the lightning.

Winter descended over the country, preventing further exploration until the following spring when, once the snows had melted, another scout volunteered to go and seek out the knowledge the leaders so desperately required. Months went by with no word or sightings of him and he was given up for lost long before he crawled, delirious and severely wounded, back over the border. Lapsing into a coma, it was several weeks before his broken body healed and he recovered consciousness. As his mind cleared and his scrambled thoughts regained some clarity, he told of how, after many weeks of hiding by day and travelling by night, he had worked his way towards the centre of enemy activity far away in the Subrat valley. Tracking a supply column along the valley bottom, the scout discovered a large concentration of enemy troops encamped beneath the towering peak of Mount Subae.

Taking cover on the hillside overlooking the area, the scout had settled down to watch. He soon located a closely guarded group of wise men operating in an open section near the centre of the encampment. For several days the scout observed as the Cantaén sages worked in relays, day and night, over what appeared to be a small stone resting on a pedestal in their midst. Backwards and forwards, they paced, muttering in ancient tongues whilst the object of their attention pulsated steadily. Occasionally, one would utter a special incantation and point his hand at some particular part of the valley side, or distant mountain peak. Forks of lightning flashed from the strange fragment of rock, spiralling briefly around the wise man, before darting down to encircle his extended arm and streaking away to where he aimed. Sheets of flame erupted from the intended targets, scorching vast areas around and sending clouds of thick, acrid smoke high into the atmosphere, leaving the heavy crash of thunder to reverberate throughout the valleys. One thunderbolt, landing nearby, had forced the scout to break cover directly in front of a passing patrol. Badly wounded, he had managed to evade capture; more by instinct than any conscious effort, he eventually found his way back home.

The High Council had no option now but to admit openly their darkest fears were proven. The Shintae was recovered and lying in the blood stained hands of the Cantaéns. Dreadful though this was, matters could have been worse. Lightning bolts and sheets of fire, no matter how spectacular, were only a minor sample of The Stone's power. Although the Cantaén wise men might yet be unable to find ways of making greater use of its massive energy the fact that they would, given sufficient time, was a certainty the council leaders could ill afford to ignore. The Shintae must be retrieved and if necessary the old sayings used to exploit its full potential, for they had records of all such things that the enemy did not. Once it was back in their possession, they need no longer fear attack.

Action was now a matter of urgency and the High Council sent word that Kaér should attend them with all haste. Whereas no others looked for The Stone, Kaér was the exception who had devoted much of his life to this quest. Now aged thirty, he had slipped away from home on his fifteenth birthday to commence his mission. The years that had elapsed since then had not been easy ones, the tales of his exploits spreading throughout the lands of both Maraé and Cantaé. He had, however, been left in ignorance of the events taking place in the west. His talents were unique and the council leaders had feared risking him too soon, but if anyone was capable of the task in hand, it was he.

Far to the south where the mountains met the sea, messengers had come up with him at his camp high in a rocky pass. Journeying up the coast, he had arrived at Myssous where the council leaders had apprised him of the facts, and, pausing only to replenish his supplies he had started out immediately for the border. A year of travel and dangerous adventure then followed, during which he had recovered The Shintae and made good his escape from Cantaé. Slipping secretly across the frontier to avoid Cantaén patrols, he was compelled to enter Maraé far away from any settlements, unable to call on any border scouts to act as escorts. Chance alone had dictated his route; a strange quirk of fate indeed that had not only directed his path towards his own home but had also brought him to his current predicament.

Through a pain-filled haze, Kaér's roving eyes steadied for a moment on the face of the form towering above. Deep pools of hatred gazed back as Sartae, head of the Cantaén Guard, struck him again and then ever harder, lashing out with vicious intent. Unconsciousness swept over Kaér as the agony of the blows intensified and his attacker, robbed of the pleasure of watching him suffer, aimed one final blow at the head of his helpless victim before turning away.

Many hours passed before Kaér regained his senses. The sun was approaching its peak and the forest was alive with the sounds of the creatures of the day. His face was swollen beyond all recognition, his eyes mere slits amid the bruising. A ringing noise filled his ears and his whole body ached unbearably, particularly where the ropes binding him dug deep in to his arms and legs. Despite his injuries, his initial thoughts were of The Shintae. There was, however, no need to feel for the pouch around his neck to know it would be no longer there. Rolling over in misery, he groaned aloud with the pain that greeted this manoeuvre.

"Sartae! Sartae!" screamed a voice from nearby. "Come quick! He's awake."

The guard's cry finally brought home to Kaér the gravity of his situation. Until then, his main concern had been for The Shintae, his own safety of secondary importance. Unbidden memories of the treatment he had seen inflicted on prisoners by the enemy raced through his mind; the twisted broken bodies he had stumbled across during his years of wandering. Nevertheless, it was the fate of prisoners taken by the Cantaén Guard that occupied his thoughts the most. Far more skilled in the art of making death more painfully protracted than the average Cantaén, just to be captured by them alone was horrifying enough; but to find oneself in the hands of Sartae, their chief, was unthinkable. In a land where cruelty was considered a normal part of everyday life, he was renowned for his inhuman deeds. Forcing open his blood-encrusted eyelids, Kaér stared around the room in desperation, searching for a means of escape. Had he not been trussed, he might have tackled the pair of guards by the door and the others at the window; even without a weapon it was better to die fighting than by torture. In desperation he ignored the pain and struggled with his bindings.

"Sartae!" the guard called again, a note of urgency creeping into his voice, "He's awake and moving," he shouted, advancing upon Kaér with sword drawn.

"Stop!" came the word of command, ringing from the doorway. "You treacherous dog! Don't you know no one except me is allowed to touch him? Out of the way, fool," he bellowed, thrusting the guard to one side and striding over to a now, outwardly, indifferent Kaér.

An evil grin spread across Sartae's face as he stared down at Kaér. He broke the silence with a huge guffaw. The sound was not a pleasant one but the product of a warped and twisted mind; soon the room was filled with a dozen others all chortling in a like manner, as if at some horribly demented joke. Closing his mind to the sound, Kaér resigned himself to his fate. He had tried his best, but this had not been good enough and now the penalty for failure had to be paid. Wiping the tears of laughter from his face with the back of a dirty hand, the Cantaén leader glowered down at his victim, malevolence intensifying in his eyes with every passing moment. Towering over the still form, Sartae was a terrifying sight. His long ginger beard, surprisingly neatly trimmed, brushed against the huge green leaf of authority woven into his tunic of brown. His flowing hair stretched down to the middle of his shoulders while a band of black encircled his head, holding the colossal jewel of seniority firmly against his forehead. The splendour of the jewel dazzled Kaér as he returned Sartae's stare, forcing him to cast his eyes elsewhere as he began to speak.

"So be it," he said softly, his voice containing not the slightest hint of fear. "You've won for now, but I, for one, won't give you any pleasure in your games to come," for Kaér had suffered their "entertainment" before and knew that though his body could be broken, they could never break his spirit. "Don't for one moment think of this as anything other than a temporary victory," he continued, "others of my people will come and where I've failed, they will not. Your days are numbered, Sartae, may you be cursed forevermore!"

All the while his voice strengthened as the words echoed around the room. Then Kaér began to laugh; he laughed at these despicable creatures, unable to see, no matter how hard they tried, they could not subjugate the soul of his people. He continued to laugh, releasing the tension that had built within him over the months.

Sartae's face reddened and then turned white with rage at such open defiance of him. Never before had he been faced with anything like this. Prisoners, no matter how brave an act they had put on previously, cowered in fright when brought before him, so fearful was his reputation; but this, this insignificant wretch had the nerve to laugh quite openly in his face. His anger overflowed and, in a blind fury, he grasped his sword. Raising the blade to strike, he only just managed to control his temper and stop himself from killing Kaér outright. Naked hatred shone in his eyes as he slammed the sword back in to its sheath.

"Light the fires and bring me the irons when they're hot," he hissed to the guards behind him. His voice choked with the intensity of the moment. "And as for you," he addressed himself to Kaér, "your little ploy didn't work did it? Thought you could make me so angry I'd kill you without thinking, eh? By nightfall we'll see who's laughing."

Turning on his heel he stormed out of the room, almost trampling underfoot the guard standing by the doorway. Scarcely had he left the room when, from outside, came the sound of running feet as one of the outer sentries raced towards the hut.

"Sar-tae!" came the breathless cry. "We must hurry... there's a large party of armed...Maraéns coming this way," he paused for breath, panting heavily.

"How far behind you are they?" snapped Sartae, back in full control of himself. "Come on man, speak up!"

"They're about a mile away," replied the sentry, breathing easier, "but they aren't acting like they would do if they knew we were around."

"Quick, prepare to leave while I deal with the prisoner," Sartae commanded his followers as he turned and ran swiftly back to his helpless prisoner.

"As you doubtless heard," he snarled, glaring down at Kaér, "some of your friends are on the way to pay you a visit, but they're going to be too late. You'll be dead before they arrive. It's a pity we can't take you with us to continue our little meeting later on but, unfortunately, you'd only slow us down."

"I'm so sorry your fun's been curtailed," retorted Kaér through swollen lips, his voice heavily laden with sarcasm, able in his final moments to savour the disappointment of his enemy.

"Ha! But no! I've a far better idea," mused Sartae, half to himself. "I know what I'll do." He turned to Kaér again. "It's your lucky day today," he said,

"I'm going to spare your life. Well, perhaps, you might just survive a day or two. Killing you will not slow your compatriots, but to leave you badly wounded will ensure they split their forces. They're bound to leave a fair number to nurse and protect you. With fewer in pursuit we stand a far greater chance of escaping."

Kaér was barely able to consider that the consequences of allowing Sartae a chance of freedom would be considerably worse for the world than those of his own death, when the blow fell and pain shot through his side and chest. For the second time that day, he left the world behind, sinking into a dark unyielding nightmare from which there seemed no hope of return.

Chapter Two

With Sartae at its head, the band of Cantaén Guards moved off at a furious pace, each member fully aware of the deadly peril he was in. They had all experienced the fighting abilities of the Maraéns at first hand, and counted themselves fortunate indeed to have lived to tell the tale. They may hate, despise, even fear the people of the forest, but rarely could they ever be accused of underestimating their capabilities.

Therefore, it was with genuine concern Sartae urged his men to greater effort. The enemy, even with a reduced force, would still outnumber them and, for his followers at least, the chances of escape were at best remote. He had fewer doubts about his own survival, but armed conflict was not something he was prepared to risk. Although supremely confident in his own ability, he was fully aware that a well-aimed arrow or unexpected blow from a sword could kill him as easily as any other. His courage was not in question, but the same could not be said about the safety of The Shintae. It was, like his own life, far too valuable for him to jeopardise unnecessarily.

Once safely back in the mountains, he would soon acquire the power to return, this time at the head of a conquering army. Now all that was left for him to do was to find replacements for the wise men, the Guros, slain by Kaér. The very name caused his sword arm to twitch involuntarily before he cast all thoughts of him from his mind. He was convinced they would meet again but when they did, the Maraén warrior would not escape as lightly as he had this time. Too much time, he thought savagely, had already been wasted and even more would be lost before any Guros reached the same stage of development, as had their ill-fated predecessors. Although some of the ancient words had been written down, most had merely been committed to memory and would have to be rediscovered by the new team of wise men. He would not tolerate such carelessness again.

Increasing the length of his stride, Sartae forced the pace as they raced along the winding forest paths. Over hills and down through long gloomy valleys they sped, traversing ravines by way of precarious rope bridges as, almost imperceptibly, the land rose towards the distant foothills. Day turned to night, making the paths almost impossible to follow, falls became more frequent until moonlight came to aid the racing fugitives. More darkness and tumbles followed until the rays of the rising sun brought much needed relief. By now, or so it seemed, the trees stuck out their branches, clawing at and holding back the exhausted, shambling group as it staggered down the never ending pathways. A twisted tree root seemed to spring up before him and, catching his foot, Sartae went sprawling to the ground. As the others shuffled to a halt around him, he came slowly to his feet, dazed and winded. His reserves of energy were spent and even he could go no longer without rest. His men looked to be in a similar condition, swaying drunkenly they awaited his command, some collapsing even as he watched.

"We'll rest until noon," he uttered wearily to the relief of the others, "with two men on guard at all times. One hours duty rota each pair, I'll take the first watch," he said, ignoring the looks of surprise on the faces all around. Although his need for sleep was as great as that of his followers, he needed to think without interruption and this offered the best opportunity.

As the others settled down Sartae, commanding his deputy, Traé, to accompany him, journeyed back a couple of hundred yards down the path to the edge of a wide clearing, ready to keep watch over the open ground. All remained quiet and, with the passing of an hour, it was mid-morning and Sartae returned to wake the next pair. Birds were winging overhead as the watch set off to relieve Traé. One songbird in search of food flew low over the sleeping figures. Something flashed upwards and in the next instant, the unfortunate creature was pinned, lifeless, against a nearby tree. Retrieving his arrow, Sartae settled down to sleep in a far happier frame of mind, a smile playing on his thin, evil lips.

The sun had just passed its zenith when the sentries on watch came racing back through the perimeter of the hastily constructed campsite. Dashing over to the recumbent body of their leader, they shook him urgently. Sartae suddenly came out of a deep sleep, enraged by the insistence of the agitated guards.

"What the devil is it?" he roared, staggering to his feet. "Can't I rest for even five minutes without being disturbed?" Spinning round, he reached for a stout branch lying nearby, determined to thrash them for their insolence.

"Master, spare us," they pleaded, throwing themselves down to lie prostrate at his feet, their sharply rising voices waking the sleeping company nearby.

"We've come to warn you," one of them squealed. "The Maraéns are almost upon us, we must leave at once if we're not to be taken," he persisted, cowering in fear.

"Stand up and stop snivelling," Sartae growled, the manner of his waking instantly forgotten. "How far behind and how many of them are there?" he demanded.

"Oh, great Sartae," the other sentry answered obsequiously, breathing more easily as the threat of a beating receded. "They had just halted at the far side of the clearing to talk and regroup when we set off back. Most of the warriors who came to the hut of that accursed Kaér are there," he spat at the mention of his name.

All hopes that a significant number of the enemy would remain to tend and guard the wounded warrior were shattered, Kaér was either already dead, or they thought him no longer in danger. If the latter were the case, Sartae would soon alter that.

"Traé," he called over to his trusted lieutenant. "I've a little task for you," he said, taking him to one side. "Go back to where we left Kaér," he murmured. "If he's still alive, then there can be no more than a couple of guards left to protect him. Dispose of them and kill Kaér. No! There'll be no time to make him suffer," Sartae warned as he saw the expression on Traé's face, "just finish him and make good your escape. I'm separating from the others so don't try to follow me, or join up with them. Make your own way back to Cantaé, and don't let the Maraéns capture you."

"Okay," Traé answered confidently, "I'll see you back in Cantaé." Quickly he collected his pack and slipped into the forest to circle around the oncoming enemy. Within seconds he was lost to sight.

Almost as soon as Traé disappeared Sartae had the distinct feeling he had sent him to his death. The premonition he had experienced earlier of coming up against Kaér once more had returned, but far stronger. Still, this was not the time to worry over such things. The Shintae must be delivered to the Guros and Traé must look to his own skills to survive. He was of no consequence in comparison with The Stone and could be replaced if necessary. Gathering the rest of the men together, he rapidly gave them their orders.

"I'm going on alone," he stated as they gathered around. "As you're all aware, we cannot risk The Shintae falling into enemy hands again. I want you to spread out and hide in the forest until the Maraéns have passed by. Then, after a short while, follow on behind and pick off the stragglers as you find them. If you are discovered then you must fight until they have all been eliminated. I shall personally execute any who return to Cantaé leaving even one of these forest dwellers alive. Do I make myself clear?" he spat venomously. At the nods of assent he continued, "Remember what I said," he added threateningly before disappearing round a bend in the track.

Now he was travelling alone, Sartae did not expect to be overtaken, his progress would far exceed that of the group he had left behind. He could, he supposed, just as easily have drawn ahead and left his men to escape on their own, but, by doing things this way, it almost guaranteed the enemy would be slowed down. Because his men would do exactly what was demanded of them, it was highly improbable any would live to see Cantaé again as they were too greatly outnumbered. Nevertheless, they would give him several valuable extra hours, which would be sufficient for him to increase his lead greatly. He chuckled to himself; indifferent to the fact his men could be dying for him at that very moment.

Pushing himself to the limit, he moved ever nearer the distant lofty peaks. Days turned to night and back again. Slowly the moon grew larger and then waned until it disappeared completely, leaving him to stagger blindly on, sleeping only when he could go no further. Eventually, three weeks after his wounding of the helpless Kaér, Sartae found himself standing before the mountain ranges he knew as home. He gazed intently at the towering summits that even now, in midsummer, were capped in brilliant white. Nearby, rock-strewn slopes and jagged edges stretched upwards towards the setting sun, while torrents of icy water cascaded in rivers of unimaginable fury. He contemplated the summer mist as it floated from the valleys high in the distant sierra, causing them to dance and fade as darkness descended. Sighing, he stooped to make his bed for what, he sincerely hoped, would be the last time as a fugitive on Maraén soil.

He slept late into the following morning as the fear of capture that had been his constant companion had faded the moment he stood on the threshold of the mountains. At peace with himself and temporarily untroubled by the urge to reach safety, he had slumbered on, dreaming the dreams of Cantaéns. Stirring eventually, however, he stretched to ease the stiffness in his joints caused by the hard earth. Silently he stood and, surveying the scene from his place of concealment, made plans for the final stages of his journey. Automatically he fingered the pouch containing The Shintae that hung around his neck, as indeed he had done each day since repossessing it.

Once inside Cantaé, he would journey the forty miles over the mountains to the village of Quen, this being the nearest township large enough to provide him with a substantial escort. Although he had made directly for the frontier, only deviating from his route to avoid the occasional hamlet, it was quite possible for someone to have overtaken him by some other route and raised the alarm.

Maraén border scouts were, in fact, combing the mountains for the second day now, word having reached them through Swifwulf, a runner sent on by Sartae's pursuers, that the accursed head of the Cantaén Guard was on the run. Progressing along the lower levels, Barnen, one of the scouts, was already searching the area for signs of recent passage. Any fresh tracks were to be investigated and, should the culprit prove to be Sartae, The Shintae retaken no matter what the cost.

It was noon on the second day when Barnen paused to rest and eat a little of his supplies. Settling down on a patch of coarse grass, he surveyed the land below whilst he ate. Beneath him, where the forest had thinned considerably, was a stretch of open ground cut off from the moorland above by a belt of trees, standing proud from the steeply rising bank. As his eyes surveyed the area he suddenly froze, hand half way to his mouth. Inside the clearing, where the meadow grew thick and deep, he could discern a faint line crossing from the east. He knew the trail was of recent origin; otherwise, the herbage would have sprung back into position. After a scrutiny of the terrain, he was unable to detect any similar signs of departure from the wood below, although this could be accounted for by the short wiry growth predominating above the tree line. His meal now forgotten, Barnen set off to investigate. Hurrying down the hillside, he foolishly forgot to look where he was placing his feet.

Sartae heard the twig snap and was instantly on the alert. Dropping to the ground, he rolled under the spreading branches of a nearby bush, where, concealed from outside view, he drew his sharp edged sword and waited, silently. He was prepared for anything; an animal could have caused the noise just as easily as could a man, although, on reflection, this seemed unlikely. Wild creatures, unless startled, rarely stepped carelessly. In which case, who, or what, had frightened the beast? With the enemy being the obvious choice, Sartae remained where he was, still as death, waiting for events to unfold.

Furious with himself over such a basic mistake, Barnen deeply regretted the impulse that had compelled him to rush. He could almost hear his instructor bellowing in his ear, "Watch where you're putting your feet you clumsy oaf! You couldn't surprise a dead rat the way you're going." He cringed inwardly at the recent memory and the laughter of his fellows that had accompanied it, his face flushing with shame. This was his first solo patrol and another mistake like that would certainly ensure it was his last. If someone was hiding in the trees, then the noise would surely have put him on his guard. However, as it seemed such an improbable place to halt, so close to the border, he did have reservations about anyone being there. Nevertheless, he exercised considerably more caution when he continued, drawn sword in hand. Using the cover of the dry streambed he had thrown himself into, he crawled towards the edge of the trees, now no more than thirty yards away. Gradually he attained a point a little over fifty yards from where Sartae had concealed himself, each still unobserved by the other.

Slowly, Barnen raised his head above the banking. In front of him, over the dense ground cover, he was able to peer through the widely spaced trees at the clearing far below. The faint line he had witnessed earlier stood out clearly now as a path of trampled grasses. His eyes followed the track as it entered the trees; a passage beaten through the undergrowth finishing, abruptly, inside the foliage nearest to the upper side, but with no sign of penetration to the edge. Now he knew someone was hidden amidst the bushes. Only trickery and cunning could hope to win this contest and, as he was well aware, his own skills were somewhat inadequate compared to someone of Sartae's experience. In reality, he did not have the ability to outwit him, but he had run out of options. The trail would have gone cold long before he could ever hope to return with help. Remaining where he was, Barnen kept a steady vigil, hoping to lull his foe into a false sense of security and lure him out of hiding.

Unfortunately for Barnen, Sartae had played such waiting games before and was quite content to remain safely under cover. As the minutes passed, Sartae grew more certain someone was out there; an animal would have shown itself long before now. The time was right, he decided, to set a trap. The noise had come from the northeast, out on the exposed moor and he was certain no one had entered the wood since then. The hillside, though, was full of dips, mounds and rocks where an enemy could choose his place of concealment with ease.

Studying the foliage behind him, Sartae picked out a route that could not be overlooked from the suspect area. Once satisfied it served his purpose, he grasped hold of the central stem of the bush beside him and shook it gently for a second or two. In the still air of the moment, it would be self evident no natural phenomena had disturbed the branches and, with luck, might draw an inquisitive watcher down to investigate.

His plan now in operation, Sartae scurried down his escape route and hastily found a vantage point from where he could study the area. Peering from behind the twisted branches of a fallen tree, he caught a fleeting glimpse of a figure entering the undergrowth, about thirty yards from his previous position. The bait had been taken and Sartae chuckled under his breath as he moved stealthily from tree to tree, eventually finding one large enough to conceal him. Keeping a watchful eye through the leafy cover at the base, he crouched down and waited.

The movement of the bush had caught Barnen's eye, as it was intended to, and he cast around for some way to enter the forest undetected from below, the dry streambed having inconveniently petered out. His gaze fell on a low depression behind him and, wriggling backwards, he dropped down onto the grassy surface below. Within seconds he reached the lower end and, bending double, dived across the final couple of yards to take cover inside the waiting undergrowth. Testing the edge of his blade, he moved off, employing extreme caution as he manoeuvred through the tangled branches, careful not to make a sound.

Minutes passed and then, suddenly, he was standing immediately behind his objective. Unfortunately, for him, he was also directly in front of Sartae's new location. Inching forward, Barnen heard a faint noise from behind and turned rapidly to face the danger but it was already too late. He caught a brief glimpse of a grinning evil visage and, out of the corner of one eye, a swiftly moving blur. Everything went black and then there was nothing, for nothing would ever worry Barnen again.

Standing over the body of his foe, sadistic pleasure was clearly written across Sartae's face. "Fool!" he roared aloud. "Did you really think you could outwit me?"

Without a backward glance at the fallen warrior, he climbed the hillside and crossed the frontier into Cantaé. Two days of hard struggle over the lower mountain ranges took him to the village of Quen, where, after a few days' rest he was fit enough to complete his journey. With a large escort, he headed back to the Subrat Valley and, within the month, the Guros had charge of The Shintae.

The guards, meanwhile, who had been left behind, had started quarrelling almost before Sartae was out of sight. Cynwul, the eldest and by far the most experienced member of the expedition, incensed by their lack of purpose, finally interrupted their senseless meanderings. Drawing his sword, he laid about him with the flat of the blade until he had their undivided attention.

"Shut up! Shut up! Shut up! You imbeciles," he snarled, "do you really want to bring every Maraén who lives in this vile forest down on us? Your voices must carry to the very shores of the great sea. Sartae has commanded we halt these devils, and that is what we must do, or at least hinder their progress. But what do you do? You make enough noise to raise the bodies of your ancestors and then stand around idly waiting for the enemy to arrive. Now, we'll do as our master bids, and I'll kill anyone who wastes more time by arguing. Understood?" he growled, his sword rising threateningly.

A nodding of heads indicated broad agreement and he continued. "Right, let's move out, in different directions, as if we've split to run for our lives. The enemy is almost sure to ignore us and go for Sartae's tracks; if not, we'll just have to make a fight of it here. However, once you are sure no one has followed you, wait a short while to be certain and then return to this spot. It's up to us then to remove as many as we can until we're discovered. We can't return home until they're either all dead or have retreated. Now, quickly, go hide and I'll see you back here shortly."

On his word of command, the group separated and raced away in all directions, Cynwul alone choosing to remain close to the pathway. Carefully covering his tracks, he moved through the trees towards a rock formation he had spotted earlier. On the side facing the track, the rock had an overhanging lip, a couple of feet above the ground. Easing himself down he pushed his legs and then the rest of his body beneath the overhang until he was lost in shadow. From here, he could survey the trail and overhear anything that might be said.

Silence descended and the minutes passed. No one appeared and Cynwul began to sweat. Perhaps they had seen through his subterfuge and even now were creeping up on him. Perhaps someone had been watching and knew exactly where he was. Perhaps! Perhaps! All these thoughts and many more raced through his mind. Then he stiffened as the faint sound of running feet carried through the air. A Maraén warrior, long fair hair flowing out behind, raced down the path towards him, his slim wiry body moving easily as he sped lithely by.

Puzzled by the single runner, Cynwul was tempted to go and investigate, but caution overcame his curiosity and he remained where he was. This was fortunate indeed for him as the path was suddenly filled with Maraéns, who gathered in a large group at the point where his men had rested. Nervously he licked his lips and then eased his sword gently in its scabbard, comforted by the reassuring feel of the handle in his grip. The enemy group made a hasty search of the area around the camp while their leader, a young lad with dark hair and a baggy tunic and breeches, at one point came within two paces of him, but he had covered his tracks too well and remained undiscovered.

"Listen," the leader said in a high-pitched voice as his followers gathered round him at the end of the search, "Sartae's band has separated. One of them has gone on alone; by the footprints, I think it has to be Sartae himself. Should Swifwulf overtake him then it may be all over before long. If, however, Sartae turns off along another route then Swifwulf won't follow, he must go on to the border to sound the alert." The leader paused a moment to drink deeply from a leather canteen before continuing.

"The rest, by the look of it, have taken to the woods, probably hoping we'll divide our forces and chase after them. If we stick together, they'll not dare attack. If Kaér had not recovered consciousness long enough to tell us who our adversary is, we might well have fallen for this little ploy. Come, let's concentrate on Sartae, we've delayed too long already. Hurry or we may yet be too late," he called, wheeling round and starting off at a run, followed closely by the others.

Cynwul allowed them a full five minutes start before coming out of hiding. Once a few of his men had returned, he sent three, including his chief scout Ceean, on ahead to keep him informed of the Maraéns progress while the remainder wandered back. An hour or two of hard running then followed, before one of the advanced group dropped back with a message from Ceean.

"They're spreading out now," he said, falling into step beside Cynwul, "and Ceean believes it is time to draw closer and take out a few of the slower ones."

"Excellent," Cynwul replied, "go back and tell him we'll be with him shortly."

As the messenger broke away, the others needed no urging to increase their pace. They had all overheard the conversation and their faces reflected their anticipation of what was to come. Indeed, it was not long before they came upon the leading group, hiding behind the trunk of a large tree. Indicating the newcomers to remain silent, Ceean waved them over to join him.

"Two of the swine are resting just around the corner," he whispered as Cynwul stepped quietly to his side. "There they are," he murmured, pointing to two figures almost hidden from sight behind another tree. "They've been there a little while now. We were just about to move in closer and surprise them. They'll not stay much longer."

"Come then," ordered Cynwul quietly. "You, Ceean, may have the honour of joining me in removing these fools, and if any of you make so much as the slightest of sounds, I'll deal with you when I return."

Leaving them, Cynwul and Ceean crept stealthily through the bushes, using uttermost caution, testing the ground beneath their feet for twigs and branches before each step. The tangle of interwoven scrub was silently drawn apart as they drew close to their foes. They wiped the steaming perspiration from their greasy foreheads as the afternoon sun baked the land around them.

All the observing Cantaéns saw were two swift flashes of light as weapons struck, then the Maraéns' lifeless bodies falling to the ground. The victorious pair emerged; wiping their swords in the long grass at the side of the pathway as their companions rejoined them. Blood lust was now raging freely through them all and Cynwul commanded his leading group to go on, following closely behind with the others.

They worked steadily throughout the long afternoon using either sword or bow, depending on the terrain, until by nightfall they had accounted for twenty of their opponents. Making camp near to the pathway, Cynwul mused on the consequences of the day's events. The main body of Maraéns would have halted by now, expecting any stragglers to rejoin them fairly quickly. It would take a while yet for them to realise something was amiss but, as the hours passed and no one arrived, they would soon fear the worst. Nearly half their band of warriors could not disappear without a reason. They would suspend their pursuit of Sartae and, he felt sure, turn back at sunrise to discover what fate had befallen them.

To warn him of their coming, Cynwul sent Ceean and his two companions on ahead to keep in contact with them, leaving him all of the night to prepare an ambush. Splitting his force, he placed them on either side of the path, concealing them behind any convenient rock, bush, or tree he could find. A thought occurred to him and, calling one of his men over, he hurriedly gave him instructions.

"Quick," he ordered, "I want you to go and pass this message on to Ceean straightaway. Tell him that as soon as the Maraéns begin to move back tomorrow morning, he must send his swiftest runner ahead to warn us of their approach. Then, Ceean and his remaining man must pace themselves to keep just ahead of the enemy, letting them catch a glimpse of them occasionally. It'll keep them eager and not thinking. Once they reach here, they must carry on so as not to reveal our location, only when they hear the sound of battle are they to come back and join in the fight. Do you understand?" he demanded of his messenger. "Can you remember all of this?"

"Yes! Yes!" the man replied without hesitation, proceeding to repeat the message word for word.

"Right, get off then. Don't stand around here wasting time," Cynwul barked at him. The guard shot off like a startled rabbit and was out of sight within seconds.

Sure that everything was in order, Cynwul ordered his remaining men to take whatever rest they could before morning, setting two hourly watches, just in case the enemy returned during the night. Both sides slept uneasily, one ready for battle and the other consumed with anxiety for their missing comrades.

Chapter Three

Encamped in a hollow beside the woodland path the Maraén party slept uneasily. Their leader, Angharad, stirred restlessly. Even the soothing sounds of the trickling brook nearby failed to calm her dark and troubled thoughts. With her long dark hair hanging loose, she no longer looked like the young lad Cynwul had taken her for. She was strikingly beautiful with an elfin face, short slightly turned up nose, high cheekbones and not too wide a mouth that, in normal circumstances, was rarely without a smile. The almost permanent twinkle of merriment in her blue eyes was temporarily absent, replaced by black rings of worry, her naturally pale cheeks whiter than normal. Even the baggy tunic she wore could not disguise her slim feminine shape as she rested on the ground. As sleep eluded her once more, she sat up and studied the area around. The flickering light cast by the moon through the leafy boughs illuminated the campsite and, she noted, her second in command was also awake.

"Mistrac," she summoned softly. "Come over here a moment will you."

"Yes, what can I do for you, Angharad?" He inquired, moving across and sitting on the cool earth beside her.

"I want you to warn the men we're going back in the morning," she replied. "We must know for certain what's happened to our missing comrades. If we leave at dawn, we might just surprise our Cantaén friends."

"Mm! You are of the same opinion as I am then? Those fiends have regrouped and followed on behind, butchering everyone they came across."

"Yes, I'm afraid so. If only I'd noticed earlier something was wrong and kept us all together."

"Don't blame yourself," Mistrac urged. "Nobody can think of everything and your mind's filled with thoughts of The Shintae. Don't forget, even Kaér, with all his vast experience, was tricked and now lies gravely wounded. If we hadn't stumbled across him, we would never have known about The Stone. Because of that, we stand a good chance of succeeding, so why return?" he queried. "There's nothing we can do to help the missing ones, they'll all be dead by now, but Sartae, even as we speak, is making good his escape. If we tarry too long, we'll never catch him. Surely, now we know their game, we can stay together and foil any more of their little ploys?"

"I've already considered that, but don't you see," she insisted, "if we become separated again, for no matter what reason, they'll continue to pick us off until we're no longer strong enough to defend ourselves. On the other hand, if we take the pace of the slowest to counteract this, then we will never overtake Sartae. We have no option but to retrace our steps and force them out into the open."

Mistrac considered this for a short while before commenting.

"Yes! You're right," he agreed at last, "it is our only course of action. We'd better be prepared for an ambush though; they'll be expecting us to turn back and search for our friends. If we don't keep a sharp look out we might yet come to grief," he added before lapsing into silence again. "We'll just have to take whatever comes," he said eventually, shrugging his shoulders. "I'll go warn the men and make sure they're ready." He made to leave but Angharad waved him back.

"Just a moment," she added, "I've an idea. They're sure to have someone watching the camp from a safe distance."

"I'll alert some of our best woodsmen," interrupted Mistrac, "and we'll take a few prisoners for questioning."

"No! No! No!" she interjected hastily. "Leave them where they are. When we move out tomorrow, they'll have to turn back. If we push them hard enough, they might betray their main force's position when they get there. I know we're clutching at straws but, unless you can think of anything else, I do believe it's our only chance. Go on, make sure everyone knows what we're doing," she commanded.

Long before the break of day, they were up and making ready for the journey ahead. Breakfast was a hasty affair with sufficient noise made to alert the Cantaéns to their rising, but not enough to panic them into fleeing too soon. Once the light was strong enough, however, Angharad suddenly gave the signal to move off. Lying directly in the path of the advancing group, the watchers, taken by surprise, were compelled to abandon their place of concealment.

Breaking cover, they were spotted almost immediately by the Maraéns who, with a loud cry, charged off in hot pursuit. Unprepared for such an energetic chase, Ceean found it impossible to send anyone on ahead to warn the main party. They were struggling to keep in front as it was. No matter how hard they tried, they were unable to stretch their lead to more than fifty paces before the hunters started gaining on them again. After five minutes they were breathing heavily, their pace already showing signs of easing and, for the next ten minutes or so, the Maraéns found it increasingly difficult not to overrun them. Ceean and his companions were now in full flight, desperately striving to reach safety, not one of them thinking clearly anymore. Entering the section where Cynwul had set his ambush, they spirited up one final effort and pulled rapidly away, vanishing quickly beyond the next bend.

"Stop!" Angharad cried, skidding to a halt as they disappeared from view. "Prepare yourselves, this is where they are." Letting out a wild Maraén war cry, she drew her sword and brandished it high in the air. Her rallying call was echoed instantly by her followers.

Realising his strategy had failed but unable to work out why, Cynwul stood trembling with anger. "Fire your bows," he screamed, "and don't any of you dare miss."

On hearing this, the Maraéns threw themselves down, all but one escaping the deadly hail of missiles hurtling overhead. Before another volley could be fired, Angharad leapt up, glancing at the fallen warrior.

"Follow me," she ordered, running towards the trees as the others, swiftly rising to their feet, raced after her.

Not only had his shouted command alerted the Maraéns to their danger but he had also given away his own location. Cursing aloud, Cynwul, sword in hand, launched himself at the oncoming mass, his men beside him. From over on the far side of the trail, the remainder of the Cantaén force entered the fray.

Swords flashed and the forest reverberated to the sound of crossing blades as both sides fought savagely, each striving to gain advantage over the other. First one, then another, would fall, Maraén and Cantaén blood intermingling, turning the soft earth to dark red mud. Weaving her way through the angry sea of slicing razor sharp steel, her own weapon inflicting grievous injury wherever it touched, Angharad fought her way through to Cynwul. The enemy leader stood over the bodies of three Maraén warriors while he easily kept a fourth at bay. Seeing her approach, the Maraén gratefully dropped back, sensing these two would fight it out between themselves.

Warily they circled, evaluating the strengths and weaknesses of the other. Cynwul, realising his opponent was a woman, concluded this would be an easy contest. His blade flashed in the morning sun as he took a quick step forward, aiming a vicious slice at her head. Parrying the stroke easily, Angharad riposted, striking blow after blow at the embodiment of evil before her but found herself unable to penetrate his guard. Backwards and forwards they fought, from one edge of the trees to the other, neither able to gain an advantage, all the while gradually moving farther away from the main battleground. Using every vestige of their respective skills they battled down the pathway, finally rounding the corner where Ceean and his two companions had disappeared.

Winded from the chase, Ceean's party had taken no part in the affray, content until now to observe the mêlée from the safety of the undergrowth. Upon seeing the direction of Cynwul's duel, they had continued to wait, springing out only when the combatants were lost to sight from the centre of action. Catching a glimpse of them, Angharad spun round in desperation taking Ceean's subordinates by surprise and, in one frantic sweep, beheaded them both. Continuing the swing, she turned full circle to find Cynwul with his sword high in the air ready to plunge it through the space where her back had been a moment earlier. Lunging, she ran her sword straight through the gaping hole in his guard. Cynwul collapsed instantly, the light of life dying in his eyes as he fell, Angharad's sword protruding redly from his back. Perceiving his opponent was now unarmed, Ceean launched his own attack, infuriated by the deaths of the others. Ducking underneath the slashing cutting edge, Angharad clasped her hands around her opponent's sword arm and, twisting round in one flowing movement, threw him over her shoulder.

The breath was knocked out of him as he hit the ground and, before he had chance to recover, she dived towards him, landing with all her weight on top of his head. There was a loud crack as she rolled clear, carried forward by her own momentum. Turning rapidly, she prepared to defend herself but there was no need, Ceean was already lying dead, his neck bent at an impossible angle.

Picking herself up off the ground, Angharad stooped and retrieved her sword from Cynwul's body. A deadly silence penetrated her mind and she realised the main battle must also have ended. Fearing the worst she careered round the corner, determined to take on any surviving Cantaéns should they have been victorious. Her joy at finding her own men in command of the situation quickly turned to sadness, only five remained standing. *So many*, she thought, *how could so many have fallen?* Her pace faltered as she walked fearfully towards the waiting group.

"Surely there must be more of us left?" she demanded in desperation of one of the warriors as she rejoined them.

"Yes," he replied, swaying with fatigue, "another seven lie wounded. But I'm afraid everyone else, including Mistrac and the Cantaéns, have perished."

"We can't leave the injured here to die?" implored another. "We must tend to them and let the border scouts take care of Sartae."

Angharad was caught in a dilemma. Should she put the lives of the wounded at additional risk, leaving them to fend for themselves, while they chased after Sartae, or should she turn back? Her duty, as the unfortunate Mistrac had pointed out, was to go on at all costs. Sartae had gained a good lead and could by now have taken any one of a number of pathways, covering his tracks as he went. Although it was entirely practicable to follow his trail, as most Maraéns were skilled trackers, searching for signs would slow them down significantly. It seemed extremely doubtful they could overtake him before he reached safety. She stared at her followers, who looked back expectantly. Those still standing were covered in innumerable cuts and gashes while she, herself, could feel the trickle of warm blood running down her body. Not one of them, she had to admit, was fit enough to travel at any adequate pace for some days to come. There could only be one answer.

"Tend to the wounded," she instructed sadly. "We can't possibly hope to catch Sartae in our condition. The only person capable of doing anything should the scouts fail is Kaér, if he still lives. He alone has the experience and knowledge to save us."

Opening their packs, they took out healing salves and began treating their companions, and themselves. For three days, they camped nearby the scene of conflict, looking to the needs of the living and burying the dead. One of the two most severely wounded died the first night but the other rallied, showing much improvement on the second day. Chopping down saplings, they constructed a litter for him and, on the fourth day, started back towards Kaér's cabin. Taking the pace of the walking wounded, it took them six days to complete the journey.

On arrival, they became immediately aware of a grave, freshly covered, at the corner of the clearing which they entered. Upon seeing this, their already failing spirits hit rock bottom and bitter frustration filled their minds. Now, in the darkest of hours, their one hope of deliverance from the horrors of the future lay dead and buried. Despairingly, they paid homage at the graveside until Angharad, wiping a tear from her eye, turned away.

"Come," she instructed, her voice a mere whisper, "we must sorrow no more. There are things to be done so Kaér's death shall not be in vain. Let's go replenish our supplies and find out exactly what's happened here."

The sound of her voice brought them out of their reverie and, following on behind; they helped, or carried the wounded towards the cabin. Barely had they reached half way when a figure emerged from behind the building and raced towards them. As he drew near, they recognised him as Banthrop, one of the group they had left behind.

"Angharad," he called, firing questions as he ran, "is it really you? Where are the others? Have they gone on, or are they following on behind? Did you manage to regain The Shintae?" he asked, falling into line beside her before pausing, puzzled by the looks of weariness and defeat written across every face.

"What is it?" he queried, uncertainty spreading across his face. "What has happened? You must have brought back the wounded while the others carried on?" He paused for breath and something in their expressions brought understanding to his mind. "Oh, no," he muttered to himself, "it can't be so. Say it isn't true?" he shouted at them. "Tell me it isn't so; they can't all be dead? Not all of them?" he screamed, grabbing hold of Angharad and shaking her.

"Yes, they're all gone," she replied gently, tears springing to her eyes again, "your own brother, Amaurold, too. He went bravely, saving the life of a comrade. Sit down and I'll tell you the whole story," she continued, as the grief stricken Banthrop released his grip.

By now, others had joined them from the cabin and, as they spread out around her, Angharad related the events of the last few days. The tale took almost an hour in the telling with constant interruptions and questions coming from the gathering; for all who listened were deeply affected by the news, many having relatives and friends among the fallen.

"So you see," she said in conclusion, "when we saw Kaér's grave, our spirits sank even lower..."

"But Kaér's not dead," interjected an astonished Banthrop. "He still lives."

"Explain yourself, at once," Angharad demanded after a moment, stunned by the revelation. "How can this be so? You are quite sure aren't you?"

"Well, he was alive when I came out to meet you," Banthrop replied. "Although he remains gravely ill, he improves a little each day. He's been able to talk a little and has told us much about what happened to him," he began, relating Kaér's story to the assembled group.

"Thank goodness he's alive," Angharad acknowledged when he had finished, "but if Kaér isn't dead, then who lies buried over there? Has there been an accident, has one of our own been killed?"

"There's been no accident," Banthrop answered quickly. "Once the Cantaéns realised their plot to split our group had failed, they must have thought Kaér would be poorly protected and sent someone back to finish him. He crept up on us a couple of days after you'd left and it was only by sheer good fortune we saw him sneaking towards us at dusk. One of the sentries stooped to retrieve a cup he'd dropped and out of the corner of his eye detected some movement. He alerted everyone and, when the intruder reached the cabin, we leapt out and surrounded him. He had his chance to surrender, but refused and died fighting. Luckily, none of us was badly hurt, just the odd cut and bruise. That's his grave you passed."

"Thank heavens," responded Angharad. "Now, let's move the wounded to the cabin. Once they've been taken care of, we can all eat and rest."

Kaér was sleeping when they arrived, so, mindful not to disturb him, they ate away from the building. While the wounded were made comfortable inside one of the larger rooms, the able bodied pitched tents outside. With others able to tend the injured, Angharad and her followers were able to sleep in peace. In fact, so exhausted were they that it was the middle of the following day before they awakened.

Chapter Four

Stretching out on his bed, Kaér relaxed, a gentle breeze playing around him as the clear forest air was drawn in through the partially opened shutters of his room. He felt much improved, although his memories of the first few days after being struck down by Sartae were vague. This had been a shadowy period, spent mainly in the shrouds of fevered semi-consciousness and sleep, broken only by painful stirrings as he was roused to imbibe herbal medication and liquid nourishment. Once fed, a potion of sickly sweet aromatic syrup had eased his discomfort and returned him to his dreams. Over the days, as his suffering decreased, the periods of wakefulness had been extended until now he only required help to carry him through the long and dreary nights.

His earlier feelings of lethargy had, for the moment, been replaced by curiosity. Not that there was anything he could readily substantiate but, ever since he had awakened from his nap the previous afternoon, his attendants had seemed preoccupied. On top of that, before dropping off to sleep, he was almost sure he had heard strange voices, although it was entirely possible he could have dreamt it. Perhaps Angharad had returned with The Shintae, but no, they would have informed him straightaway if the mission had been a success. Yet, on the other hand, if any of the party had arrived back and they had kept it from him for so long, then the news must indeed be bad.

He continued with his idle musings, wincing every now and then as he moved. Although his wound was healing rapidly, he was still strapped from waist to neck and his stitches itched unbearably beneath the bindings. His swollen face had almost shrunk back to normal and the bruising there and over the rest of his body was fading. Luckily, the heavy ropes binding him had taken much of the force out of Sartae's blow. Apart from a few cracked and broken ribs, he considered he was fortunate indeed not to have suffered injury that was far more serious. Today he was to be carried outside so he might benefit from the warm sunshine. Ceasing his aimless mental wanderings, he decided to concentrate on this instead. His thoughts, however, refused to be distracted for long, he was far too eager to be up and moving about. Had things not fared well with Angharad then he must soon be fit and able to go after The Shintae himself. He would not, he promised himself, be so easily surprised and foiled again.

Inside her tent, away from the cabin, Angharad turned in her sleep, groaned and then opened her eyes. Blinking, she managed after a couple of attempts to keep them open.

"Heavens," she cried, noticing the height of the sun through the partially opened tent flap, "it can't be this late already? How long have I slept? Banthrop!" she called, sitting up and stretching, wrapping a blanket around her shoulders. "Banthrop! Where are you? Ha! There you are, now tell me, are my eyes deceiving me or is the day really so advanced."

"I'm afraid so," replied Banthrop running over, "it's just on noon."

"Perhaps it is just as well you didn't wake me earlier," Angharad replied, shaking the last remnants of sleep from her mind. "I doubt I'd have felt half as refreshed if you had. The others, I take it, are still sleeping and the wounded; are they comfortable? Kaér! How is he?" Pulling the blanket more securely around her, she joined Banthrop out in the sunshine.

"The injured, like yourself, slept well and are a great deal stronger for it. As for Kaér, he's outside lying on his bed, overcome by curiosity about yesterday's visitors," Banthrop paused and, seeing the quizzical look on Angharad's face, went on to explain. "By visitors I mean you, of course. Before falling asleep in the afternoon, we think he heard something of your arrival. I have not told him anything yet as I thought you would rather break the news yourself. We took his bed out the back way so he wouldn't see any of the wounded, or your tents."

"Yes, you're quite right, I should be the one to break the news. I'll go and speak to him shortly, the longer I leave it the harder it is going to be."

Delaying only to wash and dress, she straightened her shoulders and made her way towards the cabin. The sun's rays blazed down as she left her tent, although not strongly, for autumn was drawing close. A few short months and winter would be upon them but, for the moment, no dark clouds marred the bright blue skies. A pity the same could not be said for her own thoughts. Taking a deep breath, she stepped up onto the boarded walkway at the rear of the cabin.

"Welcome, Angharad," greeted Kaér as she sat down on a bench beside his bed. "I've heard a great deal about you and, I must admit, I have been looking forward to meeting you. However, I gather from your troubled look your news is not of the best."

"If only it were not so," Angharad confessed regretfully. "But I'm afraid not only did we fail miserably in our attempt to retrieve The Shintae, but I also lost most of my men in the process. I suppose," she added, "there's still a faint chance the border scouts may track The Stone down, but I don't hold out much hope."

Kaér listened in silence as the tale unfolded and, while she talked, the other survivors ventured out of their beds to join them, interjecting occasionally with added details. Bringing food for themselves and Angharad, and also a rich broth for Kaér, they sat on the ground nearby and listened intently until she had finished talking. As she fell silent, Kaér refrained from speaking while his mind absorbed the information. Eventually, he turned his head and looked straight at Angharad.

"You did your best," he said softly, "and I doubt if anyone else would have fared much better under the circumstances. It's not as if you were prepared for such a chase, finding me here on your way back from your own mission was pure chance. If you'd hunted down the Cantaéns after they'd separated, Sartae would have escaped anyway. Normally, the others wouldn't have stopped running until they'd reached the border. I'm afraid one's best is not always good enough to counter the ploys of the enemy. You must not forget, Angharad, you were pitted against a master of cunning and deception. We both failed in our missions by underestimating him, come here and take my hand, for we are no different. But," he said, his voice strengthening, "once I'm fit, I will try again and this time only death will prevent me from succeeding."

Solemnly they shook hands, each one feeling, somehow, less burdened with guilt than before. No further words were necessary; they understood each other perfectly and, as their eyes met, a spark of friendship seemed to pass between them. The strain of the meeting, however, proved too much for Kaér and he had to be carried inside to rest. This left Angharad free to make preparations, for herself and a few of her more able companions, to journey back to the coast to make their reports. Leaving at sunrise the following day, they were long gone before Kaér awakened, although Angharad left a brief message for him. In the note she implored him, once he had recovered, to await her return so they might travel together in search of The Shintae.

    Two days later, Kaér was allowed out of bed. His wound had knitted well and, provided he made no sudden movements nor twisted too far, he suffered no great pain. On this occasion he could barely manage, with help, a few faltering steps before having to rest, exhausted. By the time a fortnight had passed he was able, with the aid of a stick, to walk all the way round the clearing. He continued to improve, despite the occasional set back, gradually increasing his daily rate of exercise, experiencing fewer twinges in his side as the days passed. Before long, he was spending several hours daily in practise with both sword and bow.

    The weeks passed swiftly and Kaér was surprised to realise three months had gone by since his wounding. Fully recovered, he was as fit, if not fitter, than he had ever been. Impatient as he was to be off in search of The Shintae, he curbed his restlessness and continued to wait for Angharad. A passing messenger from the border breaking his journey with them a few weeks earlier, had told them of the discovery of one of their scouts lying murdered at the edge of the forest. Sartae had made good his escape, Kaér concluded. He bade the courier inform the leaders of his recovery, and advise them he wished Angharad to accompany him on his next mission.

    The chilly autumn months were well advanced with periods of stormy weather becoming increasingly frequent. In the bleak light of early morning, Kaér surveyed the land around; pulling his thick fleece lined jacket more tightly about him. Soon the snows would be upon them and travel would, consequently, become more difficult. He desired to be well on the way by then. There was, however, no point in brooding, he had other matters to concentrate on for the moment.

    His hand closed over his bow and, turning briefly, he called to his waiting comrades. Suddenly the air was filled with movement as his men, by use of slings, projected targets high over the clearing. Kaér's hands flashed rapidly as he drew arrow after arrow from the quiver at his side, sending them hurtling towards the fleeting objects. Rarely, if ever, did he miss as he exhausted his supply of missiles. Giving the signal to cease firing, he retrieved his arrows and then repeated his actions, varying his stance and angle, standing, lying down or on the move. After an hour or so, they paused to rest awhile. Returning to the cabin, they stretched out on rugs and warmed themselves with goblets of mead in front of a roaring fire.

"If only Angharad would get a move on," Kaér commented moodily. "This waiting is not good for me at all."

"But Kaér," responded Wilfrum, one of the survivors of the battle with Cynwul's men, "you know full well she'll have been holding back, waiting until she hears you've made a full recovery. Your latest message must have taken quite a while to reach Myssous. Realistically, I wouldn't have thought she'd make it back here for at least another ten to fifteen days. Unless, of course, she manages to obtain one of the strange creatures that Segan brought back with him from his recent voyage, if so she could be here in no time at all."

"What manner of creature might these be?" inquired a mystified Kaér, unable to imagine what Wilfrum could be talking about.

"Sorry, I'd forgotten, you've been away so long you won't have heard about them. They're peculiar beasts, four legged so I'm told, about five to six feet in height and quite a bit longer. Their bodies are covered with short smooth hair with long tufts on their necks and flowing tails. They are extremely strong and can run for long distances without tiring, carrying someone on their backs as well. I think they're called Paéns and are supposed to be quite intelligent, for an animal."

"They sound almost too good to be true," mused Kaér. "If Angharad can get her hands on a couple of these beasts it would certainly cut our travelling time to the mountains. However, we can only wait and see what happens. Now, who's going to join me in a little practise with the sword?" he asked, dismissing all thought of strange animals from his mind and throwing himself wholeheartedly into the task of exercising his fencing skills.

The next three days followed in a similar pattern for Kaér and his group with the addition of running and hand-to-hand combat to break the monotony. The fourth day arrived and, just as they were about to break for lunch, they heard a strange pounding noise floating towards them on the wind. Drawing their weapons they came together, prepared to face whatever danger might threaten. Gradually the sound grew louder and then, with great cries of greeting, a party of Maraéns sitting astride huge panting beasts came galloping across the clearing towards them. The animals snorted and pranced about as the riders brought them to a halt before the astounded watchers. Having hoped to see perhaps a couple of the Paéns, they were stunned to witness such a gathering. Ten in all, they found when they had recovered enough to physically count them. Leaping from her mount, Angharad ran over to Kaér as the waiting group sheathed their swords.

"Welcome back," Kaér called warmly, recovering his composure and greeting her with a hug. "It's good to see you again. I was beginning to lose hope of you ever returning."

"Well I'm back now," she returned, stepping back and looking at him. "I just can't believe how well you look. The messenger assured me you were truly fit, but after seeing the state you were in before, I didn't know what to think."

"The wounds have healed perfectly and I'm ready to travel. But more about me later, let's go inside and eat. You must be feeling hungry after your ride. However, before we go in I must inspect one of these beasts a little closer." Taking him by the hand, Angharad led him over to the Paéns and, cautiously, he proceeded to acquaint himself with them.

Stepping back, he turned to Wilfrum and said, "They're just as you described, but far more powerful."

Once everyone had studied this strange means of transport to their satisfaction, the riders tethered the animals to the nearest trees and hastily rubbed them down. Hurrying inside from the cold, they dined from hot steaming dishes and drank from goblets filled with Kaér's choicest wines.

Travelling eastwards through the forest towards the coast, it had taken several weeks for Angharad to reach Myssous, even without the severely injured members of her party to slow her down. The leaders who were horrified by the loss of life had received her story with great distress. Any vestiges of hope vanished when news of the dead border scout reached them. In desperation, they had acquired the Paéns to speed her journey and charged Angharad with the task of accompanying Kaér on his quest.

The Paéns were to be spread throughout the border villages, from Waén in the north to Zenae in the south, speeding communications between there and the High Council. Kaér and Angharad intended going in by foot anyway. The advantage of speed, which might be achieved by using the animals, was vastly outweighed by the perils of being unable to hide either them or their tracks. Anything so strange was sure to be observed and the alert would spread rapidly through the Cantaén villages. When they returned with The Shintae, they could retrieve them then and be transported swiftly away from the danger area without fear of pursuit.

Kaér was well pleased with the arrangements, "Good," he said, "that sounds fine to me. We've also been busy," he added, "preparing and packing provisions enough to keep us going for a fair while. Mount Subae is still, I think, going to be our most likely target. I doubt if they will have gone to the trouble of moving camp, although security will certainly have increased considerably since my previous visit. I know many paths that not only lead in that direction but avoid the most settled areas, so we should remain unseen by all but a chance encounter on the way."

"We had better keep our swords handy, though," interjected Angharad. "I'll be amazed if we make it through without using them."

"There's nothing more certain than that," responded Kaér. "I've a couple of daggers which will come in very handy as well."

"Excellent," Angharad said. "Now I think it's time you learnt to ride. Come on, let's get you started."

Quickly Kaér pulled on his jacket and boots and followed Angharad outside. Spreading a blanket over the back of one of the animals, he soon discovered staying seated was not as easy as it looked, and he took many a tumble before mastering the basic art of riding. He persevered and, by evening, found he was able to exercise a reasonable measure of control over his mount. This gave little comfort, however, when later that night he tried moving aching muscles he had not realised existed before. After three days of intensive practice, however, Kaér pronounced himself confident enough to travel. He could control his Paén quite adequately, riding almost as well as the others.

Rising early the following morning, they were all eager to make a start on the arduous journey. Drawing back the heavy drapes covering one of the windows, Kaér pushed back the shutters and stared outside in disbelief.

"Come over here" he called to the others as a chill breeze blew through the opening. "It's snowing! The ground's covered and it has already started to drift. We could have done without this," he added in frustration.

Opening the shutters on several other windows, the occupants gazed out upon a brand new world. The land was blanketed in white, the swirling flakes propelled through the trees towards them by the gusting wind. Already, a two foot drift had built up against the side of the cabin as the beholders stood, fascinated by the sight. The Paéns, however, were not so easily impressed and stood heads down, tails to the wind. Forcing themselves away from the view, Kaér and his guests prepared breakfast. Subdued by the weather, they ate in silence, everyone engrossed with their own thoughts for the future.

"I think we should leave now," Kaér advised as they finished eating. "The longer we delay the more difficult the travelling will become."

Leaving the table, they put on their outdoor clothing and collected their possessions. Once outside, those who were to accompany him to the border said their good-byes to those who were to remain. Kaér bade a particularly warm farewell to everyone who had nursed him back to fitness, especially Banthrop who had taken charge of his recovery. Finally, when all that could be said had been uttered, the travellers placed blankets on top of their Paéns and mounted, awaiting the order to move off. Delaying a moment to gaze one final time at his home, Kaér gave the signal to move and, with a final wave to the assembly, they were off. Within minutes, they entered the forest and the clearing was lost to sight, hidden behind trees and driving snow.

They journeyed through the storm that, in varying degrees of severity, continued for most of the morning. By lunchtime, however, the clouds had begun to lift and their spirits likewise. As the snow ceased falling, their rate of progress increased and despite the heavy going, they managed a good twenty-five miles before darkness began to fall. Pitching their tents, they ate a cold meal in weary silence before turning in for the night. Kaér had to admit there was nothing quite like being bounced up and down on the back of a strange animal to jar every bone and muscle in your body; he just hoped he would still be able to move next morning.

Awakening stiffly from the cold, they breakfasted early before breaking camp, ready to ride at the first signs of daylight. Snowfall had been lighter here and the Paéns trotted easily along the trail, managing a good fifty miles before darkness overtook them. By dawn, the leaden skies had produced near blizzard conditions. Travel grew progressively more difficult as the hours crept by and, just after noon, they were forced to call a halt. Clearing snow from a patch of grass to allow the Paéns to eat, they rubbed the animals down and tethered them securely.

These were not the conditions for cold fare, Kaér declared, and so, accompanied by Angharad, he left the men to pitch tents while they went in search of firewood. They made several trips, each time returning fully laden with dead wood. It did not take long for them to produce a blazing fire nor the accompanying, mouth-watering, smell of cooking. The remainder of the afternoon passed slowly as they sheltered from the storm. Most of them taking advantage of the delay by rubbing waxes and oils deep into their outer clothes to ensure they remained waterproof.

"The weather doesn't appear to be improving," commented one of the men next morning. "I wonder if it's worthwhile even starting out!"

"Of course it is," responded Kaér straightaway, "it's vital we reach the border as soon as it is physically possible for us to do so. While we are fresh from a good night's rest, I think we should at least make the effort and see how we go. It's good practice for Angharad and there'll be far worse to come in the mountains."

Angharad readily agreed, collecting her pack together even as they spoke. The driving flakes eased to a trickle by mid morning and, eventually, abated altogether. By then, the path had veered in a slightly different direction and, with the trees forming a windbreak; the trail was relatively free from deep lying snow. Increasing their pace, they even managed a canter in places and, by evening, had gained back some of the time lost the previous day. The weather continued to stay kind to them and, even with the intense overnight frosts, they made good progress. Three days later found them passing through fortified walls as they entered the border village of Nemae, a journey of just over two hundred and fifty miles from Kaér's home.

Once through the gates, a cheerful group of villagers, fascinated by the sight of the Paéns, swarmed around them. The milling crowd swelled as they approached the central square, young and old alike, all trying to catch sight of the visitors at once as children screamed and shouted in excitement, running every which way. Dismounting, they saw to the needs of their mounts before the headman escorted them to his house to rest while a feast was organised in their honour.

Later that evening in the communal hall, after they had all eaten their fill, Kaér and Angharad answered as many questions about their plans as they thought prudent to do so. The curious villagers seemed satisfied with what information was given; politely declining to press deeper when the replies were somewhat vague. Most appeared delighted at having one of the beasts stabled in their village, although the odd one or two had to be reassured they represented no danger to their families. As they exhausted their questions, Rin, the headman, pushed back his chair and stood up, rapping the table in front of him to silence the general clamour.

"Quiet!" he called and, as the room fell silent, continued, "would everyone please rise to their feet? I would like to propose a toast. To, Kaér, and, Angharad," he said turning towards them and raising his goblet, "may your mission be a resounding success."

"Kaér! Angharad!" came the response from the assembly followed by a round of applause. Standing, they acknowledged the toast and thanked their host.

Seated once more, Rin turned to his guests and said, "Well, you would appear to have planned well, Kaér. As always, you look ahead leaving little to chance. But more of that another time," he added, noticing Angharad stifling a yawn, "you must be weary after your journey, I've had rooms prepared throughout the village for you and your followers."

"Rin, your hospitality is kindness personified," Kaér returned graciously. "We dared expect no more after this sumptuous meal than to be left to sleep in our tents. You are indeed generous and I humbly accept your offer of a room, not only for myself but for my companions as well."

Now the little courtesies had been observed, the gathering broke up as various villagers collected members of the group and escorted them to their dwellings. Kaér and Angharad were to be the personal guests of Rin and he, himself, took them to his home and showed them to their rooms. Both were similar, each containing a bed of thick blankets and furs laid on top of a stout wooden framework. Reed mats covered the floors while heavy drapes masked the windows to keep out the cold. Over in one corner of the room, a small blaze glowed in the hearth of a fireplace, emitting just sufficient heat to keep the air at an even temperature. Outside, the timber walls were thickly layered in mud and straw to cover any cracks.

Retiring, they fell sound asleep almost instantly. There they stayed until noon the following day. Kaér, rising first, dressed swiftly before knocking loudly on Angharad's door to awaken her. Making their way back to the communal hall, they were greeted by Rin and Sereca, his wife. Seating them at one of the empty tables, Sereca placed a plate filled with tasty morsels before them. Taking his leave, Rin went off to concentrate on village business and, looking round as they ate, Kaér was surprised to see just one other of their companions in the room, seated next to the fire.

"Goodric!" he called. "Where are the others? Surely they're not all still in their beds?"

"They certainly aren't," answered Goodric, laughing. "They were up, breakfasted and away hours ago. They decided you needed to rest and left quietly without disturbing your sleep. They asked me to pass on their best wishes for a successful mission."

"Oh, thanks! Well, if they've moved on to other villages, then why haven't you?" queried Angharad.

"We drew lots to see which hamlet we were to be stationed at and I struck lucky, I picked Nemae," Goodric replied in satisfaction.

"It would seem," returned Kaér with a smile, "that only Angharad and I are the lazy ones today."

Finishing his meal, Kaér moved over to the fire where, shortly afterwards, Angharad joined him and Goodric. There they stayed for a while, talking and planning, with Goodric throwing in a few suggestions every now and then.

Suddenly Goodric spoke up, "Don't you think," he said, "you'll be rather conspicuous in your dark clothes against the snow."

"Yes, that's true," replied Kaér, "but what else can we do? I rarely travel through Cantaé in winter and, when I have done in the past, I've always kept to the back ways and not concerned myself about it. Obviously, I've been seen occasionally, but only from a distance; usually they mistake me for one of their own and don't bother to investigate." He studied a moment before continuing. "Things are bound to be different this time, however, they'll be on the alert and expecting an incursion. Anyone they see, especially off the main trails, will be challenged immediately. Why, have you any ideas?"

"Well, I think I might have a solution," Goodric considered. "This morning, while out exploring in and around the village, I came across a bundle of white lightweight cloth. I'm sure if we asked the local tailor, he'd be able to run up some loose fitting garments to go over the top of your outer clothes."

"It's a marvellous idea," Angharad said, throwing her arms around him in delight. "We can waterproof the material and, if there's enough left, we could get him to stitch a layer over one side of our tents so they won't stick out when we make camp. What do you think, Kaér?" she asked, releasing a blushing Goodric.

"No, it's not a marvellous idea," Kaér said firmly, waiting as he watched their faces fall. "It's an absolutely brilliant one," he added with a smile. "How soon do you think you could get this done for us, we can't delay here much after today?"

"I would have thought it could be done straightaway. Come, let's go and find the tailor now and see about getting you both measured," Goodric said, dashing out of the room to find Sereca and ask her for directions.

Later that same day, before the evening meal, the new clothes were brought to them. Trying them on over their outdoor clothes, they found them a perfect fit. Thanking the tailor profusely for his efforts, he confirmed there was sufficient cloth to cover the outside of their tents and it was agreed he would complete and return them before morning. Moving outside, they made their way to the edge of the village. Walking forty paces or so across a snow-covered field outside the walls, Angharad suddenly dropped flat onto the powdery mass beneath. The watchers shouted excitedly, for it looked as though she had disappeared into thin air. Regaining her feet, Angharad continued to walk away and, before she had covered another thirty paces, it had become difficult to pick her out against the white landscape. Whenever she halted, it became almost impossible to pinpoint her and Kaér called her back, secure in the knowledge their outfits worked well in the fading light of evening. Broad daylight was another matter, however, although he felt confident they would not be as easily seen when moving.

Following much talk and discussion over their evening meal, they decided to take their leave of Nemae just before daybreak. Nothing more could be achieved by sitting around, so the two travellers retired early to rest and gather as much strength as they could. They would, after all, find few other opportunities to sleep in such peace and relative safety during the coming months.

They slept soundly until being awakened by Rin a good two hours before dawn. Swiftly they rose, dressed and partook of a hearty breakfast. Once their appetites had been sated, they retrieved their packs, now fully laden with fresh provisions of dried food, kindling and wax for their clothing. The tents and been returned as promised and they each strapped one to the top of their packs. Once the packs were ready, they donned their fleece-lined jackets and white outer coverings, which Kaér named Aralpos after a small white furry animal of the mountain peaks. With their supplies in place, they were ready for off, bidding farewell to the villagers who, in spite of the early hour, had materialised from out of the darkness. Goodric accompanied them to the village perimeter where, overcome by emotion, he wished them luck before turning back.

With a final wave, they stepped through the gateway and started up the hillside leading to the mountain ranges. Suddenly, Sereca came dashing up behind, calling on them to wait. On reaching them, she fastened two pieces of white cloth securely over their packs. Realising earlier, she explained, their supplies and equipment would stand out against their Aralpos; she had rushed to make covers for them. Expressing their gratitude, they waited until she was safely through the gates before continuing on their way.

Something cold and wet touched against their faces and, looking skywards, they saw it had started to snow again. Within minutes the fine white flakes were swirling all around and, on looking back, Nemae was lost to sight, their tracks fading as the snowfall grew heavier. Finally, undetected, they crossed silently over the border, on the road to The Shintae at last.

Chapter Five

Four long months had passed since Sartae's triumphal return and the initial euphoria of his escape had evaporated. In its place, uneasiness had taken root and this continued to grow insidiously. The Maraéns, he knew, could ill afford to take the loss of The Shintae lightly, certainly not without attempting to recover it. There had, however, been neither retaliatory raids into Cantaé nor signs of any such expeditions even being mounted. Having no clue as to what the enemy was planning, meant it was extremely hard for him to instigate counter measures.

The only news, of even minor interest, had come in a routine report several days earlier. A number of strangers, riding on the backs of some very strange creatures, had been observed entering and leaving several of the Maraén border villages. The great snowstorm had started shortly afterwards, cutting off all communications for a full week and making it virtually impracticable for any further movement to be noted. Surely no foreigner would have attempted to negotiate the mountains in such conditions when even the inhabitants stayed indoors: especially Maraéns whose knowledge of the sierra was non-existent? The latest information just received indicated the strangers and their beasts appeared to have settled at their respective destinations. He sent a messenger to the border immediately with instructions for the watchers, commanding them to monitor the situation and eliminate any who tried to enter Cantaé.

No matter what action he took to improve security, he could not shake off a feeling of foreboding. Lack of sleep, caused by nightmares in which the enemy protagonist, Kaér, was the driving force did not help either. Sartae was now positive that Kaér had survived his wounds and would, somehow, come in search of The Stone of Power. He could not, must not, be allowed to succeed a second time.

Since the return of The Shintae, the Guros had worked over it day and night and, finally, had begun to make progress in uncovering its secrets. Unfortunately, they had not attained the same state of advancement, as had their ill-fated fellows. Although The Stone could be made to pulsate and cause thunder and lightning to appear overhead, the combination of sounds and noises that would enable them to create and direct this phenomenon at will eluded them. Sartae drove them like a man possessed, ranting and raging if he so much as suspected them of slacking. The camp itself had become a virtual prison with soldiers of the Cantaén Guard constantly patrolling the perimeter and sentries set every ten paces. During the night, patrols were doubled and when the Guros took their turn to rest, guards surrounded them at all times. Once back at work they were again encompassed by a ring of armed sentries and unable to make a move without an escort.

Wherever he was, Sartae incessantly shouted orders, pouncing on any who misunderstood or failed to carry out his instructions; inflicting the severest of punishments on those who transgressed. Floggings were a daily occurrence and his followers walked in fear of his every move, word, and thought.

Suddenly Sartae decided to do something about the problem that worried him the most. Storming over to the entrance of his tent, he called over one of the guards on duty, "Hey! You! Yes you, you idiot," he thundered. "Go fetch Biren over to me, at once."

Biren had taken over as second in command after Traé had failed to return from his mission, which in itself was a pointer to Kaér still being alive. Not that Traé's demise worried Sartae in the slightest, but Kaér's continuing existence was another matter. Suppose, just suppose, he had actually managed to slip through the watchers on the border and was, at this very moment, advancing towards the camp. Sartae decided he would do well to prepare for such an eventuality.

Pacing fretfully outside his quarters, Sartae stamped his feet impatiently in a vain attempt to keep them warm. Now the snow had ceased, it had become bitterly cold with a frost as cruel as it was hard. After what seemed to him an intolerable length of time, the figure of Biren came running towards him, feet pounding over the blackened hard packed pathways. His long dark hair flowed out in his speed of travel and his face turned purple with exertion. Reaching his master's side, he stood to attention, panting heavily as he tried to regain some measure of composure.

"I came…as soon…as I heard you…wished to see me," he gasped.

"Rubbish!" snapped Sartae in reply. "If you'd tried you could have got here sooner. However, we will discuss this matter later, for the moment, I have other, far more urgent, matters to talk about. Follow me," he commanded, stomping back inside his quarters.

Realising his master's mood was not of the best, Biren followed without comment, inwardly seething at his treatment in front of the sniggering guards. Not for the first time did he wonder if being second in command to an absolute dictator placed him only one step away from that of an errand boy. Selecting a large comfortable chair Sartae seated himself beside the glowing fire, indicating to Biren that he should pull up one of the smaller wooden benches nearby. Sensing that the mood of a few seconds earlier was abating, Biren asked what was required of him.

"I've been wondering," Sartae replied slowly as he settled himself more comfortably into his chair, "what would happen if any of those wretched Maraéns managed to avoid the ever watchful eyes of my scouts and border patrols, and steal across the border without being seen, how would they reach here?"

"By using our network of roads and pathways I presume," responded Biren thoughtfully as he cast his mind over the problem. "The mountains are virtually impassable by any other means at the moment, all the high passes are blocked by snow and will remain so until spring."

"Yes, that's the most obvious way," Sartae agreed, his temper now under control, "but remember, Maraén scouts have travelled widely over our eastern lands. Perhaps not as far as this, but Kaér, as we know to our cost, has ventured here and beyond. What worries me most of all is this. How does he manage to enter, wander at will and yet be seen so rarely?"

Pausing to let his words sink in, Sartae helped himself to a goblet of wine from a flagon standing on a table next to him. Glancing across at his deputy, he found him deep in thought. On seeing this he filled another, much smaller, goblet with the dark green liquid, and offered it to him.

"Have you come up with anything yet?" he demanded as Biren readily accepted the goblet.

"Well, as I see it, the only way they can move about so readily is by routes that are rarely used, disused or unknown to us," Biren said, stating the obvious before sampling the wine and continuing. "We occasionally stumble over trails made by the Ancient Ones, pathways that apparently lead nowhere. I cannot think of anyone who has bothered to explore them, as you well know, our people tend to travel by the easiest routes. So, if you kept well away from the main trails, watched out for goat herders or shepherds and weren't afraid of difficult conditions, then you could travel virtually anywhere with relative impunity."

"Mm! That must be it," mused Sartae, draining his wine and helping himself to some more. "They must have discovered an all-weather passage over the tops, an ancient trail perhaps, most probably a difficult one, but one that allows them freedom of movement."

Standing, Sartae began to pace, muttering heavily to himself. Wisely, Biren fell silent. There were easier ways of incurring Sartae's displeasure than by interrupting him whilst he was deep in thought, but few more certain. Greed, however, overcame his caution and, whilst his leader's back was turned, he furtively helped himself to another generous measure of wine from the nearby flagon. Fully aware of the consequences should he be caught in the act, he was unable to resist the temptation; wine of such fine quality was hard to come by. Swiftly he downed a good third of the wondrous liquid before replacing his goblet on the desk at his side, confident no attention would be paid to the partially filled container.

It was some time before Sartae ceased his aimless pacing and took refuge in his chair again. Casually he glanced at Biren's goblet, a frown fleetingly crossed his brow but then he relaxed, certain no one would dare to help himself behind his back.

"I've decided what must be done but, before I tell you, drink up and have some more wine," Sartae insisted, to the delight of Biren, who could scarcely believe his good fortune.

"Pick a squad of your best men," he continued, "and take them into the mountains and circle around the camp, up to a distance of about three or four miles. You must explore everything you come across that remotely resembles a trail. Whenever you find something that you consider a possible pathway, leave three or four guards in a convenient spot to watch over it. Give them a tent and sufficient provisions to last for at least a month . Under no pretext are they to move from their base unless they detect someone travelling their way. I will not have them leaving tracks all over the place to warn intruders," he stipulated. "Make sure they fully understand that. Then, after a month…" He paused to clear his throat and recharge his goblet.

"Let me see, where was I," he resumed. "Ah! Yes! At the end of a month, if I deem it necessary, I shall send out a relief party, otherwise a messenger will recall them. What do you think?" he demanded.

Biren remained silent for a moment as he sipped his wine, savouring its exquisite flavour. Ceasing his reverie, he applied himself to answering Sartae who was becoming increasingly impatient at the studied silence.

"I've just one little query," he said hesitantly, not knowing quite how to put his criticism to Sartae. "How exactly do we find trails, which even under normal conditions are barely visible, when they're covered in drifts? Some are so deep they could bury a standing man more than three times over. The rest of the plan is indeed excellent, but perhaps you've already thought of this and have a solution?" Biren concluded, pleased to have passed off his censure in such a way that Sartae, even if he should resent it, could say little without losing face.

"Don't you listen?" Sartae shouted angrily in reply. "I've already told you once that when you discover something that might be considered a trail, you've to set a watch on it. If you should miss one and an intruder makes his way through," he added vindictively, "I'll hand you to the guards myself for their entertainment. There, does that answer your query?" he sneered.

Pulling himself to his feet, Sartae indicated the meeting was at an end and Biren, wishful not to incur any more of Sartae's wrath, departed rapidly. Returning to his tent he cursed himself repeatedly for sneaking the extra wine. Far stronger than anything he was accustomed to, it had clouded his judgement and loosened his tongue, foolishly tempting him to try to outwit his leader. Back under his own roof, he washed his face in icy water to clear his mind. Venting his anger on his subordinates, Biren handed out beatings for even the slightest delay in carrying out his demands. In due course he assembled his force and, with ample supplies, left the encampment for the mountain slopes lying deep in the shadow of Mount Subae.

Alone in his tent, Sartae reviewed his talk with Biren. Initially, he was pleased with himself for turning the tables on him, but after a while, this feeling deserted him. Again, the presentiment of meeting Kaér was strong within and he shivered involuntarily, drawing closer to the fire. Lost in a world of melancholy, he gazed into the comforting flames for some considerable time. These recurring black thoughts of late were disquieting, not least because, as he was fully aware, if he failed again and the Maraéns retook The Shintae, it could well be himself and not Biren who was given to the guards for disposal. The coming of night brought a return to his normal spirits and berating his servants for not bringing his evening meal sooner, he ordered them to be flogged at dawn.

By the time Sartae's food had been placed before him, Biren was already some distance away and had already stationed two separate groups to guard what looked to be likely spots for a trail to end. Calling his men together, he ordered camp for the night, watching idly while they erected his tent first. Once a fire had been started in the centre of the encampment, Biren warmed himself while the others prepared something to eat.

Later, sitting alone at the entrance to his tent, flaps thrown open so he might reap the benefit from the flames, Biren ate in silence, his mind filled with dark thoughts. If only he had curbed the drunken impulse that had prompted him to speak out, he might, possibly, have been able to depute someone else to come and watch over these bleak, inhospitable fells. Back at the main camp, they would be eating in warmth and comfort, discussing the evening's amusement to come. Half a dozen prisoners had just been brought into camp and Biren knew his comrades would be planning an interrogation session for the luckless captives.

Biren contemplated on this, eyes gleaming with sadistic thoughts. Suddenly he shuddered as he recalled Sartae's words, if he failed then he would be the one on the rack. His chances of success were solely dependent on luck, and this was not something that seemed to be running his way. No one, certainly in these conditions, could be expected to find all the paths, which may or may not lie around. Should intruders happen to pick a route where there was no sentinel, they would easily slip through the line of watchers. Even if they did select a way that was under observation there was no guarantee of them being seen (particularly if they came at night), nor their tracks noticed until long after they had gone by.

Repeatedly he had given strict instructions that, if anyone was spotted, one of them must go for help straightaway whilst the others attempted to detain the intruders. Knowing his men as well as he did, Biren was sure that in the heat of the moment they would all engage in battle, each one determined to claim the kill. If one of their opponents turned out to be Kaér, Sartae having convinced him he was the only Maraén capable of penetrating this far, then it seemed doubtful that a mere handful of his own men would be able to stop them.

Biren made a vow to himself there and then. If any Maraén slipped through the net then he, for one, was not going to suffer the consequences. Should any mistakes be made and it proved at all possible, he would attempt to escape from

Cantaé. The distant lands to the west seemed a likely destination. Having questioned wanderers from those regions, he knew of numerous kingdoms far away from Cantaé, where he could seek exile without too many questions being asked.

His decision made, Biren sat back and relaxed in a happier frame of mind. With the improved mood came a desire for wine, perhaps not of the quality of Sartae's, but one from his own stores would prove agreeable. Walking over to his baggage, he discovered that, in his haste to leave, he had neglected to pack any. Furious with himself and cursing loudly, he strode out of his tent and commandeered the supplies of one of his officers, striking him savagely about the head when he dared to complain.

Chapter Six

Sweeping down over the land, darkness found Angharad and Kaér weary in the extreme. After leaving Nemae that morning they had penetrated, albeit with ever increasing difficulty, well into the lower reaches of the mountains, crossing the unmarked border under cover of the swirling blizzard, unmolested and unobserved. After becoming separated for a short while early on, they had roped themselves securely together before moving off again. For many hours afterwards they had clambered blindly upwards, grateful for the spikes strapped beneath their boots as they negotiated the ever-steepening ground, eventually stumbling across a narrow valley. With no obvious landmarks visible, Kaér was unable to say with any certainty whether this was the way. In the end they decided to follow its course as, if nothing else, it would guide them farther into Cantaé. Initially, the vale sheltered them from the driving winds, enabling them to make steady progress, until a slight change of direction caused them to take the full brunt of the storm once more.

The snow was settling much deeper here than on the mountainsides and before long, they were floundering through the numerous drifts. After much endeavour, their minds numbed by the constant buffeting of the wind, Kaér regained sufficient control of his senses long enough to lead them both to the shelter of a rocky spur. Recovering their breath, they ate a little from their supplies. Kaér, on checking his pack, began to exclaim loudly.

"What an idiot I am," he remonstrated angrily with himself.

"Anything the matter?" inquired a curious Angharad, bewildered by the outburst and a little amused at the expression on her companion's face.

"You won't believe what I've just found," Kaér continued, somewhat shamefaced. "You remember Sereca, Rins wife, dashing after us when we left Nemae. When she covered the packs, she covered everything on them," he elucidated profoundly, but unfortunately making little sense to Angharad.

"Well, that sounds fairly logical to me," she commented. "When you wrap something properly, you do tend to find it hides everything beneath. Now, why don't you take a deep breath and start again, I might be able to understand what it is you're trying to tell me then."

"Perhaps you're right," responded Kaér finally. "What, with the constant howling of the wind and the driving snow, my mind must have been addled by the time we hit the valley. On my pack, neatly hidden beneath the covers are, would you believe, two pairs of snowshoes," he confessed, miserably.

"Snow shoes!" exclaimed Angharad in amazement. "You mean we've ploughed our way through all this and you're carrying snowshoes? I certainly do see what you mean," she acknowledged, "you've completely lost your wits. How could anybody just happen to forget about them?" she added in mock severity.

"I'm afraid I could," Kaér had to admit, thoroughly disgusted with himself over his negligence. "In the dark with the crowd milling round before we left, it's not surprising you didn't notice them, and then later, of course, they were out of sight. They were specially made for us. As you can see," he said, uncovering them completely, "when folded they are half normal size, making them easier to carry and no protrusions anywhere," he sighed and shook his head. "How incredibly stupid can a person be? No, don't bother answering," he added sharply as Angharad opened her mouth to speak.

Upon seeing his woeful expression, Angharad could no longer restrain herself and burst into laughter, which Kaér—after a few moments of hurt silence—joined in heartily. In better spirits, they allowed themselves a short while longer to rest before braving the elements again, travelling far more easily with the aid of the snow shoes. By nightfall both were suffering from the onset of fatigue that, combined with the rapid temperature drop, could easily have proved fatal had they tried to continue. Searching round for a sheltered spot, they came across a large rock formation protruding from the valley side behind which, in a tiny area free from snow, they pitched Kaér's tent.

From the remains of a dead tree nearby, they obtained sufficient wood to enable them, with the aid of kindling from their packs, to start a small fire. There was no risk of a blaze being observed in this uninhabited region in such a storm.

While Kaér collected more fuel, Angharad hung a shallow dish from a tripod stand she had erected over the flames and managed to produce a hot meal. Neither showed much inclination for talk and, once they had finished eating, they crawled, fully dressed, into their sleeping rugs.

They slept fitfully throughout the long night, waking frequently shivering from the cold. Taking it in turns, one or the other would add wood to the fire to afford a little extra warmth. Daybreak found them out of their beds, the land around barely visible as the wan light filtered through the threatening clouds and falling snow. After eating a hot breakfast, cooked with the last of the readily available fuel, they re-coated their Aralpos with waxes to reinforce the waterproofing. The sky gradually brightened to a dirty shade of grey and, as there seemed little prospect of any further improvement, they decided to break camp. Putting out the remains of the fire with handfuls of snow, the spot would soon cool and be covered over. Securing their supplies against damp, they strapped on the snowshoes and stepped out under the leaden sky.

Keeping to a slow but steady pace, they worked their way higher up the valley, pausing only for a few minutes in each hour to rest and catch their breath. Around mid-day, they halted, taking a short break to eat. Slipping off the rope which linked them, Kaér removed his pack and partially erected his tent as a windbreak. Angharad procured food from her pack, frowning with distaste at the thought of a cold lunch in such appalling conditions.

"Why don't we pitch tent properly?" she shouted above the roar of the wind. "The weather's not improving and if we don't stop soon, we'll be exhausted."

"No! Not yet," insisted Kaér, staggering under the force of a vicious gust from an unexpected quarter, "we have to go on. If this is the right valley and I am sure it is, there's a cavern up ahead. I've taken refuge there before and always left a good supply of food, blankets and firewood. It's a chance we have to take. This storm might go on for days and without a fire to keep us warm, we could easily freeze to death."

The prospect of sanctuary was an irresistible draw and Angharad readily agreed, smiling in anticipation. Joining Kaér behind the shelter of the windbreak, they ate sparingly, aware of the need to conserve their supplies. Should they be unable to locate the cave, it might be a very long time indeed before they were able to replenish their stocks. Packing away the tent, they roped themselves together again and continued, laboriously, on their way. Desperate not to miss the cave entrance, they were compelled to move in closer to the valley sides, increasing considerably their difficulties in moving.

Spurs and protrusions intruded onto their passage, forcing them to either go round or climb over, all of which severely depleted their reserves of energy.

By late afternoon, their movement had degenerated so much it could, at best, only be described as an erratic shuffling gait. At no point had they sighted the cavern and both were near physical collapse. Time ceased to have any meaning as they staggered on with no conscious realisation as to what they were doing, or even why they were doing it. Finally, Angharad sank to the ground, incapable of moving further. Kaér, pulled up short by the rope tied around his waist, turned and stared blankly at her for several moments before shaking off the lethargy that engulfed him. Going back, he knelt down and lifted her head clear of the snow.

"Go on, leave me," she whispered. "I can't manage another step. Save yourself. One of us must get through."

"No! Never! I can't. I won't," Kaér screamed out in anguish, shaking his fist at the storm.

As if in sympathy the wind took pity on them and veered to one side, briefly leaving the way ahead clear. In astonishment, he ceased his outburst as, in the murky light, he dimly made out a dark shape against the walls of snow not more than fifty paces away.

Turning back to Angharad, he spoke urgently to her. "Listen," he said, "I think the cavern's directly ahead. I'm going to take a quick look and then come straight back for you. Don't worry, I won't be long."

Untying the rope that bound them together, Kaér hastened towards the opening, tumbling over the threshold towards the darkness beyond. Dropping to his knees, he gasped for breath as his abused muscles cried out for rest. He recognised his surroundings immediately as the shelter he had been seeking but, before succumbing to his desire to sleep, he had to return for Angharad. With great difficulty, he struggled to his feet, swaying as his chest heaved and his eyes blurred. Taking a deep breath to clear his mind, he turned to leave when, from high above on the valley side, came an almighty crack closely followed by a deep-throated roar. Instinctively he threw himself backwards as the world around suddenly went mad. A vast wall of snow and ice came plummeting down from the peaks, shaking the very earth beneath. Kaer was swept deeper inside the cave by a sheet of densely packed snow that pinned his legs to the ground. Pressing his hands tightly over his ears, he tried to shut out the dreadful cacophony that assailed him. A terrific thud nearby jarred every bone in his body but he was too shaken to realise what the sudden drop in sound that accompanied it might mean.

Gradually the vibrations ceased as the avalanche passed down the valley, leaving him trembling in reaction. His mind in a stupor, he was for a long while incapable of doing anything to ease his position. Slowly the nervous shaking left his limbs and, instead, he started to shiver with cold as his brain, albeit on a basic level, began to function again. Realising damp was penetrating the folds in his clothing he scrabbled free from the mound of snow and, in total darkness, felt his way through to the main chamber. Colliding with a stack of firewood helped to concentrate his thoughts and he removed his pack. More by reflex action than conscious effort, he extracted a lamp and tinderbox from amongst his belongings and with hands made clumsy by the cold, managed finally to obtain a light. Gathering sufficient kindling together, he built a fire and lit it from his flickering lamp. His teeth chattered incessantly and he stripped off his wet clothes, hanging them from a makeshift rack to dry. Pulling his sleeping rugs from his pack, he pulled them tightly around him and ate a little food. Eventually, his body warmed, his eyes closed and he sank into a troubled sleep.

Chapter Seven

Almost thirty-six hours passed before Kaér surfaced from the slumberous depths, stretching out and yawning, revelling in the rare luxury of a warm bed. This indolent mood soon faded as awareness of his surroundings encroached upon his mind and hazy thoughts of the day before, as he presumed it to be, began to trouble him. The cavern was in darkness and so, forcing himself to rise, he draped the furs around his waist and went in search of a fresh lamp, barely aided by the faint light radiating from the dying embers. Luckily, it was not long before he came across a lamp, buried deep within his supplies. At some point during the night, probably several times, he must have added fuel to the fire, although he had no recollection of having done so. Blowing some life back into the ashes, he lit the lamp from the glowing remains, the flame flickering in the cool draft emanating from the numerous holes and fissures in the cavern walls and roof. Shivering, he retrieved his dried clothes and dressed quickly.

With light to work by, he raked out the ashes and rebuilt the fire that, after a little gentle coaxing, crackled back into life. As he crouched down to warm his hands against the leaping flames, the mists of shock began to lift and a dreadful thought occurred to him. Where was Angharad? Why was she not here, inside, with him? For a brief moment, his mind remained blank and then everything flooded back. Stricken with horror, he remembered leaving her in the snow while he came on ahead to check the cavern. Not only had he left his companion to die alone but, in his traumatized state, he had even forgotten her very existence.

Perhaps, he tried convincing himself, she had not perished after all and was even now awaiting rescue. No matter how unlikely this hypothesis might be, he seized hold of the lamp and headed directly to the cave mouth. Dashing round the corner, he came to an abrupt halt, gazing in disbelief at what had once been the way to the world outside. Instead of an opening, or mound of snow through which he could tunnel, there stood a wall of solid stone. Triggered by the avalanche, a rockslide had deposited a huge boulder inside the entrance, blocking the passageway completely. Stunned, he put down the lamp and began to heave and strain against the barrier, but it remained firmly wedged. Gasping for breath and shaking with the effort, he was forced to abandon the uneven struggle.

As his breathing steadied, Kaér reconsidered his options. This was no longer just an attempt to rescue Angharad, but a struggle to escape alive from what might yet become his own tomb. Although the situation was precarious, he refused to surrender all hope; he would have to dig his way out from around the edges. Before this he required food. His exertions had left him strangely weak and light headed and an uneasy feeling crept over him that, perhaps, he had slept far longer than he had initially suspected.

Adding more wood to the fire, he noted with dismay the store of fuel had already dropped significantly. Putting this to the back of his mind, he looked around for something he could use as a tool to help him in his enterprise, eating as he searched. Unearthing a broken spear, a trophy from an encounter with the Cantaéns, he returned to the entrance where, after placing a lamp on a nearby ledge, he began attacking the edges of the cave mouth. Gradually the earth, packed solid by the rockslide, gave way and hope began to stir in Kaér's heart, but before he had penetrated an arms length, his spear tip struck against solid rock. Not disheartened, he tried higher up and then over on the other side, but always with the same result.

An hour later, he stood back panting heavily and soaked with sweat. Before him stood the boulder, fully exposed and covering every square inch of the entrance, whilst all around stood the mounds of soil and rubble he had cleared away. He had tried going over, under and around, only to be foiled by bare rock at every attempt. With his shoulders hunched more than normal, Kaér retrieved his lamp and wandered back to the main chamber. Convinced of the utter hopelessness of his position, he sank down at the edge of the fire and buried his head in his hands. Some time passed before he moved again, crossing over to the small stream that flowed down a narrow channel at the far end of the chamber. Washing the dirt and filth from himself and his clothes, he gazed absent-mindedly at the tiny hole through where the water drained away. If only he was small enough to follow it, he thought wishfully.

Later, whilst resting on his bed, he stared dejectedly at the roof, illuminated by the shifting, murky light of the lamp. How the idea occurred to him, he did not exactly know, but he suddenly found himself concentrating on a spot near the top of the cave wall. The smoke! That was it! The way the smoke was drawn through an opening high above. There had to be an exit for the fumes, and probably not too far away, where he might be able to affect his own release. Rising to his feet, he gazed intently at the hole as if by looking he could be transported there. Unfortunately, the opening, although large enough, was well over twice his height above the cavern floor, the walls were smooth at that point with neither a hand nor foothold in sight.

"Of course!" he muttered aloud. "The rubble at the entrance."

Lighting a second lamp, he took it with him to the blocked exit and placed it on the ledge he had used previously. Now, with all areas of his prison illuminated, he began to implement the first stage of his plan. For an hour or more he laboured, carrying, rolling, or dragging stones and boulders through to the main chamber before seating them beneath the opening, packing them tight with soil. Slowly a platform rose from the ground. The increase sometimes almost imperceptible and then, as he came across larger items, it would grow rapidly, each precious inch gained a victory. Exhausting his supply of readily available building materials, he stepped back and admired his handiwork.

Although weary from the toil, he was impatient to put his idea to the test and see if he could reach his goal. Scrambling up the steeply rising steps that formed one end of the mound, he gained access to the platform above. Almost as high as himself, the construction remained firm and did not crumble beneath his weight as he feared it might. Resting for a moment or two, he prepared himself and then leapt, his outstretched arms clawing desperately for the tunnel lip. With a resounding crash, he dropped back and hit the platform. His feet skidded on the uneven surface as he landed and he ended up, on his back, precariously hanging over the edge. Recovering his breath, he sat up cautiously. Despite having jumped with all his might, he had missed his goal by a good eighteen inches. Staggering to his feet, he winced with the pain from his rebelling muscles, bruised by the fall and strained from the hard work.

He decided against trying again. He acknowledged it probably would have been wiser to rest before making his first attempt. Gingerly, he dropped down to ground level where he became aware of how neglected his fire had become.

The feverish pace of his labour had kept him warm before, but now he could feel a chill in the air. Stirring the charred embers, he perceived a faint glimmer of red and, kneeling down, swiftly he blew the remains back into life. Having obtained a satisfactory blaze, he sat and warmed himself before the flames. As the chamber warmed, he stripped and applied some healing salve over his limbs. Too tired to eat, he wrapped his rugs around his aching body and was soon asleep.

When he awakened, many hours later, Kaér felt much refreshed and, apart from the odd twinge, free from all aches and pains. Although the day felt new to him, outside it was noon on the third day of his incarceration. With difficulty, he refilled and relit the lamp in the dark before coaxing the fire back into life. Working on the principle that every little bit helps, he collected the ashes and threw them on top of the platform. Taking full advantage of his long stored supplies, he cooked a large breakfast. After eating his fill, he was about to throw the last of the firewood on the blaze when he realised he could make better use of it. Tying the logs together, he piled them on top of the rubble wall, filling and smoothing out the gaps with bundles of spare furs. Standing back he surveyed the mound and was well satisfied with his work; the platform was now high enough to provide an adequate springboard for his purpose. Now all he required were some extra provisions to take with him.

With skills acquired over countless other journeys, Kaér carefully added sufficient dried food to his pack to sustain him for two weeks—not enough to be indulgent but at least he would not starve. Lamp fat was a necessity and he packed as much as he could carry, complete with spare wicks. If he was lucky, he would be out within minutes, but he dare not take that for granted. Pouring away the stale contents from his canteens, he refilled them to capacity from the stream, corking them tightly against leakage. Taking his lamp, he returned for a final look at where the cave mouth had been. The boulder remained and he knew it was hopeless to make any further efforts to dislodge it. Lingering for a few seconds, he paid his last respects to his missing companion, picturing again her warm smile and laughing blue eyes. He experienced a sudden and wrenchingly deep sense of loss and, to his surprise, realised he was going to miss Angharad far more than he had ever thought possible.

"I will come back for you, Angharad," he promised aloud, "and make sure you have a decent burial, one befitting someone as brave as you."

Overcome by emotion, he turned abruptly and strode back to the inner cave. Collecting his possessions, he ascended the steps to reach the platform without a single backward glance. Looking upwards, he shuddered involuntarily.

Normally thoughts of the unknown troubled him not at all, but Kaér knew that on this occasion the fate of his homeland rested squarely on his shoulders. Instead of being free to choose his route at will, he stood entombed inside a tiny hole beneath a mountain—his only means of escape an even smaller opening leading to who knew where? No matter what he found, he would have to follow, even if it led him to his death.

Steadying himself, for the upper layer was not as stable as the ground and stones beneath, he swung the heavy pack round and round. Taking careful aim, he launched his possessions and, with a sigh of relief, watched as they sailed gracefully up to disappear inside the passageway, landing with a dull thud. Removing his jacket, he wrapped the canteens inside. Tying a short length of rope around the bundle, he repeated the previous exercise and was gratified to see it, too, vanish through the opening with barely a sound as the fur absorbed the impact. Now, one thing remained to be done, he had to join his belongings. Despite unbidden fears coursing through his mind, he forced himself to concentrate, taking a deep breath before leaping. Time almost seemed to stand still, the whole manoeuvre appearing to take place in slow motion while his arms felt incredibly tired for, try as he might, they would only rise slowly. His eyes picked out every detail on the chamber wall, every mark and crack registering as he slowly crept by the bare rock. Finally he drew near his goal but his arms would rise no faster, his thoughts raced, each one insisting he had failed and all that remained was an ignominious fall to the rocky floor.

Then, taken by surprise, he was there. His mind switched back to normal and suddenly everything was happening far too quickly. His lunging hands grasped the lip of the entrance, struggling for a hold even before they had connected. Snatching hastily at a barely definable crack inside, he managed to prevent himself from falling backwards but then he started to slip and Kaér believed himself lost. Thrusting even deeper with his right arm, his questing fingers found another fissure, deeper than the first, and he was able to halt his downward movement. Pausing, he took a deep breath and, in spite of the difficulties created by the greasy perspiration on his hands, he managed to pull himself over the edge, aided by his feet gaining purchase on slight irregularities on the cave wall. Sitting back, he allowed the pain from his grazed knuckles to subside and the tightness in his muscles to relax.

Although the chamber below remained illuminated, he found himself lying in a state of semi-darkness. Opening his pack he removed his tinderbox and a lamp that, on the third attempt, he succeeded in lighting. Placing it on the ground beside him, he checked to see whether the canteens had survived the landing. Unwrapping the bundle, he was relieved to find no signs of seepage anywhere. A cool draught flowed through the passageway and he pulled on his jacket and outer furs to ward off the chill. Fixing the pack comfortably over his shoulders. With a length of rope he tied the canteens around his waist. Satisfied his possessions were secure, he scooped up the light and crawled off into the dark.

Within twenty yards the tunnel opened out and he was able to stand upright, his head easily missing the rock above. Unlike the world outside where, no matter how dark it seemed, one could usually make out some vague shape or outline. Inside there was only blackness away from the reach of the lamp. Trying to maintain any kind of pace at all became increasingly difficult. As he progressed, Kaér kept his eyes constantly on the move, searching for dangerous protrusions from the roof and walls or for any sudden dips or rises in the floor that might cause him to stumble. Unfortunately, the longer he stared through the glare of the uncovered light, the more his eyes ached with the strain and the shorter the distance he could see. Shading his eyes with his free hand helped a little, but this was not practical for any length of time. Giving up the struggle, he sat down and decided to do something about it.

Taking a large white pot goblet from his pack, he chipped out a hole in one side of it. Carefully, he enlarged the opening until it reached the lip and almost to the base before standing it upside down over the top of the wick. Forcing it firmly down through the fat to keep it stable, he turned the lamp around with the opening facing away from him. The light, with the reflected glow from the goblet shone away into the distance leaving him in shadow with no direct glare to discomfort his eyes. Highly delighted with the results, Kaér re-fixed his pack and continued on his journey, advancing now at a much more rapid pace.

Many hours passed before he decided stop. To be perfectly honest, his body had decided enough was enough; his stomach was rumbling and, most of all, his legs ached abominably. He had marched for miles through the subterranean passages, scrambling over rock falls, going uphill one moment and downhill the next; winding and twisting one way and then the other so that by now, he had no idea as to which direction he was travelling in. For all he knew, he could be heading back towards Maraé instead of the centre of Cantaé. One thing seemed certain: it was not going to lead him to the outside world as readily as he had hoped.

Dropping his pack, Kaér quickly pulled his furs around him as he became aware of a cool breeze flowing towards him. At least walking had kept him warm. Taking out some of his dried provisions, he chewed stoically at the unappetizing fare, thankful to wash it down with a mouthful of water. Taking a thick rug from his pack, he settled down and covered himself. Using the ground as his mattress and his pack as a pillow, he did his best to make himself comfortable. As it might prove difficult to relight in pitch-blackness, he decided against blowing out the lamp. Having just refilled it, it ought to see out his sleep. With one final check on the level, he closed his eyes and, ignoring the discomforts of his bed, was soon asleep.

Chapter Eight

The heavy scent of the forest permeated the atmosphere, the fragrance of the Pazeili trees intermingling with the sweet and heady aroma emanating from the scattered clusters of woodland flowers. Traversing a small glade, Kaér paused a moment as the blazing sun beat down upon his back. Barely a few strides separated him from the relative coolness beneath the swaying branches, but he harboured no desire to move. Peace and tranquillity encircled him, leaving him in perfect harmony with the world at large. As to why he was in the forest or, indeed, by what means he had reached it, was a mystery beyond his comprehension. He was quite content to remain in ignorance.

This state of euphoria diminished rapidly as an uneasy feeling settled upon him. His eyes were drawn inexorably towards the west where, far away over the distant misted peaks, something indefinably evil had started to materialize. Unblinking, he remained motionless, hypnotized as the patch of darkness swirled and twisted, transforming itself, even as he watched, into the monstrous resemblance of a clenched fist. It was a strange and eerie manifestation that seemed to threaten every living thing around. Birds fell silent and creatures of the forest ceased their hurried rustlings. As the apparition grew ever greater in size and power, an uncontrollable urge to turn and run came over him but when he tried to move, his body froze. Beneath the malevolent image a wrist developed, then an arm. Ascending even higher, the fist turned and the fingers opened to become claws, pointing towards him with unconcealed menace. Towering high above the mountains, the spectral shape increased to cover most of the sky before changing character and, in one short flowing movement, the avenging talon came hurtling down towards him.

Instantly, paralysis and forest disappeared as he found himself racing across a vast rocky plain where, in the distance, stood a pillar of crystal pulsating with a white shining light. Safety, he instinctively knew, stood within the radiating column, but no matter how hard he ran he came no closer to its sanctuary. Glancing over his shoulder, he saw with dread that, despite his efforts, the evil image drew nearer. Sweat poured down his face and body while the sun, which only moments ago had been his ally, burned deep within his mind. Exhaustion slowed his pace as the darkness crept overhead in readiness to pounce. Raising his eyes, he perceived salvation was at hand but, even as he threw himself desperately towards his goal, the deadly enemy sprang at him. He stumbled, the ground opened up and suddenly he was plummeting headlong into a great abyss, his shadowy antagonist in hot pursuit. The talons opened wide, surrounding him, closing in from all sides.

Waking abruptly, Kaér, as in his nightmare, was soaked with perspiration, shivering as the dampness cooled against his skin. Wrapping his blankets tighter, he lingered awhile, waiting until the frantic racing of his heart had eased. His mouth was dry and, as he reached out for his canteen, something registered on his consciousness. A noise, so faint as to be almost imperceptible, came echoing down from far off passageways. Realisation came almost immediately; the sound was that of running water. Not knowing if it would prove pure, should he ever manage to trace the source, he resisted the urge to drink his fill. Reluctantly, he took only a small sip before replacing the stopper. Rising, he replenished the lamp before eating sparingly. Fully aware of how easily it was to become disorientated, he had scratched an arrow on the wall to show his direction of travel before retiring. He had thought it would be extremely foolish to journey for another day and then find himself back at his starting point.

Later, as he progressed along the winding and undulating path, one moment walking free, the next crawling on hands and knees, squeezing through the narrowest of gaps, Kaér wondered as to what time of day, or night, it might be on the surface. For all he knew, it might still be snowing or, if the weather had changed, it could even be fine and warm. As the passage angled upwards, a dreadful thought occurred to him: what if a rapid thaw had set in? He could not remember another blizzard as severe as this one and the land above must be under several feet of snow. A swift rise in temperature, so early in the season, was not entirely unheard of and, should this happen, a great deal of melt-water was bound to find its way underground. That the flow had changed course was self-evident and the faraway stream, which could now be heard much clearer, was in all probability the same one that had raced through here in the distant past. For a moment or two, he speculated on what might happen if an excessive input of water engulfed its present channel—would it be forced back along its old ways? A most disquieting conclusion considering he was standing in such a place.

Such thoughts afforded him little comfort; it was not as if he had been over enamoured with his circumstances in the first place. The irony of his position did not escape him either. Here he was, searching for water to drink and simultaneously hoping not to drown. Although he attempted to put such thoughts out of his mind, his anxiety forced him to try to increase his pace. This proved easier said than done as the gradient became gradually steeper and, in the end, he had to resort to scrambling on hands and knees.

At one point, whilst rushing to negotiate a rockslide, he slipped on the loose ground. Unable to maintain his balance, he tumbled, bringing rocks and boulders bouncing down behind him, finally coming to rest pinned against a projection in the passage side. Half buried in debris, barely conscious and badly winded, he fought for breath, unable to move. Slowly his breathing normalised and his wits, which moments before had deserted him, began to recover. He rapidly became aware of two things: first, he was lying in the dark, the lamp having disappeared and, secondly, when he tried to move he found his legs were trapped.

Blind panic swept over him and he tore frenziedly at the rocks that pinned him down until his fingers were raw and bleeding. As the pain penetrated through the temporary insanity that beset him, he made himself stop and reconsider his position in a calmer frame of mind. Something cold and wet, he realised, was trickling down his back and his blood ran cold at the thought of a flood. The trickle, however, remained just that, and shortly afterwards ceased altogether. Not melt-water after all, merely one of his canteens bursting under the strain. Although not of immediate concern, if it turned out to be irreparable then the consequences could be dire.

Forcing such worries to the back of his mind, Kaér concentrated his mental and physical energies on more immediate matters. With much wriggling about and moving of rubble, he managed to gain a sitting position, but was still unable to move his legs. At least he could remove his pack and, having done so, found his movements far less restricted. He cursed the folly that had allowed him to bring a plentiful supply of spare fuel and wicks, but had neglected the minor consideration of bringing an extra lamp. Self-recrimination, however, would not free him. He rued the earlier panic, though, for his hands were a mess and everything he touched sent a current of agony shooting through his arms. Although the pain was excruciating, it at least served to keep his senses alert. The mound of rubble covering his legs soon went down until only a single, large boulder remained, resting on the passage floor to one side of him and on some smaller rocks at the other. These fragments, combined with a slight depression in the ground beneath, were all that had prevented his legs from being crushed.

Scraping away the remaining debris from around his limbs, Kaér found he was able to move them and, carefully, he eased them towards him only to find his ankles became wedged against the rock. Try as he might, he could not extricate them and, without his lamp, it was proving difficult to solve the problem. Drawing his dagger, he hacked at the ground beneath where, for once, his luck changed for the better and he found himself chipping away at a layer of compacted silt. Taking care to avoid slicing his flesh, he loosened the earth around his ankles, releasing first one foot and then the other. After massaging his cramped and aching muscles, he pulled himself shakily to his feet just as, from nearby, came the sound of crumbling rock. Feeling about at the base of the boulder, he discovered the supporting rocks had given way. It had been an extremely close call indeed; he had escaped permanent incarceration only by a matter of seconds.

Shouldering his pack, which he dared not leave behind in case he was unable to locate it again in the darkness, he went down on hands and knees and hunted around for any trace of the missing lamp. After a long and extremely painful fingertip search, he eventually came across it lying on its side, minus its cover. His injuries caused him to fumble numerous attempts at producing a spark. Relighting the lamp, he paled, as he realised just how large had been the boulder that had trapped him.

Placing his lamp on top of the slab of rock, he carefully inspected the canteens, finding, to his relief, that none had suffered any significant damage. A stopper working loose during his descent had been the cause of his moment of terror. Opening one of the others, he washed the dust out of his mouth and plucked up enough courage to examine his hands more closely. Regretfully, he poured some of the precious liquid on to a strip of clean cloth and wiped as much grime away as was possible. Rubbing in some salve, he sat back and gritted his teeth until the anaesthetic properties of the ointment temporarily deadened the tortured nerve endings. As the agony in his hands receded, the aches from the rest of his body became more intense, though not as debilitating.

Resting, he contemplated the rockslide that had almost ended his journey. Perhaps it was the rocks he had dislodged that made the gradient appear gentler, but it certainly looked nowhere near as difficult. Once he was ready to try again, he accomplished the ascent comparatively easily and without further mishap. At the top, the passage levelled off and became far more straightforward. Thankfully, he was now faced with the minimum of obstructions, apart from the light shining directly onto his face. Not wishing to reopen his pack, he wedged a flat, sharp edged rock fragment down the side of the lamp, which to a certain extent shielded his eyes from the glare. Progress now became swifter, with the sound of running water urging him on to greater effort.

Suddenly, the passage forked for the first time since Kaér had started out on his underground journey. Previously he had passed a variety of cracks and small openings but none had been large enough to accommodate him. Taking the left hand fork, he found it dropped steeply away and, after awhile, the sound of water became less distinct. Retracing his steps, he tried the other way and found the noise gradually grew louder. The passage started to rise and then straighten out the higher he went, hardly twisting at all as the going became steeper. The sound of rushing water increased rapidly; the floor levelled out and the way in front opened up. Halting in astonishment, he found himself standing at the entrance to a vast cavern.

On the far side was a large pool of water, fed by a swiftly flowing cascade originating from a point high on the cavern wall. The falling water glistened in the light from his lamp. It sent myriads of coloured sparks flashing over the walls and ceiling as he stepped inside. The pool fed a rushing stream that channelled across the gently sloping cavern floor, only to disappear down a shaft into what seemed oblivion. Finding the water cold and pure, he emptied his own stale supply and refilled his canteens straightaway. Once his thirst was satisfied, he took time to study his surroundings in greater detail. His lamp cast flickering shadows around the walls and distant domed roof. Looking back he noticed two small exits to the right of where he had entered.

The walls, which from a distance had appeared a uniform grey, on closer inspection turned out to be streaked with motifs of green and crimson. His heart lifted at the sight. This was not the work of nature, but of living flesh, albeit from long ago. He had come across similar sights before during his travels, often wondering about those long forgotten people who had spent much of their lives etching and painting petroglyths deep underground. Why they had felt compelled to leave this evidence of their passing was something he had never understood, but the fact they had been here at all raised his spirits. If nothing else it signified there was, or had been, a way to the surface. Apart from the opening he had entered by and the two beside it, he could see no other means of exiting. Therefore, with no clues as to which way was correct, he selected the middle egress and, holding his lamp out before him, moved out of the chamber.

Once inside, the roof gradually became lower and he was soon crawling on hands and knees. The passage began to veer to the right and sharply upwards. *About time too,* he thought as it rose higher still, it really was going to take him to the surface. The roof began to rise and the path widened until he was able to walk upright once more and, shortly afterwards, found himself inside a smaller version of the gallery below, but one devoid of any water. He searched the whole area, but nowhere could he find another way out. The walls were covered with more of the strange drawings and hieroglyphics. Although disappointed, there was always the other tunnel; the people who had decorated the walls must have come from *somewhere.*

Returning proved far more hazardous than the outward journey. Once the passageway had diminished, he was reduced to crawling downhill and this, as he soon discovered, greatly upset his balance. Unfortunately, the tunnel had narrowed far too much for him to be able to turn round and descend feet first. Repeatedly he misjudged the angle of descent, pitching forward onto his face while his lamp slid away before him. He prayed the ray of light would not be extinguished and each time his prayer was answered. Finally, thoroughly disgruntled, he was able to stand and walk the remaining distance back to the main chamber.

Taking a long satisfying drink from the icy cold pool, he decided to eat and rest a little before making an attempt on the final outlet. Spreading out his bed, he glanced down at his clothes that, by now, were showing obvious signs of wear and tear. *Just what all the best-dressed Maraéns are wearing this year,* he thought wryly to himself. Finding the stress of his travels was catching up with him, he pulled his rugs around himself and closed his eyes.

Chapter Nine

Striking down through the snowy mantle and penetrating deep into the ground below, the intense cold tightened its icy grip over the land. Above the crisp and frosted surface, not even the faintest breath of air dared disturb the still and silent world. Far beneath the frozen surface safely cocooned against the elements, something moved. A pair of eyes opened and, stretching out, Kaér groaned aloud as he eased some of the stiffness from his aching limbs. He groaned again as he struggled to his feet. There must, he thought, be better ways of spending a night than by sleeping on a rocky bed; especially when one was already battered and bruised. Not until he had performed a number of exercises to restore his circulation did he even remotely feel able to face the future. On checking his hands, he found the salve had worked wonders whilst he had slept. Although they would take a while to heal fully, the pain and swelling had eased and the cuts were no longer inflamed.

After breakfasting, he drained his canteens and refilled them from the stream; heaven only knew when he would come across another source. Gathering his belongings together, he recharged his lamp and made a final circuit of the gallery, checking one last time for another escape route. In the state he had been in earlier, he would probably have missed anything he had not fallen over. Nowhere could he find one and, after working his way round to the untried opening, he entered without hesitation.

The passageway was straight, though narrow, with ample headroom. After a few minutes of steady walking, the way began to bear to the left and climb gently. The higher he progressed, the more the lamp began to flicker in the chill draught that started flowing towards him. As the route became more twisted and winding, he noticed the smoothness of the walls and floor was not entirely the result of natural phenomena. Here and there, illuminated by the dancing light, he could discern faint grooves where tools had chipped away the rock to make the passage easier to negotiate. He felt sure that, long ago, this had been a route of some importance.

The way continued to meander, ascending gradually, for some considerable distance before entering yet another long gallery. Kaér, pausing a moment to rest, gazed open-mouthed at the vast range of the ancient artists' skills exhibited before him. The walls and roof were adorned with some of the strangest sights he had ever been fortunate enough to observe. Interlocking spirals twisting round and round, interlacing with similes of the sun and moon, seemed to dominate. A myriad stars, squares and triangles in a many faceted display intermixed with symbolic spheres, carved into the rock and then painted in a mix of bright and pastel hues, fascinated and delighted his eyes. Walking slowly, he tried, without success, to make sense of the hieroglyphics carved beneath in a script totally alien to him.

Gazing and gasping aloud at the sheer magnitude of this astonishing spectacle almost caused his downfall. Completely absorbed in the wondrous surroundings, he failed to watch where he was treading. One moment he was wandering in a daze, the next he found himself falling. Reflex action took over from conscious thought, throwing his body backwards in a twisting movement to land, heavily on the floor. He sprawled face down, his lower limbs hanging over the edge of a gaping chasm. As his lamp spun wildly away, he clawed at the ground, struggling desperately until he had dragged himself to safety.

His breathing steadied and he crawled a little farther from the edge. *All this excitement is likely to be the death of me yet*, he thought acidly, easing himself up. By some miracle, the lamp remained lit and, in its light, he carefully retraced his steps. He found himself looking out over an abyss stretching the whole width of the chamber. Casting around, he searched fruitlessly for something, a pebble or stone, to throw into the crevice to determine its depth. In the pale light, he could just discern the far side and the distance was too great to even contemplate leaping. If the drop was not too bad, he could always descend and walk to the other side but, as all beneath the reach of his lamp was in total darkness, it was impossible to establish just how far beneath him the ground might be.

A solution occurred to him and he removed a spare wick from his pack. Smearing it well with fat, he knotted it thoroughly at one end to give it some substance before setting it alight by the lamp. Swinging his arm, he hurled the blazing torch out towards the centre of the crevice, only to watch in horror as the flickering flame tumbled deeper and deeper. Soon all that remained was a faint pinprick of light that was extinguished far below in a shower of sparks against one of the sides. Shocked at the depth, Kaér was prompted to move away from the edge. He presumed the gap had been formed by water forcing its way through a weakness in the base rock, as it did not extend to the wall sides. All this must have taken place long before the carvings and paintings had been attempted, otherwise they would have been erased by the raging torrents. The artists, therefore, must have had some method of bridging the opening.

Moving over to the right hand side, he spotted two irregular rows of black marks running across the wall and out over the void. Standing closer to the edge, he found the marks were, in reality, hand and foot holes chiselled out of the rock, albeit for someone slightly larger than himself. By stretching, he was able to place his hands and feet in the appropriate places, the inside of the hand hole having been cut with a lip at the front for an easier grip. Convinced a safe crossing was feasible, he swung back to the gallery floor.

Deciding against delay, he collected his lamp and returned to the starting point, when he encountered yet another problem. Once on the far side, he would require light to continue with his journey. Unfortunately, he could neither leave the lamp behind, nor carry it whilst he moved from handhold to handhold. Attempting to traverse in the dark held no attraction whatsoever, the trip would be hazardous enough with his pack swinging behind him. Stamping on the ground in frustration, he discovered a small indentation in the floor. Dropping to his knees, he filled the tiny hollow with fat and inserted a short length of wick firmly in the centre. Lighting it, he was satisfied the flame would burn at least long enough for his purposes. Nipping out the lamp, he waited until it had cooled a little before storing it carefully inside the top of his pack. With everything strapped firmly in place, he began to swing from hold to hold over the apparently bottomless pit. With light from the makeshift beacon glowing behind, he experienced few difficulties and crossed quickly to the safety of the far side. Without undue haste, he relit the lamp before the light behind diminished.

The gallery continued for another fifty yards, walls and ceiling wonderfully decorated as before. Although he studied the sights intently, he paid a great deal more attention to the ground this time. The scenes of splendour ceased abruptly with the chamber's end and he found himself back inside a narrow, high-roofed passage. This continued to ascend as it meandered back and forth, again showing signs of having been worked. Continuing without incident, he progressed at a steady rate. The tunnel appeared endless as he carried on, hour after weary hour, periodically breaking his journey for a brief rest, a sip of water and occasionally to partake of a bite to eat. He had long since lost count of the number of times he had halted.

On the surface, it was rapidly approaching the middle of the afternoon while not so far underground now; an extremely weary traveller was resting. *It must be near midnight*, Kaér thought. His legs ached unbearably, his feet were sore and he had serious doubts as to whether he would be able to walk for much longer. Taking a final sip of water, he raised himself painfully off the ground. The toils and strains of recent days had taken a severe toll of his strength and he found himself unable to call upon the extra reserves of stamina he had once possessed. Perhaps they no longer existed? What he desperately needed was a few days respite and plenty of fresh food to restore him to his former self, not that he was likely to find either buried in the middle of a mountain. Notwithstanding the urgency of his mission, he was aware of the need to be in as good a physical, and mental, condition as was possible before attempting to enter the Subrat Valley, provided of course he ever managed to reach it.

With his mind preoccupied and his body exhausted, he staggered along initially oblivious to the fact he had started shivering. He had removed his outer furs long ago, as the temperature inside the tunnels had remained fairly constant. Now, with an icy blast flowing strongly towards him, his tired mind came slowly to the notion that the surface might not be so far away. Pausing only to unstrap his outer clothes from his pack and wrap them tightly around him, he shuffled off as quickly as he was able. As the movement in the air increased, his lamp flame flickered ever more wildly before eventually succumbing to the inevitable, leaving him in total darkness. There was no chance of relighting it so he packed it away, muttering angrily.

Pulling his sword, he set off blindly, waving the weapon in front to warn of obstructions and treading gingerly, testing the ground carefully each step before trusting his full weight to it. If there were any more surprises lying in wait, a little more warning than before would not go amiss. Then, in the distance, he caught sight of a faint glow. Drawing nearer, he abandoned all caution and broke into a run as he realised the luminescence was caused by sunlight, striking against the passage walls as the tunnel curved. Moments later he rounded the corner, only to be blinded by the rays of a late afternoon sun.

Protecting his sight from this forgotten glare he turned away, rubbing tear filled eyes until the pain subsided. Gradually he reopened them and, as they became accustomed to the internal brightness he had them well shaded as he moved to face the outside world. Squinting a little, he stared towards the tunnel's end that, some twenty yards away, framed the golden orb as it hovered over distant peaks. The storm had blown itself out, or so it appeared, although the evidence of its passing lay heavy on the mountains. Of the ground, he could see nothing; presumably, it dropped away from the exit.

Nearing the opening, Kaér became aware of a vast cliff wall, over nine hundred feet in height, facing him across a wide valley. The rock face dropped sheer to a plain covered in lush thick grass a good six hundred feet beneath him. He could detect no signs of snow down there, although the cliff tops were covered in white. His field of vision widened as he gained the exit and he was able to observe that the valley itself was broadly rectangular. Both of the other visible sides were a continuation of the towering crags in front, which from this distance, appeared unscalable. Below, on the valley bottom, pools of water bubbled continuously with steam rising steadily from their surfaces. Obviously, the land below was warmed from the volcanic depths, which certainly explained the lack of snow. Far to the left, a torrent of water poured out of the cliff base feeding a tiny lake, which itself was drained on its far side by a narrow stream that shortly disappeared underground.

The vale, itself, was roughly half a mile across by three quarters wide. The grassy meadow was crisscrossed by dozens of tiny game trails, many of which converged on the lake. Such tracks meant although they were small animals they would provide him with much needed nourishment. The main problem, as far as he could see, was the valley bottom itself. It was only a couple of hundred yards away, as he discovered when he finally stood on its edge, but that was straight down and he could see no obvious place where he might descend.

Disheartened, he stepped back and sat down, eating a little as he watched the sun sink from view. He did not even want to contemplate having to retrace his steps back to where the passage split while the abyss, in particular, was something he certainly had no desire to tackle again. The light faded and he shivered involuntarily as the air chilled rapidly. Retreating down the tunnel, he prepared his bed. Sleep did not come easily to him, despite his weariness.

The weak light of dawn, reflecting off the cliff face beyond, penetrated the tunnel causing him to stir and open his eyes. Even though yesterday's breeze had eased, the air remained bitterly cold and the passage was covered in a layer of white. As he stood, his sleeping rugs slid to the ground, crackling with frost, and he stared miserably towards the tunnel mouth, thinking of all he had endured to reach it, only to find himself still trapped. His mood improved somewhat after breakfast; it never ceased to amaze him how much brighter his outlook appeared on a full stomach, even when the food was barely palatable. Outside, the sun had risen higher, its pale light casting back the shadows from the far side of the valley.

Striding out onto the ledge, he revelled in the light of day, delaying his return underground for as long as possible. Suddenly, his attention was caught by a regular pattern on the cliff face over on the far side. The figuration went obliquely across the scar from ground level, halting abruptly at a black mark three quarters of the way up. The image blurred and shifted in the steamy atmosphere and, puzzled, he squinted against the glare for a few moments before he realised it was a flight of stairs and the dark smudge another cave. No wonder he had missed it the previous night with the sun in his eyes and the cliffs deep in shadow.

If there were steps leading out of the valley, he concluded, then there ought to be a way in from here. There had been a great deal of work done to the route he had taken to make it easier to use. Why go to so much effort if there was nowhere for it to go? It was not logical. There had to be a way down. An initial cursory glance showed nothing, but moving towards the left hand side and nearer the precipice, he found the ledge did not end at the side of the cave mouth after all. From his current perspective the illusion was quickly dispelled, a narrow pathway curved round beyond the entrance before vanishing from sight. Cautiously, he stepped out and started to follow its course.

The trail clung precariously to the cliff face as he shuffled along, only able to manage certain parts with the aid of hand holes conveniently cut out of the rock. Kaér proceeded for some forty yards, climbing steadily until he reached a tiny platform. Having attained this point, he found himself staring down at a flight of crumbling weather-beaten steps, carved into a rock fault standing proud of the cliff face. Before venturing any farther, he decided it might be advisable to retrieve his belongings. Very carefully he back-tracked to the tunnel. The staircase might not be appealing, but there was nowhere else to go apart from back. Therefore with his possessions strapped firmly on his back and in some trepidation, he started back towards the platform.

It was whilst re-negotiating the pathway he remembered something he had not thought upon for many years. Long ago, returning from an expedition, he had stumbled across an aged Maraén and tarried for a while to pass the time of day with him. During the conversation, Kaér had cause to mention his recent travels through the mountains and the old man had said something to him then. *Now what was it?* he asked himself, pausing a moment while he concentrated deeply. Ah! Yes, he remembered now. The old one had recited a tale, passed on to him by his father, who had heard it from his father before him and so it had been passed down from antiquity. Some of the words floated back into his mind.

"If, whilst passing through the dreaded mountains, danger threatens, seek sanctuary in the caverns of the deep. Through the tangled web of passageways with their vestiges of long forgotten splendour, lies a secret pathway to the fiery mountain in the west. Along the way, hidden from the world, sits a valley where the travellers of old would break their journeys to rest in peace and comfort. If filled with good intent then wander freely, but should you intrude with base mind, then the spirits of the ancient ones will guide you deeper and deeper, leaving you to wander blindly until death."

The tale had, perhaps, been related in finer detail, but Kaér had been unable to elicit the actual whereabouts of the caverns, the directions for finding them having been lost in antiquity. Dismissing the story as a combination of fable mixed with the ramblings of an old man, he had promptly forgotten about it. However, if the information was correct, as it now looked almost certain to be, then he was about to descend into the hidden valley. He just hoped the spirits of the ancients approved of his motives and would allow him to leave; it was too late to worry about it now, he had already encroached upon their territory.

On reaching the platform, he began to descend, only to discover every step was an obstacle in itself. He could feel the stone crumbling beneath his feet as the runners took his full weight, causing fragments to splinter and fall away. Almost hugging the wall to his left, he was grateful for the handholds in the rock. After one near fatal incident when a step disintegrated beneath him and the hand hole collapsed with the sudden extra pressure almost throwing him into oblivion, he tested each one very carefully before applying his full weight to it. In spite of the problems, he made steady progress and once he had descended a couple of hundred or more steps, the stairway widened out. The soft, flaky stratum was left behind, replaced by hard rock, and the hollow, created by the tread of countless feet, was slight compared to the flight above.

Everything now went smoothly. He was a almost two thirds of the way down before he noticed the staircase stopped at a narrow ledge, some little way below him. Although the shelf apparently extended around a small buttress in the cliff, when the rock face curved outwards again from the far side, neither steps nor ledge were visible. This was somewhat disconcerting and Kaér descended the remaining distance at a much-increased rate, stumbling at the bottom and propelling himself head first onto the rocky spur. Rubbing his nose, he followed the trail round to find the ledge ended at the entrance to a cavern, one that sloped steeply away underground. Around the entrance and almost worn away by wind and rain, were yet more of the strange motifs.

Dropping to his knees, he peered over the edge and saw at the base of the cliff, a hundred and fifty feet lower down, a small flight of stairs leading up from the valley floor and ending at a small platform. The passage, he concluded, must spiral down, coming out at the point below where the steps ended. Taking out his lamp, he prepared to light it. He was destined to journey forever through the depths of the earth, or so it seemed.

Chapter Ten

The steeply twisting passage created few difficulties for Kaér as he descended. Indeed, within minutes it had levelled out and, for quite a while, led him back beneath the mountains before bearing towards the right, dropping gently as it curved. Suddenly, without warning, the roof and walls opened out and, after negotiating a small flight of steps, he found himself at the edge of an immense cavern. Running through the centre, cutting him off from the vaguely discerned far side, was a gaping chasm, from the depths of which echoed the sound of a raging torrent. A natural stone arch spanned the intervening space, rising from a point near to where he stood. Drawing closer to the divide, he explored in each direction but could find no other means of crossing. Although steps had been cut into the swiftly rising curvature, he was filled with misgivings concerning its strength, particularly where it narrowed towards the centre.

Mounting cautiously, the risers became progressively shallower the higher he went, ceasing altogether as he approached the upper section. With arms outstretched to aid his balance, he eased his way along what was now merely a slender beam. Poised precariously at the very peak, he steadied himself. But before he had chance to move further, an ear splitting crack rang out and the perilous platform began to sway alarmingly. Dropping the lamp, he launched himself towards the far side as the central section collapsed beneath him. His fingers made contact with the splintered remains, but then the lamp hit the river below leaving him to struggle in the stygian darkness to maintain a grip. His efforts were to no avail, the rock fragmented beneath his grasp and, with a cry of despair, he plummeted down towards the hungry waters.

Plunging deep below the surface of the turbulent flood, he was swept away as his air filled pack and clothes dragged his struggling body back to the top. Gasping for air, he barely managed to fill his lungs before the surging flow carried him over a roaring cataract. The pressure created by the falling water forced him under and pinned him down, or so it seemed, for an eternity until his plunging, spinning motion carried him free. With the easing of the cascade's murderous grip, the current snatched him away, claiming him for its own.

For how long, or indeed how far, the river maintained its reckless downward chase he had no idea, he was just grateful for the occasional brief interlude that allowed him to gasp for air. As the torrent succeeded in its fight to find a lower passage, the watercourse broadened out and the flow eased considerably. Several minutes passed during which he was content to float, allowing the stream to carry him where it willed. This proved merely temporary, however, as the channel narrowed shortly afterwards and the current seized him once more in its deadly grip. Fighting for air, his hands made contact with the overhang and, almost instantly, he was dragged under as roof and surface came together. Frantically, he tried warding off the rocky surrounds as a strange buzzing noise grew louder and a fuzzy, detached feeling came over him. With lungs at bursting point, all appeared lost until, in the distance, he perceived a faint glow. Moments later he was disgorged from the mountain and, out in the open, found himself floating free.

Coughing and spluttering, he cleared the water from his mouth and nose, gulping fresh air deep into his oxygen starved lungs. The fog lifted from his mind and, with the return of his senses, he found himself being drawn towards the far side of a small lake. A clear image filled his thoughts, as witnessed earlier from above, of a stream and sinkhole draining the icy waters. Striking out in panic, he made towards the nearest edge before the pull became too strong. Severely hampered by his waterlogged clothes, the effort exhausted him and, once clear of the danger area, he found himself unable to do little more than tread water. The icy cold liquid numbed his fingers, making them too weak and clumsy to allow him to strip off the sodden garments. His sword was jammed, its weight pulling him down, and he realised he was in imminent danger of drowning. Somehow, from out of the depths of his inner self, he found the courage to fight off the overpowering fatigue and painfully struggle on towards the bank. Crawling clear, he managed to pull off his outer garments before collapsing onto the soft sand beside them.

A combination of warm earth and a mild breeze dried the clothes he slept in and, as the moisture evaporated, his body thawed out. Consciousness returned and, sitting up, he stared around, still somewhat dazed from the ordeal. Collecting his thoughts, he remembered where he was and what had happened. Noticing his surroundings, he shivered as he gazed at the torrent pouring out of the cliff base, certainly a journey never willingly to be repeated.

At the sand's edge grew some of the tallest grass he had ever seen. Cultivated by the heat latent in the ground and the ample supply of water, the vegetation had taken on truly colossal proportions. Standing, he looked around and, over to his right, could make out two stairways, one high above the other; it was a pity he had bypassed the lower one so disastrously. At least he now had his bearings. Retrieving his pack from the mound of still wet outer furs, he opened it to see if there was anything inside worth salvaging. Surprisingly, the waterproofed covers had protected the bulk of his supplies and only a small amount of food, which he discarded, was damp.

Spreading his furs out to dry, he ate a little before deciding to take a closer look at his surroundings. Following a game trail, he clambered up the banking to reach the valley floor itself. On all sides, cliff walls soared skywards whilst chest-high grass covered the terrain. Clouds of vapour billowed from the numerous heated pools dotted about. Kaér formed the impression the vale had been created by a whole section of land sinking into the earth. From his vantage point he could now see the valley bottom was not quite as flat as it had appeared from above.

Over to his left he could make out the other flight of stairs and, as the food had gone a little way towards restoring some of his depleted energy, he felt strong enough to carry on towards the stairway. Nevertheless, he would stick to the game trails; his body was not yet up to fighting its way through the long grasses. Returning for his pack, he hoisted it into place. His over garments were almost double their normal weight and he toyed with the idea of leaving them behind, returning later when they had dried. However, not knowing what kinds of wildlife inhabited the area, he dreaded the thought of returning to find his clothes half eaten or ripped to shreds.

Slowly, he picked a route through the maze of trails, switching from one to another. The wide variety of animal tracks he observed in the soft ground delighted him, particularly some of the larger ones. He might yet provide himself with a satisfactory meal. Within half an hour, he found himself standing beneath the escarpment of the west cliff. In front were the steps that would lead him, or so he hoped, out of the valley. But before scaling them, he would rest a few days. There was also the matter of a lamp; it was unlikely he would ever find his other.

Taking him by surprise, a wild pig came snuffling down the path in front of him. On seeing this strange being, the startled animal fled squealing through the grass, long before Kaér managed to free and draw his sword. Determined to be ready in future, he removed the short bow that had been securely tied to his pack and, after much digging around amongst his possessions, found some fibre dry enough to re-string it. Taking an arrow from his quiver, he was now ready should another beast foolishly come within range.

The afternoon was well advanced and shadows cast by the mountains had climbed high on the cliffs at the other side of the valley. Gazing back over the valley, he observed, above the eastern crags, fast moving ragged wisps of cloud heralding the oncoming of a storm. Within minutes, the sky took on a green hue and the vale darkened rapidly as the sun's rays were swiftly quenched. Casting around for shelter, he could find none and, turning to the right, pushed his way through the herbage. Following the west wall along its base, he attacked the grass relentlessly, slashing at the thick woody stalks with his sword. Large heavy raindrops started to fall, an omen of ill to come. The light faded perceptively as the cloud base thickened and settled lower down the mountains. Over to the east the crags were barely discernible, vague impressions of something darker and heavier than the mist that swirled around them. He had almost resigned himself to another soaking when he stumbled over something in the grass. Picking himself up from the ground, he gently rubbed a bruised and battered shin.

Parting the long grass, the object on closer inspection turned out to be the bottom riser of a flight of stairs. With nothing to lose and, perhaps, shelter to gain, he ascended rapidly. After fifteen steps or so, the stairway levelled out onto a narrow ledge and, on following it round, he came up against a cave entrance. Once inside, it widened considerably and in spite of the gloom, he could just make out the far wall. There was nothing much on his right, but to his left the floor sloped upwards for twenty yards before flattening out into a high roofed room. There was no other exit, apart from where he had entered, but at least it was dry. The outside wall had been fenestrated and, in the weak light, he could see two tiers of bunks chiselled out of the bare rock facing the openings. In the centre stood a large, flat-topped slab of stone presumably intended for use as a table. It might not be home but, in the circumstances, this

scarcely mattered and it certainly satisfied his n[eed].
    Weariness overcame him and he struggled to s[tay awake long enough to] eat. With eyes drooping, he finished his meal barely con[scious. Ab]andoning his still damp sleeping rugs, he staggered gratefully towards [a bunk]. Rain was bouncing on the ground and Kaér uttered a thankful prayer [for the instin]ct that had prompted him to turn in this direction. Rolling up his ja[cket to fo]rm a makeshift headrest, he placed it on top of the nearest lower bunk an[d o]nto the stone ledge behind it. He was asleep as soon as his head touched th[e pillow] and it was extremely doubtful he would have wakened had all the hor[des of] Cantaé come screaming across the valley.

    The storm clouds dispersed during the early hours of the following morning, the wind eased and with clear skies overhead the temperature dropped rapidly in the mountains. Deep inside the valley, the atmosphere cooled, but only slightly, the warmth inherent in the ground easily counteracting the frost from above. The change in atmosphere could be the reason that Kaér stirred in his sleep but, in reality, it was probably his senses detecting another's presence.
    Over by the entrance, sitting cross-legged upon the floor, someone kept watch. He was a man of indeterminate age, but with a lifetime's experience written across a pale distinguished face. Had he chosen to stand, he would have been seen to be tall and slim, but sturdy. His hair was silver grey and straight, encircled with a band of pure gold. He was clothed in a flowing tunic of deep yellow; decorated with motifs similar to those Kaér had witnessed beneath the mountains. His body shimmered with a strange luminescence while his deep blue eyes glowed with an inner strength.
    The guardian of the cave maintained his place throughout the long night, as indeed he had for many ages past. His ancient race may have left behind the troubles of the world, but their spirits still roamed freely, walking forever the labyrinth they had frequented and adorned in life. Forsaking the paths of his memories to watch over the rest house, the sentinel had kept it safe for those who travelled the hidden ways. The sleeping stranger was his first guest for a considerable number of years.
    As dawn broke far away to the east and the sun's rays filtered faintly across the top of the valley walls, the figure passed from human sight to continue its solitary vigil unseen. His disappearance coincided with the sound of movement within the main chamber as Kaér, near to waking, began to stir. Finally, as the light strengthened, shining through the window directly on to his face, he opened his eyes. Time passed slowly and still Kaér made no attempt to move.

⌐rag himself out of his reverie and only the pangs of hunger
He felt ⌐im to rise, stiffly, to his feet. His breakfast of dried food
eventu ⌐an ever and, he decided, his priority must be to find fresh
taste ⌐ough his meal was over, his mind resisted the idea of leaving the
sup ⌐l seemed, somehow, part of a general feeling of lethargy. Perhaps
re ⌐rely a reaction to his painful experiences.

⌐ssing to one of the windows, he looked out over the valley. To his left,
⌐ol with steam rising from its surface caught his eye and, for the first time,
⌐ became aware of a faint sulphurous odour in the air. Yesterday, he had been too exhausted to notice anything. At the pool's edge, where no vegetation grew, he noticed a stone platform had been built with steps leading down below the surface. The idea of a warm mineral bath appealed greatly as he had heard much of its recuperative powers. Casting his eyes further afield, he perceived five more pools and, far away to his right, the lake of fresh water where he had surfaced.

Coming down to earth, he selected some snares from his pack and, taking his bow, arrows, and sword, he made himself walk outside onto the ledge. As soon as he passed through the portals the feeling of security he had experienced inside vanished and, for a moment, he stood irresolute. It wasn't long before his sense of purpose returned and he headed for the steps. He wondered why he should have felt so completely secure within the chamber and so exposed out in the open, even though he could sense no threat here. The spirits of the ancients, he believed, roamed endlessly through the subterranean passages. Perhaps, on occasion, they also took refuge in their resting place of old? Their very presence might, conceivably, have induced his feeling of well being, as well as draining him of his will power. He must, on his return, try to communicate and assure them his was not an evil path. After all, he did not intend to trouble them for any longer than was necessary.

scarcely mattered and it certainly satisfied his needs.

Weariness overcame him and he struggled to stay awake long enough to eat. With eyes drooping, he finished his meal barely conscious. Abandoning his still damp sleeping rugs, he staggered gratefully towards the bunks. Rain was bouncing on the ground and Kaér uttered a thankful prayer to the instinct that had prompted him to turn in this direction. Rolling up his jacket to form a makeshift headrest, he placed it on top of the nearest lower bunk and crept onto the stone ledge behind it. He was asleep as soon as his head touched the pillow and it was extremely doubtful he would have wakened had all the hordes of Cantaé come screaming across the valley.

The storm clouds dispersed during the early hours of the following morning, the wind eased and with clear skies overhead the temperature dropped rapidly in the mountains. Deep inside the valley, the atmosphere cooled, but only slightly, the warmth inherent in the ground easily counteracting the frost from above. The change in atmosphere could be the reason that Kaér stirred in his sleep but, in reality, it was probably his senses detecting another's presence.

Over by the entrance, sitting cross-legged upon the floor, someone kept watch. He was a man of indeterminate age, but with a lifetime's experience written across a pale distinguished face. Had he chosen to stand, he would have been seen to be tall and slim, but sturdy. His hair was silver grey and straight, encircled with a band of pure gold. He was clothed in a flowing tunic of deep yellow; decorated with motifs similar to those Kaér had witnessed beneath the mountains. His body shimmered with a strange luminescence while his deep blue eyes glowed with an inner strength.

The guardian of the cave maintained his place throughout the long night, as indeed he had for many ages past. His ancient race may have left behind the troubles of the world, but their spirits still roamed freely, walking forever the labyrinth they had frequented and adorned in life. Forsaking the paths of his memories to watch over the rest house, the sentinel had kept it safe for those who travelled the hidden ways. The sleeping stranger was his first guest for a considerable number of years.

As dawn broke far away to the east and the sun's rays filtered faintly across the top of the valley walls, the figure passed from human sight to continue its solitary vigil unseen. His disappearance coincided with the sound of movement within the main chamber as Kaér, near to waking, began to stir. Finally, as the light strengthened, shining through the window directly on to his face, he opened his eyes. Time passed slowly and still Kaér made no attempt to move.

He felt powerless to drag himself out of his reverie and only the pangs of hunger eventually drove him to rise, stiffly, to his feet. His breakfast of dried food tasted worse than ever and, he decided, his priority must be to find fresh supplies. Although his meal was over, his mind resisted the idea of leaving the refuge. It all seemed, somehow, part of a general feeling of lethargy. Perhaps it was merely a reaction to his painful experiences.

Crossing to one of the windows, he looked out over the valley. To his left, a pool with steam rising from its surface caught his eye and, for the first time, he became aware of a faint sulphurous odour in the air. Yesterday, he had been too exhausted to notice anything. At the pool's edge, where no vegetation grew, he noticed a stone platform had been built with steps leading down below the surface. The idea of a warm mineral bath appealed greatly as he had heard much of its recuperative powers. Casting his eyes further afield, he perceived five more pools and, far away to his right, the lake of fresh water where he had surfaced.

Coming down to earth, he selected some snares from his pack and, taking his bow, arrows, and sword, he made himself walk outside onto the ledge. As soon as he passed through the portals the feeling of security he had experienced inside vanished and, for a moment, he stood irresolute. It wasn't long before his sense of purpose returned and he headed for the steps. He wondered why he should have felt so completely secure within the chamber and so exposed out in the open, even though he could sense no threat here. The spirits of the ancients, he believed, roamed endlessly through the subterranean passages. Perhaps, on occasion, they also took refuge in their resting place of old? Their very presence might, conceivably, have induced his feeling of well being, as well as draining him of his will power. He must, on his return, try to communicate and assure them his was not an evil path. After all, he did not intend to trouble them for any longer than was necessary.

Chapter Eleven

Beating a way through the swaying grassland, Kaér headed towards the nearest game trail, a far easier path to tread. His general level of discomfort might have improved after a good night's rest, but his left leg, as he was painfully aware, had fared badly during the struggle for survival. Gritting his teeth he limped for quite some distance before setting the traps. He was wary of scaring away wildlife from around his shelter in case illness, or injury, found him unable to venture far. Although he disguised the snares, he did not seriously expect to encounter any difficulties, at least not initially. It was, after all, highly unlikely that any of the creatures had been hunted in living memory. Later, perhaps, when a few had been caught, then they might become suspicious of the devices.

Satisfied with his handiwork, he retraced his steps, perspiring freely in the warmth of the midday sun. A cloud of steam rising from the pool nearest to the cavern caught his eye and, he decided, it was high time he indulged in the luxury of a hot bath. Slowly, he cut a way through to the platform he had seen earlier. Kneeling at the water's edge he gazed down, his eyes following a line of steps leading beneath the bubbling surface to the pool bottom. Gingerly, he tested the water with his right hand and found the temperature not unbearably hot; touching a drop to his lips, its strong salty taste, intermingled with various other undefined flavours, certainly made it unfit to drink.

Stripping, he hobbled down the steps, gasping as the water crept around his waist. Once accustomed to the heat, he waded round to the far side where the bottom sloped gently upwards, although he was careful to avoid the deeper sections towards the centre. Lying down, he rested his head on the banking and, stretching out, let the mineral waters swirl around his body, easing his aches and pains as if by magic. A massive contusion on his left leg was clearly visible through the rippling surface, although the rest of him, particularly the lower half, was almost as badly marked, almost certainly a legacy of the rockslide. The wicked scar, his permanent memento of Sartae, ran across his chest and right side. It seemed almost unbelievable anyone could receive such a blow and still survive; it must, surely, be ordained they would meet again. Despite the warmth of his surroundings, he shivered at the thought.

Pushing all thought of Sartae from his mind, he stretched out and relaxed for a good hour before feeling any inclination to move. Wading back across the pool, he climbed onto the platform and towelled himself dry with his tunic. Putting on the remainder of his clothing, he collected the dampened garment and returned to the main trail. On impulse, he branched off on to a smaller well-defined track, which meandered towards the cliffs, not too far away from the chamber. The sound of rushing water caught his attention and, on entering a crescent shaped area where the valley wall fell back, he discovered a tiny stream cascading down the rock face. It explained why living quarters had been created so far away from the lake.

Contained by a natural reservoir at the base of the cliff, the waters drained along a narrow channel, finally disappearing down a pothole some distance away. Stooping, he tasted the crystal clear liquid and found it pure and icy fresh. Drinking his fill, he returned to the cavern to collect his canteens. Once inside he was again overcome by lethargy and it was only with a great effort of will that he made himself move. The weariness, as before, disappeared the moment he stepped outside. On his return, he really would have to commune with the spirits he felt sure resided within.

The afternoon was well advanced when he deposited the newly filled canteens beside the stairway leading to the cavern. Leaving the containers there, he went on to check his traps. The first couple remained untouched while animal tracks passed close by a third. Coming to the last one, he discovered the body of a small wild pig. Removing the beast, he reset the trap and, after skinning the animal, wrapped the meat inside the hide. Gathering the remains, he turned back towards the rest house, collecting his canteens on the way.

The energy drained out of him as he passed through the entrance and, lowering his catch, he began to explain to the unseen presence his motives and reasons for being there. As he spoke, the lethargy lifted and, although still aware of a benevolent aura, his mind was freed from all interference. Thanking the spirits, he set about preparing a meal.

In one corner of the chamber was a small, smoke-blackened opening that, he surmised, had been used as a hearth. A shaft led off at the back through which a steady draught of air was drawn up into the cliffs above. During his travels that afternoon, as there appeared no other means of sustaining a fire in the treeless vale, he had collected a considerable amount of dried animal droppings. In the fading light and with a small blaze burning brightly, he searched the chamber for some means of constructing a lamp. In two or three places he discovered small blackened cut-outs in the walls and, after filling the hollows with lamp fat, he planted a wick inside each one and lit them using a piece of burning wick ignited from the fire. Turning his attention to the carcass, Kaér cut out a couple of generous steaks, roasting them gently over the flames. As the smoke disappeared up the shaft, the odour of cooking meat filled the cavern, almost driving him to distraction with anticipation. Steadily, he fed fuel onto the fire and within half an hour, his meal was ready. Despite eating slowly, savouring each tender morsel as it passed between his lips, the meat was consumed all too soon and he was left with only fond memories and a tantalizing smell. At least his hunger was appeased and besides, there was insufficient fuel left to allow him to cook more.

Lost in thought, he remained seated, his back resting against the cavern wall. Succumbing to weariness, he yawned and stretched. Provided he did not overexert himself, a few more days should see his recovery complete. Limping over to the bunks, he spread out his sleeping rugs and, blowing out the lights, retired for the night. Gradually, his breathing steadied and his muscles relaxed.

Over by the entrance, the faintly glowing figure became visible again, someone who certainly not was resting peaceably, indeed quite the opposite. The spirit of Stakirum was deeply perturbed by the news his visitor had related earlier. The Shintae, The Stone of almost unimaginable power, was in the clutches of the most unworthy and evil people he had ever encountered.

Stakirum knew well the power of The Stone, for it was his own people who had encountered it first, long before the demise of their culture. This strange object had fallen from the heavens as a ball of flame with a fiery tail, creating panic and consternation among his ancestors who to begin with had left it well alone. This, probably, had been the wisest course of action as the meteorite;

tiny though it was, pulsated and periodically emitted rays of a strange light that scorched and burnt everything it touched. Gradually, The Stone's energy declined until, several months later, it fell dormant. Even then, it took some time before the people could be persuaded it was safe to move. At that point, the Chief Elder claimed it, giving it the name Flaming Star or "Shintae" in their tongue. Once adopted as part of the Chieftain's chattels, the deep purple stone, flecked with crimson, eventually became less important, and in the end was known merely as an unusual curio. Nevertheless, it held a certain fascination for the younger ones and for many generations of leaders' children, it was a popular plaything.

Nine, possibly ten, score years passed without incident until, one fateful day, whilst walking in the mountains with his father, a young boy named Jinost managed to mislay the object in the thick grasses growing beside the path. His father, Chief Elder Elfric, understandably incensed by this carelessness, commanded him to search the area until The Stone was found. Making his own way towards a mound of rocks, a few hundred yards away, he sat down and rested, all the while keeping a careful eye on his son's progress. After a diligent search, the youngster retrieved the missing heirloom and, holding it aloft, shouted out his success. Pleased, Elfric stood up, calling and waving at his son to rejoin him. At that moment, a huge, shaggy mountain bear ambled over the rocks behind. Normally, the beast would have ignored him or, perhaps, growled a warning, but the animal was with cub and the sight of this noisy, gesticulating object startled her. Sensing danger towards her unborn progeny, she charged instantly.

Seeing his father's imminent danger, Jinost screamed a warning and pointed vigorously towards the rapidly advancing bear, The Shintae clasped tightly within his hand. In his desperation and blind panic, the words and syllables became jumbled and, in their tongue, came out as, "Disupp-sens krosp gronst wepsz!"

Reacting swiftly to the note of urgency in Jinost's voice, Elfric spun round but was far too late to save himself; the outraged animal was almost upon him. Frantically, he tugged at the heavy sword strapped to his waist as the beast reared up and towered over him, its razor sharp claws already striking down towards his unprotected head. Throwing himself backwards, he prayed aloud as he felt the bear's hot foetid breath on his face.

Suddenly, Jinost's clenched fist sprang open, palm uppermost with The Shintae, glowing brilliantly from some strange inner energy. There was a brilliant flash, followed by a thunderous crack, which echoed around the peaks, as a streak of lighting flew across the hillside from his hand. One instant the bear was ready to strike, the next a pungent odour of scorched flesh and a charred patch of earth, smoking gently around the edges, was all that remained. Stunned with shock, both stayed motionless for several moments before racing towards each other. Lifting up his son, Elfric hugged him tightly before setting him down and, gently, removing The Shintae from his shaking grasp.

They stared nervously at The Stone half afraid it would explode into action again. After awhile when nothing else had happened, Elfric pointed The Shintae at a distant rock and asked Jinost to say again what he had said before. Repeatedly, he tried but to no avail, The Stone remained inert within his hand as he struggled to recreate the exact jumble of words and sounds uttered in his earlier panic.

It took awhile but, eventually, the correct combination was rediscovered. The Shintae flashed and a bolt of lightning leapt towards the distant rock, splitting it down the centre with an almighty crash. The noise of explosion echoed all around as Elfric attempted to perform the experiment himself. Copying the sounds made by Jinost, he was able, with a little practise, to achieve the same results at will. Filled with excitement, they hurried home, impatient to spread the news.

Over the centuries that followed, generations of wise men explored The Stone's potential. Hundreds of phrases and sounds were discovered to produce a variety of effects ranging from short bursts of explosive power, as experienced by Elfric, to long concentrated outputs of almost incredible energy. The Shintae's power had enabled them to enlarge greatly the natural tunnel systems beneath the mountains, creating direct routes to the now infamous Mount Subae, a place they held sacred. Much use had also been made of it during the construction of their vast cities in the north, places that had long since yielded to the desert sands.

During the invasion of their homeland by the Encorians, The Stone proved itself a weapon of devastating force, wiping out the invaders to a man. After this they had lived contentedly, trading peaceably with their neighbours until, one dreadful day, they came under attack again. Warlike tribes swept through the country, destroying all before them. Unused to warfare, they put up a gallant, though futile, defence and were rapidly overcome. Before The Shintae could be brought back from the south where it was being employed to open up more tunnels, it was already too late. After making a desperate race for home, the workers found a land reeling under foreign domination. Swiftly dispatching the conquerors to their doom with The Shintae, they found few of their people had come through the wholesale slaughter.

The shocked survivors split into smaller groups and scattered to the four winds. Whether any descendants of the once proud race still lived, Stakirum had no knowledge. His party had journeyed south to the mountains where, not being blessed with children, their line had died out. The Shintae, taken with them for safekeeping, had been secreted deep underground with precise instructions as to its use. They guarded it well during their lifetime, and continued to do so with their spirits after death.

A lengthy period of solitude descended until, centuries later, a party of Maraéns stumbled across one of the outer passages. Searching the innermost thoughts and memories of the adventurer's minds as they slept, the spirits discovered much about them and their people. Finding them worthy custodians of its care, they were led, unknowingly, to The Stone itself.

Delving deep into Kaér's subconscious as he slept, Stakirum learnt of the original loss of The Shintae and its subsequent rediscovery by the Cantaéns. He was thankful they had not yet passed the stage reached by Elfric, but as time progressed so would their knowledge. He hoped they would never discover the most horrifying trigger of all, the one his people had exploited to wreak vengeance upon the invaders of their land. The command, a long complicated series of sounds, caused The Shintae to emit high energy beams that sought out and annihilated all enemies of the one who uttered it. Having been witness to this before, Stakirum had no real desire to see this command used again—even on the Cantaéns, unless no other means could be found to halt their advance. The Maraéns must be saved and to this end, he implanted the deadly phrase deep within Kaér's subconscious mind. Only if his people faced a final and irrevocable destruction would it rise to the surface of his mind. He prayed they would never find themselves in such a parlous state.

The next evening, Stakirum decided, he would reveal his presence and offer his guest as much help as he was capable of giving although this would probably not amount to much. The most constructive thing he could provide had already been instilled inside Kaér's mind. Unable to do anything more at this time Stakirum removed his thoughts from the present, transporting them back to the past and, within his imagination, he was alive again, roaming free through the cities of his youth. Contentedly, he remained with his memories until, with dawn's faint glow encroaching on his dreams, he passed from sight on to a higher plane.

Hunger pangs drove Kaér out early to procure fuel enough to cook a hearty breakfast. Once his meal had settled, he bathed again in the mineral pool, allowing the waters to continue their healing ways. Taking the day at a leisurely pace, he emptied his traps and brought them and their contents back with him. He now had ample meat to feed him for several days, with sufficient over to dry and cure for his pack. By dusk he had collected a considerable amount of fuel and, lighting the fire, prepared a broth. Having discovered earlier a variety of pots stacked away in a corner he had selected and cleaned out a medium sized one. Half filling it with wild vegetables, he added water and the remainder of the meat he had roasted that morning. Setting it down amidst the flames, he waited for it to cook.

Eating his fill, he covered the pot, leaving the remainder for the following day. Daylight was failing rapidly as he relit the lamps in the wall and, using a small metal dish and goblet he found at the back of the cave, he fashioned a lamp similar to the one he had lost. Filling it with fat, he inserted a wick and lit it. After a few minor adjustments and with the doctored goblet shielding his eyes from the glare, he was able to see quite clearly as he moved it around.

Jumping back, startled, he almost dropped the lamp as he discovered, illuminated by the flickering flames, a stranger hovering silently by the doorway. It was a man, tall and slim, someone who was dissimilar to anyone he had ever seen before. The man emanated a certain majesty as he glowed with an ethereal light. A thought struck Kaér and he realised immediately he was in the presence of one of the ancient people. He bowed deeply to the resplendent figure.

"Please, forgive my intrusion into your resting place of old," he apologized, straightening up. "I sincerely hope I've not disturbed your peace too greatly with my comings and goings."

The man returned his bow with regal dignity and advanced towards him, although Kaér was quick to note the stranger's feet never moved, nor quite seemed to touch the ground.

"The Rest Hall of my people, the Ancients, as you choose to call us, is at your disposal friend and I, Stakirum, welcome you," the figure replied floating nearer. His lips moved soundlessly as the words appeared directly inside Kaér's head. "I've taken my ease now for many a long age and your coming is a blessed relief from solitude," he continued. "My friends prefer to wander the passageways and seldom bother to visit me here in the old sanctuary. Come and sit down, we have, I fear, a great deal to discuss and you still look somewhat weary."

Doing as he was bidden, Kaér sat down in front of Stakirum who seated himself likewise. They talked well into the early hours of the following morning, discussing a great many things, as Kaér learnt the history of Stakirum's people and the story of The Shintae after its fall to earth. Finally, when asked what he proposed to do next, Kaér's brow furrowed as he studied for a second or two.

"Well," he replied slowly, "we'd planned to travel lightly and quickly, using the more remote valleys and cutting across country when necessary. There are numerous routes to choose from, many of which I have scouted over the years, but then, of course, the blizzard hit which put survival temporarily at the top of our priorities," he paused before continuing. "We'd not really formulated any definite plans for gaining access to the main camp below Subae. Without actually seeing how much it has grown and what type of defences have been added, we'd decided to leave our options open. The intention was to move in at night and, with luck, retrieve The Stone and make good our escape under cover of darkness. Once The Shintae was back in my possession, I could always have used its power to force a way out if necessary.

"Perhaps if I'd done so earlier when I had the chance," he added bitterly, "then all this trouble might have been avoided. But, having escaped without any difficulty, I never once imagined they'd track me across Maraé. Still, I will not make that mistake again. Even so," he continued sardonically, "having said that, not only do I not know where I am, but I've no idea as to how, when or even if, I'll ever find my way out. All I do know is that the threat posed by Cantaé must, somehow, be eliminated forever."

Sitting quietly, Stakirum pondered hard upon what Kaér had said. He had, himself, long ago reached the same conclusion regarding the Cantaéns. An evil such as this, if allowed to flourish unchecked, would spread and eventually infect the whole world. With the power of The Shintae to support them, they would first enslave and then eliminate all they came up against; anyone not put to the sword would be corrupted into their service. It could take centuries before humanity resurfaced from an age as dark as this. The problem had to be tackled now, head on, before the ultimate path of terror and destruction had been embarked upon.

As he turned to face him, Kaér could hear Stakirum's words inside his head. "My friend," he said, "I'm afraid there's not much I can do to help. Sadly, we are unable to venture beyond the boundaries of our underground world. It is only here, within the confines of this valley, may we gaze upon the sun and wander through the meadows. However, once you've recovered fully, I'll be happy to guide you through the maze of tunnels to the world outside."

Kaér thanked him from his heart, for no one else but the ancient ones could hope to know these passageways. "Once outside," he added, "I'll be able to continue on my way provided, of course, you point me in the right direction."

Stakirum laughed and replied, "You'll not need me to direct you."

"Why ever not?" questioned a bemused Kaér. "I've no idea where I am now, never mind where I'll be when I get out of here."

"There's no need to look so perplexed." Stakirum continued, smiling broadly. "Didn't I tell you earlier that your "accursed mountain" was sacred to my people? The main reason for opening up the passageways was to provide an easier route through the mountains, particularly during the winter months. Many are interlinked and, as long you know the correct sequence to follow, you will find they all lead, one way or another, to Mount Subae itself. Most come to the surface little more than a good half day's walk from your goal."

Bowing low before Stakirum in acknowledgement of this welcome news, Kaér smiled in delight. Although eager for more information, he could not manage to stifle a yawn as tiredness crept up on him.

"But, enough for the moment, we can always discuss these matters in finer detail later," Stakirum commented as he became aware of his visitor's exhaustion. "As for now, I think I should take my leave and let you sleep. I'm afraid it's been inconsiderate of me to keep you up so late, but I haven't had anybody new to talk to for a hundred years or more. Rest now and recover your strength, we will speak again tomorrow," he promised, fading from sight.

Over the next few days Kaér took things at a steady pace, gradually rebuilding his strength with the plentiful bounty from the land around. A part of each day he spent in replenishing his supply of dried food required for the journey to come. Stakirum taught him how, with the use of certain herbs and lichen, he could make his dried meat stay edible for many months, and still taste appetizing when eaten. Mostly, however, he spent his days out in the open, breathing in the invigorating mountain air. An hour or so each afternoon was spent bathing in the mineral waters. This was something that, to his surprise, resulted in his aches and pains disappearing far more quickly than he had ever experienced before. Within a couple of days, the stiffness had left his legs and the bruising over the remainder of his body had almost disappeared. After several more sessions in the pool, much to his surprise, his scar from his wound had diminished until only the faintest of white lines could be seen across his torso.

By now he felt fitter than he could ever remember; his reactions, certainly, had never been swifter. With a bow, he had always considered himself an excellent marksman, but the speed with which he could take an arrow from his quiver and send it flying through the air amazed him, as much as did his startling accuracy at this pace. He exercised daily with his sword and, again, his actions were smoother and far surer.

A few days later Kaér declared he was fit enough to travel, only to discover Stakirum now counselled strongly against leaving so soon. He was unable to define clearly any logical reason for this request but, for several days, he had been in contact with his fellow spirits. The general feeling for which even they could offer no explanation, was that he should tarry a little longer. They were attuned to the very rock where they dwelt and some strange intuition persisted that now was not the time for action. Delay would certainly create no problems for him, indeed the very opposite would be the case.

Despite his desire to be away, Kaér respected the judgement of the kindly spirit and with a great effort of will managed to curb his impatience. Adopting a strenuous routine to maintain his fitness, he found the days passed swiftly and, during the long evenings, he had Stakirum for company. Occasionally other members of the ghostly community stopped by to talk and, though they differed in countless ways from one another, the overall impression he gained from both men and women was of a tall, slim and noble royal household.

So successful was he at concentrating his mind and energies on keeping fit, it came somewhat as a surprise when, as they were conversing one evening, Stakirum warned him to be ready to leave the next morning. The pleasure at being able to resume his journey was, nevertheless, tinged with sadness at the thought of never again strolling through this haven of peace and tranquillity. Sensing Kaér's mood, Stakirum left him alone to prepare for departure.

By sunrise Kaér was up, fed, and impatient to be off. Wandering to the doorway he looked out over the grassy meadows and bade the valley a silent farewell. He marvelled anew at the strange twists of fate that had brought him to this moment. Shaking his head in wonder, he turned sharply and squared his shoulders. Before he could make another move, a resounding crack rang out and, as his whole body quivered, he found himself standing as straight of back as his new found friends.

"All things are possible here," Stakirum murmured softly, appearing at Kaér's side as he stretched in absolute disbelief at the miraculous change to his body. "Come," he commanded firmly, "collect your pack and fill your canteens afresh, we must leave."

Hastily Kaér complied with Stakirum's instructions and shortly afterwards, with his mind still in a daze, he found himself standing at the bottom of a stairway, one that would lead him to his destiny.

Twelve days later, he took his leave of Stakirum. The intervening period had passed in steady travel, with Kaér witnessing great wonders by the light of his lamp. There were, so he was told, far greater sights to be found in many of the passages they had by passed and he longed to stay and explore, but his sense of duty prevailed. He promised to himself one day, if he survived the perils of his mission, he would return.

Reading Kaér's innermost thoughts and desires as he bade him farewell, Stakirum turned and said, "Don't worry my friend, I've looked into your mind and know your hopes and fears. Although it is not within my power to bring you back safely, my companions and I wish you to know that you are welcome to return whenever you so desire. Indeed, we look forward to the day when you re-enter this world of ours with news of your success."

"Dearest Stakirum," Kaér replied, his voice choked with emotion. "There's nothing I would like more. The thought of being able to return will help sustain me through the dark days ahead."

Stakirum pulled himself up to his full height, and in a strange forgotten tongue, said an incantation of good fortune over him. "Until we meet again," he said softly as he finished. "May your mission be successful. Farewell." And with that he was gone.

"Goodbye my friend, goodbye," Kaér called out after him.

Abruptly, he turned and walked towards the beckoning light at the tunnel's end. Nearing the exit he pinched out his lamp and he stored it away. He was now ready to face the outside world, the dangers of which he knew all too well; a place that punished without mercy the careless and the unprepared. With this thought in mind he carefully checked his sword, ensuring it moved freely in its scabbard ready for instant use.

Stepping towards the opening, he studied the terrain beyond, long and carefully. He was surrounded by white-coated mountains and, in the distance, the smoking peak of Mount Subae seemed to leap out over the skyline before him. The very sight of the fiery summit caused his resolve to waver. Only by concentrating on the reasons behind his journey did he overcome the almost overpowering feeling of dread.

Suddenly the faint sound of voices penetrated his thoughts. Checking his Aralpos were in place, he leaned a little farther out of the tunnel mouth and, without exposing himself unduly, looked down the steep hillside towards the valley bottom.

From up the valley leading down from Mount Subae, a trail had been beaten through the snow leading to a small hollow, directly beneath him, where a tent had been pitched. From his vantage point, he could discern a group of Cantaéns scurrying out from their shelter with swords drawn. At the lower end of the hollow, a steep ridge jutted out across the valley where, on top, a Cantaén warrior crouched behind a natural snow wall, keeping a watch on the area beyond. Apart from a small gap, the ridge covered the whole valley bottom. As he watched, the bloodthirsty mob took up position on the far side of the gap to him. Careful not to disturb any snow within sight of someone passing through, the Cantaéns waited, now in total silence, their ambush complete.

Staring intently down the valley, at first he was unable to observe anything that warranted such a speedy deployment by the enemy. Then, in the distance, rounding a slight curve in the valley, two figures came into view. The lookout, although lower down, clearly had a wider field of vision. Who they were, Kaér was unable to see as they were wrapped heavily in furs with an outer layer of white similar to his own. Moving steadily along, their snowshoes sliding over the crusted surface, the strangers made their way towards the gap, oblivious to the danger ahead.

Climbing the steeply rising pathway inside the cut out, the high walls closed in around them and they were now only yards away from their fate. Kaér desperately wanted to shout a warning, but common sense prevailed as his mission was of far too great an importance to risk throwing away his life needlessly. They were probably Cantaéns anyway, the homicidal nature of the people making them just as liable to be attacked by their own as anyone else. Reaching the upper end of the passage, they paused to catch their breath and, as they halted, the waiting group sprang their ambush. The travellers, Kaér had to acknowledge, reacted instantly, placing their backs against the low nearside wall, swords drawn at the ready.

As the ambush party fanned out in a semi-circle around them, the hood of the taller one fell back and the defender released a war cry of such magnitude that Kaér heard it quite distinctly. Stunned by recognition of a call he knew so well, he stared in amazement and then in mounting horror as the Cantaéns charged. This was why Stakirum had urged him to wait. Still unable to believe his eyes and ears and with no thought for his own safety, he hurtled down the mountain at a suicidal rate, his sword clenched firmly in his hand.

Chapter Twelve

Something strange had taken place during the night, something very strange indeed and Hap, the old Rituen—the only survivor of the people of Ritue—could not work out what it was. Then it came to him, the silence. The howling of the wind, which had threatened to drive him insane these last few days, had finally eased. He stretched out in his bed as peace, perfect peace, engulfed him, relaxing in the total absence of noise.

A solitary creature, he lived in a cave situated high in the side of a valley located within the lower reaches of the Cantaé Mountains. Hap was remarkably old. In fact, he had been remarkably old for an exceedingly long time. Many years ago, maybe three centuries or more, a plague had swept across his homeland, wiping out all before it. Only Hap and one other, Guthrum, had survived. Why they should have been spared whilst countless others perished was a mystery they had never been able to comprehend.

Both had become infected by the pestilence but, inexplicably, had recovered. For many years, they scoured the land seeking traces of other survivors, but without success. No matter how remote the area they came to, the results were always the same. In each town or hamlet a burial mound could be found where the earlier afflicted had been interred. Elsewhere, scattered throughout the lonely buildings, lay the bodies of the last to succumb. Despairingly, they had buried the remains and hastened on to the next settlement. They knew if they ever found a place where all the dead had been buried, there was a good chance someone still lived, but they never did.

Gradually towards the end of their wanderings, they became aware the plague had affected them in some strange way. Hap it was, who first realised that Guthrum, in spite of the years of search, looked no older now than the day they had started. His hair should be streaked with grey and his youthful face reflect the inner maturity he now possessed. As for himself, although having reached an age where the ravages of time made little significant alterations to his wrinkled appearance, he should have been either dead or infirm. They came to realise that, although the last of their race, for a considerable number of years to come they might yet provide evidence of its existence.

With their quest at an end, they had to decide how to spend their lives. As Hap had been a skilled healer and Guthrum his pupil before the troubles started, they resolved to go out and use their talents to the full. Turning sadly away from their beloved homeland, now empty of all but scavengers, they went out into the world, travelling extensively before settling in Maraé where they were greeted with much friendliness.

They toured the land, together or separately, healing and teaching as they went. Decades passed until Guthrum, answering a call for help from an injured hunter, was set upon and slain by a Cantaén raiding party. Hap was now truly alone. Burying Guthrum where he found him, he remained near the graveside of his friend for many weeks. Overcome with grief, he was at a loss as to what to do. Welcome among the communities of the forest, he could always go back or, perhaps, return to the nomadic life he had known before. Neither course of action particularly appealed to him. The Maraéns had acquired sufficient knowledge from Guthrum and himself to care for their own, and would not suffer without his presence. Gazing across the intervening distance, he could, faintly, make out the tips of the mountains. Somehow, he felt drawn towards them, some irresistible urge pulling him in their direction. The more he thought about it, the stronger the impulse became.

"The mountains," he decided, speaking aloud. "That's where I'll find peace of mind."

Revenge was not the motive that drew him to the land of Guthrum's murderers; he had cast such thoughts away after taking up the calling of Healer. He could never take the life of a Cantaén unless his, or another's existence was endangered. Nevertheless, no matter how great his dedication to his calling, it was extremely doubtful he would apply his skills to help them. No, he seemed to be called to the mountains for some other purpose. Obeying this strange urge, he made his plans and quietly slipped out of Maraé, heading for the beckoning peaks. After much wandering, avoiding all contact with the deadly inhabitants, he stumbled across the cavern that was eventually to become his home. In all the time since then, he had not shown any sign of ageing.

For a while the Maraéns wondered where he had gone and speculated as to his fate. Those who had known the pair quite well, suspected Hap might still survive but by now, of course, no one lived that had met them and their names and deeds of healing had taken on mythical properties. The stories had grown over the years and many bore little resemblance to the original facts, although it was still said one day Hap the Healer would return. Without doubt, it was a good tale to amuse the children with around a blazing log fire on a long, cold winter's evening. In spite of his self-imposed isolation, Hap came to hear many of the myths that sprang up about him. Stealing into the forest on occasion to replenish his supplies of food and herbs, he often came across the camps of border scouts or hunters. Under cover of darkness, he would move in close and listen to the conversations, the occasional references to himself bringing a smile of wry amusement to his face.

Over a period he learnt about the discovery of The Shintae by the Cantaéns, and the subsequent adventures undertaken by Kaér. The warrior's recovery from his wounds showed the Maraéns had mastered the healing skills they had been taught. The latest piece of news, gleaned before the snow's arrival, was that Kaér and Angharad were about to enter the mountains. Unfortunately, since then, Hap had been cut off from all sources of information.

Of Angharad, he knew nothing but, on rare occasions, he had observed Kaér from afar during his wanderings through the mountains. From conversations overheard in both Maraén and Cantaén campsites, he had pieced together the story of Kaér's relentless quest. The history of The Shintae was familiar to him but, having heard no mention of it for many years, he assumed it had faded from memory. His interest in the lonely Maraén increased with his knowledge and, unbeknownst to Kaér, he had, on occasion, rendered him valuable service.

Concealed high above the spot where the avalanche finally came to rest, Hap's home was situated lower down the valley from Kaér's refuge. The roar of the hurtling wall of snow had come clearly over the top of the storm but, wisely, he had refrained from investigating in the dark. Taking advantage of the lull in the blizzard early the following morning, he wandered to the entrance and gazed down over the confusion of ice and snow beneath. Studying the haphazard mounds he spotted something that caused him to take the unusual step of risking the perilous descent to investigate.

Slithering down the hillside, he approached the object that, as suspected, turned out to be a body, surely dead. Slipping his hand between the frozen furs, he found, to his surprise, the skin, though icy cold was dry and soft to touch. Damp and frost had failed to penetrate the thick layers of clothing and, on testing for a pulse, he discovered a faint beat. Old though he was, the ancient Rituen was still possessed of amazing strength and, using his bare hands he clawed the snow away from the half buried victim and, hoisting him on to his shoulder, he carefully climbed back up the snow covered wastes of the valley side.

Once back inside, he gently lowered the unconscious stranger to the ground and cut away the frozen outer garments. Stripping off the remainder, he was startled to find the victim of the storm was a woman. Quickly, he carried her over to a bed of furs and, wrapping her well with blankets, placed a fur hat over her head. Satisfied she was well insulated against further heat loss, Hap stood back. Not that she had any particular body heat left to lose, he mused, but every little would help. The comatose figure certainly needed all the assistance she could get, plus a great deal of luck, if she was to survive the next few days.

During the first few hours, he detected no appreciable improvement in the condition of his patient who remained icy cold to the touch. Indeed, on numerous occasions he actually thought she had expired. Rushing to her side, he would check anxiously for a pulse and find, to his immense relief, the faintest of beats. The hours passed slowly for Hap who, as night fell, was afraid to sleep in case his skills were required. As he struggled to keep awake during the early hours of the following morning, all appeared lost. The victim's breathing, at best a whisper, faded to nothing and the flickering heartbeat died away altogether. The experience of all his years was to no avail and, try as he might, he was unable to reverse the situation. Admitting defeat, he finally abandoned the struggle; his patient was dead.

Sitting hunched beside the fire, he stared bleakly into the quivering, leaping flames, his mind far away. He struggled in vain to recall any remedy that might have saved the stranger's life. Tiredness overcame him and his eyes started to droop. When the noise came it did not, at first, register and it was only after the sound was repeated he recognised it for what it was. A low moan! The corpse lived! Rushing to her side, Hap felt for a pulse. Yes, there it was and her chest was moving perceptively in short, shallow movements. Whatever had caused this revival was beyond his knowledge, unless her heartbeat and breath had been there all along but too weak to detect.

During the next few hours her pulse grew stronger and her breathing more regular. Her body heat rose steadily and the icy touch of death receded. Deeming the time to be right, Hap warmed some thin, wholesome broth and, ensuring it was not too hot, spooned some slowly down her throat. Convinced she was going to live, Hap succumbed to exhaustion; it was, after all, almost a day and a half since he had slept. Covering himself with his blankets, he stretched out. Within seconds, the only sounds within the cavern were those of breathing and the crackling of the fire.

Under cover of darkness, the snowstorm finally blew itself out. The storm clouds were swept away and, by first light, the air was still and cold. The sun appeared low over the snow capped landscape. Little warmth came with the golden orb, but the very sight of it added an extra dimension to the cruel world. Inside, stretching comfortably in his bed, Hap still revelled in the newfound silence and continued to doze. In the background, the dying embers of the fire hissed and crackled, barely emitting sufficient heat to keep the chamber warm. Eventually, the temperature dropped low enough to register on his mind.

Remembering his patient he leapt out of bed and soon had a cheerful blaze going. Turning, he checked his guest's pulse and found it, like her breathing, firm and steady; she certainly seemed to have a sound constitution. Her body, though, was covered in a mass of bruises, minor cuts, grazes and with a particularly nasty bruise across her forehead, Hap was wary of moving her. Although he could find no obvious broken bones, he was unable to gauge the extent of any internal injuries.

He chewed on a piece of dried meat to ease his hunger pangs as he warmed and then spoon-fed a broth to his patient. Afterwards, while his own meal cooked, he wandered towards the entrance. A passage curved away from his living quarters for twenty paces before opening up on to the valley side. At various points, Hap had strung curtains across the way, in part to eliminate heat loss and draught but mainly to prevent any reflected glow from inside illuminating the cave mouth. A beacon to attract the unwelcome attention of his enemies was something he could well do without. The entrance itself was part of a rocky outcrop and, from most angles, gave the impression of being a darker extension of this. A bush, planted nearby soon after his arrival, broke up the outline even more and, unless you actually walked right up to it, it was impossible to recognise the opening.

Passing through the final curtain he strode outside and, under cover of the bush, surveyed the scene before him, amazed at the change in weather. Gone were the overcast skies to be replaced by glorious sunshine. Although too high in the mountains for the sun's rays to have any real effect, its very presence served to lift his spirits. Even so, it was bitterly cold and, shivering, he pulled his clothes more tightly round him. From the sun's position, he estimated it to be an hour past noon.

He experienced a moment of anxiety as he remembered his trip to fetch the stranger; the tracks he had made would point straight towards his refuge. Keeping well stocked with provisions he did not, normally, move around outside after the snows came. In spite of the area's isolated location, away from the main centres of Cantaén activity, the threat of discovery was still too high. Looking downwards he found no sign of his passage; a fresh fall of snow had covered the area leaving him secure. Breathing a sigh of relief, he returned to his living quarters where he stirred and tasted his lunch. He ladled a generous portion into a bowl and, shortly afterwards, emptied his dish for the third time and declared himself full. Washing the food down with a flagon of fresh water from the stream at the rear of the chamber, he swilled out the dishes and stored them away.

Now his immediate needs were satisfied. He checked his patient once more and found little change, although he sensed the recumbent figure was no longer in a coma and was now in a deep, more natural sleep. Feeling more at ease, Hap sat back and relaxed. As the afternoon progressed, the stranger began to show signs of movement. By evening, she was tossing and turning with frequent incoherent mumblings and cries. Hap, fearing she had gone down with a fever, made numerous checks, but finally concluded she was suffering from nightmares. Placing his ear close to the stranger's lips he could, occasionally, discern the odd word and sentence, the most predominant of these being Kaér and Shintae. Hap, certain now his guest was non other than Angharad, became concerned as to what fate had befallen his intrepid traveller of the mountains.

From what he had seen and heard of Kaér, Hap was sure he would never abandon a companion, yet he had seen no tracks of a searcher in the snow. There was also the mystery of the rope that had been tied around Angharad's waist when he found her. The other end showed no signs of wear and tear. Re-examining it, he found each end in perfect condition. He was positive the pair had, at some point been roped together. If not, then why tie one end around Angharad? There were too many unknown factors. They might have encountered a party of Cantaéns, or just about anything to cause them to separate.

It was useless to speculate. The only thing that did seem certain, however, was that by now, Kaér was either incapacitated or dead. The more he thought about it the more convinced he became it was the latter. Somewhere, outside, Kaér must lie buried under tons of snow and ice. Even if he had come to the surface, it was far too late to do anything for him now. Angharad had herself barely survived the few hours she had spent in the snow. No, there was no other solution; Kaér had perished leaving Angharad as the sole survivor of the expedition to Mount Subae.

Perhaps this was why he had been drawn to the mountains so many years ago. He, Hap, must travel as companion to Angharad. One alone stood little chance, but two, together, made the likelihood of success far greater. He considered the dangers of the mission for a moment and then dismissed them. Death no longer held any fears for him; it was, after all, nearly four hundred years too late. Indeed, there were moments when he could almost welcome it. Since Guthrum's murder and his self imposed-exile, life had become somewhat wearisome. Not that he regretted the unfortunate illness, which had already extended his life far beyond the bounds of possibility. He had seen so many things, learnt much to help his fellow man, but now he was starting to feel his age.

The hours sped by and suddenly Hap realised it was time for the evening meal. Feeding some broth to his increasingly restless patient, he felt sure she would awaken before too long. Banking up the fire he blew out the lamps and sought sanctuary beneath the blankets of his bed. Once Angharad awakened he would be fully occupied and rest might not be as easy to find. The glow from the fire spread a soft radiance throughout the chamber. Sharp edges blurred, outlines became distorted and, as if by some ethereal power, the years fell away from Hap's face and the visage of a young man appeared. The countenance of youth with neither cares nor worries to blemish its tranquillity. A log flared, the firelight flickered and the illusion was dispelled.

Morning arrived and, inside the cavern, a figure stirred and moaned. Moments passed and then the figure moved more positively and, suddenly, a pair of eyes flickered open. Eyes that were numbed by suffering, glazed with a remembrance of pain and cold. Behind those eyes, a mind sparked back into life, a mind that carried an almost unbearable memory of a racing, white wall of death, of spinning round and round, of suffocation under great pressure and finally, a numbing blackness. The eyes focused slightly and all that could be seen was a deep red glow, a vision of death. The mouth opened and from it uttered the shrill despairing cry of one lost to the world. Angharad screamed and screamed.

Chapter Thirteen

As Angharad's anguished cries shattered the silence of the chamber, Hap was torn unmercifully from his slumber. Leaping from his bed, he raced to his patient's side where his immediate reaction was that the young Maraén had lost her sanity. Somewhere in amongst the dreadful mix of snow, ice, and rock, something must have struck her head a terrible blow, causing the bruise across her forehead and damaging the delicate mind behind. The body, which had shown such tenacity to survive, was, apparently, nothing more than an empty shell.

Speaking softly, he tried to calm her, telling her she was safe, but the words failed to pierce the waking nightmare within Angharad's mind. Only the flickering flames of death registered within her confusion. Suddenly a sharp pain stung her cheek, closely followed by another and the images of her mortality faded as rapidly as they had come. Throwing up her hands to protect herself, her cries were abruptly stifled. Hap ceased his slapping and, as the hysteria subsided, he filled a goblet with water and offered it to her.

"Here, drink this," he urged, steadying the vessel and pouring a little of the liquid into her mouth. She coughed and spluttered as she tried to swallow. "Gently. Take it slowly and you'll manage much better," Hap advised.

She obeyed and Hap was gratified to see some measure of intelligence register in her eyes. Allowing her a little more to drink, he placed the goblet on the floor, stooping low to catch the faint words she struggled to utter.

"Where am I? What happened? Who are you?" she whispered, shivering despite being swaddled in piles of thick blankets and furs. Over in one corner a fire was burning brightly and the cold, she realised, came from within, from the very marrow of her bones.

"Well," he replied in slow and measured tones, "you're safe for the moment inside my home. I'm afraid you were caught in an avalanche. You received a nasty bang on the head and have lain half buried in the snow for a whole night before I found you. I'm Hap," he added, "and I think that will have to do for the moment. No! Don't try to speak," he cautioned, "rest yourself and have a little more to drink."

Angharad took another sip but it was icy and she felt even colder inside. She shivered and Hap realised what was wrong.

"Lie back," he said, standing up. "I'll heat some water and mix a drink for you."

Crushing some dried herbs, he dropped them inside an earthenware pot before adding boiling water and leaving it to brew. Once it had cooled sufficiently, he strained some of the brown liquid into a goblet and, propping Angharad up; he left her sipping the drink. Quickly, he set about preparing a broth. All the while he worked he kept up a constant stream of chatter insisting, however, his patient did not try to respond. Calling her by name, he asked if it really was hers. Angharad nodded in reply, wondering how this stranger could possibly know. Sensing her bewilderment, Hap explained about his trips down to the forest. Hap declined to mention his certainty of Kaér's demise and Angharad, in her weakened state, never inquired, just assuming he had gone on alone.

The warm drink was like nectar to her parched throat but, once the broth was ready, her appetite soon faded and she could only manage a few spoonfuls. If nothing else, it went a little way towards warming her bones. Weariness swept over her and within seconds of laying her head back on the pillow, she was asleep. Hap smiled as he looked down. A few days of good food and rest should see her up and about.

After finishing off the remains of the broth, Hap began searching through his store of herbs and specially cured lichens for the ingredients he needed to mix a potion for Angharad. One leaf of this, two of that, a pinch of another and five grains of something else; he continued in a similar manner until satisfied he had missed nothing. Throwing everything together into a mortar, he pounded it with a pestle until he had a fine powder and added the resultant mixture to a pot. Pouring in some warm water, he left it to infuse. Later, using a large wooden spoon he stirred the resultant mass into a wet and sticky paste. Adding more water, he heated it gently over the fire and let it simmer until the concoction was ready. Removing the pot, he placed it on one side and selected a large jar with an airtight cork.

Once the mixture was cool enough to handle, he lined a large bowl with a piece of muslin and emptied the contents of the pot over it. Folding the cloth over the top, he twisted the ends together and continued to twist. As the bag became smaller, a thick amber liquid began oozing from its sides and, shortly afterwards, the bowl was a quarter full. Unable to strain any more, Hap disposed of the bag and its contents before draining the amber liquid into the jar and sealing it. A drop of this every day would help restore Angharad's strength and ensure her recovery was not marred by disease.

As the sun set over the mountains Hap, who had been dozing in a corner, was startled by a voice calling his name. After living alone for so long, he was slightly bewildered.

"I'm sorry to make you jump," apologized the weak voice of Angharad, "but I'm rather thirsty and I don't appear to have enough energy to fetch a drink myself."

"Oh! It's quite all right, I was just a little confused for the moment," Hap returned, gathering his wits together. "Visitors are something I haven't entertained for quite an age, in fact young lady, not since long before you were born," he remarked, refilling the goblet with more of the brown liquid he had left to keep warm beside the fire. "In future I'll leave a drink nearer to you."

Propping her up he passed the goblet whereupon Angharad promptly spilt a little.

"Never mind, you'll soon be fit and strong again," Hap called as he observed the look of frustration on her face.

Going over to the jar, he removed the stopper and added a couple of spoonfuls of the amber syrup inside to a cup before diluting it with a little warm water.

Giving it to Angharad, he said, "Here, drink this medicine, it will help you recover all the more quickly."

After initially screwing up her face at the mention of medicine, Angharad made herself try a little.

"Oh! It's quite pleasant," she commented after her first sip. "In fact it's excellent," she whispered after a second try, her voice starting to ebb.

"That mixture was a much respected remedy in my day; you may fear no illness whilst you continue to imbibe its goodness. Now finish it and your other drink while I warm some more broth. No! Don't talk," he admonished severely, "conserve your energies."

Hap's scowl was so severe that Angharad fell silent again. Later when food was brought to her again, she managed to consume slightly more than her previous attempt, but was so weak that Hap was forced to spoon-feed much of the meal to her. She had always been strong, as far back as she could remember, and this weakness frightened her. Even her first encounter with a Cantaén war party was nothing compared to this. For someone who was used to a healthful outdoor life suddenly to find she could not summon the strength to raise a portion of food to her mouth, held all the makings of a nightmare. Hap sensed his patient's mood as a look of self-derision passed over her face. If she continued to feel sorry for herself and afraid for the future, then recovery would indeed be slow and tedious.

"Listen carefully and remember what I say," he commanded sternly. "I know your strength appears to have deserted you but don't worry, it's only temporary. No one could expect to go through what you have experienced without any after effects; indeed, most would not have survived. In fact there were periods when even I seriously doubted you would ever regain consciousness; it was only your general level of fitness that brought you through. Inside a couple of weeks you should be back to normal and all this will be a distant memory.

"I know you're ashamed at having to be fed but it won't be for much longer. Indeed it'll be sooner still if you keep eating, so come on, try some more, it'll do far more good inside you than in the dish."

Angharad managed half a smile and intimated she would try again. To her surprise, she had soon emptied half the bowl. Hap acknowledged the attempt before fetching another of his many jars from the ledge at the rear of the cave. Opening it he took out a spoonful of a thick syrupy substance.

"Try this," he ordered, but in a more kindly tone. "It will help to stimulate your appetite. If I'd thought earlier, I could have given it to you straight after you'd regained consciousness."

Angharad swallowed the proffered spoonful that seemed to have all the flavour of the earth and woods of Maraé, the ingredients having, in fact, been gathered there. Her eyelids drooped and, lying back, she slept again. Hap was delighted with her progress. Two nights ago he would not have believed it possible but now, provided she kept up her spirits, she was well on the road to recovery.

When Angharad next awakened it was already early morning and Hap had just returned from checking outside. He was shivering as he warmed his hands by the fire, having not bothered putting on his top furs, he was now suffering for it. Turning, he noticed his patient was stirring.

"Brrr!" he exclaimed. "There's a heavy frost outside; anything that escaped the snow is covered with ice. The skies are clear though and there's no sign of cloud. How do you feel today?" he asked, changing the subject. "I think you slept well enough, at least you didn't disturb me during the night."

"Considerably improved," came a reply in a manner much more positive than Hap had expected. "I feel so much better than yesterday. The coldness inside has gone and I actually feel hungry. I've even finished the drink you left for me," she indicated the empty goblet.

Angharad's voice was indeed stronger and the note of self pity, Hap was pleased to hear, was noticeably absent. Recharging her goblet and giving her some more of the potion, Hap paused a second to reflect that the admonishment seemed to have done the trick. Food, though, was another problem and Hap was forced to help her again towards the end, but at least she managed to empty the dish. The syrup appeared to be working and so he gave her another dose.

They talked for a short while, or rather Hap talked and Angharad listened, interrupting occasionally. As he told of his long life, his patient was astonished to discover he really was the 'Hap the Healer' of Maraén legend. Half an hour passed quickly before he realised he was losing his audience, Angharad's head was starting to droop.

"Please forgive me," he apologized contritely. "I'm afraid I've rambled on far too long. You need to sleep, it will do you far more good than listening to me."

"You do yourself an injustice," retorted Angharad stifling a yawn. "I really found it most interesting, if I wasn't so tired I'd gladly sit and listen to your stories all day. I knew the desert had been inhabited in the past, but not so extensively."

"You humour an old man," replied Hap, secretly pleased at the compliments. "But, if you're still interested when you awaken then I'll tell you more. We were not the first to live in the desert region either. Sometimes when the sand moved in the wind, the remains of great cities could be found, the likes of which I've never seen anywhere else. Who built them, or what became of the inhabitants, we had no knowledge, but enough of this, you're weary."

Angharad acknowledged this by simply falling asleep. Eating his own breakfast in silence, Hap remained lost in contemplation. Thoughts of the future lay heavy on his mind, particularly as his own now seemed inextricably tied to that of his guest. Angharad might well be resourceful and experienced in the ways of the enemy but she did not know the region. Only Hap could guide her to where she wanted to go with any reasonable chance of success. By using ways unknown to any other, including Kaér, he could reach the lower reaches of Mount Subae from where they were now in about eight days. Most would be hard pushed to manage it within the month.

His mind made up Hap walked resolutely towards the rear of the cavern and, from beneath a bundle of furs, retrieved a couple of objects stored away inside dusty greased cloths. Striding back to the fire he knelt down and uncovered them. Inside was a pair of swords of a most unusual design. Hap had never discovered from where they had originated, nor how the Cantaéns, who had tried to kill him, had acquired them. Although sworn to fight only in self-defence, he had kept them both, not wanting them to be rediscovered and further defiled by the mountain people. The unsheathed blades gleamed in the light with their edges honed to an almost impossible sharpness. He had no desire to take life but once engaged upon the quest he might find his options severely limited. The Shintae was too important to risk through his inaction. One sword he would keep himself, the other he would give to Angharad to replace the one lost during the avalanche. Returning them to their wrappings he placed them out of sight. It would be soon enough to show them when his guest was able to hold one; the sight of them now would simply stir up her impatience.

The remainder of the day passed in a rush of activity for Hap. Whilst seeing to his patient, he took a length of charcoal and wrote out on a piece of hide a list of items they would need for the journey. Although Angharad's spirits continued to rise during the day, by early evening she was tired out. Hap, unaccustomed to so much exercise, was also exhausted and, once his guest had settled down, retired to his bed.

Chapter Fourteen

The days passed quickly as Angharad continued to recuperate. By the third day Hap had found some old clothes to fit her and, while she dressed, he went out to check on the weather. On his return, Angharad was allowed out of bed for the first time, staggering once around the cavern holding on to his arm. Afterwards, sitting back on her bed, she just could not believe how weak she felt. Hap commiserated, but also reassured her the worst of this would soon be over. Much to her surprise, Angharad found this true and, as the week progressed, discovered her energy slowly returning. Once she became more active, Hap taught her a set of exercises, which seemed miraculous in the way they toned her muscles.

With the revival of her strength had come a renewal of her mental faculties and Angharad began asking the questions that Hap dreaded most having to answer. Where was Kaér? Had he gone on ahead to scout for The Shintae? Was he coming back for her, or was she to meet up with him nearer to Mount Subae? Hap remained silent for a moment, unable to tell Angharad anything more than that she was alone when he had rescued her. Angharad confirmed immediately that Cantaéns had not been the cause of her separation from Kaér.

"Why then did Kaér leave?" demanded Hap. "Surely he didn't desert you? But the rope that tied you together doesn't show any signs of being torn in two?"

"Of course he didn't abandon me," retorted Angharad indignantly. "The blizzard was severe, we were close to collapse and it was only the thought of Kaér's refuge that kept us going. Although we were beginning to fear we might have passed it by. I had just fallen when Kaér, who was not quite as badly affected, spotted what he thought might be the entrance.

"After loosening his end of the rope, he went to check. After all it was only a matter of a few steps. Then, as he disappeared inside the opening, the whole world erupted and the next thing I remember is awakening in here...Oh no!" a terrible thought entered her mind. "He could still be in there, trapped by the snow."

Hap paled at the idea, such a scenario had not occurred to him. Pausing only to put on his outer furs and collect a pair of snowshoes, he rushed outside and raced up the valley, oblivious of the tracks he was making. *If only I am in time,* he thought, spurring himself on. Within twenty minutes or so, he had slithered his way to where the valley veered. Rounding the corner, he found himself in a landscape totally alien to the one he had known so well. The avalanche had been far worse than he had imagined, completely changing the character of the land hereabout. At the point where the entrance to Kaér's hiding place should have been stood a huge mound of rock, three hundred yards wide, fifty high and nearly a hundred deep. The snow must have come initially, sweeping Angharad clear just before the mountainside collapsed. From what he could see, Kaér's body must lie crushed beneath the landslip.

Clambering over the rubble until he was roughly above the spot where the cavern mouth had been, he began tapping loudly upon the rocks. Pausing to listen, he tapped again, continuing all around the area until satisfied he would never, ever, receive an answering call. Not that he could have done much had he heard a reply. There was certainly no possibility of digging through to the entrance, assuming it and the cave behind still existed. Some of the slabs of rock were twenty to thirty feet across. He just hoped Kaér had died instantly in the rock fall, not slowly in the dark, badly injured and suffering from hunger and thirst. He shuddered at the prospect. There was nothing more he could do here. Retracing his tracks, he prayed that snow would fall and disguise the signpost to his home he was creating. Looking back he thankfully realised the gusting wind was already covering his trail with powdery crystals.

He was away for almost two hours and Angharad was frantic by the time he returned. Hap broke the news immediately and she flinched as tears welled in her eyes. She remained morosely silent throughout the remainder of that day and for most of the next. Hap left her alone with her grief; she had to work it out of her system in her own way. During the following evening she suddenly brightened and though Kaér often came into their subsequent conversations, the subject of his death was never mentioned.

Angharad took some persuading before she agreed to let Hap accompany her on the remainder of the journey to Mount Subae. She was reluctant to expose her benefactor to the toils and rigours she expected to encounter on the way. Hap, though, was adamant, declaring if he could not join her then he would go by himself. Under such pressure Angharad finally capitulated, secretly pleased to have someone to act as a guide. Her knowledge of the mountains was slight and without Kaér to lead, she had little idea of where she was making for or, indeed, in what direction to go. She would have found her way eventually, but whether in time to save Maraé was another matter. Delighted with the outcome, Hap decided to show Angharad the pair of swords. Never before had she seen such workmanship and from this point on she became positively enthusiastic.

Clasping one of the swords in her hands, Angharad was surprised at its lightness. The metals of its manufacture were unknown to Hap, but it rang true and was of exceptional strength. The blade had been pattern welded, a method almost unheard of in those days but one of which Hap had some knowledge. A bundle of metal rods, he told her, were twisted together, forged, re-forged and beaten to form a flexible nucleus. After this, hard, untwisted sections were added to form the cutting edge. The blade between the edges was herringbone patterned, a result of the original forging of the rods. A large metal pommel provided perfect counterpoise. Angharad noted Hap's was of a similar design although the guard on his was straight whilst hers was curved. The grip, she noted, was inlaid with silver in an intricate design. Regretfully she slid it back inside its sheath of leather covered wooden laths. Returning it to Hap, she decided to concentrate on recovering as swiftly as she could; a weapon such as this deserved nothing but the best from the person handling it.

In the week that followed Angharad's condition showed a vast improvement. She passed most days in exercising, performing both her own exercises and ones that Hap taught her. The sword was never far from her side. Its lightness enabled her to practice for longer periods than would have been advisable with the slightly shorter, but far heavier Maraén ones.

They cured and dried meat for the journey while other vegetable foods were prepared in a way previously unknown to her, the result being a concentrated block of sustaining food. Their packs soon filled with supplies. Angharad's furs were repaired and, from pieces of cured hide and finely woven material lying amongst Hap's stores, she made herself a set of clothes to replace those lost in the avalanche. Sets of Aralpos were made from white fabric and then thoroughly waterproofed, as was a tent constructed from the same cloth. Although barely large enough to sleep them both, it did mean their joint body heat would help keep them warm. Upon Angharad's insistence, they manufactured a second tent in case they became separated.

A third week came and went as they completed their preparations. The suppleness returned to Angharad's sword arm and, as she exercised, she could almost feel the power growing inside her muscles. Initially she had tried too hard and tired herself but, with Hap's counselling, she had curbed her enthusiasm, making steady progress comparatively painlessly. Now fully recovered, she was eager to be on her way.

On the morning of the twenty-third day after the avalanche, they took their leave; Angharad waiting down below in the valley bottom while Hap bade a solitary farewell to his home. Whatever the future held for him, be it good or bad, life or death, he had a feeling he would never return. The refuge had served its purpose well, but now it was time to move on.

Angharad, sensing Hap's mood, tactfully remained silent as they made their way up the valley. The silence was companionable and both were glad of the opportunity to collect their thoughts. They made good time and by noon had traversed a good six miles. The surface of the snow was powdery and flew about with each step they took, but underneath it was firm and made for good travel. They were downcast as they passed the scene of Kaér's incarceration but, leaving it behind, they concentrated on what lay ahead.

By evening, although weary, they were not over-tired. They pitched camp in the confines of a cleft at the edge of the valley and, while Angharad kept watch, Hap lit a small fire and cooked some of the food they had brought with them. Once the meal was ready, they extinguished the flames and ate in silence. By now there was a distinct chill in the air and, by the light of the setting sun, they retired to their tent to sleep.

They spent a miserable night, frequently woken by the whining of the wind and the cold, which despite the thickness of their furs, seeped up from the ground. Mercifully, dawn arrived and they dragged themselves shivering into the open. This time while Hap kept vigil, Angharad cooked the last of their fresh food over a newly lit fire. From now on they would not risk a fire unless they could find a cave to hide it in. The deeper they penetrated enemy territory, the greater the risk of discovery. Breaking camp, they were four miles away before the sun had stretched its weak skirt of light half way down the valley walls.

Keeping to an even pace they were careful not to overexert themselves.

The intense cold would soon freeze the perspiration on their bodies and death was always ready to welcome another careless victim. The day passed without event and with the coming of darkness, they managed to locate a small cave where, in spite of being unable to find any wood for a fire, they spent an easier night out of the howling wind.

The next day, shortly after noon, they came to a fork in the valley and Hap went to the right. It soon became apparent that luck remained a companion, for, after a mile of heavy going, the valley veered slightly to the left and they discovered most of the snow had drifted to the far side of the vale. Removing their snowshoes, they were able to walk for the remainder of the day unencumbered.

Once more they were lucky to find a cave for the night, although this one had seen habitation in the past. Clearing away the grimmer evidence of Cantaén occupation, they discovered a large supply of cut wood, stacked in a corner out of the way. After building a fire they spent a comfortable night, fortified by a hot broth that raised their spirits. The embers were still glowing the next morning when Hap awakened, alerted by the sound of distant excited voices. Beams of sunlight filtering in through the entrance alerted him to the fact they had greatly overslept.

The sound of the Cantaén tongue sent a deadly chill running down his spine although, from the volume of noise, they appeared to be only a small party. Where they had come from he did not know, but they had obviously discovered Angharad's and his footprints in the shallow snow. He estimated the Cantaéns were still some way off, for the valley carried sound quite well. Although excited, they did not sound particularly alarmed. He supposed they expected to find fellow Cantaéns, rather than enemies. Placing a hand over Angharad's mouth to muffle any noise, he shook her awake.

"Shh!" he whispered as she struggled back to reality. "Don't make a sound. We're about to have company."

Angharad listened intently as the foul tongue echoed along the valley. Rising, she drew her sword, but then an idea struck her and she sheathed it again before kneeling down beside her bed. Quickly she pushed, pulled and folded the rugs to make it appear as though someone were still sleeping there. Hap quickly followed suit with his own bed.

"It wouldn't fool anyone in good light," Angharad murmured, "but they'll be coming out of bright sunshine into the dark. It'll be some time before their eyes adjust and the flickering light from the embers gives an impression of movement as well."

Hap glanced at the rugs and they did indeed seem to stir as if someone beneath were dreaming. He nodded in agreement and, silently, they moved over to the shadows by the cave mouth. With swords drawn but held tightly behind their backs so no gleam betrayed them, they stood rigidly at either side of the entrance, scarcely daring to breathe. Slowly the voices drew nearer and Hap could make out most of the conversation that was going on.

"I wonder who they are?" came one voice.

"How should I know?" someone answered. "Some down valley trash no doubt."

"Who cares anyway?" said a third. "If they're friendly we'll let them share their breakfast with us an' if they aren't, we'll just take it and leave 'em nothing."

They all sneered horribly as Angharad and Hap shuddered at the sound.

"And why not?" interjected the original voice. "After all we're the ones who have to go down to that wretched forest to spy on those miserable Maraéns for Sartae. We deserve the best, and we're going to get it," he declared.

A different voice joined in the conversation, "I hope they won't share," it said wickedly.

"Oh. Yeah!" exclaimed yet another in some surprise.

"Because we can have some fun with 'em then, stupid," came the response.

"Mm! Nice idea," commented the third voice, "but shut up now. There's no need to alarm them is there? We might just have some fun anyway."

After one final, dreadful cackle, they fell silent and all Angharad and Hap could hear was the faint tread of their feet as the Cantaéns crunched through the snow towards them. Then came a sudden expectant lull as the enemy stood outside, closely followed by the sound of someone entering.

"There's just the two of them," the Cantaén whispered to his companions outside, "sleeping like babies they are, so come on in quietly and no tripping over your feet any of you. Let's giv' 'em a little surprise," he chortled as they followed him in.

They spread out inside the cave, six of them, leaving the silent observers, unseen, behind them. The leader strode over to the 'sleeping forms' and with quick movements kicked the outer furs away.

"Right, let's have a look at you," he roared. Then his voice trailed away and he stared in disbelief at the empty beds. "Where'd they go?" he wailed as the others shuffled about uncomfortably, as much at a loss as their leader to explain this strange twist to their plans.

"Right behind you, my treacherous ones," came a clear, sharp voice, causing the Cantaéns to jump at the sound. "Ready and eager to make your acquaintance."

As one, the Cantaéns wheeled around and saw two shadows by the entrance holding large swords gleaming redly in the dim light. The leader was the first to recover and, with a loud cry, drew his blade and launched himself forward, the others following on behind. Angharad easily parried a swift, sideways slash of the Cantaéns' sword and then with a short thrusting blow finished him. As he slumped to the ground the next Cantaén, tripping over his body, went flying straight on to Hap's blade and was run through. The remaining intruders backed off, stunned by the rapid loss of their two companions. Their only means of escape was the opening through which they had entered by and that meant passing the guardians. Plucking up courage they flung themselves in a fury at their mysterious enemies, four against two. The resulting fracas did not take long, Angharad claiming victory over her opponents with little difficulty but Hap, even though he had the upper hand, was not finding it as easy to finish off his antagonists.

Drawing off to one side, Angharad engaged one of Hap's assailants in combat. There was a short, sharp exchange of strokes before Angharad, slipping on a stone, went down. The Cantaén, sensing victory, raised his sword for a final, fatal blow. Angharad rolling smoothly as she landed threw her sword straight at her attacker's unguarded body. The blade went true, and the Cantaén collapsed heavily on top of her. By the time she struggled free and retrieved her weapon, Hap had already triumphed over his adversary. Standing back, they surveyed the scene. The Cantaéns had certainly paid dearly for their want of "a little fun."

Hap looked across at Angharad and said, "Come. Let's pack and get out of here, this is no place for decent folk."

She nodded in agreement and, within minutes, they were on their way, not pausing to eat until much later. By the middle of the afternoon, they were many miles away when Hap, who had for half hour now been studying the valley sides as they progressed, stopped abruptly. Angharad waited patiently for him to continue, leaning on the bow she had taken from one of the dead Cantaéns. They might have need of one later and it was of excellent quality; one of the few things the Cantaéns took any care of in the making was the requisites of war. She watched closely as Hap concentrated intently on the far side of the valley, hoping he had not lost his bearings. Never before had he hesitated as to the direction they were to take. Still, not having the faintest idea as to where they were, even the remotest glimmer in the mind of Hap was an improvement on what she had to offer.

Hap mumbled to himself as his eyes searched the landscape. Then the frown left his brow and a smile came to his lips as he found something to his satisfaction.

"Things look different in the snow," he commented as if in explanation. "I rarely come this way in the depths of winter. Can you see the shadow of that large outcrop of rock over there?" he pointed towards a spot on the left hand side of the valley, about a hundred yards away.

"Yes," replied Angharad cautiously, "is it significant?"

"It most certainly is. That is the entrance to a short cut through the mountains. In the far corner there's a crack in the rock that takes you over the mountain into another, hidden valley. I was here only last year. There were no signs of discovery by the Cantaéns then and I'm fairly sure it will have remained that way. I found the entrance quite by chance one blazing hot day, many summers ago, and took shelter there from the sun. It appeared to be a dead end but, out of curiosity, I followed it all the way to the top and came out on a most astounding sight. But this is something you will be able to judge for yourself later."

Angharad looked upwards not fully convinced. Elsewhere the sky remained clear but the mountaintop was wreathed in mist and cloud, certainly a daunting sight.

"Is it always like this," she inquired.

"In winter? Yes! Though in summer, when the sun is stronger and the air much warmer, occasionally you do find the skies clear," he replied as they made their way over to the outcrop.

Although they had encountered deep snow lower down the vale, the area around here was reasonably clear and they were able to climb without leaving tracks for prying eyes to find. The rocky ground higher up would show no signs of their passing either.

"No wonder the Cantaéns haven't discovered it," Angharad said as they neared the entrance. "Their superstitious natures would lead them to believe there are demons lurking in such an inhospitable looking area as this, especially a place where the land is always covered in cloud."

"Mm. That's certainly a possibility; although I should imagine the main reason is that they generally take the easiest route when travelling. The only ways in and out of the valley that I'm aware of, are here and at the far end, and both are naturally concealed from the eye. The route we followed to reach here, as you know, splits and the other fork leads directly to the south. They have no need to find additional routes over the tops."

Hap finished talking as he reached the hidden way and Angharad nodded in acknowledgement, hoping he was correct in his assumptions. The Cantaéns were unpredictable and it was unwise to underestimate them.

The crack, Angharad realised as they began to ascend, was only wide enough for one body between the rocky walls that towered on either side. The path was steep and, in places, they had to resort to climbing as it twisted back and forth. After a while, she no longer knew, nor cared, in what direction they were travelling. The journey seemed never-ending with the temperature dropping the higher they went. An hour went by, and then another and still they struggled upwards. Finally, after another long and weary hour had passed, they entered the bank of low cloud covering the top of the valley side. Night was falling as they fought their way through a shroud of freezing mist.

Although Hap assured Angharad there were no sudden drops to worry about, they had difficulty in keeping their foothold as the moisture from the atmosphere was squeezed on to the frozen ground, creating an icy sheet beneath them. The faint light from the setting sun had faded and the mist was now so dense that Angharad was becoming anxious.

"We must pass over the top before we make camp," Hap insisted when questioned about the advisability of continuing. "Otherwise, we'll spend a cold, miserable and potentially dangerous night out here. The mist permeates everything and, at this height, we risk freezing to death. The path levels out soon, and then begins to descend. In another hour or so we will be out of the cloud and down to a much warmer climate."

Angharad grunted to show she had heard, although how Hap was going to find a warmer environment was beyond her. She was becoming increasingly exhausted the higher they went. The air was much thinner here, and the long climb had drained much of her energy. Unlike Hap, she was not accustomed to such a rarefied atmosphere. Until now they had ascended steadily since leaving Hap's home and gradually they had become accustomed to the change. To Angharad's great relief the path levelled out shortly afterwards and, as promised, soon started to descend. Hap borrowed his companion's bow and, feeling the ground before him in order not to be taken by surprise on the steeper sections, carried on.

They descended rapidly; Angharad soon found her breathing easing. Although still considerably higher than in the other valley, the drop in altitude was beneficial to them both. Breaking through the cloud level, they carried on for some distance to ensure they remained clear. In the end fatigue compelled Hap to call a halt and, despite feeling much the same, Angharad pushed herself to erect the tent. Both had gone beyond hunger but, once Hap had rested and recovered a little, they made themselves eat something from their supplies before stripping off their dripping outer coverings and crawling gratefully under their sleeping-rugs.

As she drifted off to sleep Angharad was vaguely aware that the biting chill in the air was no longer apparent and although cool, it was still many degrees warmer than it had been before. They had not encountered any snow since shortly after starting to descend but, whatever this might or might not signify, she was far too tired to think about it now.

Chapter Fifteen

Awakening in the grey light of dawn, Angharad stretched and yawned, finding to her delight the mildness in the air was real and not merely a dream. Sitting up, she looked across at Hap who opened one eye and, realising the hour, immediately closed it again. Yesterday's climb had taken a great deal out of him and he was in no mood to make any effort just yet. Thankfully their bodies had acclimatised overnight to the increase in altitude and their breathing was no longer as laboured.

Drawing back the tent flaps, Angharad came to an abrupt halt, open mouthed, as she gazed in wonder at the sight that greeted her. Watching through half closed eyes, Hap smiled at the expression on her face; the view still had a similar effect on him, even though he had seen it often enough. Beneath the swirling banks of cloud the barren, frozen wastes of Angharad's imagination did not exist. Instead a thickly wooded vale spread out before her. A broad river meandered gently westwards along the valley bottom, steam curling skywards from its surface. The forest continued as far as she could see, until land and cloud merged.

"It's not what you expected, is it?" inquired Hap after a moment.

"I must confess, it's far beyond anything I could have possibly anticipated," Angharad replied, looking around her in awe. "We'll certainly travel more rapidly in the woods than we did in the snow. It feels like we've been transported back to Maraé. How far does it go on for?"

"The forest? Apart from an occasional break it covers nearly the whole length of the valley. This whole area is volcanic. The heat from below keeps much of the land clear of frost but be warned, there are stretches where it's much cooler and then we'll have need of our furs. The river, though, is fed by hot springs and never freezes over, even in the coldest parts.

"We'll be travelling on the river, which will save us a considerable amount of time. In fact, four days or so from now, with luck, we'll be at the other end. Once there, we're little more than a good day's march away from the outer reaches of Mount Subae itself."

Absorbing this information, Angharad decided to leave any further questions until later. With breakfast in mind, she went in search of fuel, staggering back shortly afterwards, arms fully laden with dead branches from the woods below. Collecting her bow, she vanished again, returning half an hour later with a brace of large rabbits. Lighting a fire, she quickly prepared the meat. The aroma of cooking finally dragged Hap from his bed and, whilst she looked after the meal, he packed away their equipment.

The setting of their encampment worked wonders for Angharad's spirits. The slightest hint of a woodland scent was sufficient to send a tingle of excitement running through her. She wanted to dance, sing and shout, but wisely refrained from doing any such thing. Hap would have thought she had taken leave of her senses. Instead she contented herself with smiling and whistling whenever her mouth was not filled with food.

"Come on then," Hap said eventually, "let's make a move. It's mid-morning already and we ought to be many miles away from here before we make camp tonight."

"Surely," Angharad responded, "if we're going by river we'll have to construct a boat of some description?"

"Certainly not!" he answered, a smug expression on his face. "During my visits, I've been working on a raft. I put the final touches to it last year, but then didn't bother using it. So, fortunately, it's still at this end of the river."

Angharad smiled in acknowledgement and went off to finish sorting out their packs. Later, as they made their way to the river they surprised and killed a deer. Wasting no time, they skinned the beast and cut out as much meat as they could carry between them. Depositing the meat and their supplies near to the raft, they returned for the rest of their kill. Arriving back at the river's edge, Angharad was finally able to inspect their mode of transport. It consisted of a three yard square platform made from stout logs lashed together. A pole was fixed in each corner with a larger central one from where a canopy could be stretched for shelter. They could always utilise one of their tents for this purpose. Strapping down their possessions, they set about launching the craft.

Hap had assembled the construction on top of a row of loose logs that was to act as rollers. Even with their combined efforts, they had a struggle to move it. Taking out the rear log and placing it at the front as they went along, they eventually managed to manoeuvre the craft to the riverbank. Hap mumbled something about this being the reason he had decided to walk on the previous occasion, at which point Angharad burst out laughing. The idea that Hap had not considered how unwieldy it would be tickled her sense of humour. Her companion, conversely, was not amused and it was some time before he was able to appreciate the humour of the situation.

Before giving the raft its final push, they lashed a rope to one of the uprights and secured it to a nearby tree to prevent the craft from being swept away. Then with one final effort, the raft slid gently into the water, floating satisfactorily with the deck standing proud of the surface by a good eighteen inches.

"Tomorrow we'll strap our packs and food high up on the centre pole," Hap informed Angharad. "We won't hit any rough stretches today, but later on the river narrows in parts and the current increases quite rapidly. There's a good chance we might become awash and there's no point in risking our supplies."

Casting off the mooring rope, they leapt on board and, even before the steering oar had been lashed into place, the current had swept them midstream. Another stage of their travels had begun. The river was swift moving and they took it in turns to steer the raft. The craft was awkward to control and a great deal of sweated effort was expended before they became adept at the task. Although the intention was to keep midstream, when negotiating bends they were occasionally swept up against the riverbank. A couple of times, after becoming badly entangled amongst the overhanging growth, they were left with no alternative but to hack themselves free with their swords.

In spite of such set backs, they made a good twenty-five miles and with darkness imminent, they cast about for somewhere to land. At one point the river broadened considerably and on their left they spotted a shingle beach. They almost grounded the craft before realising it would probably sink into the soft riverbed making it difficult, if not well nigh impossible to re-launch the following day. A few hundred yards beyond, however, they came to a point where the river veered sharply to the right. The current swept them over to the left bank and, with barely enough light left to see by, Hap noticed an outlet from a tributary stream. The opening was wide enough to accommodate the raft and the water seemed deep enough to take its draught. More by luck than skill, they managed to turn the raft towards the channel. Taking hold of the rope they had used during the launch, Angharad leapt onto the banking and, exploiting the crafts forward momentum, dragged it clear from the main stream. As Angharad secured her end of the rope to a nearby tree, Hap fastened another hawser to the stern and, jumping ashore, did likewise. Once moored, Angharad built a fire and started to roast a little of their venison while Hap procured a selection of wild vegetables. An hour later, they had eaten their fill, erected a tent and, exhausted, retired for the night.

The next couple of days passed uneventfully as they covered considerable distances, starting at first light and continuing until dusk, eating cold fare as they went. During the late afternoon of the first day, they entered a cold region and remained with it until the following morning. Travelling here was a miserable affair. Unable to move around to keep warm they were forced to spend the time shivering inside their furs. At dusk they pitched camp beside the river where they spent the night in relative comfort, keeping a fire burning throughout. With a return to warmer climes, camp the following night was a much more cheerful concern. Their river journey was now almost at an end and by noon on the morrow, Hap estimated they would be back on foot and in the cold again.

"Why can't we float all the way to the end of the valley?" Angharad asked over breakfast the next day, just before daybreak.

"I wish we could," Hap replied, "but, unfortunately, the river widens and becomes so shallow we'd run aground. But before we reach there we'll have to make sure the packs are tied securely."

"Why's that?" inquired Angharad, somewhat warily.

"The river passes through a narrow gorge, before opening out," Hap explained. "There's no hope of going around it at this time of year, even in summer it's not the easiest of ascents. Everything will be covered in ice now as it's in a cold area and, without proper equipment, it would be foolhardy to try. The far side is far gentler and, if we return by the same route, we can easily lower ourselves down this end by rope."

"Yes, I can see the sense in that, but is the gorge all that bad?" Angharad demanded, warily. In spite of coming from the coastal region, she had always felt safer on dry land.

"I'm afraid so," Hap confirmed. "On top of the current's speed, there are plenty of rocks, large and small, sticking up from the riverbed. If we hit one of those, we will really be in trouble, even if the raft doesn't break up on impact it could easily capsize. Our only chance if things do go wrong will be to hang on to any debris large enough to keep us afloat, otherwise our furs will drag us under."

"We should rope ourselves to the central pole then," Angharad suggested, "it might prevent us from being washed overboard. But," she advised, "you'd better make sure your knife's handy, if the raft does come apart you'll need to cut yourself free in a hurry."

Angharad was careful to double-check everything as she secured their packs, even adding extra lengths of rope as a precaution. She hoped the perils had been exaggerated but, as Hap had a tendency to understate, she had the distinct feeling she might be glad when the river journey was over.

"How were you going to manage by yourself?" Angharad queried as they cast off from the river's bank. "Surely it'll take all our combined strength to handle the steering oar! You'd never have been able to control it by yourself!"

"It was summer then," Hap replied, once they were underway, "and I'd intended to tie up the raft before the gorge, there was no ice then and I could have easily climbed around it. What's more, I couldn't launch the wretched thing, as you're fully aware," he growled, as he saw the look of amusement cross over Angharad's face. "Don't forget," he added testily, "I'm a healer, not a practical person like you. How was I to know the thing would be so heavy and awkward when I'd finished?"

He scowled so much with embarrassment that Angharad was a little contrite. Even so she had to look away for, try as she might, she could not stop the laughter bubbling up inside and she had no wish to hurt Hap's feelings any further.

Within half an hour of their departure, the landscape had changed, becoming bleaker and more barren as they drifted back towards the bitter cold of winter. Taking it in turns to control the steering oar, their hands soon became numbed by the biting frost. By mid-morning Angharad became aware of a narrowing in the river and an increase in the speed of the current. In the far distance, the snow covered plain seemed to end abruptly at the base of lofty cliffs. From here the gap between looked dreadfully small indeed. A shiver ran down her spine and she shuddered with apprehension. Hap was resting on the deck and, bending down, she shook him fully awake.

Moving rapidly to his feet on the swaying platform, Hap, after a quick glace downstream, gathered up the free end of one of the ropes he had attached earlier to the central pole. Tying it firmly around his waist, he took over the steering oar while Angharad did the same with the other.

With each fleeting moment, they drew nearer to the gorge as the raft gathered speed. All too soon the towering walls closed in on either side and they were swept into the roaring semi-darkness of the passage. Tossed first this way then the next, they fought to hold the oar steady in the boiling water as they struggled to keep their footing. The roar of the rapids assailed their ears as the movement of the raft became increasingly erratic and the deck awash with foaming water.

Time and again they were forced to throw themselves hard on to the oar to steer themselves clear of huge, jagged rocks protruding from the angry surface. Then in the midst of the furiously raging torrent, they hurtled over a submerged obstruction and the oar was crushed to pieces, hurling them to the deck as the craft spun crazily and dipped sharply over the edge of a small cascade. As the raft slipped sideways, the river poured over them and Angharad, who had lengthened her safety rope to allow her more freedom of movement, was swept overboard. Hap, though severely buffeted by the pounding water, remained on board as his lifeline took the strain. Positive buoyancy pushed the stricken craft to the surface and Hap succeeded in crawling to the centre. Bracing himself as best he could against the main post, he grasped hold of Angharad's rope and began to pull, hand over hand.

Hap was gratified to find a burden still attached to the other end, all was not yet lost. Looking over his shoulder, he could see, barely a couple of hundred yards away, the river was streaked with white, indicating yet another bad stretch of water. If Angharad were not on board by then, the river bottom's deadly teeth would rive her to pieces. He renewed his frantic efforts and, almost at the last moment, a hand appeared over the edge and, as Hap took the strain, Angharad dragged herself on board to lie gasping and retching until the insistent tugging of the rope around her waist roused her. The seething mass of water was only yards away as she crawled to the relative safety of the centre. Back to back with their arms linked and the post between them, they braced themselves for the next onslaught.

Their luck returned, albeit temporarily, as they negotiated the watery maze. The rapids were soon left behind as the travellers were propelled as if by some demonic power before, with a sudden crash, the raft was dashed against a massive outcrop. Two logs shattered instantly with the impact and were swept away as the raft reared up, high against the rock, before sliding away and righting itself. Miraculously, the remaining logs stayed intact leaving the raft still relatively stable.

Although Angharad had more or less recovered from her near drowning, she, like Hap, was soaked to the skin and shivering from the cold. They had begun to despair of ever reaching safety when the river widened out and the current slowed its lethal race. The cliffs came to an end and, nearly three quarters of an hour after entering the gorge, the travellers were back out in the open. Still alive they might be, but not for much longer, if they could not find shelter and warmth before their clothes froze to their skins. The battered remains of the raft drifted over to the left and ground to a halt on a sand bank. With knives held in unfeeling fingers, they clumsily cut the ropes holding them and their supplies before picking up their packs and wading ashore.

"There's a small cave over there," Hap said through chattering teeth as he indicated a black hole in the side of a nearby cliff at the valley's edge. "I always leave a good supply of firewood inside."

Moving through the snow, they could feel their clothes stiffening and hear the crackle of frost upon them. Stumbling inside, Angharad built a fire while Hap fumbled open his pack searching for a tinderbox. He was pleasantly surprised to discover that the contents, including a spare set of clothes, had faired quite well and suffered little water damage. With their whole bodies shaking uncontrollably, Hap had numerous unsuccessful attempts to light a fire before success favoured him. Building the flames as quickly as they could, the cave slowly warmed as Angharad collected her pack and vanished into a nook at the rear of the cavern. Hap stripped off and towelled himself dry with a couple of lengths of rough cloth. The brisk rubbing restored some of his circulation and, after a few short exercises, his body began to tingle. The fire had really taken hold now and he fed more logs on to it, the heat reflecting back from the cavern walls as he dressed in his spare outfit. Angharad joined him shortly afterwards, her long hair hanging damply over a fresh tunic and, after spreading their wet clothes out to dry, they warmed themselves and some food before the flames. Luckily, being well waterproofed, their furs had escaped the worst effects of the river and soon aired off while they rested.

Several hours later, their wet clothes dried and packed away, they bade farewell to their refuge. For three hours they worked their way down the valley and, as the shadows lengthened, they approached the far end of a large lake that marked both river's and valley's ends. Soaring mountains bordered three sides whilst the valley floor, which led back the way they had come, marked the fourth. Skirting the boulder-strewn shoreline, Hap pointed towards a dark shadow looming thirty feet or so above the nearside edge at the end of the mere.

"That's where we're heading," he indicated, "it's an old drainage hole. The lake, at some time, must have been considerably deeper. The passage leads down through the mountains for about three miles, eventually coming out above a dry water course on the other side."

"Where does the water from the lake come out now?" Angharad asked curiously.

"I've really no idea," Hap replied. "There are no rivers of any great size at the other side of this mountain, none that could possibly be taking the volume of water coming from here. It could end up just about anywhere and, I suppose, in almost any direction."

"What's the passage like?" queried Angharad. "I mean, is it dry or wet, can we walk through it or do we have to crawl for most of the way?"

"It's certainly not damp but we do have to crawl occasionally. There are, however, one or two steep drops to negotiate and we will need to take extra care there. We can tackle the first section tonight, it shouldn't take us more than an hour to complete."

Twenty minutes later had they clambered their way up to the entrance and, upon lighting a lamp, began the long descent. The first time they had to crawl, it was for a short distance only and even then Angharad found the experience somewhat unpleasant as she squirmed along, dragging her pack behind. The next occasion lasted for over a hundred yards and, feeling increasingly uneasy as the passage pressed in all around her, she was thankful to finally reach the end of the section. Hap laughed when she told him so and warned that some of the passages they would come to tomorrow were twice as long. Angharad groaned inwardly and refrained from comment. Tired and staggering from weariness, they reached a point where Hap said it would be dangerous to continue in their present state. They dined from cold fare and laid out their beds. Checking the lamp, Hap added enough fat to ensure it would burn for at least another twelve hours before they turned in for the night.

Much later, on opening her eyes, Angharad checked the fat level beneath the burning lamp. From what remained, she estimated she had slept for about nine hours, which would put the time somewhere between five and seven in the morning. Turning towards Hap, she decided to leave him a little longer. Despite his incredible age, the old Rituen had acquitted himself admirably during the journey but his care-worn face was looking drawn and haggard. He was not possessed of unlimited reserves of energy and even though he might be prepared to push himself to the absolute limit, she had no desire to see him reach such a state. Hap's potions and fitness regime had worked wonders with her stamina and, despite the passage through the gorge being a considerable drain on her strength, a good night's rest had left her feeling greatly refreshed.

Nevertheless, it was doubtful whether Hap would feel the same way when he awakened, and she decided to try to persuade him to rest for a day. Not that she held out much hope of the idea finding favour with him. He would certainly not desire the journey to be interrupted on his account.

After eating a cold breakfast, she put herself through a series of exercises until a few grunts and groans told her Hap was beginning to stir. His eyes flickered and then he sat up abruptly, looking at the lamp.

"Seven thirty-ish," he commented. "Have you been awake long?"

"About an hour," Angharad replied. "I decided to let you sleep on a bit. In fact, why don't we take the opportunity of resting today and continuing tomorrow? We could both do with a break after yesterday."

"Mm! It sounds good, but no. We must go on, the sleep's restored me and once I've eaten, I'll be ready to leave."

Angharad tried her uttermost to persuade him to take the day easy, but got nowhere and in the end gave way. To fall out over the matter was senseless and she did, at least, manage to extract a promise that if any point he did feel fatigued, they would make an early camp. With Hap still chewing on his breakfast, they set off. The going, for a short way, was straightforward enough until Hap halted suddenly. The floor dropped away and, half blinded by the light from the lamp, Angharad knew she might well have blundered over the edge had she been leading.

"It's about sixty feet to the bottom," Hap informed her. "You'd better go first while I hold the rope. It'll be easier for me to go down unaided as I know all the hand and foot holes."

"All right," Angharad said, admitting defeat. It looked as though there was nothing she could do to ease things for Hap at this stage. "What do we do about light? We'll need some form of illumination, but I don't know whether we'll manage to hold on to a lamp while we're descending."

"That's no problem," replied Hap. "I've the solution here in my pack."

While Angharad tied a rope around her waist, Hap produced two straps, each with a small spiked dish attached, sticking out at right angles. He fastened one around Angharad's head with the dish protruding from her forehead and then did the same with the other strap to his own head. Lighting two small candles, he pushed them firmly onto the spikes before blowing out the lamp. As Hap took up the slack, Angharad lowered herself over the edge. The candle lit sufficient area for her to see and, with Hap calling out instructions; she soon made it to the bottom. Looking up she could see the faint flicker of Hap's candle reflected from the cavern roof.

Untying the rope she gave three gentle tugs whereupon Hap hauled it back to the top from where, shortly afterwards; he lowered down their packs. As soon as they touched the ground, she dragged them clear and tugged once more on the rope, jumping smartly back as it came snaking towards her. Taking out the lamp from her pack, she relit it from the candle before extinguishing it. Lamp fat they had in plenty, candles they did not. Hap made short work of the descent. At no point did he appear to rush but one moment there was the distant flicker of candlelight high above and the next, or so it seemed, he was stepping down beside her. Even with the security of the rope around her waist, the descent had taken Angharad over twice as long.

The next section was exceedingly narrow, though high. There was a ledge some six feet off the ground and Hap climbed up to it, Angharad passed him the packs and followed suit. Once they were there, the way widened slightly and they were able to squeeze through. After ten minutes or so, they came up against a rock wall and were forced back to the lower level. A small opening beckoned and, dragging their packs behind, they crawled for some distance. Finally, the way widened out; the roof angled upwards and they were able to walk freely again.

The passage continued to widen, opening out until the roof and far walls disappeared into darkness. Keeping to the left hand side, they maintained a steady pace over the uneven floor. Before long they came across an arrow pointing towards the roof, marked on the wall by Hap on a previous visit. The rock face was pitted with small fissures and as Angharad held the packs, Hap stretched out and began to climb, working his way upwards for twelve or fifteen feet before pulling himself through a small opening. Throwing up the packs, Angharad clambered up behind him.

The passage opened out after a few yards and, apart from the occasional drop or section where they had to crawl, became reasonably straightforward. In time the roof bore down on them and, as the ground dropped steeply away, the floor turned to ice and they began to slide. Hap, having never before travelled this way in winter, was taken completely by surprise while Angharad, who was leading, tried to scramble back up the slope. The thrashing of her legs, however, destroyed any remaining hold and she disappeared from sight with a low cry.

The lamp flame flickered out and she could feel the rocky walls flashing by as she accelerated, hurtling blindly down the shaft. Suddenly, it became lighter up ahead and, careering through something soft, cold and damp, she found herself fighting for breath as snow pressed in all around. Her rate of descent decreased rapidly and, bursting through the powdery wall, she came out into bright sunshine, spinning wildly in midair. After a moment she landed on her back in a cushioning snowdrift, where, much to her surprise and relief, she found herself unharmed.

Scarcely had she time to worry about what might have happened to Hap when he appeared overhead, hurtling down to land unhurt in an ungainly heap over to her right. Both had retained their packs and Angharad, somehow, still clutched hold of her lamp. Sighting a snow free patch of ground nearby, they ploughed their way towards it. Fortunately, none of their belongings had suffered serious damage during the rapid descent.

After resting for a short while, they strapped on their snowshoes and, under the glare of the mid-morning sun, strode out. Keeping to the left hand side, they followed the narrow valley for a good mile as it veered towards the south, leading them away from the direction of Mount Subae. The snow was firm underfoot as they advanced cautiously, keeping to the shadows wherever possible. Nothing could be done to disguise their tracks and they prayed no one would spot them. Fortunately the surrounding land did seem deserted. The valley dropped steeply away before opening out into a larger vale heading slightly west of north.

"In summer," Hap informed Angharad, "this is a well travelled route, but, as you can see from the lack of tracks, it's seldom used at this time of year. It takes the Cantaéns to and from the mines in the south, but, as they can't transport the ore over snow and ice, they shut down production during the winter months."

"Let's hope it stays like this until we're long gone," was Angharad's solitary comment.

Turning northward, they set a steady pace, halting briefly around noon to eat. As mid afternoon approached, the valley narrowed slightly and, in the distance, they could see a low ridge, sixty to ninety feet high, spreading out from the west wall, but stopping short of the eastern edge. The barrier was far too precipitous to climb easily and so they made for the right hand passage. An uneasy feeling settled on them and, as they drew nearer, they scrutinized the ridge top for any signs of danger. The area appeared clear and, apprehensively, they approached the gap. As far as they could see, nothing was amiss at the entrance and satisfied, they started up the narrow pathway.

They paused just before the passage opened back out into the main valley and studied the lie of the land. Again, there was nothing in sight to cause alarm, so they moved off warily. To their left a large mound obstructed their view and

Angharad was about to suggest she scale it to have a look ahead, when half a dozen dark shapes broke cover from on top. With swords drawn, they hurtled down towards them.

Chapter Sixteen

Biren, the Cantaén, was feeling rather sorry for himself, worrying about the consequences of failure should his mission prove unsuccessful. He was convinced Sartae would carry out his threat of execution if any Maraén breached the defensive line, once the Cantaén Guard had finished with him that is. Staggering to his feet he groaned aloud. The wine he had purloined the previous night had been of particularly poor quality as the steady thumping of his head testified. Every movement brought on a vicious stabbing pain behind his aching eyes. He swayed for a few unsteady moments until his vision cleared and he reeled towards the tent flap. Crouching outside, he scooped up handfuls of snow and wiped them over his face and head. Gradually his condition, if not his humour, improved.

Daybreak was still some time away as he worked his way through the tents of his followers, kicking, shouting and cursing until they were all awake. His mood brightened considerably as he watched the wretched troops crawl from their warm beds into the freezing air. Wrapping his furs more tightly around himself, he callously refused to allow them to dress in theirs, laughing as they shivered in the biting chill. His head was clearing rapidly and some of his old, evil spirit had returned.

"Cold are you?" he sneered. "Pity isn't it? What do you think this is, a training exercise? We're supposed to be on a vital mission and look at you lot standing there, half naked. Living in camp has made you soft—soft in the head if you think you might undress for bed. Just suppose a group of Maraéns had crept up on us during the night," he ranted, "you wouldn't have survived five minutes in this weather."

"From now on you'll all sleep fully clothed, your weapons beside you and then, if anything does happen, you might just be ready for it. I shall visit you all from time to time, no matter where you're stationed and if I find anyone bending the rules, heads will roll. Do I make myself perfectly clear?" he roared. They nodded in affirmation as he continued, "Now, get out of my sight, and somebody bring my breakfast," he demanded.

Dismissed, they fled to dress and warm themselves before their fires. The cooks swiftly brought Biren his meal but, despite their speed, he berated them for taking too long. Whilst Biren ate, a servant packed his leader's equipment and then cleared away his empty plate. Swaggering outside, Biren watched as his tent was taken down. Noticing most of the others were barely halfway through their meals, he knocked the dishes out of their hands and forced them to break camp immediately.

Dawn flickered over the peaks as Biren and his motley band advanced through the mountains. Every now and then, he would dispatch a group to set up an observation post, usually over the most difficult of terrain. He had kept to the easier routes and in the end was left with only five others. Working their way through the hills surrounding Sartae's headquarters, they reach a point about three miles, in a straight line, from the main camp. Dropping down towards a steep sided valley, they kept to the right hand side and headed south.

Biren had a place in mind and not long after noon, two miles farther on; they arrived at his destination, a small hollow in the valley bottom at the base of the western cliffs. The depression was situated on top of a ridge, which jutted out from the western edge, separated from the eastern side by a small gap. A large snow-covered bank beside the northern entrance of the gap effectively screened the hollow and most of the upper valley from anyone passing through.

After instructing Kriel, one of his followers, not to make any tracks in the snow that might be seen from the other side, Biren sent him to the top of the ridge to keep watch. Setting the others on making camp, he had them erect his tent first and, as soon as his belongings were installed, took immediate occupation, leaving them to sort themselves out with much grumbling and complaining. As Biren would not hear of a fire being lit now they were in position, they made do with cold fare.

Mid-afternoon was upon them when Kriel called down a low warning as two figures came into view, moving along the valley towards them. Without undue haste, they left their tents and, swords at the ready, hid themselves behind the banking overlooking the gap.

"Careful, you stupid oafs," Biren hissed at them. "If one of you so much as makes one flake of snow fall over the other side I'll have him flogged. I don't want any noise either. When Kriel gives the signal, we'll all lie flat in the snow and wait until they've gone by, then we can attack 'em from behind.

"If they turn out to be Maraéns, Kriel will slip away and return to base as quickly as possible with the news. I don't want any of you taking a shot at him because you think he's deserting. Any questions?" no one dared speak. "Right, not another sound."

They waited in silence, hardly daring to breathe. Biren's threats were not to be taken idly, he was, after all, quite capable of carrying them out. Every eye was upon Kriel, waiting for his signal. Suddenly, he waved his arm frantically. The travellers had entered the gap. Dropping down, they listened intently for the sounds of movement to reach them.

Five minutes passed and then another five. The strain became intolerable. *Had the strangers turned back?* they wondered. Then, in the distance, came the gentle swish of snowshoes slithering over the frozen surface. Muscles tensed as they drew nearer, grips tightened on swords. For a moment the noises ceased altogether. *Did they suspect something?* Movement started again and the sound of breathing came to them over the still air, it came nearer and, as it passed by, they launched their attack.

Biren became aware immediately that some freak acoustic of the valley had played a cruel trick upon him. The intended victims had not gone by but were directly below. Even as this registered, the strangers caught sight of their attackers. Retreating instantly to stand inside the entrance to the gap, the travellers waited with swords drawn and their backs to the far wall. The Cantaéns advanced over the snow towards them and, for several moments, they weighed each other up, the light of battle glinting in their eyes. On closer inspection, Biren realised only one of them was a Maraén the other, who appeared old and weary, was of a people unknown to him. The Maraén would be the main danger and he hissed at his followers to concentrate their energies on him.

The hood of the younger one fell back and, as it did, long dark hair was released and, startled, Biren realised the Maraén was a young woman. Perhaps he would not kill her straightaway, he thought, but then she let forth with an ancient Maraén war cry and, in a blind fury, his followers fell upon her. The sound of steel upon steel echoed throughout the valley and Biren soon discerned he had underestimated the capabilities of the old one. Whilst he and two others had attacked the woman, the remaining pair had engaged the elder and already one was dead with the other hard pressed.

At that moment, the old one slipped, cracked his head against the rocky wall and fell to the ground, stunned. Now they were four against one, the Cantaéns redoubled their efforts. The defender fell back slightly to stand over the unconscious body of her companion, ready to defend him to the death. Swiftly her sword flashed, darting, slashing, slicing, and cutting until the entire enemy had been bloodied.

No matter how hard they pushed, Biren disgustedly observed, not once had they been able pierce her guard, in fact she appeared to be enjoying herself. He had a dozen cuts and scratches himself and although none were serious on their own, if he continued to receive them at this rate they would soon become so. Standing back for a moment, he observed the skirmish, noticing as he did the deadly enemy seemed to be tiring.

Lulled into a false sense of security by this apparent sign of weakness, one of the attackers stepped in to inflict a fatal blow, only to be cut down instantly by the slicing blade of a suddenly alert and energetic foe. Enraged, Biren decided to put an end this rapidly developing fiasco. Drawing away from the mêlée, as another of his men went down under the flashing blade, he took the bow from his back and plucked an arrow out of his quiver. With only one of his followers left, Biren took aim, waiting for a clear shot. Twice he almost let fly, but stopped himself as his view became obstructed. Then came a momentary suspension of hostilities and he had a clear sight. Easing back the bowstring, he took a deep breath, slowly exhaled and then released the deadly missile.

At the very instant of release, a white-coated apparition manifested itself at his side in a cloud of powdery snow. He did not know who, what, or where it came from and was destined never to find out. The figure cannoned into him and his arrow was spent harmlessly in the air. Before he could recover, a blow from a sword sent him reeling unconscious to the ground.

When he finally came to his senses, he found himself lying in the snow with only the bodies of his followers for company. From the height of the sun, he estimated an hour had elapsed since he had been struck down. His head ached abominably and he shivered uncontrollably in the cold. Staggering to his feet, he was violently ill before managing to stumble back to camp. The tents had been thoroughly searched although the food, inedible to Maraéns, remained. Before he did anything else he must have warmth. Lighting a fire, he concentrated on driving the frost out of his bones. The fiery pain inside his head lessened and he found himself able to warm and keep down some water.

Luckily the cold had slowed the bleeding from his wounds and dressing them, he considered his options. There seemed no sense in carrying out his duty to warn Sartae. His only reward for such diligence would be execution for failing to prevent an incursion. No, after a good night's rest he would follow his original plan and head south towards the deserted mines. If his luck held, by spring he would have crossed the passes into the west and be firmly ensconced in some distant land.

Travelling in easy stages Biren was wary. Sartae was a bad enemy to make and, after a couple of weeks, Biren was at a loss to account for the lack of pursuit. His head troubled him for some days, forcing him to take things steady but even so, he never saw a soul. One strange thing did occur. During the third night after the debacle at the gap, he was brought suddenly awake by the ground shaking and the distant roar of avalanches triggered by the movement.

The tremors continued for most of the night and, occasionally, during the days that followed, he could sense the earth moving beneath him. Crawling out of his tent the next morning, he found a dark cloud covered the sky to the north. In the direction of Mount Subae, huge columns of smoke seemed to be rising skyward to feed the darkness. For many nights afterwards, a glow could be seen emanating from the same direction and the skies above him became covered in a smoky blackness. An acrid, sulphurous smell hung in the air for many days until the winds changed direction and blew the clouds away. Whatever it was that had occurred, Biren could not begin to surmise, but, if this was the reason for his being left in peace, he was grateful for the reprieve.

He rested for a week at the mines and then started westwards, never to be seen again by anyone from the mountains or forests. Far away though, in a land so distant the sun had almost set in the mountains before it rose there, a wanderer eventually settled down and made his home. Betraying the hospitality of his hosts, he fomented strife and rebellion before being hunted down and put to the sword. Biren was called Birnel in those parts.

Long before these events unfolded, at the very point Biren lay senseless at the gap, Hap had recovered sufficient of his senses to discover the fighting was over and the remains of the enemy were spread all around. Gingerly, Hap felt the back of his head and discovered a tender lump the size of an egg. His vision blurred as he pushed himself to his knees and finally staggered to his feet, anxious as to the condition and whereabouts of Angharad. Shaking his head, his eyes cleared and he gazed in wonder at the sight of his travelling companion, embracing and dancing about with a stranger in noisy celebration. As they parted company and stood at arms length, Hap caught sight of the newcomer's face and immediately recognised his lone traveller of the mountains.

"Kaér," Angharad whispered eventually in a tone of bewilderment. "How can it be?" she stuttered before words failed her.

"Yes, Angharad, it is I," Kaér replied, as much overcome by emotion as she was.

"But you're dead," Angharad managed to collect her thoughts. "I mean, we believed you were dead. The whole mountainside collapsed on top of you."

"I thought you, too, were gone but I couldn't dig my way out to make sure," Kaér paused for a moment, shuddering at the memory. "Yet! Here we are, each of us very much alive and mourning for the other!" Then both were laughing as they buried the dark thoughts that had haunted them since that dreadful night, only now able to admit how much each had missed the other.

Into the middle of this came a loud cough. Kaér and Angharad started at the sound, so unmindful of their surroundings had they become.

"As Angharad is not going to offer any introductions, I must make my own," Hap interjected, beaming all over his face. "My name is Hap and I am so pleased to meet you."

Kaér strode over and shook the proffered hand. Like he had discovered Stakirum, Angharad too had found a friend in the mountains when she needed one most.

"I'm terribly sorry Hap, I'm afraid I forgot all about you in the excitement. Kaér, Hap. Hap, Kaér," she said belatedly as she introduced them, tears of happiness in her eyes.

"I forgive you," Hap acknowledged graciously, "and now you two have put each other down, perhaps we can move on to somewhere more agreeable," he indicated the bodies, "and continue our discussion."

"That seems like a sensible idea," Angharad agreed, collecting the equipment they had dropped during the fight.

In the excitement of the moment, they never thought to check the bodies and took it for granted all had perished. Had they done so, things might have ended very differently for Biren. Before leaving the area they did search the Cantaén camp and remove as much firewood as they could strap to their packs. The food they ignored, not even daring to think about what it might contain. Departing, they headed up the valley where, after a hundred yards, they came upon the body of another Cantaén lying in the snow. Kaér explained how he had seen the man making a run for it and had brought him down with a single arrow before joining the fray. Kriel would never make it back with news of the intruders, leaving Sartae to sweat it out in uneasy ignorance.

Employing great caution, they advanced further, sticking mainly to the tracks made by the Cantaéns. Eventually, with the coming of darkness, they reached the spot where the enemy had entered the valley from a western tributary. Moving off the trail, they made a cold camp, a fire was something they simply dared not risk. Kaér sampled some of Angharad and Hap's supplies while they partook of his, all relishing the exchange.

Over the meal they swapped tales of their adventures since the avalanche had separated them. The spirits of the ancients fascinated Angharad and Hap, Stakirum in particular. Kaér related all he had discovered about the origins of The Shintae and Hap was amazed to find the country of his youth had once been a green and fertile land. Overcome with curiosity, Kaér asked how it was that Hap could call the desert region home when nobody had lived there for hundreds of years. All Maraé knew the story of the great plague and its consequence for the desert dwellers.

"Let me think," he studied for a moment. "There were just two survivors, one an old man and the other much younger. They eventually came to live in Maraé and, so legend has it, neither one of them aged a day in all the years they lived there.

"Still, legends are always greatly embellished and nobody really believes that part of it. If I recall correctly the younger one was a healer. In fact, they both were and, so the story goes, they passed on much of their medicinal knowledge to our ancestors. The younger one died in a Cantaén ambush while the older one, after collecting the body, vanished. He was never seen again and must have died a long, long time ago. Now what was his name?"

Kaér fell silent, his forehead puckering in concentration. Angharad deliberately refrained from prompting him. She knew he would recall the name in due course. Hap, meanwhile, was enjoying himself immensely. Angharad's face had been a picture when she had found out who he really was and he did not expect Kaér's to be any different.

"I've got it," Kaér announced, just as Angharad was beginning to think she might have to point him in the right direction. "Hap. That's it. I knew I'd remember in the end."

Angharad could no longer restrain herself and burst into laughter with Hap joining in. Kaér stared at them as if they had lost their minds. His companions could see the struggle going on inside his head, mirrored on his face, as he tried to accept the idea.

"You're called Hap!" he exclaimed.

"Correct so far," laughed Hap in reply.

"But you can't be The Hap of legend. It's just not possible. No one could have lived so long. I know you look old. Oh, sorry, I didn't mean it quite like that. But it would make you hundreds of years old. No, I can't believe it. Well I mean, I mean..." his voice trailed off in confusion. "Oh! I don't know what I mean," he growled in frustration and sat back dumbfounded.

"Let me introduce myself fully," Hap said, drawing himself up to his full height. "I am Hap, formerly of Ritue, a healer by choice, a traveller by circumstance and, unfortunately, the last of my nation. I'm also, as you so kindly noticed, somewhat elderly," he added facetiously, "but if I hear any more aspersions regarding my looks, or years, you'll find I'm not so far gone I can't give you a good hiding," he concluded with a smile to take the edge off his words.

Kaér shook hands with him in astonished silence and, though he recovered soon enough, they could occasionally hear him muttering to himself about it. They talked long into the evening as Hap and Kaér became better acquainted with each other. Kaér's respect for the elderly Rituen grew as he learnt of how he had observed him during his mountain trips. There were not many who had the ability to do so without him becoming aware of them. Hap, he realised, must indeed be a master of concealment.

About nine o'clock, Kaér stood up and began to dress in his outer furs and Aralpos. Angharad, watching in some surprise at his actions, suddenly realised what it was about him that had been puzzling her ever since they had met again.

"Your back!" she cried. "Why, it's straight. How did that happen Kaér? It's a miracle."

"I'm not really sure," he replied. "As I was about to leave the Valley of the Ancients, there was a loud crack and it just straightened. Stakirum said all things were possible there and I didn't like to question him, I was scared I might be dreaming."

"How strange a place it must be," murmured Hap in amazement. "But where are you going now? Surely not to that wretched mount?"

"Yes, I'm afraid I must. Someone has to scout around and see what's going on. They are sure to have changed the system since I took The Shintae. Security is bound to have increased and we must find a safe way in. Hap has never ventured to the base of Mount Subae and you, Angharad, certainly haven't. I have been there on several occasions, although not from this direction."

"But surely we may accompany you," interjected Angharad, a little put out at being left behind.

"No, it would be safer if I went alone," Kaér continued. "If I don't return, you'll get your chance soon enough. Apart from anything else, knowing something of their tongue, I can pass as one of them if challenged, especially in the dark. Once inside the outer perimeter area, I hope to find a secure place for us all to hide out, one from which we can observe the camp. With a safe route scouted, we should all be able to enter unseen."

The others saw the wisdom of this and, curbing their disappointment at being left behind, wished him luck as he moved out, his Aralpos soon making him invisible against the snow in the darkness of the night. With Kaér out of sight they decided to keep a lookout, indeed it had been remiss of them not to do so earlier. Deciding on four-hour shifts, Hap took the first watch. The fight and subsequent meeting with Kaér had put fresh life into him and he no longer looked the same worn out person he had that morning.

Leaving Angharad to settle down, he crawled out of the tent and, keeping to the tracks the Cantaéns had made, entered the smaller tributary valley. Fifty yards inside he came across a snow free rocky area leading to a ledge that doubled back to the main valley. From this vantage point, the tent was almost directly beneath him and he could observe both up and down the main valley as well as the smaller vale. Unfortunately, the overcast sky meant he could distinguish little detail. Cantaéns, however, were not renowned for silent travel and he felt confident they would betray their presence long before they became a danger. He shivered in the cold. The chill of early evening had eased to be replaced by a damper atmosphere that, if anything, felt even worse. Snuggling down inside his furs, he remained motionless, studying the land.

After an estimated four hours, Hap took a long and careful look around before descending stiffly back down to the valley. Angharad was already stirring as he entered the tent and took little waking. As soon as he had divulged the location of the ledge, he covered himself in his blankets and went straight to sleep. Finding the observation point without difficulty, Angharad, fully refreshed, decided to extend her watch until daybreak. Then, in the grey light, just before dawn, a faint movement caught her eye and she realised someone was coming down the main valley. From the darkness of the shape, she knew it must be a Cantaén, Kaér would never move around without his Aralpos. Slipping carefully down, she hastened to alert Hap. Luckily, the way to the tent was cut off from view of the upper valley by a small scree slope. Entering, she shook Hap gently awake.

"Hush!" she whispered. "I think we have company."

"How many of them are there?" he questioned, struggling out of his bed.

"Only one, as far I can tell. We can take cover behind that mound just above the tent."

Loosening their swords, they made their way to the top of the bank. Angharad had brought her bow and, as the figure drew nearer, she placed an arrow in position. The intruder seemed determined to head straight towards them and, in the dim light, she decided to wait until the target became clearer before loosening her shot. They were still unable to make out the features of the advancing figure when he halted and looked uneasily about. Somehow he sensed danger and Angharad knew she could hold back no longer. The enemy was wary and they could not risk him escaping to raise the alarm. Taking careful aim, Angharad took a deep breath and then let the air go in a loud sigh of relief.

"Angharad! Hap! Is that you? What are you doing?" came the familiar voice of Kaér over the snow towards them.

"Over here," Angharad called out as she and Hap gained their feet. Beads of perspiration forming on her brow as she thought of how close she had come to releasing the arrow.

"Whatever do you think you're doing wandering about without your Aralpos?" she expostulated as they drew closer. "I almost shot you for a Cantaén just now."

"I'll explain over breakfast," responded Kaér a little startled. "The Cantaéns, by the way, are confined to camp or guard duty. Those out on watch, like the group we encountered yesterday, are under strict instructions not to move about. Even so, we should keep a lookout. If we take some food to where you've been keeping an eye on things, I'll tell you everything I've discovered."

Chapter Seventeen

Leaving the camp well behind, Kaér travelled swiftly over the virgin snow. There was no point now in trying to cover his tracks; nothing could be more guaranteed to put the enemy on the alert than an obvious attempt at concealment. This way his trail would be taken as that of a messenger from the lower camp. After half a mile, the valley angled sharply eastwards and he came across a well-trodden path coming down from the western hillside. Not to use it would arouse suspicions and, as it was going in his direction, he stepped boldly out on to it. Stealth would only invite harmful curiosity and so he removed his Aralpos and hid it behind a large boulder.

He marched brazenly up the valley. He was confident in his knowledge of the Cantaén dialect and knew he would be able to bluff his way past any outposts. By eleven o'clock, he was nearing his destination. The path had split some distance back, with one fork carrying on along the valley bottom. He chose to take the other route, one that veered sharply left and started climbing the rocky slope almost immediately. Once over the top, unless his sense of direction had completely deserted him, he would find himself directly above the Subrat Valley.

He could expect to be challenged at any point from now on and, taking a deep breath, he eased his sword in its scabbard. Moving forward, his instincts soon warned him he was under observation, although no sentinels betrayed their presence. Finally, standing on the brow of the hill, he gazed down into the darkness below. From the profusion of fires, he located the enemy camp, or settlement as it now gave the appearance of being, down to the west, while in the east towered the huge black bulk of the infamous Mount Subae. A cold shiver ran down his spine as he gazed at it. The banks of cloud, which swirled around the summit, glowed dimly red and, for a moment, he pondered on the luckless innocents whose lives had ended beneath its demonic shroud.

Suddenly he became aware of two dark shapes, detaching themselves from behind rocks over to his right and moving towards him. Fighting down the instinctive reaction to draw his sword and attack, he stood his ground and waited until they drew closer to him.

"So there you are," he snapped, adding all the arrogance he could muster as he conjured up the commanding tone of a Cantaén leader. "Have you been sleeping on duty? I've been standing here so long now I'd almost given up hope of you ever arriving."

The two guards stopped, flustered by his directness. That they took him for one of their own was self evident by their attitude. Kaér's swaggering stride, dark clothes and hood had deceived them. During his previous travels he had learnt to disguise himself and, back down the trail, had fixed a false beard to his chin. It might not have passed close inspection in daylight, but for now it was ideal. All mountain males sported beards and he would have immediately aroused suspicions without one.

"We were just waiting to see what you'd do," replied one of them, regaining his composure.

"In any case," interjected the other. "What do you think you're doing, wandering about in the middle of the night? There are strict rules governing movements outside the perimeter, punishable by death if contravened," whereupon he drew his sword and advanced threateningly on Kaér.

"You'd better come quietly, or it'll be the worse for you," growled the first one doing likewise.

Kaér thought furiously for some way out of this predicament. It had never occurred to him that Sartae might restrict movement so close to the camp. Disposing of the guards would defeat his purpose, they would soon be missed and search parties scouring the area were something he could do without.

"Put those swords away now," he commanded, drawing himself up. The straightening of his back had added inches to his height and he now found he was somewhat taller than his adversaries. "Do you dare threaten Cerdic, Chieftain of the Westlands? By all that's evil I'll have your heads once Sartae hears of this."

The guards stepped back a pace in surprise and indecision as Kaér praised the name that had sprung unbidden to his mind. Cerdic was chief Cantaén warlord in the west and it was most unlikely these two Northerners, from their tongues, would have seen him before. He rarely, if ever, ventured to eastern Cantaé and the reputation of his warriors was so fearsome even Sartae, himself, had never felt confident enough to assert his authority over them. If such a personage as Cerdic could come, alone by the look of it, all this way then it must be a matter of great importance.

Bowing deeply, the sentries sheathed their weapons. They had only been doing their duty, but would Sartae look at it in this light. If they had done anything to hinder his plans then his wrath would know no bounds.

"We're most humbly sorry," apologised one.

"Yes, we really are," agreed the other, cowering in trepidation.

"All right," Kaér began in a slightly more conciliatory tone, "I can see now you were just following orders, but I am here on a matter of great secrecy," he lowered his voice and continued in a conspiratorial tone. The guards moved closer, listening intently to what he had to say.

"Heed carefully my words and never, even under pain of death, repeat anything of what you are about to hear. I have journeyed at night so that I might remain unseen by your fellows. Even my armies remain encamped some twenty miles south of here. Only two others accompanied me and they wait just down the valley until arrangements for their safety can be agreed with Sartae," he paused for breath as the guards waited, agog, for the rest of the tale.

"My companions are of great importance to the cause against Maraé," he spat at the mention of the name. "On the strength of their knowledge I have journeyed this far to settle any differences with Sartae and to join forces with him against those forest devils. One, a stranger to these parts, has lived with those woodsmen for many years whilst the other, a Maraén woman, bears a grudge against their accursed High Council.

"They stripped her of her land and property for some slight misdemeanour, throwing her out, destitute, on to the streets to beg for a living. The stranger was her friend and together they decided to journey to the lands beyond the mountains. Fortunately for us, they fell into my hands on the way and, quite willingly for revenge offered to aid our cause."

Kaér was well aware none of his people would do something like this; in fact, they would never have had their land confiscated in the first place. This type of thinking would appear quite normal to the Cantaéns to whom such a course of action was an everyday occurrence.

"They have knowledge of a secret way to Myssous," his voice dropped even lower, "and are prepared to guide us through it. Once we have destroyed their High Council, we will advance inland against a leaderless nation and, with an army coming towards us from the mountains, we will crush them.

"Now can you see why I came at night? If word were to leak out it might eventually filter down to the forest and put them on their guard. All I require from you is a pass enabling me to enter the camp without having to announce to all and sundry who I am."

This was the point where he discovered if they had been taken in by his story. Should they not believe him, he would have to dispose of them and risk any complications this act created. He need not have worried. Like most Cantaén soldiers, the sentries were trained to accept orders without question from their superiors and, as Kaér had cast himself convincingly in this role, they had no cause to distrust his authenticity. Without further ado, one of them felt deep within his pockets and brought out two pieces of hide, one slightly larger than the others.

"The larger one allows the bearer to enter the camp," the sentry explained as he handed them over. "The other gives direct access to the central area where Sartae dwells. You'll have to make yourself known to the guards outside his tent, but they're hand picked and your secret will be safe with them."

"Excellent," acknowledged Kaér, keeping his relief under tight control. "Now! One final request before I leave. Tomorrow night, I shall bring my companions with me. It would be foolish at this stage for them to enter the main camp. The woman in particular is bound to create a stir. Is there some place, perhaps on the way down, where they can remain safely hidden? They could be there for some time while Sartae and I make preparations for war."

"I know just the place," one of them answered quickly, desperate to please. "As you follow the main trail down, you'll come to a junction where a track bears off to the left. If you follow it round, it will take you to the storage caverns. The path is well trodden and your footprints won't give you away. Right at the far end are the empty caves. Once they're cleared," he continued, "no one goes near them again until restocking takes place next autumn. Your companions will be safe enough and, provided they don't make it too obvious, they can always obtain supplies from the other caverns during the night."

"Excellent, my dear fellow," Kaér responded pompously, as would be expected of him.

"Do you require one of us to accompany you down to camp and show you the caves as well?" inquired the other sentry.

"No, that won't be necessary," retorted Kaér hastily.

The last thing he wanted at this juncture was to enter the enemy stronghold. All he needed to do was find the caves, check their suitability and return. There was, he suddenly thought, something he could do to ensure the fullest co-operation of the sentries.

"Now, if you'll give me your names," he requested, "I will pass them on to Sartae and recommend you receive promotion, once the need for secrecy is over. Men as astute as you should not be wasted doing sentry duty. I shall personally see to it that you become Unit Commanders when we invade the forest."

Both guards were obnoxiously ingratiating as they bestowed their thanks upon him, leaving him feeling queasy at the sight and sound of them. Finally, he elicited their names, Triamun and Deet, before taking his leave as they continued to bow and obsequiously mumble their gratitude.

Well pleased with the outcome of his subterfuge, he was soon over the summit and moving downhill. The path dropped steeply away and, in places, steps had been cut to make the descent easier. Following the lie of the land, it wound its way down and Kaér soon realised he was out of sight of the watchers on top. Clouds were gathering overhead and he knew they would never be able to see whether he entered the camp.

Before branching off the main trail, some twenty minutes after leaving the top, he checked to make sure there was no one on either path. Deet had assured him no more guards were sited between there and the valley bottom but Kaér, knowing the devious nature of Sartae, would not have been surprised to find a sentry post had been secretly positioned at some unlikely spot. Once satisfied he was alone, he turned onto the side road and, soon after midnight, reached the first cave.

As no tracks led towards it or the numerous ones that followed, he knew they must be filled with untapped stores. He passed them by without a second glance until a couple of hundred yards farther on, he came to one with tracks in profusion leading into it. He confirmed by sneaking a look inside and finding it piled high with boxes and crates at the back and rubbish at the front, this was the one in use. Moving on, he rounded the base of a scar, jutting out from the hillside, that effectively cut him off from view of the other caverns and, he hoped, the prying eyes of Cantaén supply teams. A well-trodden path led sharply away to the left and headed steeply upwards. No more of the main trail had been cleared and, not wishing to attract attention by leaving footprints in the virgin snow, Kaér decided not to carry on to seek out further empty caverns. Those storage areas must have been exhausted before the great snowstorm struck.

Turning up the side path Kaér, after twenty yards, found himself at the entrance to a cavern. Turning round, he looked down and found the settlement directly in front of him. He could not have found a more ideal place had he searched all night and, silently, he thanked the unwitting sentries who had sent him here. He was barely three hundred feet above the valley bottom and the encampment was about five hundred yards away from the base of the hill.

Once inside the cavern, Kaér was surprised at its size as he wandered about. Not daring to risk a light, he used his bow as a guide stick. The Cantaéns, as was their way, had left the floor strewn with rubbish. Broken crates, bundles of cloth and odd lengths of rope were everywhere and, even with his bow to aid him, he still took a tumble or two. Heading back to the entrance, he settled down, lying on his stomach to gaze steadily at the campfires below. He had about four hours to waste before he could contemplate returning. It would invoke the guard's suspicions if he did not allow sufficient delay for his mythical meeting with Sartae to have taken place.

He studied the layout of the settlement as best he could, but the campfires were burning low and gave little away from this distance. An hour passed and then another with still no sign of The Shintae. Surely, they would be working on it night and day and their Guros must have discovered some of the trigger phrases that activated it. A third hour dragged by and still nothing happened. Then, just as he was beginning to think he might have to leave without confirmation of its location, a flash of light arched skywards for six, nine, and finally twelve-hundred feet before descending back to earth. The silence of the valley was shattered by a tremendous thunder-like peal, closely followed by the shrieks of a group of perimeter guards as the bolt landed nearby.

Although he could provide general details from what he had observed, he knew he would be unable to give the sentries at the top specific details of any injuries and damage. Therefore, if he timed his arrival at the top so it appeared he had started back just before the flash, he would be able to answer their questions without having to commit to anything specific. He estimated it would take about an hour to reach the top from the valley bottom and just over half that from his location.

Twenty minutes later, he vacated the cavern and walked back down the trail. Within half an hour, he was standing on the summit where his greeting from the sentinels was far different from before. They marched smartly towards him and saluted in the Cantaén manner.

"Greetings, Lord Cerdic," Deet called, bowing low. "I trust your mission went well?"

"Of course," Kaér snapped, "did you doubt it would go otherwise for me?"

"No, no, certainly not," Triamun interjected hastily, rapidly changing the subject. "Was the cave to your satisfaction my Lord?"

"Oh! That! Yes, I briefly inspected it on the way down and it will be adequate," Kaér replied, turning to go.

"What happened back there sir, if you don't mind telling us?" questioned Triamun before he could depart and, as Kaér fixed him with a steely stare, he added quickly, "The noise I mean, your business and how it went is entirely your own affair, of course. You've already honoured us by telling us so much about it already. We heard a blast and a few faint yells and wondered if any of our fellows were killed."

"I've really no idea," Kaér said unconcernedly. "I'd already left by then. From where I was walking, it appeared to land somewhere along the perimeter. Why, surely you're not concerned are you?"

"No, it's not that, but we're stationed here for a week," explained Deet, "and we get little or no news at all from down below. There's just us for night duty and the other two for days."

"There are more of you?" demanded Kaér warily. "I've heard no mention of this before. Am I likely to meet them tomorrow night when I bring my companions with me? I merely confided in you because I needed help in getting in and out without the common herd discovering my identity. Don't tell me I have to tell more people about my plans. I might just as well stand on the cliff tops and shout it to the whole world."

"It's all right," squeaked Triamun in panic, quaking at Kaér's supposed anger, "we're on permanent night duty; the others will never know anything about you. Your secret's safe with us and, as Sartae was asking for volunteers, we'll put ourselves forward to do an extra week in case you require us longer."

"Good," Kaér said, pleased at the outcome. "Don't forget to keep your mouths shut. Sartae has agreed to my recommendations and, unless you fail me, you'll find yourselves promoted to Unit Commanders shortly."

Once again, Kaér suffered the guard's effusive gratitude before he was able to depart. To begin with, he was conscious of their eyes on his back, but the feeling soon left him and he knew he had gone beyond their vision in the dark. Removing the beard, he stored it carefully away inside his pocket and by five o'clock he was well on his way. Retrieving his Aralpos from their hiding place, he rolled them up tightly and attached them to his sword belt before, minutes later, rejoining the trail through the snow he had made earlier. An incredible weariness came over him and it seemed an age now since he had woken inside the mountain passages. He thought about putting on the white coverings but decided against it, from what he had learnt it seemed unlikely there would be another observation post in this valley. At least he would be able to sleep all day while the others kept a lookout.

A lookout! It suddenly occurred to him that, in the excitement of their meeting and subsequent discussions, they had failed to set a watch. He felt sure they would have done so after his departure, but yet again, they had talked of enjoying a good night's rest. All thoughts of tiredness left his mind and, in a state of high anxiety, he quickened his pace.

It was almost daybreak as he neared the camp, and, when there was no greeting, he feared the worst. That they would be expecting to see him wearing the same clothes he had left in did not occur to him. Drawing closer, his hunter's instincts had warned him he was under observation. The hairs prickled on the back of his neck as he stopped and looked around, feeling distinctly uneasy. Calling out, urgently, it had been to his immense relief that Angharad had answered.

Kaér, his story at an end, struggled to stay awake long enough to answer all their questions. Eventually, their curiosity satisfied, he left them and, yawning, returned to the tent. The day passed uneventfully for the other two as, either alone or together, they kept watch above. The sky remained overcast and a slight thaw set in, as Angharad found to her cost when part of the snow cornice above the ledge collapsed and half buried her. Struggling to free herself, her violent efforts almost took her over the edge. For a few frightful seconds, she swung crazily on the brink before managing to find a secure hold and restoring her balance.

As evening descended, Angharad came down from her final watch and found Kaér awake. They ate and, apart from occasional desultory snippets of conversation, remained content with their thoughts. They waited several hours before breaking camp and then, following Kaér's example, the others removed their Aralpos and stored them away inside their packs. The earlier rise in temperature had allowed them to restock their canteens but now, they observed, the tiny streams were again coated in ice.

Walking steadily, it was close to midnight when they reached the hilltop overlooking the Subrat valley. To Angharad and Hap's amusement, Kaér had donned his false beard again. Even the deadly necessity of its use failed to make them see the serious side of it. Nevertheless, they had their mirth firmly under control long before they reached the summit where Deet and Triamun awaited them. Kaér had warned the others to treat him in the manner befitting a Cantaén warlord and, in front of the guards, he must always be addressed as Lord Cerdic. Apart from a comment from Hap that "the poor lad's got delusions of grandeur", they proceeded to treated him with true deference. Kaér also thought it wise for the others to split his pack between them at the bottom of the climb; a warlord would not encumber himself with baggage when travelling with lesser mortals.

"Greetings Lord Cerdic," Deet said respectfully, bowing low as Kaér strode arrogantly towards him. "Are these the two with the knowledge of the secret way?" inquired Triamun, his curiosity getting the better of his judgement.

"Of course they are you stupid oaf," snarled Kaér with a note of exasperation in his voice. "Who did you think they'd be?" he paused ominously as Triamun cringed in fear. "I told you never to mention them again. Could I have misjudged you, I wonder? Perhaps you don't wish to be Unit Commanders after all?"

"I meant nothing by it, my Lord," Triamun stammered in alarm, his chances of promotion receding rapidly. "We've mentioned it to none bar you. We haven't even discussed it between ourselves in case someone should come and overhear."

"I sincerely hope not," Kaér responded ill temperedly, before relaxing the severity of his tone a little and continuing. "In that case I shall make no mention of your indiscretion to Sartae, but don't take me lightly. If you ever speak of it again, even if only to me, you'll not live long enough to command anything. Do I make myself clear?" he snapped.

"Yes! Yes!" cried Triamun and Deet together. They were now so greedy for promotion and scared of Kaér, in his guise of Cerdic, they would have done virtually anything he asked of them.

"Right," he announced, "remember what I've said," and then, turning to Angharad and Hap, commanded. "Come! We still have some distance to go before we reach your quarters and I must meet with Sartae again tonight."

"Yes, my Lord Cerdic," Hap said with true servility in an accent befitting a newcomer to the mountains.

Angharad said nothing but bowed low in reply and, leaving the quaking guards behind, they marched down the path. Leaving the main trail at the junction, they arrived shortly afterwards at their destination. Exhausted, his companions settled down to sleep while Kaér, who had slept all day, kept watch.

Chapter Eighteen

As dawn broke, the valley was revealed in ever increasing detail. The sprawling encampment Kaér had discovered on his previous incursion had altered beyond recognition. Studying it with interest he found to his surprise that it was now set out in an orderly fashion, a rare accomplishment indeed for Cantaéns. Pathways crossed at regular intervals, dividing the area into rectangular segments. The region's main east-west communication route ran through the valley, passing to the north of the camp and Kaér was amazed the sentries had not queried why, in his guise of Cerdic, he had not made use of it himself. The element of secrecy in his story must have convinced them totally.

As the light strengthened, he discovered each segment contained on average four large straight-sided tents with angled tops and, from what he could estimate, upwards of a thousand sections were located within the perimeter track. Not all tents, by any means, would be used as living quarters, but it still meant a probable concentration of maybe ten thousand or more Cantaéns down below. The thought of such a grouping made him shudder, although he took comfort in the fact their knowledge of The Shintae had not advanced anywhere near as rapidly as the population had. Apart from intermittent pulsations of light during the hours of darkness, he had seen no evidence to suggest the Guros could do anything apart from play with The Stone.

Kaér continued to watch and was soon able to make out greater detail. Having established The Shintae's approximate whereabouts from its meagre nighttime's activity, Kaér scrutinized the area around the centre of the camp. An open courtyard encircled by tents occupying a complete section caught his eye. Standing at the midpoint of the enclosure was, or what appeared to be, a pedestal from where the occasional flash of light could be witnessed. Two or three sections away a single, large, circular tent with a conical roof was sited.

This, he surmised, would be Sartae's headquarters.

As the morning advanced, an increase in movement became obvious and around nine o'clock the perimeter guard was relieved. Kaér made a note of the hour; this could be of significance when they came to gain entry later. A stirring came from the darkness behind and shortly afterwards Angharad, wiping the sleep from her eyes, moved up to join him. The sounds of the supply detail arriving for work could be heard from the nearby caverns. The worker's voices carried clearly in the still mountain air and, consequently, both of them kept their own conversations low and movements to a minimum. Hap awakened soon after and joined them at the entrance. While Kaér went off to rest, the others tried to formulate some ideas for the coming incursion, studying the layout of the camp until it was imprinted upon their minds.

The guard changed again at one o'clock and, after noting it down, Hap returned to the rear of the cave to rest. Angharad's mind wandered as the afternoon dragged by; nothing of interest was happening below and, with her mind far away, she was almost taken unawares. Dimly she became aware of voices drawing closer and, glancing across; saw two Cantaéns walking down the pathway towards her. Ducking backwards she grabbed the packs, which were lying nearby, and scrambled towards the darkness beyond. Silently alerting the others, Angharad dropped to the floor beside Kaér and together they waited in the deepest reaches of the cavern for the visitors to arrive.

Within seconds, or so it seemed, two menacing figures were silhouetted against the light. Fortunately, taking no interest in anything beyond the threshold, they seated themselves at opposite sides of the entrance with their backs to the walls. Producing dirty bundles from their pockets, they ate the contents with relish. After greedily forcing the last remaining crumbs into their mouths, they sat back, belched and then began to grumble about conditions down below. The observers settled down quietly to listen to the foul tongue and it soon became apparent, at least to Hap and Kaér who understood the language, that they might be able to turn a part of what they were hearing to their advantage. Eventually their talk died away and, in response to some distant shouting and swearing, they scurried back to work.

"What was all that about?" Angharad asked after making sure they were out of earshot.

"They appeared to be complaining," Hap replied. "It seems Sartae has developed a whim for his personal supplies to be brought down, specially, each evening for his meals the following day. One was bemoaning his luck because he'd been selected, along with a couple of others, to fetch it tonight."

"That's right," Kaér mused as they kept a lookout by the entrance. "I think we ought to change places with them. I already have a pass given to me by Deet and Triamun; we can acquire a couple more from those who are on supply duty tonight. With a little judicious beard trimming of our captives, we ought to be able to disguise the pair of you quite adequately. Can anybody else think of a better plan?" he inquired.

The scheme met with general approval and Angharad suggested that, if they waylaid them on the return journey, they would discover exactly how the Cantaéns split the burden amongst them. The others readily agreed; they could not hope to pass unnoticed if they acted out of character.

The sky remained leaden all afternoon as the milder weather persisted. The thaw had set in with a vengeance and the pathways below soon degenerated into a sea of mud. It was going to be a sticky night in a number of ways. As the light faded the Cantaéns stopped work for the day and silence returned to the hillside. The evening fires were lit below as the cloud cover dropped lower and a thin mist floated in wisps around the caverns.

The mist continued to thicken by the hour and, by early evening, they had moved back down the trail and now lay concealed beneath an overhanging rocky outcrop. Not long afterwards, the muffled sound of feet, squelching through the mud, came towards them. Three vague shapes, the leader carrying a flaming torch, loomed out of the darkness and passed by, unaware of the presence of the watchers. Twenty minutes or so later the noise of their return came filtering through the fog. As before, there was no talking, the inclement conditions proving too much for even their garrulous tongues.

Creeping out of hiding, the watchers pounced on their unsuspecting prey. The ensuing action was brief and within moments, their victims were lying bound, gagged, and unconscious at their feet. Hurriedly they transported the Cantaéns back to the empty cavern. All three were carrying packs and, removing them, Angharad grimaced at the stench emanating from within. Gritting his teeth, Hap cut away the Cantaén's beards. Using a glue-like substance, which Kaér produced from his pack, Angharad and Hap managed to stick sufficient hair onto their own faces to look reasonably convincing in the dark. Kaér fixed his own disguise and with hoods up to keep out the mist, they should not invite any comment. Wrapping most of the Cantaéns' evil smelling supplies in cloth, they placed them at the top of their own packs. They would not pass a serious examination, but a cursory inspection, if any, was all they anticipated. They were, after all, expected.

With the final part of their masquerade complete they moved off towards the main track. Walking through mud, slush, and mist made for heavy going and twice, despite the torch, they nearly went over the edge. Nevertheless, by nine o'clock they had left these difficulties behind them as the track levelled out onto the valley bottom. The guard, they calculated, would have changed by now and with the torch marking their location, any hesitation now would look suspicious. Taking deep breaths they marched out over the exposed ground, all three praying that the relief watch would not realise their line up was different to the one that had left earlier.

The mist at this level was nowhere nearly as dense as on the hills, but the constant drizzle did little to raise their spirits. The track was a quagmire and all three slipped and slid as they tried to walk. The faint glimmer of campfires brightened as they drew nearer and then, almost before they were ready, they were approaching the sentry post at the southern entrance.

Initially the sentries, huddled round a tiny fire, failed to notice the arrival of the food detail. There were only two of them at this point, the circling patrols being out of sight for the moment. Gazing into the flames had robbed them of their night sight and they started guiltily at the sound of the trio struggling towards them.

"Hey! You! What do you think you're doing, wandering about at this time of night?" one of them shouted, drawing his sword as he vented his spleen at being caught unawares. "Come on! Speak up man! Let's be having your excuses, not that they'll do you any good. Isn't that right Streef?" he demanded of his companion who drew his blade likewise.

"Aye, that's right," Streef replied chuckling, "no good at all."

"Grow up you stupid oafs!" Kaér snapped back at them. "We haven't walked half way up that wretched mountain to fetch food for the boss to be stopped by a pair of buffoons like you. I wouldn't like to be in your boots when he wakes in the morning and finds 'is breakfast isn't ready for him." He stared insolently at the guard who shuffled uncomfortably until he averted his gaze.

"That's right," muttered Streef, trying to calm the situation. Whenever one of Sartae's meals arrived late, those responsible were publicly flogged and Streef, for one, did not intend to suffer the same fate. "The last guard, when we relieved them, told us to expect them back any time now. For the sake of a bit of peace and quiet, let 'em through."

"Huh!" the other snorted. "I think we ought to check their passes, just to make sure they are who they say they are."

"Of course they're who they say they are," Streef snarled, deliberately siding with the arrivals. His partner was a hot head and deserved all he was likely to get. "Let 'em through," he continued heatedly, "if you keep this up you'll bring the captain down and then we'll have to explain everything to a committee tomorrow. If you haven't already forgotten, it's our day off. Just let 'em through."

It was the idea of having to sacrifice a part of his day off, rather than the fear of a flogging that finally persuaded the sentry to back off, mumbling.

"I should think so too," complained Kaér with asperity, waggling his finger at Streef, "another few moments and I'd have reported you. I won't bother now unless Sartae says something, I don't want to waste my day either, but don't ever try a trick like that again," he threatened, poking him in the chest.

Storming passed the quarrelling guards they hurried away along the roadway. Coming up to a set of tents they lost sight of the pair, although they could still hear them arguing in the distance. Approaching the first junction they were aware their direction of travel would take them directly to Sartae's headquarters, an area that circumstances would not permit them to avoid. If the supplies they carried failed to reach his cook, Sartae would have the camp turned upside down looking for the missing bearers. They would be incredibly lucky indeed to escape the ensuing upheaval.

Checking they were free from observation, Angharad and Hap transferred all the strange food to a pack they had taken from one of the original bearers. Kaér changed his pack for this, handing his own to Hap for safekeeping. In the darkness they were indistinguishable from most Cantaéns as they marched boldly down the centre of the road. From all around came the sound of raucous laughter and the coarse licentious songs of the mountains, bellowed forth by wine-slurred discordant voices. Fires burned inside the tents and, on occasions, in the open spaces at the centre of a section of four tents. From here the noise was at its greatest as celebrations appeared to be taking place and the intruders could see the weaving shapes of soldiers outlined against the flames. Whatever anyone could find to celebrate in these conditions, Angharad could not even begin to dare to imagine; Cantaéns were peculiar creatures at the best of times.

An occasional voice called out to them, but Kaér shouted back that they were on duty and would see them later. His answer seemed to satisfy the drunken louts who promptly forgot all about them, as indeed was his intention. Carefully they counted each section as they came to it, not wanting to go too far. The sentries around Sartae's abode were bound to be more alert and less easily intimidated than those on the perimeter. Kaér's disguise and accent might pass all but the severest of tests but, unfortunately, the same could not be said for the others.

The nearer they came to the danger area, the more Kaér's sword arm twitched. Dearly would he like to force a final showdown with his deadly enemy but The Shintae came first, no matter what. Forcing himself to relax, he had his thoughts firmly under control by the time they reached the ninth section. All appeared still. Sartae would not want the sound of revelry close to his quarters and the sections that bordered him would be filled with the camp's elite: warriors who considered themselves above the common herd. A decree from Sartae that he would personally hang anyone who disturbed his peace might, just possibly, have had some bearing on the matter as well.

"Okay, here I go then," Kaér whispered as they halted. He had a sudden thought, "Hang on a moment, though, you'd better tell me where you're going to wait, otherwise I might never find you again."

"We'll be down there," Hap said, pointing to the left where all was quiet and still. "When I studied the area from the cavern, I found a group of sections where no one came and went. You'll find us inside the first tent of the third section down from here, the one on the right hand side."

"Yes, I know where you mean," Kaér replied thoughtfully, "but take care. It'll probably be where they store their weapons. Once under cover you ought to be safe enough, but keep a careful look out on the way, it's certain to be patrolled regularly."

"Right, we'll do that," came Angharad's acknowledgement. "Good luck," she whispered, kissing him lightly on the cheek.

"Thanks, I'll need it," Kaér responded warmly, gazing into her eyes for a second or two before striding purposefully away.

Chapter Nineteen

Holding back for a moment Angharad and Hap turned away as Kaér headed off down his chosen route. After the raucous gatherings they had left behind, it was unnervingly still and the noise of their passage through the mud seemed unnaturally loud. They slowed their pace to quieten their footsteps, careful not to attract the attention of a patrol. Without making it too obvious, they studied the area around, eventually satisfying themselves that no one had them under observation. Nearing a crossroads they moved over to the right and took shelter beside a tent where, from within, the sounds of snoring could be heard plainly. Crouching low they inched quietly forward and checked the roadways for anything untoward.

Everything appeared clear and Angharad made to step out but, before her foot had chance to touch the ground, a hand shot out and pulled her back. Hap whispered for her to stay silent as they dropped to the ground. Initially, she could hear nothing, but then the distant sound of trudging feet caught her ear. Easing deeper into the shadows, they waited for the marching group to pass. Fleetingly the path was filled with silent shapes and then they were gone.

Once the patrol became lost to sight in the mist, Angharad and Hap slipped safely across. Now safely inside the storage area they negotiated another junction without incident, walking to the middle of the section before entering the central tent through an opening they found on the northern side. Once over the threshold, the pair trod carefully, mindful that knocking over a row of weapons would soon bring someone to investigate. Running down the centre was a clear passageway and they moved swiftly down it, turning into an aisle between the mounds of weaponry that led towards the eastern side. On reaching the canvas wall, with his knife Hap made a small slit in the fabric and, as they settled down to wait, he proceeded to keep a watch through the opening.

Kaér, meanwhile, had not glanced back after leaving his companions. He walked as if he had every right to be there, a soldier lawfully executing his duty. Appearances were of paramount importance now; the guards ahead would be vigilant and heedful of any slip. Fortunately the likelihood of their knowing the individual bearers was slight indeed. The elite rarely mingled socially with the lower orders and the evening teams, or so the Cantaéns at the cave had said, were changed almost daily.

He was conscious of being watched long before a shadow detached itself from an opening between the tents on the seventh section. These guards were certainly competent, Kaér thought, as another did likewise from the other side of the track. Neither of them spoke nor drew their swords, but the aura of menace they projected as they positioned themselves a couple of paces behind, sent a shiver down his spine. He was in no doubt at all, should he try to make a break for it or attempt a move towards a weapon, they would pounce on him. In front the glow of many torches drew nearer and a sentry, with sword drawn, stepped out from beside the main entrance flap of Sartae's tent and moved towards him.

"What do you want at this hour you snivelling wretch?" he demanded. "The master does not wish to be interrupted by the likes of you. Speak your business and then be off."

Kaér stood with head bowed down, in what seemed a posture of fright and terror. It would have seemed odd if he had not for most Cantaéns quaked when confronted by Sartae's special guard.

"I...I...I've come w...w...w...with his food," he squeaked in a high-pitched voice. "I...I've got a p...p...pass here," he continued, fumbling in the folds of his furs. With trembling hands, he passed it over to the sentry for inspection.

"Huh!" the sentry grunted as he studied it, waving the others away. "It's all right! He's harmless," he called to them, sheathing his blade. Turning his attention back to Kaér, he grumbled ill temperedly, "Don't they tell you lot anything back there?"

Kaér shook his head dumbly, just another peasant to be bullied and mocked without fear of retaliation.

"The food has to be delivered round the back where the cook works, not the front you idiot. You lot don't have many brains, do you? Now, I suppose I'll have to show you where to go. It'll be too much to ask for you to find your own way."

Kaér nodded meekly, following on behind as the guard stormed off towards the rear of the tent, mumbling to himself.

"Are you the best they could find?" the guard asked contemptuously, before a thought occurred to him and he came to an abrupt halt, suddenly, suspicious. "Why is there only one of you anyway? There's always supposed to be three. Don't tell me they let you out by yourself because I don't believe it. Come on now, what's happened to them?"

"Ra...Ra...Raale slipped and hurt his leg and Dralin's helping him back to his tent," Kaér replied, hurriedly conjuring up two names.

"Rubbish!" the guard exclaimed ominously. "Whoever heard of you lot helping one another? I bet they've deserted and you're covering for them so as not to get into trouble yourself. The truth, now, and be quick about it or I'll have you flogged for the rest of the night," he threatened, advancing, a hand resting on the hilt of his sword.

"No, no, it's nothing like that," cried Kaér, feigning panic. "It's true what I said. Raale did fall and hurt 'imself. We was going to leave him, but he grabs Dralin by the legs and pulls him down. Before Dralin can get out of his clutches, Raale produces a knife and holds it to his throat an' says if you don't help me, you great stupid pig, I'll slit you right 'ere. So Dralin 'as to carry 'im back down. I left 'em at the entrance."

"That sounds more like it," the guard acknowledged in disgust.

The elite always looked after their own, a peculiarity of their select group. He accepted the fuller explanation without question; it was, after all, typical behaviour among the ranks. Reaching the rear of the tent, he called out.

"Hey! Chef, where the devil are you? You've got a visitor."

A flap opened and a head poked out. Ignoring Kaér, the cook spoke directly to the guard.

"See he doesn't come inside with those dirty boots," he snapped. "In fact, take his pack and fetch it yourself," he added before disappearing back inside.

The guard's eyes flared angrily but he refrained from answering back, self-preservation deemed he did not upset Sartae's personal chef too much. Roughly, he snatched the pack from Kaér and rudely told him to go. Kaér happily obliged and beat a hasty retreat into the mist. Drawing near to where the guards had appeared previously, he could feel their presence but, recognizing him, they remained out of sight.

Relief swept over him as he left them behind. Nevertheless, the release of tension was not without effect and he struggled to repress an almost irresistible urge to laugh aloud. He could just imagine the look on Sartae's face if he ever discovered the identity of the person who had brought his provisions.

With an effort he restrained himself and before reaching the junction where he had left his companions, his mirth was firmly under control. The patrol was elsewhere and he arrived at the place where the others waited without any difficulty. Angharad, alerted by Hap, came rushing out to greet him. "Thank goodness you're safe," she said grasping him by the hand.

"Yes! Indeed," agreed Hap, stepping up beside them. "We were beginning to imagine all sorts of things."

Turning back inside, Angharad led the way to where they had concealed themselves and, while Hap kept watch, Kaér told them his story. Half way through the telling, Hap motioned them to be silent. The guard was making its rounds again.

"I make that about twenty minutes since the last patrol," he noted. "If they keep to a regular routine, we should be able to slip out of here with ease." Kaér had to repeat his story at least twice before the others were satisfied. This was certainly a tale to tell around the campfires, provided, of course, they lived long enough to find one that had friendly people around it.

"You'll never seek for employment when you arrive home," Hap commented after the re-telling. "So consummate an actor as yourself will be able to put his sword away forever and become rich and famous as a strolling player. You'll never want for anything again."

Kaér chuckled at the idea; it would certainly be less stressful than his current occupation.

"Maybe you're right Hap," he considered, "you might have hit on something there. You could manage the company while Angharad sews the costumes and sweeps the stage!" he added with a smile.

"I think," snorted Angharad with a twinkle in her eye, "you're afraid I might upstage you. Anyone could fool a Cantaén, but it would take a genius to act convincingly in front of our people, someone more like me."

"What rubbish," interrupted Hap with grin as Angharad threw a pack at him while they made themselves comfortable, still laughing at the exchange. Gradually they fell silent as they waited for the camp to settle down.

"I've just had a thought," Angharad, said breaking the silence suddenly. "I know we've said we would prefer there to be no noise before we actually reach The Shintae, but there's likely to be a real uproar once we do. The whole camp's going to be roused and they'll be after us like a pack of wolves."

"That's true enough," mused Kaér, "but it has always been a weakness in our plans, what do you suggest?"

"What we really need is a diversion, something that will stir up the camp, but not at us. The three of us dashing about by ourselves will soon attract attention, but if we're just a part of the general crowd then no one will pay any attention to us."

"That would be helpful," Hap acknowledged, "but how do you propose we create this instant panic?"

"There's an area in here free from clutter," Angharad replied. "If, when the patrol's gone by, we start a fire and arrange the fuel in such a way it takes a little while before the tent goes up in flames, it will allow us to get well away before anyone notices it."

"Yes it certainly would," admitted Kaér as the possibilities struck him. "Set up correctly, it won't really get going until we get closer to The Shintae. If we keep under cover until the alert is given, we'll be able to mix with the crowd. Come on let's get ready."

After stacking arrows and wooden shafted weapons to form a pyramid shaped mound, they erected a smaller one a little distance away. The second was constructed in such a way that, once well alight, it would spill over onto the main pile and ignite that. Spreading combustible material from there towards the stacks of weapons, they estimated the whole tent would be in flames before the patrol returned.

With this task out of the way, the minutes dragged slowly by with only the regular passes of the watch to break the monotony. By midnight, however, the sounds of distant revelry had diminished considerably and, eventually, faded altogether. Even so, they waited a while longer to ensure the camp was fully asleep. Just before one o'clock, the patrol marched by and the trio was ready to move. Lighting the fire, they held back until it was blazing to their satisfaction before they stepped outside.

From where they stood The Shintae was just five sections due north. Cautiously they emerged on to the roadway and then, more boldly, marched along the path. After a muttered word from Hap, they slowed their pace and began to stagger and weave about from side to side. To a casual observer, they were just three drunken revellers trying to find their way back to their billet. Nearing the end of the third section, Kaér glanced behind and could see a faint glow through the mist. They decided to shelter here until the alarm had been raised then, if questioned, they could always say they were going for water from the streams to the north. Looking back again, the glow had increased considerably; the tent must be well alight by now. With luck it would spread to some of the others. Silence persisted for just a few more minutes before cries of "Fire, fire," came drifting towards them.

Leaving the storage area behind and, with the sounds of movement coming from the other side of a canvas wall, Hap said, "Come on, let's stir things."

Swiftly they raced around the nearby area shouting out at the top of their voices.

"Fire!" they screamed. "Fire, everybody get out."

As if to emphasize their words, the smell of burning wafted across and the Cantaéns, sniffing the air, leapt from their beds.

Within moments the area was filled with a milling throng and Kaér called out, "Hurry, raise the camp. You lot," he indicated a group from one tent, "fetch water and the rest of you go and try to beat out the flames."

The gathering broke up in disorder as the disorientated, sleepy Cantaéns hurtled off in all directions. No one took any notice of the perpetrators and, within minutes, it seemed as if the whole camp was running wild. The mixture of smoke and mist helped ensure chaos reigned and, in the confusion, the infiltrators made off northwards. Running into a crowd of Cantaéns, they found their way blocked. As none of the enemy seemed prepared to take the initiative, Kaér, fearing his group might become trapped, hurriedly shouted out a set of instructions to them. Trained to accept orders without question, the pack scurried off to carry out the commands, leaving the path clear.

"This way," Kaér indicated to the left. "We want to be up here on the right."

With the drifting smoke thickening all the while, a wide area behind was now aglow and, looking back, Kaér feared they might have started something far bigger than initially intended. If they were not careful, they could find themselves caught up in the conflagration. The glimmer of a lamp hanging from a frame caught Angharad's eye and she pointed it out to him. Heading towards it, they found the duty guards darting nervously about, unable to decide on what course of action to take. They had strict orders not to leave their posts but surely, if the camp was in the process of burning down around them, they ought to do something about it. Kaér resolved their problem for them.

"Sartae's sent us," he gasped, pretending to suffer from the exertions of running. "Never mind the tent, go help fight the fire before the entire camp's destroyed."

The guards, never thinking to question the authenticity of the order, fled. As they disappeared from view, cloaked by the swirling smog, Kaér's group dashed through the entrance unchallenged. The rug covered sides and floor of the tent were dimly illuminated by lamps hanging from support poles. Several tables had been overturned and food trodden into the floor. Cushions were strewn about and the whole area looked as if it had been abandoned in a hurry. Leaving Angharad to watch the entrance, they hastened round the tunnel-shaped tent as it followed the outer edges of the section. Moving through various dormitories and what looked to be the private quarters of the Guros, they found everywhere was emptied of people. The sound of voices could be heard through the heavy canvas separating them from the courtyard. Hurrying round they came to an opening that gave access to the inner sanctum.

There had been no evidence of The Shintae all evening but Kaér had an idea. "Quick," he said, "go back and tell Angharad to cover her ears. You do the same. Press the fur of your hoods in tightly until you're as deaf as it's possible to make yourselves." Hap opened his mouth to as if to interrupt but Kaér continued, "Hurry, there's no time for questions. Oh, and keep your eyes shaded as well," he added as an afterthought.

The urgency in his tone sent Hap scurrying back to Angharad who, staring in amazement, complied with the command. Kaér, pausing only a moment to allow them sufficient time to prepare, took a deep breath and stepped out into the open. Initially, he went unnoticed by the Guros who were much too busy arguing amongst themselves at the far side of the dimly lit courtyard, casting apprehensive glances skywards and anxiously sniffing the air. In the centre, lying on a pedestal of marble, lay The Shintae and Kaér's heart skipped a beat as he gazed down upon The Stone. For a moment he thought he might be able to walk over and take it without any trouble, but then one of the Guros turned round and, noticing him, began to walk in his direction. He was, from his mode of dress, the senior member of the group and the others fell silent as they noticed his withdrawal.

"Guard," he demanded imperiously, "what is happening? We are told to remain here but nobody will tell us anything," he complained bitterly. "Is the camp on fire or not and, if so, is it dangerous to us, or our charge?" he indicated The Shintae.

"Yes, I'm afraid it is, there's been a serious outbreak," he answered grimly. "It started in the arms stores and now threatens the whole camp. You are to make your way to the perimeter on the eastern side and await further instructions. Sartae has commanded me to take The Shintae and hold it for safe keeping until the situation has clarified."

The Guros turned as if to carry out Kaér's orders but then paused in mid-stride. A thought occurred to him and uncertainty filled his mind, turning back he addressed himself to Kaér.

"We'll go," he said, "but The Shintae comes with me. Lord Sartae, personally, entrusted it to me and I will not release it to anyone without his spoken order, especially a common soldier like you. You're not even a member of his bodyguard," he sneered disdainfully at Kaér. "By whose authority do you issue these orders," he demanded, "and where's your authorisation, in Sartae's own hand, to enter this area? Come on now, speak up and present your orders."

"I have the sanction of the High Council," he answered abruptly and the wise man stared at him in bewilderment.

"The High Council!" he spluttered finally. "What Council? Are your brains addled, we have no Council here? You're mad, you hear, mad."

"There is a High Council where I come from," Kaér continued, his voice like ice. The other Guros', who had moved up behind their leader, ceased shuffling, stilled by the intensity of his tone. "A truly democratic institution," he continued to the shocked audience, "and not a petty tyranny led by some perverted, evil degenerate like the one who rules your every move. Yes, indeed, I have the authority of the High Council to take The Shintae and to employ whatever means I deem necessary to repossess and hold it."

The enraged Cantaéns moved towards him and Kaér unsheathed his sword. Unarmed, they fell back as he carried on with scarcely a break.

"This Council of which I speak is The Stone's rightful heir and to them and only them are entrusted the awesome secrets of its power. It is not to be used for wanton mindless killing and destruction, which is all you are capable of, but for healing and building. Never, at any point since it came into your possession, have you sought anything other than its destructive qualities. Your claim is forfeit. Stand back!" he thundered. Moving swiftly, he grasped hold of The Stone and held it aloft before the dumbfounded group could react.

"In the name of the High Council, I reclaim it," he cried triumphantly. "The High Council of Maraé."

The Guros' fell back cowering, blood draining from their faces at the sight that confronted them. Kaér, The Shintae in his hand, seemed to swell in size and fear flowed through them all. Their leader quickly recovered some of his badly shaken wits as thoughts of Sartae's retribution for The Shintae's loss overcame his fear.

"At him," he screamed, his face contorted with fury. "He must not escape. Stop him or Sartae will skin us all alive," but, even as the words left his lips, he knew he had left it far too late.

The intruder uttered some strange incantation and The Stone glowed brightly orange in his hand.

"Inshilinga da vaal ylas indish," he chanted, pointing the object towards the northeast.

The leader was almost upon him when The Shintae started pulsating rapidly, changing to a deep purple colour. A beam of tremendous energy and intensity shone out, parting the mist and smoke for several seconds before a thunderclap rang out, the likes of which had never been heard before. The Guros, temporarily deafened and blinded, fell stunned to the ground. Fortunately, for Kaér, the one who held The Stone remained immune to its effects. As The Stone reverted to its inert state, he thrust it deep inside a pouch hidden within the folds of his jacket and, stepping over the unconscious Guros, re-entered the tent. Sprinting round the inside, he soon reached his friends, their hands still clasped tightly over their hoods. Shaking them gently on the shoulders, he indicated it was safe to release the pressure. Shielded from the worst excesses of the noise, they had suffered little discomfort and were full of questions. Time, however, did not allow for them and so, without a word, they stepped outside. In any case, it was obvious from his expression Kaér had been successful.

Out on the roadway, Kaér began to realise just how effective the use of The Stone had been. Everywhere, Cantaéns blundered about, blindly tripping over any obstruction in their path. Nearly all held their ears as if in agony while some had given up trying to walk, crawling around in despair. Unfortunately the smog would have prevented much of the camp from being affected by the light, but the hearing of the residents would be impaired for a while.

Half the camp seemed on fire now with flames shooting high into the air to the south and east of them. Sartae would soon discover the loss of The Shintae and instigate a search for the culprits, even if it meant leaving the camp to burn. With this thought in mind, Kaér headed westwards, away from Maraé. Sartae would look for them in the east and, by the time he discovered his error, Kaér's party would be far away, working their way back from a completely unexpected direction.

Without warning, the ground suddenly began to move beneath their feet and, from the distant heights of Mount Subae, came an explosion of spectacular magnitude. The noise died away to a deep-throated roar that rumbled on and on, never ending. Already in a state of shock and confusion, the inhabitants gave way to total panic as they attempted to escape the sounds and tremors of doom. Then, added to the smell of burning, came the foul acrid stench of sulphur. The Cantaéns, to a man, abandoned the camp, fleeing in all directions. Through the smog, a shower of fine, hot ash began to fall, cutting visibility to almost zero. More tremors shook the ground and, struggling to keep their feet, Kaér loosely roped the three of them together. If they became separated now, they would never find each other again.

Inadvertently, the instigator of this latest trouble had again been Kaér. Unknown to him, the beam from The Shintae, had curved away from the camp and landed deep within the crater walls of the infamous mount itself. Cutting down through the fiery surface it had released the molten core below. Subae was now in full eruption. As rivers of lava spewed out from near its glowing top, ash, stones, and boulders were hurtling skywards, some to fall considerable distances away. The flows of lava would, eventually, come together until, in the end, only two would remain, one moving east while the other followed a course that would take it on to engulf the entire camp area.

The trio struggled westwards and, leaving the encampment behind followed the lie of the land. There was little chance of their identities being discovered and so they removed their uncomfortable disguises, everyone was uniformly covered with a layer of ash and no one they came across took any notice of them. Everyone was too preoccupied with self-preservation to care. The fall of ash became heavier and, in places, they experienced difficulties walking. On and on they stumbled, gradually overtaking the straggling groups who had made it out before them. Dawn came, but the change in light was barely perceptible, the sun's rays scarcely able to penetrate the darkness that covered the skies.

A couple of hours after dawn found them exhausted, the combination of walking over ash-covered ground and the foul air conspiring to sap them of their energy. They were all suffering badly from swollen eyes, irritation in the nose and, despite having wrapped cloths around their mouths to keep out the dust, their throats and chests felt raw with a persistent tickly cough now affecting their breathing. Finding a hollow at the side of the valley, they managed to pitch a tent and, while one kept a watch, the others slept. Luckily, few Cantaéns managed to struggle that far whilst the trio slept and, as the tent was rapidly camouflaged with ash, they escaped detection. The lookouts, though, had to work hard to keep the tent from becoming buried. They could so easily have suffered the same fate as many Cantaéns who suffocated after collapsing with fatigue.

By mid afternoon they had all managed some sleep and, after a hasty meal, packed the tent away. The fall of ash had eased a little, but the land was thickly covered. In the end, they resorted to using snowshoes to stop them from sinking into the layer. They travelled without incident for three or four hours before

Kaér, who was leading, tripped and tumbled down a steep gully. The others, still attached by rope, were dragged down behind. Angharad and Hap sat up at the bottom, uninjured but coughing and spluttering up the dust they had swallowed.

"Yuk! That tastes awful," complained Hap as he cleared his mouth of the foul deposit. "Come on, let's go," he said rising.

"Yes, let's," agreed Angharad.

Pulling on the rope that connected them to Kaér, they called for him to hurry but he remained motionless. Worried, they dropped to their knees beside him. His head, they could now see, had struck hard against a point of a rock that pierced the covering of ash. Blood poured down his face from the wound and his breathing sounded terrible. Gently they raised his head and cleared the ash from his airways allowing his respiration to return to somewhere near normal. Unfortunately he remained deeply unconscious, leaving them in a quandary as to what to do for the best.

Ideally, to care for him properly, they needed to pitch camp and remain where they were but it could be hours, or even days, before Kaér regained his senses. The cloud and mist might lift at any time to leave them exposed and vulnerable. The fleeing Cantaéns would not remain in a state of shock forever and the sight of strangers, one of whom could not even speak the language, would arouse suspicions straightaway. The consequences of moving him, though, could be just as serious. They had absolutely no idea how badly hurt he was. Hap might be highly skilled as a healer, but even he could not predict with any accuracy what the outcome of a head injury might be. Furiously they discussed the matter but, in the end, the safety of The Shintae had foremost consideration. The decision was made; they would move and seek shelter away from the valley.

Praying the move would not kill him, Hap gently lifted Kaér over his shoulders while Angharad collected their packs. Moving north to the valley side, they began climbing. Higher and higher they stumbled and staggered in the dark, breaking regularly to swap burdens and, occasionally, to carry Kaér between them. Eventually, moving out of the mist, they left the valley far below. A thick cloud of smoke and dust hid the moon and stars. There was no change in Kaér's condition and, as the air began to lighten faintly, they searched around for shelter. They saw no sign of the enemy who must have kept to the valley bottom. As she looked back, Angharad was relieved to find their own tracks were rapidly fading under the falling ash. Even the most skilled of Cantaén trackers would be unable to follow the trio's trail now.

Stumbling across a cave in a scar high up on the valley sides Hap entered and carefully laid Kaér on the dry, ash free ground inside. Angharad tended to him while Hap regained his breath. It was no easy thing carrying a dead weight up a mountainside. They could not afford to stay here for long as they needed to put more distance behind them. One day, two at the most, was all they dared risk. If he had not regained consciousness by then, they would have to continue carrying him. Neither of them could bring themselves to leave him to his fate, even though this would have been Kaér's wish.

Preparing a little food, they ate in silence. At Hap's insistence, Angharad laid out her bed and tried to rest. Why such a thing had befallen Kaér now, when their mission had successfully gained its objective, was beyond her comprehension. After all the dangers they had experienced, to simply slip and have this happen was unbelievable. She shook her head in despair, slowly falling into a fitful sleep as Hap remained at Kaér's side, never moving.

Outside in the twilight like gloom, ash, and dust continued to rain down, as the remnants of their tracks were lost to sight. With the disappearance of their footprints, so Hap, Angharad and the injured Kaér passed beyond the knowledge of Cantaé and thus it remained for many a long day. No trace was found. They had, apparently, vanished from off the face of the earth.

Chapter Twenty

Two extremely long and wearisome weeks had passed since the devastation of the Subrat Valley and until the previous evening, Sartae had remained in ignorance as to what had actually transpired that dreadful night. The chaos created by the fire and mist had turned to panic when, after The Shintae's violent discharge, half his followers had suffered temporarily blindness, deafness, or a combination of both. At the time, he had been delighted that the Guros' had finally made some progress, but was far too concerned with preparations for flight to find out the exact circumstances. In fact, at the first calls of alarm, he had commanded his guard to gather supplies of food, water and tents in case evacuation became necessary.

The heavily draped tent had spared them from the intensity of the light beam, although the accompanying blast still caused great discomfort. But moments later the mountain had exploded and, as the tent collapsed around them, they had staggered out into the open. With the ground moving beneath their feet they had made a desperate attempt to reach The Shintae but, barely able to see a hand in front of them, they had became hopelessly disorientated in the smog and general hysteria. A shower of ash had started falling, cutting visibility even further and, eventually, they found themselves at the perimeter. Sartae, feeling sure the wise men would have fled with The Stone, had decided to carry on and put as much distance between him and this rapidly unfolding nightmare as was physically possible.

Initially he had intended to try to make contact with the Guros along the way but, with conditions continuing to deteriorate, Sartae realised he would be fully stretched concentrating on his own survival and must trust to fate to look after theirs. Struggling blindly on, they had pitched tents whenever exhaustion had overtaken them. Like Kaér, they constantly had to guard against being buried alive by the volcanic fallout. Occasionally groups of half crazed soldiers desperate for water, loomed out of the darkness but Sartae had them driven off. They would be hard put to make their own provisions stretch as it was, and he considered his own existence to be of far greater importance than anyone else's.

Three days after the eruption, the shower of ash and dust, which had greatly reduced over the previous twenty-four hours, finally ceased. The mist lifted and, although the sky remained masked by a layer of smoke, they were soon able to work out their position. To their amazement, they found themselves only thirty miles away from their starting point. The valley, though, was wide and they could quite easily have gone around in circles for some of the time, their muscles certainly felt as if they had travelled at least double that distance.

In need of a respite, Sartae decided to call a halt and rest. Searching round, a spring of fresh water was located, well away from the heavily polluted streams running through the centre of the valley and camp set up nearby. Selecting two of his fittest guards, Sartae dispatched them back to the encampment, mainly to establish the extent of the damage and, secondly, to see if any trace of the Guros could be discovered. If the area was still habitable, he intended returning. There were stores a plenty in the caverns on the hillside, ample food as well as spare tents and clothing. The dead and missing could easily be replaced and any survivors reinstated to their duties. To return without The Shintae, though, was pointless and so later that same day, Sartae commanded two more of his followers to go on ahead. If the Guros were in front, then they must be found.

The remainder of the day and night passed without incident for those who took their ease. Even Sartae had not fully recovered from the shocking events. His vindictive temper was, most unusually, in abeyance and not once since fleeing the camp had he shouted at, beaten, or threatened any of his followers. He stayed like this for some days, although his old nature was quick to re-assert itself after then.

As evening fell on the second day, the Guards who had travelled back along the valley returned to make their report. Throughout the whole of the journey, they had seen no other living creature, nor discovered any trace of the wise men. A few bodies, partially buried in the debris, had been found and examined, but to no avail. As for the countless other missing men, thousands could lie hidden beneath the blanket of ash. It would be an impossible task to sift through it all to find them. No, if The Shintae was buried along with the Guros, it was there to stay unless some miracle occurred to fetch it to the surface and guide them towards it.

The encampment no longer existed, its place taken by a vast lake of steaming lava. Rivers of molten rock still flowed freely from the peak, but no longer pushed towards the valley bottom. Black smoke billowed skywards from the crater above while the air around was foul and deadly. Any waterholes and streams not covered in lava were blocked or heavily silted with ash, the water poisoned by the sulphurous emissions. Considering everything, the scouts thought it highly inadvisable to head back. Dismissed, they took their leave, leaving Sartae with much to think about.

Nowhere, or so the scouts said, could any tracks to be found more than ten miles east of their location. Those who had escaped must, therefore, have passed that point before the ash stopped falling. Despite the early mass panic, it was unlikely that many would have attempted the highly dangerous enterprise of ascending the valley sides, especially the non-athletic and mainly elderly Guros. Turning eastwards would have put them directly in the path of the lava flows. No, they would have headed straight down the valley. If The Shintae was not in front then it was lost forever, either buried under the ash or absorbed into the molten lava.

Alternative plans must be put in place. If The Stone was gone then its loss could not be allowed to interfere with his or, indeed, every Cantaén's main objective in life. Maraé must be finished as a nation, its people put to the sword or enslaved. This was the priority now, no matter what the cost, the undertaking must go on.

Although his force from the valley was finished as an effective fighting unit, it represented only a small percentage of the men at arms spread throughout the land. The Cantaén Guard, alone, was a vast organization and Sartae, as commander in chief, could direct them and the ordinary troops at will. In effect, he ruled Cantaé and no one dared challenge him except, perhaps, just one, the actual person whose name Kaér had used so successfully to gain access to the Subrat valley.

Cerdic feared no one, including the head of the Cantaén Guard. The large body of troops that served under him, although swearing allegiance to Sartae, in reality took their orders from him alone. On several occasions, Sartae had been tempted to enforce his authority but, unsure of a favourable outcome, had backed off from direct conflict. Now, he would have to beg for help; there was no way he could carry out a full-scale offensive without the extensive resources of his arch rival. Even for the pleasure of fighting the ancient enemy, Cerdic was bound to extract numerous concessions before agreeing to any pact.

Sartae could already tell who his next second in command was going to be, and only then if he was lucky. Cerdic would, in all probability, insist on higher status. Yet, on the other hand, this might not be such a bad idea. If things went badly, then the blame could always be laid at Cerdic's feet or, as and when victory seemed assured, he could always sustain a fatal injury during battle. A dead hero? How sad! Oh, he would really enjoy making those arrangements. Yes, any concessions would be paid back in full. He had actually managed a smile.

Contemplating the immediate future, he estimated it would take at least another week to reach the stronghold of Grenishov, the nearest town of any importance on his route. Once in residence, he would send messengers throughout the land to summon reinforcements and arrange a meeting with Cerdic. With his thoughts much clearer, he had retired to bed, only to spend a restless and uneasy night. Waking at dawn, he felt little refreshed but, shaking off his mood of despondency, he had ordered an early start.

Over the next couple of days the cloud thinned and, on the third day, the wind changed direction driving the last of the darkness away. The sun shone brightly through clear blue skies and a thaw began, continuing daily with increasing rapidity. Countless streams, freed from their icy prison raced full to join the ever-expanding rivers below. The snow may well lie deep on the mountain tops and in the high passes for some time yet but here, in the valleys, large tracts were now free from ice.

Daily the party expanded as numerous bands of soldiers joined with them. They were mostly well disciplined troops who, since the cessation of the ash storm, had been able to trap and hunt with some success. These differed greatly from the ravenous hordes they had come across earlier, and Sartae, desirous of sampling fresh food, had welcomed them to his side. But even with this influx of strays, the company barely reached four hundred on arrival at Grenishov. With ten days having passed since the eruption, he had expected to find a considerable number of survivors in and around the town but to his surprise, no more than a few hundred were there. For a little while, odd groups and stragglers arrived to increase the tally but, in the end, nearly seven thousand men were posted missing, presumed dead.

Four days later, Sartae's foul temper was back with a vengeance, chiefly when he reviewed the events of the previous fortnight. Inside the manor house, secure behind the fortified city walls of Grenishov, Sartae sat alone at the dining table in the great banqueting hall. In frustration, he smashed his fist down hard upon the wooden surface in front of him. Originally believing the whole debacle a combination of natural disaster and accident, he had now been apprised of the truth. A small group of Guros, staggering into town late yesterday afternoon had enlightened him, after a little persuasion, of the actual truth of the matter. Their tale had caused such a fury that those who witnessed it were certain he would die of apoplexy.

The fire, the supposed advance by the Guros, everything, in fact, was now clear; all were the work of a saboteur. Even the mountain's eruption seemed to have been triggered by the use of The Stone and, as he was fully aware, only the Maraéns had the knowledge to exploit it in this way. From a description extracted from the unfortunate but now far wiser, wise men, he realised immediately, notwithstanding the disguise, it had to have been Kaér who had out-manoeuvred him. Calming his instinct to execute them all, he flogged and imprisoned them instead. Kaér would, most likely, have perished in the aftermath of his incursion, but survival was still a possibility and the Guros might yet have their uses. Troops were ordered out to search the mountains for any signs of his deadly foe, with strict orders to kill from ambush if they found him. If he saw them first, he would, without doubt, use The Shintae to make good his escape.

His fist crashed onto the table again, sending a full goblet of wine flying across the room as Sartae vented more of his rage. As he stood abruptly, his chair tipped over and hit the wooden floor with a resounding thud that echoed throughout the stone walled chamber. Noisily he stomped towards a nearby window from where, down in the square below, he observed as a captain issued last minute instructions to a group of soldiers. At the word of command, they marched off towards the mountains, eager to supplement the searchers already there. Turning towards the city gates, he could see streams of fighting men entering the stronghold from nearby districts. Three thousand were shortly to be dispatched towards the east, to strengthen the forces there and seal off the border. More would follow over the next few days and should Kaér survive the mountains, they would stop him there.

His servant, Skingol, entered and righted the chair as Sartae, calling for more wine, returned to the table to contemplate the future. Within a couple of months, once the weather had improved, he would have an army of such magnitude nothing could prevent its advance through the forests. Unless The Shintae was not lost after all and it had reached the Maraéns. But by then he would have a good idea either way. If the manhunt proved fruitless and no signs of passage appeared along the border, then it was almost certain his enemy no longer survived. Kaér was a man of action and would not remain in hiding for long. He would feel honour bound to make an attempt at escape. If, by some weird chance, he managed to slip through the net. The Maraéns would soon indicate their possession with a demonstration of The Stone's powers. Now, all he needed was a reply to the message he had dispatched to Cerdic.

Fifteen days passed without an answer and Sartae became increasingly anxious. Unfortunately, for those whose daily activities brought them into contact with him, a troubled Sartae made everyone else's lives unbearable. Even without the arrival of Cerdic's soldiers, Grenishov was bursting at the seams. Battalions from all over Cantaé were answering the call. Officers were billeted in every available house, barn or cowshed throughout the region, while a huge tented metropolis had spread out around the city walls to house the troops. Sartae and his aides were kept busy organizing supplies as, day and night, convoys of carts pulled by oxen disgorged their loads into hastily erected storehouses. The town's forges had been greatly enlarged and extra smiths brought in to operate them to capacity. Working long shifts throughout the day and night, they repaired old weapons and made new ones. Large stockpiles of arms and general goods were spread throughout the city and the countryside around. Sartae had learnt his lesson the hard way and would never again risk placing all his reserves in one place.

Smoke from innumerable campfires and forges lay heavy on the air and the constant smell of cooking pervaded the atmosphere. Troops continued to flow in as the camps outside spread farther up and down the valley. Patrols kept a vigil on the hills but without success, sending back regular reports; but still no messenger came from Cerdic. Night fell and all along the valley bottom, campfires burned brightly like a myriad stars. The bustle of the city eased not at all with the coming of darkness, with the sound of hammers on anvils ringing out above all else.

From down the valley came the sudden, strident call of a horn. Leaping to his feet, his uneaten meal scattering in all directions, Sartae dashed to the open window just in time to see one of the outer sentries race across the dimly lit square in front of him. As the sentry passed from sight, Sartae could hear him talking to the guards at the door before passing through the entrance below. Striding across to the hearth, he turned his back on the roaring flames and awaited the sentinel's arrival. The pounding of feet on the wooden staircase ceased, to be followed by a loud knock.

"Enter," he shouted as the door flew open. Bowing low, the sentry waited until commanded, before marching smartly over and saluting.

"What's all this noise about?" Sartae growled ill temperedly. "Are there intruders loose? If so, I'll personally cut to a shred the ones responsible for letting them through."

"Oh! No! There's no intruder, Master," the sentry answered quickly. "Lord Cerdic has come, in person, to speak with you. He ordered me to go on ahead, to advise you of his arrival."

"Is he alone?" queried Sartae with eager anticipation. If so, he would arrange for his execution now. Tomorrow, after concocting a suitable story of course, he could go west and bring Cerdic's troops back under his own command.

"No, your Excellency, he's brought his armies with him. There are thousands of soldiers stretching down the valley as far as the eye can see. The leaders are making camp a couple of miles away."

"What a pity," he muttered to himself.

"Pardon? Sir," the sentry said, looking puzzled.

"Oh! Nothing!" Sartae replied quickly. The removal of Cerdic would have to wait. To assassinate him now, with his troops just down the road, would trigger a rebellion, something he did not have time to deal with just now. "How far behind you is he?" he inquired.

"About fifteen minutes, Master," the sentry estimated.

"Right, return to your post. On the way out tell my servant I require him, immediately."

The sentry bowed low and left directly as Sartae began pacing backwards and forwards before the open fire. Skingol hurried in and Sartae swiftly gave him his orders. He must get someone to clean up the mess from his dinner, someone to fetch his finest goblets and two, no, three jars of his special reserve wine. The cook must produce a special meal for later and many, many more instructions were reeled off to the astonished attendant. Leaving Skingol running round like a man possessed, Sartae went and changed into his finest clothes. A good show had to be put on for Cerdic, Sartae needed his troops badly.

A quarter of an hour later found the room spotlessly clean, Sartae having taken command of the operation away from his flustered servant. Wines and goblets were placed on the table, whilst others brought in bowls brimming with delicacies. Extra lamps to brighten the chamber were lit and hung around the room. Once everything was to his satisfaction, Sartae waved the servants away and sat down. Other chairs had been placed at the opposite side of the table and at various points around the room. If one looked carefully, none of the other seats was raised quite as high as Sartae's, it might only be of minor advantage but it would certainly do him no harm.

Ten long minutes went by and Sartae, impatiently, began to pace the floor. The minutes continued to pass and he forced himself to take a deep breath and sit down beside the open fire. Plainly, Cerdic was deliberately goading him. Nobody else in the whole of Cantaé would dare such a thing and he could feel his anger rising again. From outside came the sound of movement and Sartae composed himself, his anger cooling rapidly as he realised this exasperation was Cerdic's exact intention. An adversary whose judgement was clouded by rage would be greatly disadvantaged against one who had his thoughts and emotions clearly under control.

Heavy footsteps could be heard on the stairs, closely followed by a knock as the door swung open and Skingol entered. Bowing low, he ushered in Lord Cerdic. Sartae stood and turned to greet his guest and, although the two had not met for several years, both found the other little changed. Of the two, Sartae was slightly the taller and, subconsciously, he pulled himself up to his full height, exaggerating the difference. His dark hair, flecked with grey, flowed down his back, spreading out over the black cloak, draped across his shoulders. The jewel of authority, affixed to the black band around his forehead, reflected the lamplight in sparkling brilliance, adding greatly to his presence. His ginger beard covered the upper part of a full-length silver tunic, almost hiding the huge leaf embroidered into the material. The tunic swished along the wooden surface beneath as he moved over to the doorway.

Accepting the outstretched hand coolly, Cerdic removed his white fur jacket and thrust it towards Skingol who quickly took it away. Beneath the jacket, Cerdic wore fine hide breeches and a short grey tunic, which, to Sartae's fury, a green leaf had already been embroidered. He certainly could not be accused of hiding his ambition. Like Sartae, his beard was neatly trimmed and his hair swept back on to his shoulders. His face was thickset and swarthy with a scar running across his brow and down his left cheek, parting a bushy eyebrow on the way. His deep-set black eyes gave no intimation of his thoughts as he stared at Sartae who, controlling his ire, returned the scrutiny without betraying any sign of his hidden anger.

Nevertheless, Cerdic was fully aware of the effect he was having and allowed a little amusement to show in his eyes. Let the overstuffed, pompous old fool suffer, he thought wickedly. The time was almost ripe for a new order and he was now well placed to make demands of the 'Great' Lord Sartae. Let him squirm and suffer, like so many others had done before him. Once he was joint commander, he was well on the way to realising his own ambitions. Just as Sartae had plans for disposing of Cerdic, so too had Cerdic for removing Sartae from power. Which one, if at all, would succeed was a question only the future could answer.

"Ah! Welcome Lord Cerdic," greeted Sartae politely, master of his feelings again. "I see you've decided to come yourself instead of sending a messenger."

"Yes, I thought it would be more expedient this way," Cerdic answered, just as cordially. "Once I'd decided to join forces with you, it did seem rather pointless not to come at once and, at the very least, bring a part of my army with me."

"That is excellent news," Sartae responded with mock enthusiasm, "it will certainly save us a great deal of time. Together, we'll grind them into the ground and burn their forests down around their ears. Still, we can discuss this later, come, and sit down. A goblet of wine?" Sartae inquired and, as Cerdic nodded in answer, he clicked his fingers at Skingol who was standing silently by the door.

Skingol swiftly filled and brought over two brimming goblets to where the men were seated, at opposite sides of the fire, tasting the dark green liquid before offering it to them. The testing of food and drink by servants, in front of important guests, was customary as the use of poison to remove a rival, although rare, was not exactly unknown in Cantaé. Sipping his wine, Cerdic waited for Sartae to continue with the conversation. He knew exactly what he desired and Sartae, who was not a complete fool, would be fully aware of these aspirations. So, let him do the talking for the moment. Sartae would obviously try to sidetrack him in the hope he would accept something subservient, but Cerdic was not overly worried. The result would be exactly as he and not Sartae wanted.

"Yes, indeed," Sartae continued after taking a long drink from his goblet. "It's certainly good of you to put your men at my disposal. How many did you say you'd brought with you, five, ten thousand perhaps?" he inquired innocently.

"I didn't say," Cerdic replied smugly, "but it approaches eighty thousand. I had to leave half my forces behind to protect the western approaches."

"Well, they'll certainly come in useful," Sartae had to avow, astounded by this revelation. "I wasn't aware you had so many under your command!"

"We have great need of them in the west, it is, after all, a large area to patrol," Cerdic said blandly.

"Mm! You remember my second in command, Traé, don't you?" Sartae asked, suddenly changing the subject.

"Yes," came the wary reply, "we met on a couple of occasions."

"I thought you had. Unfortunately he failed to return from a mission inside Maraé. I appointed Biren to take his place, but he was proving unreliable and then went missing during the eruption. As you can see, I've been unable to find anyone else suitable to deputise for me since then," he paused a moment, to let the significance of his words sink in before continuing. "Neither of them could be held worthy of comparison with you, though. You're a born leader and strategist, skilled way beyond their wildest dreams. Not only that, but you have raced here with a large complement of troops to aid me. Such loyalty is deserving of high reward. You know, I cannot honestly think of anybody finer, or more qualified, to succeed them than you. I really do think you ought to accept the position," he proposed. Even if he did not succeed in his ploy, it was undeniably worth a try.

"Well, thank you for the offer," acknowledged Cerdic, "but I'm afraid I must decline. As you are aware, my troops have tremendous pride in their abilities and, under my leadership, have known numerous victories. To become a mere deputy, particularly when you consider the shortcomings of your previous ones, would seriously undermine both my credibility and their status with the other battalions. Indeed, it really constitutes a severe loss of face to us all. No, they would feel a far more valued and essential part of this campaign if I were to be given equal responsibility. You do, of course, want us to stay and fight, don't you?" he raised an eyebrow, smiling as he delivered the thinly veiled threat.

"But of course," Sartae agreed, capitulating gracefully, "I wasn't thinking straight. We must make you joint commander, alongside me. Come. Let's drink to your new role?" he added, standing to make the toast.

Cerdic joined him and, with smiles that never touched their eyes, they raised their goblets in mock salute. Even so, it was probably a good thing neither was able to read the other's mind.

Sartae's messenger had left before the Guros' arrival in Grenishov and Cerdic was unaware of the fate of The Shintae. This being the case, he asked the question that his newfound partner would much rather not have had to answer.

"The Shintae, what's the latest news regarding its fate?" he inquired, sitting down again.

"Ah! The Stone," Sartae murmured, coughing a little to hide his embarrassment. "It's a long story," he explained. "Why don't we have some more wine?" he suggested. "Skingol, bring the jar over here and refill our goblets."

Whilst their drinks were being replenished, Sartae mused over the best way to put over the sorry details, one that might cast him in a slightly more favourable light. Unfortunately, that option did not appear to exist. Leaving the jar in the middle between them, Skingol left the room as bidden, closing the door quietly behind him. Sartae wanted no witnesses to what promised to be a session of some considerable discomfort for him.

Relating the events leading up to the eruption and beyond took Sartae quite some time, throughout which his guest remained unusually silent, stirring only occasionally to top up his goblet. Nevertheless, contempt crept into his eyes as it became clear how easily Sartae had been outmanoeuvred. On the other hand, it was, perhaps, just as well Cerdic never discovered exactly how Kaér had gained entry to the Subrat Valley in the first instance, Deet and Triamun having perished during the excitement.

His tale complete, Sartae sat back and awaited comment from Cerdic, whom, it seemed, was in no hurry to furnish any. Eventually, after resting his goblet on the floor, he shook his head in disbelief and turned to face him.

"What a mess," he sneered disdainfully. "You allow an ignorant nonentity from the backwoods of that peasant land, Maraé, to relieve you of The Shintae, not just once but twice. You really are out of your mind," he added scornfully.

In reality, he was enjoying himself. There was no one else who could talk to Sartae in this manner and live to tell the tale. Lack of seniority had not always prevented him from voicing his opinions in the past, sometimes at great personal risk, but now he was joint leader, Sartae could do nothing about it. The target of his derision, meanwhile, was struggling hard to hold down his rising temper. Only the thought of eighty thousand heavily armed and highly dangerous troops outside the town prevented him from drawing the knife, concealed in the folds of his tunic, and plunging it through his guest's black heart. Cerdic, seemingly unaware of his host's mood, carried on.

"I just hope, for your sake, The Shintae is either retrieved or lost forever with Kaér in the ashes. If he lives and makes good his escape, your days are numbered. Once the people learn the truth about this sorry affair, they'll tear you limb from limb. But don't you worry, someone else will be running Cantaé by then, someone who's not so easily duped by a stupid oaf straight out of nowhere. Someone like me!"

"Absolute rubbish," Sartae retorted hotly, unable to contain his anger any longer. "What chance do you think you'd have against one such as he? He'd run rings around you; you wouldn't even know how to begin to stop him. You know nothing of him, or anything about him, so don't make rash assumptions. It doesn't go with your reputation."

"To hear you talk, anybody would think you admire this Kaér?" responded Cerdic savagely.

"Admire him? Yes, to some extent I suppose I do. Anyone who can travel our lands at will, eluding capture for as long as he has, must have some merit. He has fooled the best of our trackers for years now. If any do come across him they find, to their cost, he's probably the most skilled fighter in existence today. Most consider themselves lucky to escape with their lives.

"You've never had to deal with people like him in your western lands. All you tangle with are ignorant savages who have neither the wit, nor the skill to compare with that of your men. The main struggle is going on here, in the east. Oh, yes I know, only too well, that Kaér took The Shintae once before. Do you know how we managed to retrieve it from him? No? We caught him asleep, safe in the middle of his own lands. Even then, the results might well have been far different had his senses not been dulled by fatigue. Never before has anyone got closer than fifty paces without him waking, alerted by some sixth sense.

"Yes, I admire his fighting spirit, even though I curse the mention of his name. Place him before me now and I'd have him put to death before your eyes. Don't ever again even so much as hint I'm a Maraén devotee because, army behind you or not, I'll have your hide for it," he thundered, eyes blazing with fury.

"You make a grave mistake, you know, in not trying to understand the nature of the enemy," he carried on in a milder tone. "Kaér may be the greatest of all Maraén warriors, but there are tens of thousands more with similar strengths and abilities. Just because they have no permanent military force, doesn't mean they are easy prey. This isn't an afternoon's hunting trip we're getting into but a fight to the death, you do realise this don't you?" he added sarcastically, pausing a moment to sip his wine before warming to his subject once more.

"When we're finally ready to attack, we'll have almost two hundred thousand men at our disposal, and even then might find ourselves struggling to beat them. The only way we'll ever achieve dominance is by strength of numbers, by taking out small hamlets, one by one, allowing no one to escape and raise the alarm. We will need to move fast and adhere to a strict timetable. Before their leaders in the east realise something is amiss, it must be too late for them to erect defences. We have to be already there, amongst them, victorious. Stealth will win the day, not direct battle, army against army, as you are used to.

"Certainly, without The Shintae it's not going to be as easy as originally intended but, provided they don't regain control of it, we can win through. Personally, I think the eruption was unintended. Pure chance guided the lightning bolt to the centre of the mountain, not Kaér. With no sign of him since, especially considering the number of men out searching, I'm convinced he's perished in the aftermath, The Stone with him.

"So, in future, keep your criticisms to yourself and wait until you know something about the foe before airing your views. Never forget that, through circumstance, you might have been made joint commander, but I've been leader far longer and I didn't come by it as easily as you. Out of necessity I've promoted you, but take care not to overstep the mark."

Shocked by the intensity of Sartae's anger, Cerdic sat rigidly in his chair. He had seen him in foul moods before, but never anything like this. Unwisely, he had thought himself on a par but, so he was beginning to understand, there might be more to Sartae than he had imagined. He would have to step warily until an opportunity arose to dispose of him.

Sensing he had come out on top, Sartae's mood changed instantly and he became pleasantness itself. Moving to the table, he called for Skingol and commanded their meal be brought in. Afterwards, they talked long into the night, discussing the forthcoming campaign in greater depth, managing to empty all the wine jars before retiring. Although disagreeing quite vehemently over certain matters, Cerdic managed to avoid another tirade.

Earlier on, Sartae had given instructions for a house to be commandeered, one of a size that befitted his guests' status. Whilst they had talked and planned, Cerdic's servants had taken up occupation and made it ready for him. Although it was the early hours of the morning before he finally arrived there and despite the quantity of wine imbibed, he still found great difficulty in dropping off to sleep. There was much to occupy his mind.

Chapter Twenty-One

Spring was now firmly established and only the higher reaches of the mountains still wore their cloaks of white. In Grenishov, itself, few signs of the terrible winter remained and, despite the massive influx of troops, a few sturdy trees were coming into bud, survivors of both cold and axe.

The two months since Sartae and Cerdic joined forces had flown by in a whirl of activity. As a result the bulk of a vast Cantaén army sprawled out for a good five miles around the township, billeted in dozens of tented townships, one hundred and ninety five thousand fighting men preparing for war. In the mountains beyond the Subrat Valley, a further ten thousand were still on constant patrol. The extra troops sent to seal the frontier had now been pulled back to holding areas, well inside Cantaé.

Along the border, as in the mountains, no trace of Kaér had been discovered and even the sceptical Cerdic now accepted he was dead. An enemy scout, recently captured, had been persuaded to talk and from him they learnt that the Maraéns also believed Kaér had failed. Their observers had witnessed from afar the beam of light strike the summit of Mount Subae, closely followed by the start of the eruption. They knew of only one person out there who could exploit The Shintae to this effect, and had realised straightaway that something must have gone badly wrong with his mission.

From the prisoner they learned that the massive deployment of Cantaén soldiers throughout the whole length of the border had put the Maraéns on a high state of alert. But, as the weeks passed without further incident, they had come to the conclusion that the Cantaéns had over-reacted to the natural events taking place elsewhere. From conversations amongst troops stationed on the border, overheard by Maraén scouts on intelligence gathering missions, they knew the Cantaéns had become aware of the loss of The Shintae. Convinced the Cantaéns would never dare launch an attack without it, especially as they had started pulling forces back from the border, the Maraéns had cut back greatly on their own defensive forces.

Throughout this period, a steady stream of supplies poured through Grenishov, most going on to fill huge storage dumps created some way back from the border. Weapons were repaired or replaced as necessary and thousands more stockpiled with the food, along with thousands of other items. An army on the move had a rapacious appetite and to keep it replenished would require a constant movement of provisions to the front. As this involved the use of civilian workers, the mountains, apart from farmers and hunters, had been emptied of most fit and active adults.

Despite the abrasive nature of their first meeting, Sartae and Cerdic had worked surprisingly well together as a team, although neither believed this could be anything more than a temporary truce. For the moment the success of the operation greatly depended on not allowing their personal feelings to interfere with the invasion plans. Their various armies were restructured and extra battalions formed, each one commanded by a Cantak—a highly experienced general. Each battalion was subdivided into ten companies, consisting of a thousand troops under the control of a Unit Commander. With only last minute preparations left to deal with, Sartae busied himself with those while Cerdic went out visiting the Cantaks and Unit Commanders, ensuring everyone was fully informed of the final campaign plans.

Although aware of the object of the exercise, the Cantaks had been kept in the dark as to how it was to be achieved. Now, as Cerdic revealed the master plan, they began to nod in agreement. The stratagem was simplicity its self, Sartae had no desire for a long drawn out campaign. The longer it went on, the greater were the chances of the enemy realising what was happening. He would much prefer the Maraéns to be so depleted in numbers as to be as near ineffectual as possible when finally making a stand.

The essence of their plan was a combination of speed and stealth. There would be two main groups, comprising of four battalions each, one striking eastwards towards the coast from the south and the other one similarly from the north. As they advanced they would fan out, widening their path of attack until, on reaching the coast, the southern troops would head north and the northern ones march south. The remaining battalions would spread out in between, in groups of company strength. The mountain searches were being abandoned and those involved regrouped to form another battalion. They would wait alongside those already withdrawn from the border for the arrival of the main forces. The border guards, redundant once the invasion was under way, were to be redeployed throughout the main battalions as scouts.

Maraéns were, in the main, a sociable people and who, unlike Kaér, lived in close knit communities. Communications between villages, however, were irregular at best, except from the border and even those had been scaled down as the threat of war had eased. If they moved quickly, the lack of travellers coming out of the west would not be commented on. To ensure every village was wiped out, the size of each company was such that each settlement could be overrun quickly, crushed by sheer weight of numbers.

The leaders were fully aware no one could hope to get away with this forever. By the time the Maraéns discovered the nature of events, the pincer movements of the outer groups would be nipping together as the central groups joined forces with them. They would be close to the enemy's capital and its pathetic High Council by then, and Sartae would take great delight in personally hanging any council member who survived the onslaught. Yes, once his armies came together, they would be invincible. Any remaining Maraéns would be squeezed until they were forced under the waters of the ocean. Sartae savoured the idea with delight. By the end of the week, Grenishov would be virtually deserted as the armies moved out to assume their invasion positions. In contrast to Kaér and Angharad, they could take the shortest and easiest routes, unhindered by snow or the need for secrecy in their own lands.

Five weeks later, to the day, the Cantaén army stood poised, ready to make its first incursion into Maraén territory. The weather remained mild and, as the season had been unusually good, Sartae took this as an omen for success. Summer was not far away and by winter, he would be master of both mountain and forest.

Pacing up and down inside his tent, some four miles back from the border, Sartae waited for sunset. Over to one side, Cerdic sat, easing his nervous energy by savagely berating his servants whenever opportunity presented itself. Throughout the day, all along the border, advance units had been moving forward from their holding stations, awaiting only the coming of darkness before crossing over to take out the border villages. Highly trained teams were already moving against Maraén Scouts on duty overlooking the frontier. The sun dropped from sight and dusk crept over the land. An hour passed, and then another. The earth fell silent and then suddenly, with the light of the moon to guide their way, the advance units were gone, leaving the instigators uneasily awaiting the results.

Surprising the Maraéns as they slept, their sentries were overwhelmed and the gates seized before anyone could raise the alarm. The end was swift, few even realising what was happening and, by sunrise, from Waén in the north to Zenae in the south, not one village or villager remained in existence. The border was wide open and the Cantaéns wasted little time in taking full advantage. Messengers came racing back from nearby villages with the news and, as a series of small beacons relayed signals of success from both up and down the border, the main battalions were already entering the forest. The war had started in earnest, gathering an unstoppable momentum as the troops advanced.

The invasion progressed mainly as planned and, as days turned to weeks, the Cantaén troops moved swiftly through the forest, wiping out all before them. Village after village fell to the attacks, which came out of nowhere, leaving the populace dead and dying in the streets. The rapid advance continued for almost two months leaving Sartae and Cerdic well pleased with the results. Although they had planned it to be so, they were astounded that good fortune continued to favour them. Even more gratifying, for their evil hearts, was the look of stunned shock on the faces of their victims.

At each community, preferably just before dawn, the Cantaéns spread out, encircling the area. Scouts had kept each one under observation beforehand, noting down when inhabitants were outside the perimeter. In these cases soldiers were sent to deal with them well away from the target area. Sartae and Cerdic insisted no burning of villages took place as smoke, rising high from all directions, would alert even the most feeble witted of their enemies to danger. Not surprisingly, they suffered few casualties; the villagers were usually asleep or unarmed, their weapons stored away for safekeeping. Whenever the invading troops came up against hunting parties, however, it was a different story, the true abilities of their prey becoming immediately obvious. On these occasions, the Cantaéns paid dearly for their lives.

Both day and night alike messengers raced in and out of Sartae's headquarters bearing dispatches to and from Cantaks all over Maraé. On all fronts, the campaign was ahead of schedule and before another month was out, at the height of summer, they would be within striking distance of the coast. The risk of discovery, though, increased daily. The country was becoming much more open and densely populated as the Cantaéns drew nearer to the coastal lowlands. Large tracts of land had been cleared, ploughed and planted around most villages, leaving wide-open spaces to cross. Communications, this close to their central government, would be better organised and far more frequent. If suspicions were not already aroused, they soon would be as the non-appearance of messengers and travellers became an epidemic.

The central Cantaén forces were just over two weeks march from the coast when they embarked on the assault of the village of Rostic. The raid had been reconnoitred in much the same way as the others and, at no time, did anything appear out of the ordinary. Even Sartae himself had come to observe this operation. Under cover of darkness, the Unit Commander ordered his men to encircle the settlement and, long before dawn, everyone was in place, awaiting first light to initiate the attack.

There was, however, on this occasion, one significant difference; inside Rostic lived a chronic insomniac, Patuc, who had tossed and turned for most of the night. Finally, after his irate wife had threatened to throw him out, he decided a short stroll in the cool freshness of the early hours might be good idea. In the darkness, the Cantaéns missed seeing him. Patuc, a keen hunter, was renowned for the quietness of his step. Upon reaching the outer areas of the hamlet, he began to feel distinctly uneasy. There was nothing he could his finger on, it was pure instinct as all around was perfectly still and quiet. In fact, that was the problem, it was too peaceful, unnaturally so, not even the normal noises of the night were apparent. Then, faintly on the breeze, came the sound of someone talking softly. Patuc stiffened as he heard the coarse speech. The years he had spent as a Border Scout in his youth meant he would have known that foul tongue anywhere.

Swiftly he slipped back into the village and began moving silently from house to house, alerting the others to the danger outside. To begin with, no one believed him, but the urgency in his tone finally penetrated their sleep-befuddled minds and before long, the whole population had been silently roused. To help celebrate the headman's birthday, a bonfire had been recently constructed in the centre of the village square. Large amounts of fat and green wood were fetched and placed inside the structure. Indeed, anything that would give off smoke—thick black smoke—was added. They would light it the moment they were attacked. Breaking open the local armoury, they shared out the weapons, to men and women alike, while hunters brought out their favourite bows. Positioning themselves as best they could to give all round protection, they waited for the enemy to strike.

The first rays of light flickered overhead, objects gradually became visible and suddenly, the fields around Rostic were filled with silent moving figures. A Maraén war cry rang out from inside the village, the like of which most Cantaéns had never heard and then the air was filled with arrows as the defenders made their presence known. The attackers, abandoning the dead and wounded who had fallen under the barrage, withdrew in confusion. Sartae, beside himself with fury, stormed around until some semblance of order was regained.

Nearby, another company was resting after being moved back from the front and Sartae dispatched one of his scouts to bring them to him immediately. Twice, while they awaited reinforcements, messengers tried to sneak out of Rostic but they were spotted and brought down within yards of the perimeter. From inside the village a column of smoke was rising skywards and Sartae began to rant and rave, there would be no more surprise attacks now. Higher and higher the smoke rose, becoming blacker by the moment. The village would not last out the morning but the damage was already done. Luckily, for him, many of the groups were coming together and one or two had almost reached battalion strength. These would present a far more potent force to the Maraéns from whom resistance could now be expected.

Ten miles down the road stood the hamlet of Atwar where, an hour or so after sunrise, an excited crowd had gathered in the central square. All cast apprehensive eyes towards the west, at a loss to explain the meaning of so much smoke rising from the direction of Rostic; perhaps the village was on fire. After much discussion, it was decided to send a team to investigate. Ten men were picked from the numerous volunteers and within the hour, they set off down the road. Running into a party of eight from the nearby village of Lithros on a similar mission, they banded together and headed in the direction of Rostic.

By the time they reached the halfway point, the smoke level had decreased quite markedly. The outbreak could not be that serious if they already had it under control and, after much debate, they decided it was hardly worth their while carrying on. Pausing to eat, drink, and gossip, it was with a guilty start they suddenly realised a good hour had passed them by. The distant smoke had now petered out altogether and before turning for home; they took one final look. For a moment, as the group fell silent, came the faintest sounds of commotion, carried from afar by the breeze. Not one of them could understand what it was and when the slight breeze died, the noise disappeared with it. Irresolute, they wavered before finally agreeing it might be advisable if, after all, they carried on to check that everything was all right.

Up ahead, the battle had, temporarily, come to a halt and although they stopped frequently to listen, all was silent. The urgency of their pace slowed and, in the end, it was mid-morning before they paused for breath, barely half a mile from their destination. Without warning, the conflict flared again and the sounds of battle came distinctly towards them. Rostic appeared to be under heavy attack, but by whom? Surely, if the Cantaéns had invaded then the High Council would have issued a warning long before the enemy could possibly have penetrated this far. Having said that, the villagers suddenly realised they had heard nothing from the west for awhile now.

None of the group were armed; they had set off to fight a fire, not a war. Whatever they lacked in weaponry they made up for in courage. No matter what was taking place ahead, it must be seen and verified before they returned to raise the alarm. Separating into several groups, they moved slowly through the surrounding trees. Experienced hunters, they moved swiftly but stealthily through the woods. Within half an hour, they were all concealed at various vantage points, gazing in horror across the fields towards Rostic. The sight that greeted them was distressing, for most had friends and relatives who lived there. The village itself was surrounded by what appeared to be thousands of Cantaéns, many of whom were either dead or wounded. Within the hamlet, a fair number still lived, firing off arrows against any Cantaén unwise enough to break cover. Occasionally, a Maraén war cry rent the air, accompanied by the sound of steel upon steel.

As noon approached, the streets of Rostic became littered with the bodies of both defender and invader as the enemy made a concerted attack. Relentlessly, the few surviving villagers were driven back into a rapidly decreasing area. Smoke and flames billowed skywards again as defenders fired the buildings they were forced to surrender. The observers knew they should leave now whilst they were still able, but no one could tear himself away. It would have been a breach of faith to leave the beleaguered citizens now. These brave people, doomed to perish without knowledge of their success, had done their uttermost to warn their fellows. The watchers, although unable to help, could not let them die without a caring soul to say a prayer.

The end came shortly afterwards, but not before the remaining buildings were fired. A funeral pyre of their own manufacture it might be but, of far more significance, it was a beacon, a warning to all who saw that trouble was coming. As the last of the defenders went down under a hail of arrows, the observers fled, tears streaming down the faces of even the most hardened. Gathering back at the spot where they had separated earlier, they turned without a word and raced back down the road.

While the group from Lithros made directly for their own village, the others continued towards Atwar where a crowd gathered in the square to hear the runners tell their sorry tale. A stunned silence greeted the news and then a deep moaning started to grow but, before hysteria could set in, the commanding voice of Guthlic, the village headman, rang out.

"Silence," he roared above the sounds of wailing. "We don't have time to mourn. The Cantaéns will be upon us any moment now and we must flee without further delay. Everybody, go, gather what food, water and weapons you can carry and meet back here in five minutes.

"Go on, hurry, away with you," Guthlic commanded as the throng swayed in an indecisive mass. "Let not the villagers of Rostic have died in vain. Today we must turn and run. If we are to fight another day, then we must first live to reach it."

The spell was broken and the shaken inhabitants hurtled off in all directions, fear adding impetus to their movements. Those too young, elderly, or infirm to fight arrived back with supplies of food and water while the rest, men, women and older children all carried weapons of some description. Not one without a grim expression on his or her face.

"Families with young children must go first. Leave as a group and travel swiftly. We can only spare your own men folk to act as escorts" Guthlic ordered. "The elderly and the sick must, I'm afraid, make their own way to safety, we cannot afford to send anyone else to help them."

The square emptied rapidly. There were no complaints as the family men were grateful to be allowed to see their loved ones to safety, whilst the others accepted they were on their own. A few tears were shed as parents parted with elder sons and daughters, but their offspring stood proud and stern, awaiting their chief to command them. Within minutes only the young, the single and those couples without small children remained, apart, that was, from the group who had gone to Rostic. Despite most of these having young families, they stayed firmly where they were. Guthlic scowled in some irritation, but addressed himself to the others.

"Those of you who are left," he directed, "must spread the message far and wide. Move swiftly, but don't venture west, I seriously doubt there is anyone left alive out there to warn. One final thing before you go. It is your solemn duty to see that the warning gets through. Your fighting skills will be required, but not until later. For the moment, do not put yourselves in needless danger. A dead hero who saves one life and loses a village is worse than useless. Don't be distracted. Now go and do your best."

Leaving at a run, they fanned out in all directions, except west, allowing Guthlic to give his undivided attention to the party who had returned from Rostic.

"Why are you still here?" he demanded. "Didn't you hear what I said? If those of you with families hurry, you'll soon overtake them, and as for the rest of you, go and warn your fellow countrymen."

The leader of the group, Iryam, stepped forward and spoke in a low voice to the Chief.

"You didn't witness the things they did to our people in Rostic," he said, "but we did. We have absolutely no intention of going to safety, nor do we intend dashing about from village to village. There are already sufficient numbers for that task and more will come from the hamlets they warn. We would make little or no difference. Our families are young and fit, they will travel just as quickly without us."

"What are you going to do then?" Guthlic inquired, although he already suspected what the answer would be.

"We're all well armed," replied Iryam, "and quite capable of living off the land. We aren't large enough a unit to mount a direct offensive but once behind enemy lines, we'll do our best to disrupt their supplies and communications. We won't cease until every one of them is driven from the land, or we too are dead. Once our companions from Lithros rejoin us we'll be away, with or without your permission, although we would prefer you to give us your blessing."

"You have it," Guthlic promised. "Oh! If I were thirty years younger, I'd go with you but, I'm afraid, I would only slow you down. Look," he said, as a party of heavily armed Maraéns joined then in the square, "your fellows have arrived, go quickly before the enemy reaches here and you find yourselves trapped."

"But what about you, you can't remain," Iryam stated, keeping a wary eye on the road from Rostic. "You should have left with the others."

"Why? I've lived here all my life," the headman retorted, "and I don't intend leaving now. I'm far too old to take up running and besides, I don't see why I should. No, I'll stay and make sure they find neither shelter nor sustenance. As soon as you're off, I intend to set the whole place alight and then, if my old body allows it, I'll take a few of them to the grave with me."

Iryam made to try to dissuade him and then stopped himself. The chief had no close family ties, his wife and child had died many years ago and after their loss, he had dedicated himself to the welfare of the villagers. Now, with everyone leaving and unlikely to return, he was without purpose. Looking at him, Iryam suddenly saw him as if through the eyes of a stranger and, for the first time, he realised just how old Guthlic was. His voice may have lost none of its power, but his body was frail and bent. He could not hope to outrun the enemy so why not just let him end his days the way he wanted, performing one final act of duty. Grasping Guthlic firmly by the hand, he embraced him briefly before drawing back, standing to attention and saluting.

"Do not let them take you alive," he said in final warning. Guthlic nodded in response, there was no need to explain.

Sadly, Iryam turned away and, calling on the others to follow, set off at a run. They moved swiftly, entering the woods at the far side of the village. Glancing back through the trees, they could still make out the solitary figure of Guthlic, standing motionless in the silent square.

Two days later, Iryam and his band of guerrillas were deep behind Cantaén lines, already the victors of half a dozen minor skirmishes. Theirs was only the first of many such groups who took to the forest, creating chaos and mayhem whenever the opportunity arose. Although casualties were high, a steady stream of their fellows came through to swell the ranks of the survivors, ultimately tying down large numbers of the enemy forces as the resistance group's deeds became more daring and effective.

Cerdic, meanwhile, had joined Sartae an hour or so after the battle for Rostic had ended. Wandering through the smouldering ruins, they cast dark glances towards the distant column of smoke, signalling the destruction of Atwar. By evening, the eastern skies were rapidly filling with similar signs of warning. In his heart, Cerdic blamed Sartae for the debacle, even though chance alone had dictated the course of events but, wisely, he refrained from voicing such thoughts.

"I suppose it could have been worse," declared Sartae without a great deal of conviction. "It might have happened weeks ago. Still, there's nothing we can do about it now, except prepare ourselves for some opposition. With luck, they won't get properly organised before we reach the coast."

"Perhaps!" responded Cerdic non-committedly, his mind on other things. The scale of carnage wrought by one small village had shocked him. Sartae might not have been exaggerating after all when he had spoken of the Maraén fighting spirit. If the rest fought with anywhere near as much savagery as this, then the campaign might take much longer than even Sartae was willing to admit to.

For a few days, however, the advance continued unhindered by any opposition at all. If anything, events proceeded far more smoothly as every hamlet, town or city they came to was deserted and lying in ruins. The coastal regions were by far the most densely populated of the whole of Maraé, but nowhere did they have sight or sound of anyone. Messengers, arriving from other areas, all brought similar stories. The whole country seemed to have taken to its heels and fled. There could, however, be no escape, they were caught in a trap that was, inexorably, closing in around them.

News from behind was much more alarming. Supply trains were being raided, wagons destroyed and teamsters killed. Transit camps were coming under attack and, as the casualty list continued to mount, troops had to be pulled back from the front to protect their lines of communication. Even more were recalled to hunt down the marauding bands as, notwithstanding some initial successes, the problem escalated rapidly. Larger and larger quantities of troops were needed, slowing the rate of advance significantly.

A week after the massacre at Rostic, the first signs of real resistance came from the front. Ambushes and minor engagements became commonplace and the Cantaéns took to advancing in larger groups. Even these proved ineffective as sudden hit and run attacks took a heavy toll, the Maraéns fading away almost before they had chance to retaliate. It soon became obvious the enemy was willing to do anything to slow them down except engage in open battle. Sartae became convinced they would not face them in force until they reached Myssous, and then they would fight to the very last man, woman, and child. He would have need of all his troops then.

Despite increasingly successful Maraén attempts at slowing down the advance, a fortnight later found Sartae gazing out over the undulating farmland that would take him to the coast. Although towns and villages lay dotted over the landscape, the only visible signs of movement came from billowing columns of smoke, rising from the embers of burning ruins. The land appeared deserted but, without a doubt, ambushes were already in place, waiting to be sprung. Raising his line of vision, he perceived, far away, a vague shape on the distant skyline. Myssous perhaps? It did not matter; his objective was at hand. He only had to reach out and take it.

Chapter Twenty-Two

No Cantaén, at least none who had returned to tell the tale, had ever penetrated deep enough to gaze upon Myssous. Sartae's own mental image was that of a large village, possibly a town, with one or two impressive buildings encircled, perhaps, by a wall. Nowhere had they come across a community larger than four hundred dwellings and none of these, once well away from the border, had been fortified. Even the hamlets spread out below, numerous though they may be, were only medium-sized. Looking down, however, Sartae was still amazed at just how many of them there were.

The experience gained from his own travels, combined with that of others, was of a densely forested country whose people lived in widespread isolated communities. Like every Cantaén, he had presumed the remainder to be much the same, but in this, they had erred greatly. The coastal belt, including the twenty to fifty miles of deforested land adjacent to the ocean, stretched in places almost two hundred miles inland. Within this area, almost two thirds of the nation lived and worked. Instead of wiping out the bulk of the population during their advance they had, in fact, barely touched the areas of maximum density when the alarm had been raised.

The progress of both the southern and northern armies had slowed considerably after reaching the coastal belt. With the number of settlements increasing rapidly the nearer they came to the capital, their forces soon became overextended. At least now, with the land emptying before them, the rate of advance was building momentum. Unfortunately, both groups were still some day's march away and Sartae was in no doubt he would have great need of them. For the first time, he had Myssous in full view and even from this distance, it was quite clearly something he had neither imagined nor planned for. His blood ran cold at the very sight of it. The explanation for the rapid withdrawal of the Maraén forces was self-evident. Why risk a pitched battle out in the open when you have a natural fortress to retire to?

Myssous was indeed something special and not merely a collection of quaint buildings beside the sea housing a few garrulous old men, as Sartae had supposed. Instead, it was a large city standing at the southern end of a vast plateau that towered above the coastal plain. Originally called the Clardac Plateau, the whole area had for so long been referred to as Myssous by the Maraéns that the tableland was now known by no other name. Eleven miles long by five deep at its widest points, the plateau's sides rose sheer to a height of six hundred feet. At high tide, a mile and a half of its depth stood on the plain, five hundred yards more at low tide, with the remainder jutting out into the ocean. Over on the far side and unknown to the invaders stood a natural harbour, a place from where the Maraéns sailed to trade with distant lands.

Home to the High Council, Myssous was a city of stone built houses and chambers, a mixture of flat and domed roofs, arched doors and windows, the buildings linked by narrow cobbled streets and tiny paved squares. Well-tended parkland and public gardens lay in amongst the jumble of buildings. Other, smaller, towns occupied the remainder of the plateau, separated by open fields, many of which were covered with tents housing refugees awaiting evacuation. Along the whole length of the perimeter stood a fortified wall of stone that Sartae, quite correctly, imagined was lined with armed defenders. The wall was superfluous to the rocky cliffs below, but even Cerdic, when they drew nearer, had to admit it was impressive. Myssous itself was built on a rocky mound where, upon the summit, stood a watchtower. Even as he looked, a column of smoke rose from its tip, his forces had been spotted and Sartae imagined he could hear, carried faintly on the breeze, the sound of horns, sounding the alarm.

Thirty miles out to sea stood a chain of sparsely populated islands where most non-combatants were being evacuated. Ships, boats, and indeed virtually anything that could float, had been pressed into service, ferrying them day and night across the intervening distance. Their task was almost at an end; only latecomers still awaited transportation. All manner of game abounded throughout the islands while wild fruit, edible plants, and herbs were to be found in plentiful supply, sufficient at least to keep the refugees from starving for a while. Unfortunately, there was little natural shelter and the Council was forced to send as many defenders as it could possibly spare to help construct temporary accommodation. If things became desperate, the refugees would have to fend for themselves but, for the moment, the hundred or so thousand soldiers who remained should be sufficient for the High Council's protection.

By mid-afternoon, the Cantaén army was encamped within half a mile of the plateau's base, encircling the entire landward side with sentinels placed at closer vantage points. The cliffs looked even more inhospitable from this distance and Sartae could see two roadways had been cut out of the rocky walls. Each one twisting its way to the summit before passing through barred gates, mounted in the battlements above.

The Maraéns, with ample supplies, were content to sit out a long siege. Their ships, once the evacuation was complete, would continue to trade, bringing in cargos from abroad to replenish stocks. The enemy, despite having numerical superiority, was going to find great difficulty in scaling the heights, certainly with sufficient men to create a real challenge. Coming from a land locked country, they had no practical knowledge of boats and were unlikely to try for the far side of the plateau, at least for some time. This was fortunate indeed because the Maraéns, in the process of extending the harbour's amenities, had temporarily demolished much of its defences to make way for construction work.

A week later saw the Cantaén army back to full strength, the northern and southern groups coming up within days of each other. The remaining isolated areas of woodland around the coastal plain echoed to the sound of felling trees. Wooden covers, constructed and erected over strategic roadways around the cliff base, afforded some protection against the hail of missiles that rained down on them. From these havens of relative safety, troops were hurled daily at the heights above. Massed together they slowly climbed the paths, shields held overhead for protection and a battering ram in their midst. They were soon driven back, but the gates did appear to be showing signs of wear. From time to time, the Maraéns responded to the challenge and, before the attackers could reach the top, the defenders would charge out to confront the enemy. During the ensuing engagements, both sides suffered casualties and, overall, matters had reached deadlock.

Ten days after the start of the siege, a small party of reserve troops arrived, a group of mercenaries who had travelled widely beyond the confines of Cantaé. On a whim, Cerdic had them brought before him and inquired if any had knowledge of the oceans. One, a middle aged Cantaén called Balac, stepped forward. Slim and wiry, he had a face like wrinkled leather and, when he spoke, his breath whistled through a gap in his front teeth. Over the years, he had plied his deadly trade for various sea-going nations, making numerous voyages in the course of his duties, both as passenger and crew.

Dismissing the others, Cerdic took him on a short journey to the remains of a fishing village situated in a wide sandy bay, a few miles south of Myssous. There, leaning at a drunken angle, a fishing boat lay beached high up on the dunes. Although the vessel had suffered damage, the sailor declared this mainly superficial and well within his capabilities to repair. Leaving him to make a start, Cerdic returned to his headquarters, sending carpenters back to help with the work.

Two days later, after a successful launch Balac handpicked a crew from Cantaéns who had fished the mountain lakes in small one-man cobbles, and put them through some intensive training. The following day, he sent word to Cerdic who, after witnessing further sea trials, was well satisfied with the result. As it was the far side of the plateau that interested him most, he ordered Balac to set sail at daybreak to reconnoitre the area.

Early next afternoon, an excited Balac entered Cerdic's quarters where he quickly gave details of his short voyage. Having reached the far side of the plateau without incident, they had followed the cliff face around and out to sea, throwing nets over the side of the boat and waving cheerfully at anyone who had taken notice of them from the walls. The watchers had waved back, taking them for a local fishing crew; Cantaéns, after all, had no knowledge of sailing. The cliffs had continued for the whole way around the plateau, apart from at the centre where the land dipped down towards sea level and a narrow inlet led to a natural harbour. They had observed several ocean-going ships entering and departing from here but, inexplicably, the defences around this section were minimal, and no watch appeared to be kept.

An idea formed in Cerdic's evil mind and he dismissed Balac. After a great deal of thought, Cerdic finalised his stratagem and sent for Sartae. His fellow leader, for the moment at least, still needed to be kept informed of his plans. Now they were no longer on the move they rarely met, preferring to spend their days plotting ways of taking absolute control rather than conversing with each other. With this in mind, Sartae exercised caution and brought with him a full contingent of guards to his meeting that evening.

"Ah! Do come in, sit down, have some wine," greeted Cerdic as Sartae was ushered inside.

Once settled and the wine tested by a servant, Cerdic continued smugly, "I do believe I've found a way to enter their stronghold undetected."

"What are we going to do," Sartae sneered ungraciously, "sprout wings and fly? It is impossible; the wretched place is impregnable. The only chance we have is to wait until they run out of food and become too weak to resist, but even that's a long shot. If they're getting supplies in by sea, which I suspect is highly likely, then it could take forever before that happens."

"The sea, my dear Sartae, is the crux of the matter," commented Cerdic patronizingly. "I've found not only a boat, but someone with sufficient knowledge to sail it."

"Mm! A boat," studied Sartae thoughtfully. "How large is it? Can we use it to blockade the far side and prevent them from getting supplies in?" he demanded.

"Steady on, it's a single small boat, not a navy," Cerdic replied defensively. "Even when fully laden, it will carry no more than carry twenty soldiers."

"Oh wonderful!" exclaimed Sartae sarcastically. "We send a handful of soldiers out to sea in a tiny boat and hold the whole of Maraé to ransom. It's impracticable! They'll simply ram it with one of their ships and sink it. A great idea, remind me not to turn out again when you have another. If that's all you can come up with, I'll go now," he snarled, making as if to leave.

"Don't be a fool," Cerdic growled in fury. "Just sit down and hear me out."

Sartae, reluctantly, sat back in his chair, making himself comfortable again as he reached for the wine. If Cerdic was losing his senses, he might as well stay and enjoy himself. The time was drawing close to when he would be eliminated anyway.

"Please help yourself," Cerdic offered sardonically as Sartae filled his goblet to the brim. "Now, sit back and listen. As I was saying, I have a boat, albeit a small one, but it does at least float. Yesterday, I sent it on a mission to sail past Myssous and, when it returned this afternoon, its crew brought me some extremely interesting information."

"Oh yes! What might that be?" inquired Sartae without enthusiasm.

"On the far side of the plateau," Cerdic continued unperturbed, "lies a harbour that is virtually unprotected. Obviously, they don't anticipate trouble from that direction."

"What do you suggest," grunted Sartae, still openly hostile, "we storm the plateau from the sea? If we're lucky, twenty men might actually take less than a hundred years to complete such an operation, provided the Maraéns come at our men one at a time and they don't die of old age first."

"Silence," roared Cerdic in exasperation. "Of course I don't expect twenty men to take on the whole of the Maraén army by themselves but, if they land at night, they can infiltrate their way over to this side under cover of darkness. Whichever gateway they reach first, they'll have sufficient numbers to overpower and dispose of the guards on watch. After dark, we'll move troops onto the roadways close by each entrance and once the gates are opened, we'll have a thousand men inside within minutes. They'll be able to secure the area while our battalions follow on behind. The Maraéns will be finished."

Sartae, finally, saw the point of the meeting and nodded in understanding. The idea had some merit and, as neither he nor the Cantaks had been able to conceive anything remotely workable, they might just as well go along with it. One thing was certain; Cerdic could not be allowed to survive his triumph if the ploy proved successful. He was continually strengthening his position and, if left much longer, might become too powerful to touch.

"Congratulations," Sartae conceded eventually. "It could work quite well. When do you propose sending in your men, tonight or tomorrow?"

"Not for a few days yet," Cerdic replied. "Balac, the boat's captain, hasn't sailed, apart from yesterday, for several years. Although he managed that without incident, he would prefer to hone his skills. It does require, so I'm led to believe, some skill to dock a boat, silently, in the dark and it would be foolish to wreck it through impatience."

"Yes, I suppose so," mused Sartae as the idea really began to take hold. "Keep me informed as to how things are progressing," he insisted, preparing to leave.

Outside, the weather was deteriorating rapidly. The last few days had been overcast and cool but now a storm was building beyond the horizon. Over the next few hours, the winds increased to storm force, whipping up the ocean and sending huge waves crashing down onto the deserted beaches. Cerdic, concerned for the safe keeping of his project, sent a squad of soldiers to Balac's aid. With the additional work force, he was able to beach the craft before conditions became too severe, pulling it well away from the pounding surf.

Black clouds scurried overhead and huge droplets of rain started falling. For three days, strong winds lashed the area, bringing with them torrential downpours of rain. Tides were exceptionally high, flooding many coastal areas and forcing many troops inland.

By the fourth day, the winds had dropped significantly and Balac reported to Cerdic that if the improvement continued, he would be able to start training the following morning. Cerdic readily agreed and over the next few days, the sailor put his crew through their paces. The siege itself was still deadlocked and Sartae was impatient for a speedy outcome to the war. His troops were becoming restless, their morale dropping as, daily, they were sent up against the gates, only to be repulsed with heavy losses.

Four days later, Balac returned to see Cerdic with good news: they were ready to make their attempt. A messenger relayed the news to Sartae and early that evening, the two leaders stood on the beach, watching as the fully laden craft sailed out to sea. With nothing to do now but wait, the pair journeyed the two hours march back to Sartae's tent where they passed the time drinking wine and pacing up and down. Four, five, six hours passed without news and tensions began to rise. Thinking something had gone wrong; each started attributing blame to the other. Tempers frayed and voices became raised as another thirty minutes dragged by and then, from the distance, they caught the sound of running feet.

Although favoured with a good wind, the seas were rough as the landing party rounded the edge of the plateau, leaving the soldiers miserable and all wishing they had stayed on dry land. Having never even seen the ocean before the invasion, this, their maiden voyage, was proving rather traumatic. Balac laughed at their fears, they ought to have come with him just after the storm, this was a millpond compared to then. His passengers, however, drew little comfort from these comments as the distant sound of waves crashing against the cliffs, sent shivers down their spines. Their captain smiled complacently and continued to steer due north.

Two hours after setting sail, Balac checked his position and, leaning hard on the rudder, steered the boat towards the channel leading to the harbour. The roar of breakers grew louder and then appeared to surround them as they entered the inlet. The soldiers began to fidget nervously; was this lunatic going to kill them all, they wondered? Mercifully, the channel was short and as it opened out, they found themselves inside a natural bay where the waters lay dark and still. Sheltered from the breeze by the plateau, the sails hung limply and, after raising the rowlocks, they set the oars and silently rowed the remaining few hundred yards. Making for the south side where few buildings stood, they touched against the harbour wall with a soft bump. One member of the crew leapt ashore holding onto a hawser, which he bound tightly around a bollard on the dockside. Then, once the boat was moored securely, the passengers, to a man, fled the cause of their misery, leaving Balac to stare scornfully after them. Shaking their heads in disgust, the crew stepped off the gently rocking deck and moved over to join them.

Pausing a moment before moving off, they listened carefully for any cries of alarm. The only sounds, apart from the noises of the night, were those of merriment coming from a tavern on the far side of the harbour. Towards the centre, a large sailing ship lay tied up, its decks in darkness and no sign of life below. Out in the bay, another three rode at anchor, again showing no lights. With everybody either asleep or in the tavern, Balac and his men appeared to have slipped in unnoticed. Not daring to risk a skirmish with the Maraéns, who were now singing unconcernedly, Balac led his men quickly through the deserted streets and up onto the plateau beyond.

Once on top they progressed carefully, fearful of arousing Maraén interest. Luckily for them the route they took was sparsely populated, consisting mainly of open parkland recently vacated by the last of the refugees. Occasionally the sound of marching feet came towards them and they took cover in the shadows at the side of the roadway until danger passed. With an overcast sky and no stars to guide them, they became completely disorientated and it was luck, rather than skill, that eventually brought them to the western edge of the park.

Before them stood a town of some considerable size and they decided to try their luck on the other side. In single file, they stole silently through the cobbled streets. Most buildings were in darkness but from the occasional one came the sound of voices raised in good natured laughter or song. They cringed as they passed; such wholesome pastimes were alien to their natures. Fortune continued to smile on them as they went unnoticed and, coming out on the far side, they entered an area of woodland. Half an hour later, they stumbled clear onto a broad, well-maintained roadway that, after another twenty minutes of steady marching, brought them finally to stand in the shadow of the great castellated walls.

On either side the edifice stretched away into the darkness, a roadway running adjacent along its length. Nowhere could they see signs of a gateway. The distant sound of voices came to them from sentries, vigilantly patrolling the ramparts above. Backing away until they were lost in the night, Balac turned northwards, leading his men in a line parallel to the wall. An hour later they came to another roadway and, working their way closer, found it led straight to a substantial gatehouse. An arched passageway, illuminated by a burning torch, ran through the centre and, at the far end, a huge pair of barred gates were set into the solid walls. Over to the left hand side of the barbican stood a doorway, presumably the entrance to the guardroom, from where the murmur of voices floated clearly towards them. High above, on the battlements, a couple of sentries kept watch on the cliff road beyond while the turrets on either side of the structure seemed devoid of life.

Half a mile back down the road, lamps could be seen burning in a large village where, they calculated, the main support troops for this section were housed. Balac was fully aware that even the slightest of mistakes would alert the Maraéns at the gatehouse. The alarm would be sounded and their fate sealed. Therefore, taking care not to rattle even the smallest pebble, they drew their swords and surreptitiously advanced towards the sound of voices.

The door to the guardroom was ajar and the leading members peered cautiously inside. Half a dozen Maraéns were sitting round a table playing a game with board and counters. The game was unfamiliar to the Cantaéns but it served their purpose well. While the guard's attention was absorbed, they squeezed through the opening and crept soundlessly inside. Whether it was a draught or some sixth sense that made one of them look up, no one would ever know, but by then it was too late. A knife flashed through the air, piercing the luckless soldier through the heart. As he collapsed across the table, the others were cut down before they had chance to react. It was all over in seconds. Quickly, the Cantaéns spread out to search the areas leading off, barely pausing for breath.

Most chambers were empty and left untouched but, in one, a group of sleeping Maraéns was found and quickly dealt with. In the end, only one door remained closed. It stood at the end of a narrow corridor and in the dim lamplight, they almost missed seeing it. Opening it carefully they discovered a spiral staircase leading upwards and Balac, quite correctly, assumed they were at the base of a turret. Selecting three others to accompany him, he started to ascend. After a short climb, they reached a landing and found another doorway. Balac, blowing out the light, gently turned the handle and pushed against the wooden door, which silently opened outwards on well-oiled hinges.

Outside, leaning over the parapet with their backs towards them, were the two lookouts Balac and his men had observed from below. Stealing across the stone flagged surface, there was a brief flash of steel before their victims were dragged away and concealed inside the other turret. Looking along the ramparts, they could see no sign of anyone else, the patrols being at the furthest reaches of their beat. Leaving two men on guard, the Maraéns' cloaks wrapped around them in disguise, Balac descended with the remaining attacker to give the all clear. Ordering a dozen more to dress in enemy apparel, he sent them above to seek out and eliminate the patrols on the walls. Leading the remainder outside, Balac watched as they unbarred the massive gates. Creaking loudly, they swung inwards and, to his surprise, he discovered they were almost a yard thick. No wonder they had remained immune to the heavy pounding. With the poor run up at the top of the cliff, the puny blows from the battering rams had barely scuffed the surface.

With the way open at last, the advance party leapt out of hiding and sped over the last section of road and through the portal, setting up a wide defensive ring around it. Word soon reached the Cantak who had taken over command from Balac, that the Maraén patrols along this section of the wall had been eliminated, and he immediately sent out several heavily armed groups to scout the area. All the while thousands more troops were pouring in to consolidate their positions, spreading out as their numbers strengthened. Now seven hours since Balac and his party had set sail, a messenger was despatched to Sartae with the news: stage one had been accomplished.

The leaders were elated by their success and, before dawn, had well over fifty thousand men in place on top of the plateau. The whole of the northern half of the wall and the immediate area around was firmly under their control. During the latter part of the night, working on information received from the scouting parties, they began spreading farther afield, wiping out complete towns and villages as they slept. Soon after sunrise word reached them, apart from isolated pockets, the whole of the northern sector was in their hands.

The mist, which had descended during the early hours, cleared as a fresh breeze sprang up from the ocean. Gulls soared and screeched overhead and the scent of salt water was carried on the air. Dark clouds were swept away as the sun climbed over the clifftops. Now, Sartae decided, was the right time for them to venture to the summit and conduct operations themselves. The area was safe enough for them to travel freely and he had a great desire to see Myssous for himself.

Surrounded by their personal guards, they made directly for the plateau above. Climbing the steep switchback roadway, they heard the distant call of horns, the alarm had been raised and the fight would be on in earnest now. The call was taken up and echoed by hundreds more as it travelled south. This was a signal never before sounded, a warning of invaders within the walls. The leaders hurried their steps as, all around, siege weapons were dragged up the cliffs in their component parts. The machine operators needed no urging to greater effort. The height of the plateau had rendered the weapons useless down below and the men were relishing their chance of action.

With the enemy warned and on the defensive, the Cantaks wasted no time in pressing forward their attack. As the hours went by, the superiority in numbers of the Cantaén forces grew as battalion after battalion moved up to join the conflict. Once the other gate fell, the stream of fresh troops became a flood. Initially, the Maraéns, stunned by the sudden appearance of the enemy inside their stronghold, were driven back under the savage pressure. The farther south the invaders pushed, however, the stiffer the resistance became. Groups banded together, constantly reforming in a vain attempt to stem the ever-increasing multitudes that swarmed before them.

In a desperate rearguard action, the Maraén defenders ferociously attempted to delay the enemy while their main forces prepared the capital for the coming assault. They bought each second with their lives as countless numbers lay dead, surrounded by the bodies of their foes. Streams ran red as the slaughter continued throughout the morning. Only grudgingly did they give ground, but by noon, their backs were against the city walls and, as the gates opened for them, those that were still able ran inside and took up positions on the battlements above.

All afternoon the Maraéns sallied forth but each time, despite inflicting heavy casualties amongst the enemy, they were forced to retreat inside the relative safety of the walls. By now, the Cantaén siege weapons were in place and pounding the city with vigour. Rocks and boulders hurtled high above the walls, crashing down with devastating effect as buildings crumbled and collapsed on top of the beleaguered defenders. The city walls alone resisted the rain of destruction, but even these were coming under increasing pressure.

Siege towers, constructed in sections below and originally intended for the cliff top walls, were hoisted up and assembled. Rising above the ground, they soon passed the height of the battlements in front. Large, solid wooden wheels were incorporated into the bases and screens built to protect the troops. This work continued throughout the night and by dawn the fields around the main gate were covered by the monstrous objects. Sartae moved to the front and, staying well out of bowshot, gave the order to attack. The towers trundled across the open ground and, as they came to a halt before the walls, drawbridges were lowered onto the battlements beneath. Cantaéns charged across the narrow walkways, leaping down onto the ramparts as a steady stream of men followed on behind to replace those who died. Many more threw up ladders and began to scale the walls until, from a distance, the very stonework appeared to be in constant motion.

Many of the constructions were fired and the occupants incinerated, only to be swiftly replaced as more soldiers and towers moved forward. The fighting became severe over all sections of the wall. Ladders were sent plummeting to the ground and boiling oil poured down on the attackers, but for every one killed, another two seemed to take their place. At first the Maraéns held their own but in the heat of the afternoon, they were compelled to give way against the surging tide of soldiers coming at them. The enemy gained a secure foothold on the slippery ramparts and, as massed ranks of soldiers flowed over the top to strengthen the invaders positions, the Cantaéns gradually fought their way down to the streets below.

Reinforcements continued to pour through the towers as the Cantaéns pressed their advantage forward. The fighting became intense as they neared the gatehouse, but the momentum from behind eventually pushed them through. The gates were torn open and, with a triumphal roar, the main army launched itself towards the arched portals. As the influx of invaders became an unstoppable tide, the defenders were driven remorselessly back through the streets and squares. It was now only a matter of time before they were finally crushed. Even though all hope had been extinguished, they still fought, and with such courage, that every step the Cantaéns gained was paid for in blood.

Sartae could scarcely control the savage excitement he felt as evening approached. Although much of the town remained in Maraén hands, victory was now inevitable. The enemy had neither men nor resources sufficient to hold out for much longer. The mopping up operation did not require his presence and, he decided, it was time to pay a short visit to his quarters to change. Once dressed in all his finery, he would return to command the final moments of triumph, the one leader for all to see. He had heard nothing of Cerdic all afternoon and, in the heat of battle, had given him little thought.

With just two of his personal guards for company, he descended to the plain below. The noise of conflict faded as they set off inland, his mind already working on his victory speech. Passing through a ruined village, the sound of agonized groans brought him back to reality. Spinning round, he watched in horror as his bodyguards collapsed, arrows through their backs. His eyes lifted from the prone forms and, thirty yards away, he gazed into the unwavering stare of Cerdic. It had been distinctly unwise to put all thought of him from his mind, Sartae belatedly realised as he cast about for some means of escape. His attacker already had another arrow in place, pointing directly at his heart. Cerdic sneered at him across the intervening distance as he drew back on the bowstring even more. Sartae froze as he watched him adjust his aim, but his would be assassin was over confident. The extra strain on the bow was too much and, before Cerdic could fire it, the bowstring snapped and the arrow dropped harmlessly at his feet. A deep sigh of pent up tension exploded from Sartae's lips.

Throwing down the useless weapon in anger, Cerdic snatched his sword from out of its scabbard and charged towards him. Sartae stepped back a pace and drew his own blade, waiting in silence for his arrival. The late afternoon sun lay heavy as they circled, warily looking for the right moment to strike, sweating profusely in the sultry air. Soaring banks of cloud were building overhead and, in the distance, came the rumble of thunder. Cerdic feinted and then launched himself into the attack, but Sartae easily deflected the blow and then the fight was on in earnest. Backwards and forwards they pressed each other across the village square. One moment Cerdic was giving ground under the furious onslaught of his opponent, the next their situations were reversed and it was Sartae who was struggling for his life.

As the thunderous crashes rolled nearer, the sun was obscured behind the rising storm clouds. Huge flashes streaked across the heavens and down to earth, the light grew dimmer and the sky turned an eerie shade of green. The hair tingled on their heads as the atmosphere became electrically charged. Each of them, their skins covered in numerous cuts, was starting to weaken from loss of blood.

Sartae, wiping the sweat from his eyes, was becoming light headed and knew he must tend to his injuries soon if he was to survive. Cerdic, though, appeared to be in a far worse state; he was weaving all over and his reactions had slowed considerably. If he could just steady himself for a few moments, he could finish it now. Cerdic raised his sword for a vicious down stroke and Sartae, seizing his chance, staggered forward and ran his blade straight through the unprotected middle of his enemy, slicing upwards as he pulled it clear. For a second nothing happened and then Cerdic's sword slipped from his grasp and fell harmlessly to stick, quivering, in the ground behind. A trickle of blood ran from his mouth and, for a moment, his eyes burned with a fierce intensity as he took a step forward. The light died and, slowly, he slid to the ground. The whole affair had taken place in silence and it was only now that Sartae, swaying with fatigue, spoke.

"Goodbye, fool," he whispered over the body. "You were never good enough to wear my mantle. If only you had been content with what you had, you could have lived to savour the triumph that is mine now. Mine alone."

Unsteadily, he made his way across the village square. Forcing himself to concentrate, he started binding his wounds with strips of cloth torn from his shredded tunic. Fumbling in his haste, he struggled to stanch the bleeding from the worst of his injuries. The rain, which until now had held off, started falling in torrents as lightning flashed all around and thunder assailed his eardrums. It must be weakness, he thought, as he became aware of a steady pounding inside his head. Leaning against the remains of a house wall for support, he steadied himself, shaking his head to clear the mistiness from his eyes. Lightning illuminated the land and looking up he saw, to his horror, a pack of demons charging down on him. He shook his head again, but the image remained and, for the first time in his life, Sartae knew real fear. An insane cry left his lips and, in his dazed state, he turned and ran back across the square towards a house that had, somehow, escaped destruction.

An open door beckoned and he fled inside, panic lending strength to his movements as he raced up a flight of stairs and out onto a flat topped roof above. Crazily, he leaned over the edge as the demons spread out beneath. He raised his sword and waved it wildly about, screaming down abuse. Suddenly, directly overhead, came a brilliant flash and the air around crackled as lightning arched downwards towards the tip of his blade. The metal glowed brilliantly as the peal of thunder roared and Sartae let out an inhuman cry that carried over the might of the storm. He staggered along the edge, his clothing smouldering as sparks flew from his smoking weapon. His body stiffened and then relaxed, his legs gave way and he fell to the ground beneath, a charred and crumpled heap of rags.

Chapter Twenty-Three

Sunlight shimmered through the leafy boughs as Angharad, away on a hunting trip, paused a moment to rest. Before her was a stretch of open ground, heat rising from its sun baked grassy surface while, nearby, a stream trickled merrily through the undergrowth. Moving over to the brook, she stooped down and refreshed herself with its icy freshness. Five months had now passed since they had reclaimed The Shintae and, despite the warmth of the day, she shivered as she recalled that dreadful night. The choking ash had, at least, concealed their tracks and prevented anyone from tracing them to their refuge. As she sat down, her thoughts wandered back to their time in the cavern.

Hap had despaired of Kaér's life that first night, so ill had he been. Although the wound to his head had seemed insignificant, he remained deeply unconscious and for two days, they watched over him. Hap finally persuaded Angharad to take a break and walking round the inner sections of the cavern to ease some of the stiffness in her legs, she came across a passage leading underground. If nothing else, exploring it might help to take her mind off things and so, packing some food and plenty of lamp fat, she left Hap in charge of their patient. Marking the walls at regular intervals in case she became lost, she walked for what seemed hours, always taking the easiest route. She had almost lost hope of finding anything interesting when, in the distance, she glimpsed daylight. Increasing her pace, she hurried towards it.

Reaching the tunnel's end, she found herself at the side of a thickly wooded valley, surrounded by lofty mountain peaks. In spite of the ground being covered in snow, the air seemed relatively mild and from her elevated position, she could make out a number of game trails. Slithering down the hillside, she set off on a cursory inspection of the area. There was no trace of human occupation and, as far as she could tell, there was no other way in. It certainly would serve admirably as a hide out until Kaér was fit enough to travel again.

The hour was late and, finding a convenient natural shelter under a fallen tree, she decided to spend the night there.

Starting back early the next day, it was almost noon before she finally walked out of the tunnel. Helping herself to food and drink, she sat down wearily as Hap brought her up to date on their patient's condition. To her delight Angharad found Kaér was showing signs of improvement and, on a couple of occasions, had even regained consciousness. Convinced he was over the worst, Hap agreed. Once their patient was well enough to move, they would relocate to the valley.

The next few days passed uneventfully with Kaér waking more often and for longer periods. He remained weak but this was the least of his problems, there was something else terribly wrong. The blow to his head had robbed him of his past; his earliest memories were of waking in the cave. He even failed to recognize his own name whilst his companions were complete strangers. Hap could offer no prognosis; his skills as a healer were ineffective under these circumstances. Only time, perhaps, could cure Kaér but even this could not be guaranteed.

A week later with Kaér strong enough, physically, to move, they removed all signs of habitation from the cavern and headed underground. Mindful not to overtax his fragile strength, they took the journey at a steady pace, spending the night below ground. Arriving at the valley late the following morning, they started work on constructing a shelter, using the tunnel as a base for a few days until their new home was habitable. They talked constantly to Kaér, trying, without success, to jog his memory. He did not seem unduly worried by this lack of knowledge. In fact, his whole character had altered. Drive and energy, so essential a part of his being, were noticeably lacking and he took much persuading to perform even the simplest of tasks. Stories about his past fascinated him, but Angharad and Hap could tell he did not believe they were talking about him.

As his strength returned, they came to realise only details of his own life were affected. His ability with bow and sword remained undiminished, although rarely could he be bothered to apply himself to practise. On occasion, he took notice of the way they had constructed the shelter and passed comment on how it could be improved. The thoughts appeared to come unbidden out of his mind and it irritated Hap and Angharad considerably when, after not being able to remember the simplest thing about his life, Kaér could reel off the most complicated details about a thousand and one other things.

The one remaining, albeit vague, memory that still connected him to his earlier life was that of The Shintae. This he kept next to his chest in a leather bag, strung around his neck with twine. They had explained to him what it was and what it could do but at the time, he appeared little concerned. After much discussion, they decided to take it from him for safekeeping. This proved a grave mistake as, flying into an uncontrollable rage, Kaér drew his sword and threatened them both before taking off and hiding in the woods. When he eventually returned, several hours later, he remembered little of the incident and the others refrained from mentioning it. Hap privately concluded The Stone, having been Kaér's objective for much of his life, was so deeply entwined within his subconscious that he protected it now by instinct. One thing, nonetheless, was certain, he retained his considerable fighting capability and they risked real danger if they ever tried to remove The Stone again.

The weeks turned to months and Angharad made regular trips back to the cavern. Careful to leave no signs of her visits, she would study the land around. At first, numerous groups of Cantaéns could be observed scouring the countryside, presumably searching for them and, on still days, the sound of voices drifted over the moors from the valley beyond. Around two months ago though, all mountain top movement had ceased and she saw nothing for a while. Then, on one of her visits, a couple of weeks later, she was greeted by the sound of greatly increased activity coming from the valley, a commotion that continued for several days. At a loss to explain what was happening, she dared not investigate in case her curiosity betrayed their location. However, since then, the mountains had remained relatively silent and she had heard very little noise at all coming from below, almost as if the area had been abandoned.

Putting such thoughts out her mind, Angharad left the stream to concentrate on hunting, returning late that evening to their shelter with fresh meat for supper. After eating, they retired around the fire to keep warm as the temperature dropped rapidly so high up in the mountains. Kaér still showed no signs of recovering his memory and Angharad felt angry and frustrated at her inability to do anything about it. Gone was her friend's leadership, replaced by a meek subservience she found repugnant. As Kaér wandered off to his bed, Hap and Angharad began to discuss their situation in peace.

Both were deeply worried by the disappearance of the Cantaéns. The mountains must be deserted. If not, the profusion of wildlife Angharad had also observed on her more recent trips to the outside world, would not have moved into the district. This then was their problem: if the enemy had departed, then where was he now? Each time the question was asked, the answer was the same. It had to be Maraé and if that was the case, the High Council was in great need of The Shintae. The thing to be decided upon tonight was whether they dared set off and risk The Stone with Kaér in his present mental state, or wait a little longer in the vain hope he might recover. If the mountains really were deserted, it did not matter as they would be able to travel quickly and safely but, without Kaér's intimate knowledge of the secret ways, it would be nigh impossible if large areas were still occupied. Kaér could not even remember how to use The Shintae, never mind protect them with it. On top of everything else, he might just take it into his head to wander off. In fact, they were going to have great difficulty in persuading him to leave under any circumstances. The valley was the only home he could remember and it greatly upset him whenever the subject came up.

"There is only one thing we can do," announced Angharad in the end. "We must take a chance and leave tomorrow. We have to find out what's happening."

"No, no!" cried a pathetic voice. Kaér had not been asleep after all, he must have heard every word. "I won't go," he screamed at them in panic, leaping to his feet and fleeing into the night.

Hap shrugged his shoulders at the departing figure and turned to Angharad, a look of despair on his face. "What can we do with him?" he pleaded. "To take him with us in this condition is suicidal. He will bolt back here at the first opportunity. If he meets any Cantaéns on the way, they'll just relieve him of The Stone and everything we've done will have been for nothing,' he sighed, leaning back against one of the shelter's roof supports. He had a sudden thought: "When he returns and falls asleep, we'll have to rope him and, if necessary, drag him along with us."

From the tone of his voice, Angharad could tell Hap was not keen on the idea, but it was a potential solution. If a war was raging in Maraé, then it was their duty to return as swiftly as circumstances dictated. Even though they had great respect for the man Kaér had been, they could no longer allow this to affect their decisions. He had to come with them, either of his own volition or under duress. There was a second alternative, but neither of them felt able to voice it aloud. It remained a choice that might yet have to be made. They had tarried far too long already and the life of one Maraén could not be justifiably balanced against those of the whole nation.

Settling down they awaited his return, but it was many hours before he ventured back. Pretending to be asleep, they listened as he entered and sat down in a corner, crooning to himself as he rocked gently to and fro.

Succumbing to exhaustion, his body relaxed and his breathing steadied. Silently, Angharad left her bed and as Hap joined her, they gathered up the rope.

"I'm sorry it has had to come to this," Angharad whispered as she dropped the noose down over Kaér's head, drawing it tightly over his arms. "It's the last thing I ever wanted to do but some day, I hope, you might understand why we did it."

Quickly, while he stirred uneasily in his dreams, they bound his hands and feet together. Keeping a watch by his side, they were ready when he awakened mid morning with a start. Finding himself unable to move, Kaér began to panic. Violently, he thrashed about and it was a little while before the soothing words of his companions penetrated his mind. His struggles subsided as he realised The Shintae was still next to his skin, listening to what the others had to say. At the thought of leaving the valley, he again became agitated and they were forced to reassure him once more.

Eventually, he appeared to accept the inevitable and settled down as they made breakfast, Hap feeding him while Angharad packed their supplies. Satisfied they had everything they needed, they split Kaér's pack between them and removed the ropes binding his legs. Standing up in silence, he meekly followed on behind Hap with Angharad bringing up the rear, holding tightly on to the rope that connected her to Kaér.

The passage was a stiff hundred foot climb above the valley bottom and just before the entrance, a section of the path crumbled beneath Kaér's feet. With his hands tied, he was unable to avoid tumbling backward. Desperately, Angharad tried to halt his descent, but the rope was snatched from her hands. Rolling faster and faster, Kaér plummeted down to land with a sickening thud on the ground below. Shocked at the suddenness of the mishap, they scurried down to the still and silent figure below. By the time they reached him, however, he was beginning to stir and they prayed he was not badly hurt.

Helping him into a sitting position Hap quickly checked Kaér for injury, but nothing seemed to be broken. He must have cracked his head on the way down as, beneath the hairline, the scar from his original injury had re-opened. Stanching the flow of blood, they cleaned the wound, bound a strip of cloth around his head and helped him to his feet. He appeared a little dazed and disorientated but when asked if he was fit enough to continue, he nodded and they began the ascent again. This time he was roped front and back and without further incident, they soon reached the entrance.

Maintaining a steady pace, they worked their way through the mountain, arriving at the other side early in the evening. Here they stopped to rest and eat but Kaér, complaining of a severe headache, would touch nothing. He was, in fact, severely troubled. The blow to his head had unlocked large, though mainly unconnected, tracts of memory. As more of his past flooded back, he was left confused finding real doubts as to his identity. Was he actually this mythical figure of whom the others had spoken, or was he the person he had found himself to be in the valley? As increasingly larger pieces of the jigsaw clicked into position, he found himself discounting his recent personality. Then, suddenly, came the moment of realisation. He was Kaér, the guardian of The Shintae. Everything became clear, his life, travels, and finally, the expedition to Mount Subae. He remembered the eruption, the subsequent flight, and then tripping and falling. The recent months faded as if they were a dream and sitting up straight, he looked directly at his companions.

"I won't be requiring these bindings any more, thank you," he uttered to the astonished pair. "I'm perfectly well now, my memory's back and it's very uncomfortable sitting like this. So, Hap, do come and untie me. I promise not to do anything stupid."

Hap could do nothing but stare, dumbfounded. The firm and decisive tone of the old Kaér, likewise left Angharad stunned. The fall must have jolted Kaér's mind and brought him back to his senses but, even so, they must be sure before they released him. Recovering her wits after a moment or two, Angharad began to speak.

"Do you remember what happened?" she asked and, as Kaér replied, they both fired question after question at him about his life. He soon convinced them he was his old self and, rushing over, Angharad untied the ropes and embraced him.

"Typical!" proclaimed Kaér as Angharad released him. "Some people become excited over the slightest thing. No self control at all," he added with a smile.

There was, however, one final test to be performed and though she detested having to do it, Angharad knew there was no alternative if they were to be one hundred percent certain.

"May I have a look at The Shintae?" she requested as Hap gave her a sharp stare.

"Certainly," Kaér replied unconcernedly. "Here you are," he said, dropping it out of the leather bag into Angharad's outstretched hand.

Angharad studied The Stone as Kaér asked innumerable questions about the last few months. His memories of this period were fading rapidly as his old life re-established itself. As Hap kept him talking, Angharad, in an apparent act of absent-mindedness, slipped The Shintae into her pocket and leapt up.

"Drat!" she exclaimed. "I've dropped something back down the tunnel. I won't be long," she called as she set off back along the passage.

Hap sat expectantly, waiting to see if Kaér would rush after her, but he paid no attention to Angharad's rapid departure and continued with his questioning. Half an hour later, she reappeared and, as Kaér turned to greet her, Hap mouthed everything was all right. Taking The Shintae from her pocket, she gave it back to Kaér who accepted it without a second glance and placed it back inside its pouch for safekeeping.

"Did you find it then?" he inquired suddenly.

"Er! No, it must be much farther back," Angharad replied, shrugging her shoulders. "It doesn't matter, it wasn't anything terribly important."

"Oh! Well, never mind then," Kaér said, dismissing the whole episode.

They talked long into the night, telling of their fears for the safety of Maraé. Kaér's face grew grave as he was forced to agree with their conclusions.

"We must make haste," he stated at the end. "If you've read the signs correctly, we're at least two months behind. It will be a long, weary and dangerous road, but we must endeavour to overtake them."

Taking to their beds, they catnapped until the faint light of dawn tinted the skies. Rising quickly, they breakfasted in silence and, within half an hour, were on the move. On reaching the Subrat Valley, they descended the rocky hillside and, turning east, followed in the tracks of the Cantaén armies. Keeping a careful lookout for supply convoys, the evidence for which was all around them, they eventually moved northwards out of the valley. Nearing Mount Subae's smoking peak, they circled around the devastated area and after checking his bearings, Kaér set a course that would take them clear of the most widely travelled roadways. As these were filled with a constant movement of people and supplies, it was fortunate that he did.

The weeks flew by as they worked their way across Cantaé. Keeping mainly to the high ground, they headed in a northeasterly direction. Although not the most direct of ways, it should put them at the edge of the main areas of enemy concentration on reaching Maraé. Occasionally, on hearing or seeing enemy groups, they backtracked and tried alternative routes. Attempting to fight their way through was not worth the risk of losing The Stone and, to use it, would attract the attention of every Cantaén within fifty miles.

It took almost eight weeks before the three of them stood, desperately weary, on top of a ridge overlooking Waén, the most northerly of the border villages. Barely a week had passed since the fall of Rostic, far away in the distant east. They did not know exactly what they would find down below, but they were sure it would not be pleasant. They had recently come across the tracks of a large detachment of the enemy and, as the sun hovered over the peaks behind, they followed their footsteps down the steep and winding path.

Night fell before they reached the base of the ridge and in the darkness, they made their way along a forest trail. The air was still with only the sound of their movement to break the uncanny silence that pervaded the area. No owls hooted, no creatures rustled in the undergrowth and Kaér could sense no enemy presence, in fact there was nothing. A cold shiver ran down their spines.

"This bodes no good," Angharad whispered to Kaér as they walked side by side down the path.

"I think we ought to make camp here tonight," Hap called softly from behind.

"So close to shelter?" queried Angharad with a hint of surprise in her voice. "Another ten minutes or so and we'll be there."

"You are still young yet," Kaér spoke for the first time. "Hap and I have travelled widely and seen sights we'd hoped you might never have to experience. We will camp here tonight and pay our last respects in the morning. The things you'll witness then will stay with you forever and, if I were you, I would not willingly wish to see them by moonlight."

"But we don't know they're all dead," interjected Angharad, her mind refusing to accept the truth of what Kaér was saying. "Surely, some might have escaped and crept back after the Cantaéns had moved on or, maybe, there are some prisoners we can set free."

"We have to face facts," Hap broke in gently as Kaér spread his blanket out on the grassy banking beside the path. "Did you see the smoke from their fires when we were on the ridge? No, you didn't. Did you, perchance, catch sight of any movement from below? No, because there wasn't any. Where are the outer sentries? We should have encountered them by now. Have you forgotten so soon the lessons of your own skirmish with the Cantaéns in the forest? No, I didn't think so. Come, let's rest and try not to think of tomorrow," he ceased talking and Angharad, at last, had to admit the truth she had tried so hard to deny.

Later in the evening, she settled down but her mind was too restless to accommodate sleep and, staring at the stars, she remained lost in thought for some considerable time.

A bank of cloud moved in during the early hours and a fine drizzle greeted them at dawn, doing little to raise their spirits. All were depressed by a largely sleepless night and the thought of what was to come. None felt like eating and so, with heavy hearts, they started down the path. All too soon they found themselves on the outskirts of what had once been a thriving village. Filled with apprehension they entered through the main gateway, the heavy wooden barriers swinging gently in the breeze. At first little appeared out of place but as they entered the surrounding buildings the full horror of their expectations was realised. Angharad left hastily to await the others out in the woods. They followed shortly afterwards, faces ashen and drawn. Together they said a short prayer before retiring farther down the path.

"Shall we not bury the dead? inquired Angharad after they had come to a halt.

"No!" replied Kaér, emotion sharpening his tone. "We don't have time. We will be hard put to do anything for those who still live. I'm afraid you'll see many more sights like this before we're through."

"Yes," responded a subdued Angharad. "I suppose you're right."

"Oh, do come on," interrupted Hap, stamping his foot irately. "We can't waste precious minutes standing around discussing the dead. Forget them, they're beyond caring."

This apparent callousness caused Angharad and Kaér to spin round in amazement but on seeing the expression that lay deep within his eyes, however, they realised it was burning anger and not indifference that spurred his words. Without further ado, they turned towards the east and increased their pace.

A week passed and they began to despair as it became clear how swift and deadly the Cantaén advance had been. Although now hardened to the sights they witnessed, Angharad was almost ready to give up with Hap not far behind her in his despondency. Only Kaér's indomitable spirit kept them going. Despite his words of encouragement, even Kaér now accepted they were going to be too late to be of assistance, the final battles would be over long before they could hope to reach Myssous. He had The Shintae, though, and the knowledge to use its power. The might of Cantaé would be ended forever; he was going to make sure of that.

A fortnight after leaving Waén, a miracle happened. They had just skirted round another victim of the Cantaén advance when, carried on the wind, came the sound of hooves pounding towards them. Unsure of what to expect, they concealed themselves at the side of the road and settled down to watch. As the noise grew louder, they drew their swords, ready to defend themselves. Almost as a blinding flash, Angharad realised what it was and, throwing down her weapon, she leapt out onto the road as four snorting creatures galloped round a corner to their left. Kaér joined her almost instantly as the charging beasts skidded to a halt and stood in a panting, stomping huddle some ten yards away.

Calling softly to the nervous animals, Kaér and Angharad advanced cautiously towards them. Initially, the beasts shied away but gradually, the soothing sounds of voices distantly remembered began to calm them. To Hap's astonishment his companions moved closer to the animals, reaching up to pat their trembling necks. The remains of bridles were still in place and taking hold of them, Kaér and Angharad led the sweating creatures off to one side of the road. Hap, meanwhile, had kept well in the background; these monstrous things were beyond his experience. After much persuasion, he came near enough to pass them some rope and after picketing the beasts on a grassy bank, they quickly rubbed them down.

"What are they?" questioned an amazed Hap as they rejoined him. "And, more to the point, now you've caught them, what are you going to do with them? Roast them for dinner?"

"Cook them!" exploded Angharad with laughter at the very idea. "These aren't for eating. These fine creatures will carry us to Myssous and, with luck, do so before the Cantaéns reach there."

"Don't look so surprised," grinned Kaér, "they aren't monsters, you know, just some of the Paéns we've told you about."

"Ah! Now I understand," he replied thoughtfully, some of the doubts clearing from his mind. "I never thought I'd actually see one and now you produce four out of nowhere," he continued, peering a little closer. "I'd have expected the Cantaéns to have either killed or made use of them."

"We thought the same," Angharad said. "They must have escaped during the raids. Now, we have one apiece and a spare to carry our packs."

"Does that mean I have to ride one?" observed Hap somewhat dubiously. "That's going to slow us down somewhat."

"Only for a day or so," Kaér replied cheerfully, "and then we'll all be travelling like the wind."

Although Hap looked extremely doubtful, he listened attentively to their instructions. Raiding their packs, Angharad placed a blanket over the back of nearest Paén and, after putting off the dreadful moment for as long as possible,

Hap finally consented to be hoisted on top. They walked him around, holding on to the animal's reins until Hap became more confident and a little less unstable. There was no point in breaking their journey to let him practise as he could just as easily learn on the move. Finding blankets for the other Paéns, the travellers tied their supplies securely to the pack animal and, mounting, set off at a trot.

To begin with, Hap experienced great difficulty staying on his beast but, as the days flew by, he became more proficient and their rate of travel increased dramatically. In spite of his progress, he found it almost beyond belief that sitting down all day could make him so weary. On rare occasions, he even managed a good word for his steed, but never at the end of a gruelling ride.

Eleven days after the arrival of the Paéns, the riders gazed down upon the ocean for the first time. Moving out onto the beach, they dismounted stiffly and picketed the animals on grass-covered dunes. Angharad threw off her outer travel stained clothes and raced across the sands towards the ocean. Kaér and Hap did likewise and soon caught up with Angharad. Reaching the water's edge the trio launched themselves into the gentle waves like children. For a good hour, they played in the water beneath the midday sun before racing back to their supplies. Angharad, collecting a fresh outfit, went off to change leaving the others laughing and shouting. Towelling themselves dry, they dressed in clean clothes, their spirits lighter than for many a long day.

Cheerfully, over a meal, they contemplated the future as seagulls wheeled above, screeching noisily as they dived for scraps the travellers threw for them.

"The going will be far easier now," Kaér remarked as they finished eating. "The coast road is well travelled and by far the best maintained in the whole of Maraé. Unless we meet any unforeseen delays, we will come up with the enemy or be in sight of Myssous within eight days."

"It could be longer than that," Angharad interjected. "There's a storm brewing out there," she added, pointing to the distant horizon, "and it's going hit the coast sometime during the next few days." The others stared at her in amazement.

"Since when did you become a prophet?" queried Hap. "The day's fine, not a cloud to be seen anywhere and yet you conclude there's a storm's coming." Turning to Kaér, he grinned and said, "It must be the salt water that's affected her brain, the woman's gone mad."

"Ah! That explains everything," Kaér laughed in reply. "We'll have to tie her to her Paén to protect her from herself. Ouch!" he exclaimed as Angharad leaned across and cuffed him. "See, Hap, she's attacking me now for no reason at all. You'd better go and fetch the ropes."

"Listen, you oafs," spluttered Angharad indignantly, "I've lived most of my life by the sea and, like other such people, have developed an instinct for these things. I can tell you here and now there is a storm on the way. I feel it in the air and smell it on the breeze. Within four days you'll be scurrying for shelter and, I hope, if only for my sake, you find it, otherwise we face the prospect of a most unpleasant time out in the open. Oh, and another thing," she announced, leaping up, "it might have escaped your notice but we have a journey to finish and I, for one, intend to carry on with it. Follow if you so desire." Untying her steed, she jumped onto its back and, gathering the lead rope of the pack animal, galloped away across the dunes towards the coast road. Once there, she stayed her pace and awaited the arrival of her companions.

Following her example, they soon joined her and, together, continued on their way. The landscape flashed by as they raced on, hurtling passed village after village, each filled with its own horrific sights. Rostic's warning had been too late to save this region and the rider's earlier mood of optimism began to fade.

Chapter Twenty-Four

With a good road beneath them, the trio made excellent time pushing themselves and their steeds to the limits of endurance. Every morning Angharad would sniff the air and declare the storm was drawing nearer but, as the weather remained fine and sunny, the others continued to disregard her warnings. Before the sun set each evening, they sought out some deserted hut or cabin for shelter as nothing could persuade them to stay inside the charnel houses the villages had become.

It was noon on the fourth day after reaching the coast when Angharad suddenly reined in, calling on the others to halt. Now was the time, she said, to head for cover. Neither Kaér nor Hap could perceive any signs of a storm but Angharad remained adamant and so, with much reluctance, they followed her inland. Before long she found a stone built house, obviously abandoned for some years, standing on higher ground a mile from the coast road, sheltered from the seaward side by a small ridge. After stabling the Paéns in a stoutly constructed barn attached to the dwelling, under Kaér's direction, they started work on making the building as watertight and wind-proof as they were able. Labouring for several hours, they were compelled to finish their task by lamplight, but long before completion the freshening of the wind had become quite noticeable. The temperature was falling rapidly and, once Kaér was satisfied the work was adequate, they retired inside to light a fire. A large stockpile of wood had been discovered in the barn and they fetched ample supplies through. Huddling around the blazing logs for warmth, they could hear the wind howling by. Storm clouds were building and, shortly afterwards, the rain started beating against the cottage walls.

Overnight, the conditions continued to deteriorate and they were frequently woken by the howling gale. For two long days they sheltered from the savagery of the elements, which seemed bent on destroying everything in their path.

Trees were uprooted and large areas of the plain were under water, flooded by torrential rain and exceptionally high tides. The travellers knew nothing of this until the fury of the storm abated and they were able to venture forth once more. To begin with they passed their time in idle conversation, but it was not long before Hap noticed a subtle change in the relationship between Kaér and Angharad. He smiled to himself as they became closer, a touch of hands, a stolen kiss when they thought he was not looking. He suddenly felt very old indeed and took to spending much of his time in the other rooms to allow them privacy. Who knew what would befall them in the days to come? This might well be the only time in the world they had left to be together.

On the third day, although the air was cool and the wind blustery, only ragged edged clouds raced overhead with just the occasional shower to lash the land. The scale of damage that greeted them when they moved outside, although not entirely unexpected, still caused some surprise. Mounting the ridge, they could see that even the coast road, constructed on higher ground, had been washed away in places. They decided that for a while at least, they would make better progress by moving inland. Shivering in the cool air, they returned to the cottage for a final meal.

"Do you really think anyone can have survived?" questioned Angharad as they finished eating. "Up to now it seems as if those mountain devils have had everything their own way. Apart from the odd isolated incident, they have taken every community by surprise. Even where there has been evidence of resistance, it has been short lived and ineffective. Perhaps it is already too late!"

"Never give up hope," replied Hap, sensing Angharad's despair. "When that dies then so do we, they cannot have gone much further without the alarm being raised. Do not forget, we are coming to areas that were highly populated and someone must have seen their approach. Cheer up, have faith in your countrymen."

"I suppose so," Angharad murmured, "but a little more of me seems to die every time we pass another village, knowing what lies inside. Yes! You're right—I must cast away these gloomy thoughts. We will be in time. We have to be in time."

"Then let us depart," commanded Kaér, rising to his feet. "We must travel like we have never done before. We must be as swift as the wind, nay, swifter still. The deliverance of our people is here," he shouted, pulling The Shintae from its leather bag and holding it up aloft for them to see. "Nishrigg, Um-at-il-aa," he whispered and The Stone responded, glowing with a deep golden inner luminescence. Gently, it pulsated for a moment before becoming dormant again. "As The Stone answers its call now, then so it will again when the need is great," he said, returning it to its hiding place.

Silence descended as his outburst subsided and Angharad found new strength had entered her body. It could have been The Shintae or, perhaps, Kaér's words that rekindled her faith. Either way it did not matter, the result was the same. They seized their packs and raced outside to the barn. Leading the Paéns into the open, they mounted and galloped inland in the wake of the dying storm where, once beyond the main areas of damage, they turned south and struck out for Myssous.

Entering Priorvic, the third village after leaving the cottage, they found, for the first time since setting foot on Maraén soil, a different picture. A warning must have been given, finally. Waving her arms about, Angharad let rip a Maraén war cry. The call echoed through the ruined, empty streets, before being carried away on the wind. The residual happiness, however, remained with her as they galloped away. From there on, most communities they came across were burnt to the ground and, in time, they came across growing evidence of resistance and ambush, some of it quite recent. They avoided all contact with the small groups of enemy forces they observed, seen mainly scavenging through ruined townships. The small size of the units led them to the conclusion that Sartae must have pulled in the bulk of his troops for the final assault.

The weather continued to improve and after six days of constant travel, they halted in near darkness for a final camp before reaching Myssous. So close to their destination, all three were on edge and even when not on watch, they failed to catch more than an hour or two of sleep. In the grey light of early morn they ate a cold breakfast. Perhaps, a thought passed through Hap's mind, this could be their last meal. From here on, they were entering dangerous territory, where the enemy had concentrated his entire fighting force. Not one of them spoke; they all knew the risks they faced and until they saw how the land lay, they could make no firm plans for action.

The race was almost at an end and, mounting their steeds, they sped south keeping a wary eye out for signs of the Cantaéns. All morning they rode without sight of the enemy but in the distance, they could see columns of smoke rising from the direction of Myssous. Faster and faster charged the Paéns, sensing the urgency of the riders who held on grimly to their mount's heaving backs, the ground hurtling by at a frightening rate. The atmosphere grew heavier all the while but still they continued their chase, pausing only occasionally for the sake of the animals.

Noon came and passed as Myssous came into view, slowly growing larger as the riders weaved their way through the mass of ruined villages towards the towering cliffs. Drawing nearer, they passed by thousands of empty tents and, far away, they could make out the glint of sunlight reflecting from steel clad helmets on the walls above Myssous. In their hearts, they knew their beloved city was falling even as they rode. *Let us be in time*, they prayed over and over again.

Thick black clouds were gathering overhead and the distant sounds of thunder rolled across the plain towards them. The storm struck, catching them in its downpour as lightning flashed all around. The driving rain and mud, flying from the Paén's hooves blended both riders and their mounts into one as they hurtled towards a ruined village standing directly in their path. In a flash of lighting, they caught sight of a figure on the far side of the village square, leaning against a crumbling structure. Upon seeing them, the figure turned and staggered across the cobbled market area, disappearing through the open doorway of the one remaining building left standing.

As they wheeled into the open space and reined in before the smoke-stained frontage, the stranger appeared on the flat roof above, screaming down at them but the words were lost in the clamour of the storm. The figure raised a sword high in the air just as a fork of lightning arched down from above, earthing through the outstretched metal. Falling, the body landed at their feet as the air exploded above in an almighty crash, their startled mounts shied, plunging and leaping about. Bringing his Paén back under control, Kaér, keeping a tight hold of the reins, dismounted and stepped over to the smouldering bundle on the ground. Stooping, he retrieved something lying on the ground beside the head of the remains and, holding it aloft, strode back to rejoin the others.

"Look," he shouted over the thunder. "It's the authority of the leader of the Cantaén Guard. This has to be the body of Sartae. It must be an omen," he called, jumping back up on to his steed. "Come, let's ride while we still have time."

Cantering passed the remains of Cerdic, Kaér failed to recognise him, just another body lying on the ground. Turning towards the roads that led to the ascent of the plateau above, they raced on beneath the towering cliffs. The final meeting between Kaér and Sartae had not been as either had imagined it would be, although the result was just as decisive. With his death, the storm seemed to lose heart and as it rumbled away into the distance, the sun came out sending clouds of steam rising from the waterlogged ground. The trio had almost gained the road to the top when a group of fierce warriors leapt out from the rocks around. Desperately the riders pulled up and as they shouted aloud, the archers ceased firing on recognizing the Maraén tongue of their victims. Members of a guerrilla band, they had taken them for more Cantaén devilry.

"Stop," cried Angharad. "What makes you fire upon your own? Have you taken leave of your senses?"

"Who are you?" shouted back the leader of the group, still suspecting trickery.

"I'm Angharad," came the reply, "and these are my companions, Kaér and Hap. We have returned with The Shintae by long and arduous routes to save the nation, not to be killed by our own like some common Cantaén trash. Stand aside and let us pass, our charge is sorely needed up above."

"But you're dead!" the astounded leader replied, falling back in amazement at this revelation. "We thought you lost long ago in the mountains. Can it be true, do you really have the ancient Stone of power in your possession?"

"Yes, of course it's true. But why are you down here and not above?"

"The city's walls are breached and the gates lie open. The enemy is within Myssous and defeat is inevitable," retorted the leader in sorrow. "The Cantaéns will soon take to the sea and, once they discover the islands where our families have taken refuge, Maraé will be gone forever. We have fought from deep behind enemy lines for some months now and are returning to the woods. We intend to make them suffer for as long as we're able."

"Then raise your spirits," triumphed Angharad as she pointed to her strangely silent companion, "this is Kaér, the guardian of The Shintae."

Turning, they gasped in horror as Kaér slid slowly from his Paén, falling to the ground beneath its feet. Leaping down, Angharad threw herself down at his side, followed closely by Hap. Carefully they turned him over so all could see the dreadful wound inflicted by a Maraén arrow. How cruel was the fate that had taken Kaér through so much to save his nation, only to fall at the very hands of the ones he had suffered to save. He was still alive, but barely, as Hap tried to stanch the heavy bleeding issuing from where the arrow had torn into his side. Kaér opened his eyes and spoke in a whisper to the assembly around him.

"Make haste," he said, "before it's too late. I have so little time left and I must reach the summit and see the city for myself. Put me back on my steed now and tie me to it," his voice faded and only the bright feverish light in his eyes told them he was still conscious.

Gently they lifted him back upon his mount, arrow still embedded, and lashed his legs beneath. To attempt to remove the missile would only cause further damage and even greater blood loss. Angharad looked across at Hap who shook his head. There was nothing more they could do, except pray his determination kept him going long enough to use The Stone. Saddened, the Maraén group parted and let them pass. Kaér's steed, feeling the weakness of its master, bore him steadily up the winding road, never once putting a foot wrong on the precipitous journey. At last, they entered through the arched portals and onto the plateau beyond, heading straight for the gates of the capital.

A red mist floated before Kaér's eyes and he longed to lie down and sleep, to slide peacefully into the welcoming arms of death. The initial numbness, experienced after the pain of the arrow's penetration, had been replaced by waves of agony radiating from the wound, setting his whole body on fire. Perspiration beaded his brow as he gritted his teeth, forcing himself to continue, his hold on reality becoming more tentative with every passing moment. He knew he must activate The Shintae soon, before weakness robbed him of the chance, but some inner compulsion compelled him to struggle on across the plateau. Whatever it was, it hovered at the back of his mind and try as he may, he could not drag it from the depths of his subconscious. For some reason he had to witness with his own eyes how parlous was the state of the Maraén forces, the words *only when all is lost* kept beating inside his head and he would fight back the pain and continue.

Angharad and Hap little knew what drove their dying friend to carry on, both wept openly at the sight of his deathly pallor. Through the depredation of battle they rode, as the distant city walls grew ever larger. Approaching the open gates, a party of Cantaéns ran out, bearing the spoils of battle. Spotting the advancing riders, they threw down their ill-gotten gains and loosed off a wild volley of arrows towards them. As the fog momentarily cleared from Kaér's mind, he fumbled inside the folds of his tunic and pulled out the leather pouch. Shaking The Stone into his right hand, he held it aloft and spoke softly. It glowed with energy as fire flashed from within and the enemy fell to the ground. His vision clouded again but, with The Shintae still held tightly in his hand, he moved forwards and passed unscathed into the Citadel itself.

Scenes of destruction lay all around; Maraén bodies mixed with those of the enemy were piled high in abandoned mounds. Ruined buildings gaped wide in silent misery. From ahead came the sound of conflict and Kaér suddenly knew the time had come. A strange darkness was creeping over him and, making a supreme effort of will, he forced it back. His eyes focused as he surveyed the dreadful scenes around him and then the veil lifted from his mind as the words of Stakirum came clearly to him. Now he understood why he had to see for himself. An ironic smiled played on his lips as he thought of what he must do. He, who had only ever wanted peace, was about to unleash such destruction as had never been seen since the days of the ancients. Angharad and Hap stared in wonder as they observed a strange glow emanating from his face. Sitting bolt upright, Kaér opened his mouth and began to shout aloud in a voice so strong they forgot all about his injury. For a few brief moments they knew the Kaér of old, standing firm and strong, seemingly indestructible.

"Streen-A-Canbar-i-Alwar," he intoned, continuing in a like manner for some time, a string of meaningless sounds to any who heard them. On The Shintae, however, they had a magical effect.

The Stone swelled in size and turned deep red in colour, pulsating in a complex rhythm. Lightning flashed, thunder roared as tongues of fire flowed out from within, filling the sky with their awesome presence. Everywhere, Cantaéns fell to the ground writhing as the flaming barbs penetrated deep within their bodies. More and more energy flowed from The Stone as retribution spread throughout the forests and across the mountains, seeking out the enemy until all of a like mind had suffered a similar fate. The only one to escape was Biren, although he suffered a raging fever for many days in the distant lands where he had taken refuge and was lucky to survive.

Gradually The Shintae diminished in size and power and, as it ceased to pulsate, Kaér's whole body tensed in agony. Gripping The Stone tightly in his clenched fist, he pulled it to his chest and collapsed over the back of his sturdy mount. Flying from their own Paéns, the others raced to his side, cutting the ropes that bound him, easing him to the ground. With unsteady hands, Hap checked for a pulse and found a faint whisper.

"Has…has…he gone yet," Angharad stammered tremulously cradling his head in her lap.

"No," Hap said, covering him with a blanket, "but he can't last much longer. Only his desire to see the mission through has kept him going this long," he broke down and it was a little while before they noticed how dark it had become.

Thick black smoke seemed to be rising from all around and they realised the bodies of the Cantaéns were afire, each one blazing with a flame so bright it hurt the eyes to look. Even as they watched, the remains blackened and crumbled away, turning to a dust so fine it spiralled skywards to join the ever-increasing darkness above. Within minutes, the land was cleared of the evil desecration, as the cloud grew larger, shutting out the sun as it spread rapidly outwards from Myssous. Kaér's eyes shot open and, for a moment, he looked at his companions and smiled one final time. Putting The Stone to his lips, he whispered something too faint for them to hear. He tried to speak to Angharad as she held tightly on to his hand, but only a sigh escaped, he stiffened momentarily and then his body relaxed and Hap could no longer feel a pulse.

"It's over," Hap whispered in sorrow.

Before Angharad could speak, a beam of light shone out from The Shintae, piercing the smoke and dust above. A wind blew up from the land and the cloud was driven out to sea, lost forever over the distant waves. The beam remained for a short time in the evening sky, a triumphal beacon to those who had survived their darkest hour, before fading away leaving The Stone to shine with a brilliant silver light in Kaér's lifeless hand. Faintly, they heard sounds of surprise and bewilderment echoing through the city streets towards them but, ignoring all distractions, they tended the body of their friend.

Pulling the blanket over his face, they placed his hand, still clutching The Shintae, above his silenced heart. Improvising a bier from spears and blankets, they laid him on top and carried him through the winding streets of Myssous, to the very summit of the highest point. Crowds of survivors made way for them, staring in wonder at their burden with the brightly shining star on top. Many of them recognized Angharad, but the expression on her face and that of her companion made them draw back, their questions unasked. Dimly, they understood the silent walkers bore a grief too deep to share and that, somehow, they had wrought the miracle that had saved them. Spreading out, the crowds formed an archway of honour with their swords as the bearers approached the tower on the hill. Entering the marbled hallway, they gently placed their burden down on top of a long, carved wooden table. The Shintae had now become inert and they removed it from Kaér's icy grasp. Taking a golden tapestry from the walls, they covered him before leaving him to rest in peace.

Stepping outside, a group of councillors approached, still in an obvious state of shock, the suddenness of their deliverance beyond their comprehension. Seeing they were unable to grasp the significance of events, Angharad retained hold of The Shintae. Taking charge, she inquired if any present had knowledge of the ancient words and The Shintae. A wizened councillor, standing to the rear of the group, spoke up.

"I, Mustric, am versed in these matters," he said, his eyes brightening as he realised Angharad held the relic in her hand.

"Here, take it and go quickly," she charged the startled Patriarch. "Use it wisely; there are many lying at death's door whose lives might yet be saved. Hap," she turned to her friend, "please go with him, your skills are of paramount importance too."

They both nodded and disappeared into the crowd as, turning to the throng, Angharad shouted above the general clamour.

"The wounded are everywhere, bring the most serious cases to the healers immediately and make the others comfortable while they wait their turn. Hurry, there is still much to do," she commanded as the multitude split up, rushing to carry out her instructions. Followed by the remaining members of the High Council, Angharad returned inside the tower.

"There lays the body of Kaér," she said quietly, holding back her tears, as they looked curiously towards the table. "It is because of him you are freed this day from the tyranny of Cantaé."

"How did he die?" inquired Alfwin, the leader of the High Council, coming out of his stunned state.

Moving away and entering into an antechamber, they sat down as Angharad related the saga of their journey. By midnight, she had concluded her story, but they continued to question her until the small hours, halting when no more could be extracted from her tired mind. Turning towards her, Alfwin, who had previously been deep in thought, suddenly asked a very strange question.

"When you removed The Shintae from Kaér's body, what colour was it?" he demanded. "Was it still silver or had it returned to normal?"

"Er! I don't know," answered Angharad vaguely, confused by the question. "I think it was normal. Yes I'm sure it was," she remembered hesitantly, dismissing the question as irrelevant.

"I must go to Hap," she said, jumping to her feet. "I've spent too long here as it is, there's much I can do to assist him and you have the future of Maraé to consider. I commend Kaér to your charge. We will return to bury him with the full honour he deserves."

Alfwin made to speak but Angharad was already gone. Directing the other members of the High Council to begin the mammoth task of organizing the survivors, he went through to the entrance hall. Enlisting the assistance of two passing soldiers he placed Kaér's body onto a stretcher and, between them, they carried him out into the darkness.

Working night and day, snatching a moment's rest whenever they could, Hap and Mustric, along with other skilled healers, eventually treated the last of those in desperate need of their specialist skills. Angharad had laboured with them and, like Hap, had managed to shut out her anguish with hard work. Now, with others well able to tend to the needs of the recovering wounded, they were left with little to occupy them and their sorrow returned in full. Five days had now passed since their arrival in Myssous and it was time to inter Kaér into his final resting place. Sadly, they returned to the tower, expecting to find his body lying in state, but there was no trace of him. Approaching some of the council members, they learnt no one had seen his body since the day of their deliverance. On asking for a meeting with Alfwin, they discovered he was out of town.

Angharad was frantic with grief; surely, they would not have buried him without telling them. They dashed outside the city walls where fields had become vast graveyards, frantically asking the workers if they knew anything. They shook their heads. What was one more body among so many? A plan had been drawn up showing where those whose names were known had been placed, but Kaér's was not listed and thousands of other locations were marked unknown. In despair, Angharad and Hap walked back to the city, asking everywhere for news of Kaér, or Alfwin, but to no avail. Boatloads of returning refugees were pouring in from the far side of the plateau and the couple became caught up in the throng. The streets were alive with hustle and bustle. Everybody seemed to be looking for someone—family or friend. For three days, Angharad and Hap searched the highways and byways until, on the point of giving up, a child came racing up to them.

"Are you Angharad and Hap," she inquired shyly, "the two who brought in the body of Kaér?"

"Yes, we are," Angharad replied kindly, crouching down and looking her in the eye, "Why do you ask, do you know where they've taken him?" she asked, hope rising in her heart.

"Follow me," she said, turning round and skipping off down the road. "You may call me Alicia," she called back as they hurried in pursuit. "Grandfather sent me to find you."

"And who might your grandfather be?" Hap asked as they caught up to her.

"Why, Alfwin of course," she said as they pushed their way through the mass of people entering through the city gates, shortly leaving the capital behind them.

As Alicia dashed on ahead, they followed as best they could, filled with questions she either could not, or would not answer. Going beyond the burial grounds, they crossed a stretch of open parkland and entered a tiny village, virtually untouched by the ravages of war. A large house stood fifty yards back from the roadway and, as they walked up the garden path, the door opened and an elderly woman welcomed them inside.

"Come in," she said smiling, "my husband awaits you in his study," she indicated a doorway at the far end of a narrow corridor, "just knock and walk in. Now Alicia," she said, taking hold of the child's hand and walking away, "I've just taken some cakes out of the oven…"

Mystified, Angharad looked at Hap who shrugged his shoulders and indicated for her to lead the way. Knocking on the door they entered to find Alfwin standing by the window, overlooking the remains of what had once been a garden. Before he had chance to say anything, Angharad spoke out, unable to hold back the frustration that had been growing inside her.

"What have you done with him?" she demanded furiously. "We've searched everywhere. I just hope you have not buried him in an unmarked grave. All I ever asked was that you took care of his body until I got back."

"Why would I bury him," Alfwin answered quickly, "Kaér wasn't dead. In fact, he still lives," he added to Angharad and Hap's stunned disbelief.

"That's not possible," snapped Angharad, angered by Alfwin's reply. "How can you say that? You didn't see the wound nor watch, helplessly, as his life's blood drained away. You weren't there when, after saving you all, he collapsed. I was and so too was Hap, we saw him die," she ceased her outburst and buried her face in her hands, too upset to continue.

"It's all right," Alfwin continued gently, "I'm neither mad, nor in the business of creating false hopes. Open your minds and think back clearly to that day. The retribution Kaér unleashed upon the Cantaéns is beyond the High Council's comprehension and, as to how he came by such knowledge, we just do not know. However, what I do know is that he must have said something else, afterwards, just before a final ray of light shone out. Am I not right?" he asked softly.

Lifting her head, Angharad nodded in confirmation, a puzzled expression on her face. "Yes, he put The Stone to his mouth and whispered something but we couldn't make out what it was. How can this be of any significance?"

"Ah! Do not forget, Kaér studied the records of The Shintae for many years and his understanding of it is vast. He was within moments of death; in fact, he had almost left it too late when he finally attempted to save himself by using its natural recuperative powers. The Stone's return to normal before you removed it told me he had been successful. Had it stayed silver, it would have meant no life remained to complete the healing cycle."

"Then why didn't he use it earlier, when he was first wounded?" Hap demanded, not fully convinced.

"Because, as you discovered, the recipient goes into such a deep coma he appears to be dead. Kaér was fully aware of this and knew he had to stay conscious long enough to bring about the demise of the enemy, therefore his own life was of secondary importance."

For a moment, Angharad was rendered speechless, unable to take in the Elder's words. She had watched Kaér die, Hap had confirmed it; but what could Alfwin possibly hope to gain by lying to them?

"Where is he?" she whispered at last. "I must see him."

"This way," Alfwin said as they followed him out of the room and up a flight of stairs leading off from the centre of the corridor.

Reaching the top he took them across a landing and down a short passageway before striding through an open doorway on their left. They found themselves at the edge of a large room, their gaze drawn immediately towards a figure seated in a cane chair on the far side. The face and body were emaciated; black rings hung darkly round the eyes and the skin was almost translucent but it could be none other. Rising stiffly, Kaér moved unsteadily towards them, smiling broadly. With a shout of pure joy, Angharad opened her arms and raced to greet him, happiness spreading across their faces. As they embraced, they looked deep into each other's eyes and their lips met. Hap glanced at Alfwin and hastily they stepped outside, closing the door behind them. This was not a good time, Hap decided, for him renew his friendship with the lone wanderer of the mountains.